I0739083

CLASHING WATERS
The Obyascon Prince

MEREDITH T. TAYLOR

Grey Circle

Clashing Waters
The Obyascon Prince

by

Meredith T. Taylor

Copyright © 2018 by Meredith T. Taylor

www.MeredithTTaylor.com

All rights reserved. Except as permitted under the U.S. Copyright Act of 1976, no part of this publication may be reproduced, distributed, or transmitted in any form or by any means, or stored in a database or retrieval system, without the prior written permission of the publisher.

Grey Circle Publishing

www.GreyCirclePublishing.com

The characters and events portrayed in this book are fictitious. Any similarity to real persons, living or dead, is coincidental and not intended by the author.

Printed in the United States of America

ISBN-13: 978-0-9960637-2-2

ISBN-10: 0-9960-6372-2

~For those who still find love magical
For those who swim without a view of the shoreline
&

For those who have always believed in me

PREFACE

1

———

*"One can no more keep the mind from returning to an idea
than the sea from returning to a shore. For the sailor, this is
called the tide; in the case of the guilty, it is called remorse. God
stirs up the soul as well as the ocean."*

— *Victor Hugo, Les Miserables*

A tiny bead of saltwater glistened against William's brow as the late afternoon sun slowly began to make its descent. Even after so many months, my pulse quickened each time he drew near. My fingertips traced the details of his golden hand as I nestled closer to him.

"We have to get up you know," I said as I pressed my lips against his warm shoulder. The salt from his skin penetrated my senses, instinctively sending me in for another kiss.

"I won't be going anywhere, and neither will you if you keep kissing me like that." He groaned. In one swoop, he effortlessly scooped me onto the sand beneath him. He leaned down, ever so carefully brushing his lips against mine.

"Now you are just trying to distract me," I teased.

"Is it working?" He brushed his lips against mine again before descending once more.

"What planet are we on again?" His kiss began to make me feel lightheaded. I suddenly remembered to draw in his essence before I collapsed. He slowly pulled away from me. I leaned into him for more.

"Careful. I am still learning my limitations. One wrong move and that kiss may render you unconscious again." I thought back to months earlier when our first kiss was almost my last. Our relationship was complicated to say the least. Though William and I had discovered a way around a single kiss, he was still rightfully cautious, as I would always be half-human, and he a siren in every sense of the word.

"I think I'm adjusting to this Sironian thing quite nicely actually," I teased. William brushed a stray golden lock behind my ear.

"Yes, you are. No one that has ever existed has accomplished what you have done—faced all that you have faced. And yet, here you are rebuilding what almost destroyed you." It was impossible not to gaze at the utter perfection of the creature next to me along the shoreline or what remained of the shoreline. He motioned to his work truck resting on the broken asphalt atop the jetties. Debris from the hurricane had filled it to the brink. We had spent much of the summer cleaning out the inlet waters from Theron's destruction.

"This is my home now, not just the Inlet Joy, but the jetties, the marshland, and the sea. It wouldn't be in this condition if it weren't for me … for my existence," I sighed.

"You can't keep blaming yourself. Theron's regime is to blame," William replied swiftly.

"Yes, but I killed Maris, his daughter-in-law, Aria's mother!"

"You had no choice! Theron sent her to kill you. She would have killed both you and James. You were perfectly right to protect yourself and your friend. Besides, you forget that he directed the hurricane here well *before* you killed Maris. He was coming for you."

I knew he was right. The category five hurricane that Theron ushered towards us, almost three months earlier, was intended to end my life. I had survived but with a hefty price. The insignia etching into my wrist was my constant reminder of the agreement I had made to save the lives of those that I loved. I had contracted to join Theron's Legion someday and William to marry Theron's heir. All had assumed he had agreed to marry Aria, but by some twist of fate only known to William and Silas, he had made that vow for my hand in marriage. William and Silas both claim that I am the granddaughter of Theron and his rightful heir. Could it possibly be true? Was I the Sironian princess? The thought of losing William made me feel sick.

But despite this treaty, much of the South Carolina coastline had been left in shambles. Many of the homes along the Garden City peninsula were pushed into Murrells Inlet, washed to sea, or they were so badly damaged that they were scheduled for demolition. The high sloping dunes that once harbored the nesting wildlife were entirely eroded, leaving behind a foreign landscape so flat that the ocean waves almost broke directly into the marshlands. It was my fault. My mere existence was to blame.

"We have at least a few more hours of daylight, and I want to finish cleaning out this section of the inlet before nightfall," I groaned. William seemed to relent, as he wrapped his arm around my waist and helped me to my feet.

"You know, that would go a lot faster if you had some help," a familiar voice said as I turned to see Kirby, Toby, and Mace coming over the backside of the jetties. Kirby tossed a mud-encrusted toilet in the back of William's already overfilled truck. Mace carried a broken kitchen sink and Toby an entire rusted-out claw foot tub.

"Remodeling?" I teased my mud-covered Sironian friends.

"That's an understatement! This place is trashed!" Toby exclaimed, as he effortlessly snapped the tailgate closed. I was still astonished by the strength of my Sironian friends. The truck buckled under the weight before the rear axle snapped and one of the rear tires came loose. William shook his head.

"Oops. Sorry, Will, looks like we may owe you another truck." Toby chuckled, tossing William the displaced tire. He caught it effortlessly.

"Gee thanks! You guys are a big help," William muttered sarcastically.

"Glad to help!" Kirby smirked before winking at me. William glared at him. In truth, Theron's attack on the Protectors had solidified the group. William seemed more than appreciative of their willingness to put their lives on the line for me. Together with Silas, we had become a kind of dysfunctional family but a strong one. We were stronger together. We needed each other. But despite this, Kirby still liked to ruffle William's feathers, and flirting with me seemed to be his tactic of choice.

"I will bring around my truck, and we can start clearing out the northern canals. The guys and I finished the embankment and southern canals today," Mace stated. I was still unsure if the mutual respect between William and Mace had grown into a friendship, but the two at least were able to coexist without constant conflict.

"Ok. Marguerite and I will do a sweep of the point to survey what debris remains in this area," William replied. He had barely gotten out the words when a fourth mud-covered person appeared from around the jetties carrying several large splintered planks of lumber.

"What should I start on next?" An out-of-breath Caleb asked before hoisting the lumber in the back of the broken truck. The extra weight caused the rear to collapse completely. Caleb looked up startled. "Did I do that?" he said embarrassed.

"No, it's okay, Caleb," I reassured him. My younger brother had spent the majority of his summer here with us too. It would still be quite some time before Caleb would know if the gene would awaken inside of him as it had done with me or if it would remain mostly dormant as it had done with our father. Either way, there was no denying that Caleb was half Sironian too. Each day he was drawn deeper into the world of the Sironian, a fact that scared me immensely, but one that I knew could not be avoided. He was still able to live apart from the coast, still able to live a human life, but if the gene were to awaken inside of him as it had done with me, he would have no choice but to join us.

In many ways, Caleb already was a member of the group. He awoke each morning to train with us despite his lack of strength or skill and seemed equally committed to the inlet cleanup. The crew teased him a bit, but he seemed to be liked by everyone, and so he was allowed access into a world that most humans could only dream. Silas was the most attentive, studying him, observing vigilantly for any sign of a transformation. Like me, Caleb was one of a kind. We needed to keep his existence a secret from Theron. If he had come after me, he would come after Caleb.

"Before we go any further, we should take an inventory of which canals still need to be cleared before the weather begins to turn cold again," Mace explained. He was right. Humans usually avoid cold water—at least in the South anyway. "Once the water chills, we will have to resume at night or in the early morning hours to avoid notice." The destruction had kept most of the tourists away for the summer. In fact, aside from some overworked construction workers and a few homeowners that popped in from time to time, the area was virtually devoid of life. The crew listened as William and Mace laid out the plans to do an inventory of the remaining cleanup efforts. Silas was concerned that debris and contaminants were already having an effect on the fish and wildlife in the area.

Despite the destruction, it had been a magical summer with William. He slowly and carefully introduced me to the underwater mystery and majesty of the ocean. William spent most morning hours introducing me to an underwater world that I never knew existed. We explored the inlets first. William was cautious, fearing that at any moment Theron might send his forces to attack. But as the weeks wore on, it appeared that Theron had indeed retracted his army and kept his promise concerning me. His Legion had disappeared. My love dedicated himself to teaching me all about his underwater realm. The reefs were breathtaking. The sea life was unimaginable. His world was so physically near the world I had grown up in, and yet so far from anything I could have ever imagined. William was careful to steer me away from any areas populated by other Sironian. Occasionally, we would run across one, causing William to react fiercely, but in general, they avoided us. Whatever Theron's orders, these underwater creatures wanted no part of us.

When the final cleanup efforts were complete for the day, William anchored my beautiful wooden boat dockside at the Inlet Joy. "My boat is muddy," I pouted, still admiring the exquisite details of the small boat William had handcrafted. I cupped a small amount of seawater into my hands trying to rinse off the hull.

"Then I will make you another one," he said flatly without a moment's hesitation. His thumb traced my jawline causing my pulse to race again. I had not become immune to his touch. He smiled, sensing what his touch had triggered.

"You would do that for me?" I said, eyeing him playfully.

"I thought you knew by now; I would do anything for you." His lips brushed against the side of my neck sending shivers throughout my body. He smiled and leaned back to admire my reaction.

"Anything?" I teased again, as I rinsed the mud from my hands.

"Yes," he laughed. "For you, I would do anything that is possible … and most things impossible." His eyes narrowed. The way he looked at me still took my breath away.

"Even let me skip out on this whole high school thing?" I pleaded. He groaned.

"I knew I might live to regret those words, but I was thinking that you had something else in mind," he teased. William's eyebrows rose flirtatiously. I laughed.

"I may need to renegotiate. I didn't know those cards were on the table," I replied.

"Let me assure you; there has never been anyone as tempting as you—siren or human. Unfortunately, those cards need to stay in the deck—for now anyway." I sighed. He swept me tightly into his arms. "I did not spend all of these years as your Protector only to have you die at my own hands," he said.

I longed for a physical relationship with William. It was never far from thought, but I knew William would never let things progress that far between us. No, there would be time to negotiate that, but there was something more reasonable to request. We had three and a half weeks until school resumed for the fall, and William was determined that I join Kirby and Toby as part of the senior class. The hurricane had pushed back the start of the school year until the third week in September as parts of the school were still being renovated from the storm's wrath.

"One negotiation at a time I suppose," I sighed. "Back to the whole school thing, I could just complete my senior year by correspondence, that way I could help Silas while the rest of the Crew are in class." He laughed. I pulled him against me. "Besides, you already have twice the credits. I am guessing that the school will just mail you a diploma."

"It arrived last week," William replied. "I've done my studies. There is no need for me to make appearances any longer. I am needed here. There are many months of work remaining to put the inlet right again."

"Then I will work with you!" I exclaimed. "I would rather be here helping than stuck in a classroom all day!"

"I'm not about to let you off of the hook so easily. Mace has already graduated, so he will be relieving Silas of most of his daytime duties. Besides, it is important for you to integrate back into the human world as much as possible, not only for appearance sake but for yours as well.

"My sake? I can assure you that I am not missing out on anything. I have had seventeen years of living as a human and only a single summer as a Sironian," I huffed.

"It's more than that." William's brow furrowed. "You have seen what is out there. Those living apart from the human race have evolved into monsters!" The longer we live apart from the humans, the more like those creatures we become. As Protectors we have to become more like those we seek to protect and less like the monsters inside of us." I had seen William become the monster to which he was referring. I had observed the evil in the eyes of the ocean-dwelling Sironian. There was no comparison to the beauty of the boy in front of me to the siren creatures of the deep.

"You can't compare yourself to those creatures!" I cried. "You are not like them, and neither is the crew."

"But you see, Marguerite, we *are* siren. We all have the capability of becoming like them; we all still have those urges inside of us. Imagine a tiger bred in captivity; once that tiger is released back into the wild, its primal instincts will unexpectedly take over to ensure its survival. You are half human and still changing, but the longer we put ourselves apart from the human world, the stronger those urges become," William said. I thought of James and how I had almost taken his life there on that beach prom night. Nothing had been stronger than the desire to consume every ounce of essence from within him. Nothing that is, but the love I had for my dearest friend.

Most Sironian are deprived of love, only taught one emotion—allegiance. Their allegiance was to Theron and the decrees he had created, edicts that fashioned loveless unions and tore children from the arms of their parents, for the sole purpose of strengthening his regime.

Luckily William had known real love, though it was cut short by the untimely death of his parents, Morgan and Robert Avery. They had escaped from Theron's regime to live among the humans for the protection of their children. William's parents had lost their lives because of it. How thankful I was that he had learned love from Morgan and Robert and also that he was arranged into Silas's care at a young age. Silas had not only taught him to be the most skilled of all Protectors, but he also learned the values lacking in the others of his kind. Silas was like a father to William and the rest of the crew.

But someone was missing from their patchwork family—Aria. Her jealousy over our relationship had caused her to leave the sect. Aria's betrayal had almost destroyed us all. I wondered what her life was like now that she had returned to Theron. My mind began to race in a million directions.

"What are you thinking about?" William said tracing the lines of my creased brow.

"Do you think Aria will ever return?" I asked. The question seemed to trouble him.

"Honestly, I just don't know. Aria's remorse was evident, but her betrayal almost had us killed. How can she face us after all that she has done?"

"But she again believes she is betrothed to you. I think she will come again."

"Even if she returns, I cannot stay away from you," William whispered tenderly. His fingers brushed against my lips softly. "It is only a matter of time when she learns the truth that you are Theron's granddaughter, your father born before hers, making you Theron's heir. I could never marry Aria. The contract I made with Theron was for your hand in marriage only." The idea that I was Theron's granddaughter and heir to his crown was still like an unbelievable dream to me. Not long after the storm, I had finally gotten up the nerve to question my grandmother, and she had reluctantly verified what William and Silas had told me. I was indeed the unknown biological granddaughter to Aaron Theron, ruler of the oceanic waters of the world. What would Theron's response be when he ultimately learned the truth? How would Aria react when she learned that William would be taken from her once again?

"Certainly she will not be able to stay away from you and from the crew. They have been like brothers to her!" I cried.

"It's possible one day she will return. And when she does, together we will decide how to deal with it." He scowled. "But I have more immediate concerns."

"And what would those be?" I could hear his heart increase its pace. His eyes narrowed.

"Each time I leave your side, I know there is a possibility that they may come for you." He clinched his chiseled jaw tightly. We rarely mentioned that part of the treaty. I had vowed to spend three months under Theron in training each year until he thought it time for me to take my place in his Legion. We were both aware that they could come for me at any time.

"Theron promised that no harm would come to me as long as we follow through on what we agreed," I stated swiftly.

"How can I do that, Marguerite? How could I ever step aside and let them take you away from me?" The pain of this image was evident in every inch of his perfect face. I felt it too; the thought of being apart from William, even for a short period, was agonizing.

"There is no choice." I pleaded, looking down at the slivery mark on the inside of my wrist. "They will come," I held up my branded arm, "but not to take my life." William looked down at his matching insignia.

"No, Theron has what he wants for now. But do not be misled. When they do come, it will not be just to train you. He is taking you to induce you to follow their Legion. They will try to indoctrinate you into Theron's regime."

"It would be impossible! You of all people know how strong minded I can be."

"When the time comes, you will need all of your strength. You will need to be tough—more resilient than you have ever been," he pleaded. The sound of tires crushing shale broke the intensity. James's Blazer pulled into the drive at the Merri Mac just several houses down from the Inlet Joy. William's eyes narrowed.

"I am pretty sure I'm the only siren alive who has to share their girl with a human," he groaned.

"I think you are the only siren alive with a girl." He sighed. I could see that he was trying to hide his frustration over my bond with James. James got out of his car and motioned to me from across the lots.

"I guess this means your evening is already spoken for?" William asked. I shrugged, as I took his flawless hand in mine.

"I'll see you later tonight, okay?" William brushed his hand across the side of my neck pulling out the thin silver chain that had fallen into my shirt. The tiny rare Shiva shell dangled against my tank top, a constant reminder of the bond between us.

"Don't forget me," he whispered as he brought my fingers to his lips.

"Not a chance," I said as my fingers slowly slipped from his.

I turned to see James pulling a large duffle bag from his back seat. He immediately headed in my direction. I turned back to William, but he had completely vanished back into the warm inlet water with not so much as a splash. Guess one should expect as much from a boyfriend who was a siren.

"I thought this week would never end!" he said, as he barreled across the lawn and scooped me into a big hug.

"Welcome back! How was your week?" I pulled away, realizing that I was still covered in mud. "Sorry, we've been clearing debris out of the inlet. I haven't had a chance to shower."

"Why am I not surprised? Most girls spend their summer break working on their tans, but Marguerite Westley spends hers covered in mud," James teased.

"Someone has to do it," I shrugged. He laughed as my hair toppled into my face. "Sorry I'm such a mess."

"You are more beautiful than ever, darling." He playfully wiped a spot of mud from my nose, but I could see him looking over my shoulder. "I could have sworn I saw your boyfriend with you when I pulled up."

"Oh, yeah. William had to go clean up too," I sputtered.

"Which basically means that he saw me pull up and took off."

"Basically." I nodded truthfully. It had been a mostly peaceful summer balancing my attentions between William and James. I spent the early mornings in training with Silas or cleaning the inlet with the crew, but I usually met up with James mid-morning. I knew his feelings for me still ran much deeper than friendship, but unlike Kirby, whose flirtations were intended to irritate William, James was tactful. There would always be an underlying current between us, a history that no one could take away, but for the most part, he seemed resigned to friendship. There had been no more talk of romance since that disastrous prom night. I was relieved, especially since my feelings for William had only grown deeper through the summer months. We seemed to cling together; knowing at any moment, we could be torn apart.

"Well, I'll give you some time to shower and clean up a bit. I was hoping you were free for dinner. I've been working on my portfolio and wanted to get your thoughts on it … perhaps over a juicy Sam's Corner burger?" James eagerly awaited a response.

"Sounds good!" I replied. "I think a storm front may be pushing through tonight and rain is expected. Let's make it an early dinner. You go unload your bags, and I'll meet you at the dock in thirty minutes." We both looked over to see a mud-covered Caleb heading downstairs to the shower stall wearing nothing but a white towel. He waved to my copper-haired friend, narrowly catching his towel that had begun to slip from his hips.

"Hey, Margo! Hope you don't need any hot water!" Caleb teased as he opened the door to the shower stall. I winced.

"On second thought, we'd better make it forty-five."

2

———

"Doubt that the sun doth move, doubt truth to be a liar, but never doubt I love."

~William Shakespeare, Hamlet"

"I'll have the fish and fries," I said to the weathered man in the white apron. James appeared both surprised and hurt that I had corrected the order he had placed for me.

"I can't believe you are once again deviating from the cheeseburger," he said as he passed the guy a twenty.

"Guess I've just had a taste for fish lately." It was an understatement to say the least. The further along the gene seemed to progress, the more seafood I was subconsciously adding to my diet. It would be these subtle changes that would someday force me to tell James the truth. James eyed me curiously as he began to escort me to a makeshift table in the back. The loud sound of hammering changed our plans. The hurricane had virtually demolished Sam's Corner. The joint was still under repair with the grill open for locals and construction crews. "Let's go eat on the pier," I suggested over the deafening construction. He shrugged.

"This will be to go, please," he said to the weathered man behind the counter.

The pier had always been special to James and me, our own unique childhood getaway, but the boarded barricade blocking the entrance served as another reminder of how life had changed. James and I looked out over what was left of the structure. The storm had torn its boards from their pilings as it swallowed up the entire end.

"I'm sorry, James; I'd forgotten for a moment."

"Me too. It's hard to see this place like this. Gosh, we had so many memories here!" James sighed. My brow furrowed realizing that my memories here no longer exclusively belonged to us. It was here that I first met the crew. It was also here that I had fallen into the icy depths and taken my first glimpse of a world that was impossible to imagine—at least for a human. Those days seemed like ages ago. I was a different person now. I was no longer just human.

James and I found a sheltered spot just below the dunes where we picked at our bagged meals. The sun had completely fallen behind a blanket of dense clouds. There was no sunset, only an eerie glow across the water. Simple. Beautiful. I could see James's courage mounting. I dreaded the impending conversation that I had managed to escape from all summer. His eyes met mine, his face carrying an expression that I had not seen since the dreaded prom night. Retreat was not an option.

"I was amazed the first time I saw you were swimming—without me, I might add!" He playfully leaned back against the dune and fumbled with a golden lock of my hair. "Six years of trying to get you in the water—nothing. I let that one slide, but now you're trading up the cheeseburger?"

"Everyone changes, I guess." I said. It was a weak reply, which only seemed to fuel James's mounting frustration.

"Look. I know what's going on with you." Out of frustration, he ran his fingers through his copper hair. "I know what *this* is—what this *change* is about!" I began to sink. I felt as if I had been punched in the chest. I had envisioned how this conversation would go a million times, but I was rattled. What would I say to him? How does one even begin to explain what I had become?

"James. It is important that you know …"

"It's William. You've changed for *him*." His jaw tightened the same instant mine relaxed. I hoped that he did not notice the sudden relief spreading across my face. He did not know the truth. I sighed. Of course, James would blame my changes on William. I had fooled myself into thinking that I could have both James and William in my life. The pleasantries of the summer had come to an end.

I started to protest when out of the corner of my eye I caught sight of them. Well beyond the breaker, at a distance too far for the human eye to process, were two Sironian creatures half visible hovering atop the water's surface. They were watching me. My heart pounded loudly in my chest. Even at such a distance, it was startling to see them exposed in the daylight. They were both larger than any Sironian that I had ever seen. Their hair and skin were as pale as the oceanic whitecaps, and their large almost colorless eyes leered into mine despite the distance. These creatures were different from the ones I could recall from Theron's army. Had Theron sent them for me? Adrenaline rushed through my veins as I contemplated my next move.

"Earth to Margo! Hello?" James leaned toward me, momentarily blocking my view of them. I shifted to see around him, but all that remained was the clashing surf. He shifted into my sightline once again. "Margo!"

"I'm … sorry … I thought I saw something," I uttered.

"You haven't heard a word I've said, have you?"

"Um … I think you were somehow drawing a correlation between my fish sandwich and William?"

"You care about the guy. I get it," he rambled on obliviously.

"I care about you too," I protested. My eyes immediately searched the surf again for the creatures. The false sense of security I had developed over the summer vanished. They were watching me!

"I know that. But it's not the same. You love someone else." He took my hand in his.

"There are all kinds of love you know," I said, trying to mask my growing concern. I caught another glance of them, this time much closer to shore. Their distance, now well in the range of human sight. A chill went down my spine. Now was not the best time to be having this talk with James. Vivid flashbacks of my friend's limp body trumped any other thoughts. My instincts as a Protector began to take over. These Sironian put no value on James's life, He was their prey and being with me made James a target. I would *always* make James a target.

"Just promise me that you will stay *you*, okay? Don't let William change you," James said tenderly. I bit my lip and nodded. James would always accredit William for the changes he observed. He would always resent William for how I had changed. I wanted to make him understand, but it was impossible. To do so would only put James at greater risk by defying Sironian law. The human world and the Sironian civilization must remain separated by a veil of secrecy.

My eyes searched the mounting whitecaps behind him. There was no sign of the Sironian, but they were out there. I knew they were there watching us. I began to practically pull James off the beach. "It looks like rain on the horizon; we better head back in case a front pushes through this evening," I said quickly. He was annoyed that I didn't seem to be taking his words to heart.

"Ok," he shrugged. "Looks like we will be bagging this food 'to go' … again." I took one final glance into the oceanic whitecaps as James crammed his food back into the sack. I saw nothing, but I knew they were there just beneath the surface. James remained oblivious to the dangers around him. I knew that he was in love with me, but his broken heart would mend. I had almost sucked the life from him, Maris had almost finished him off, and now I was once again exposing him to danger. I realized what I must do. If the Sironians were watching me, they were aware of my affection for James. My feelings for him would make him a target. My close friendship with him would keep him in harm's way. My heart ached. It had to be done. I had known since the Sironian gene had awakened inside of me but selfishly refused to admit it. I had to find a way to let him go.

****

James stayed with me until the rain began, but my mood was somber, to say the least. When he retired early, I was relieved. I had spent the evening trying to say "goodbye" to the only friend of my childhood. There was no way for James to safely integrate into my world. There could be no other option, but the words did not come. I thought back over the faces of the creatures. Were they from Theron's Legion? After our last encounter, they knew our strength. The crew would stand together and fight if needed. We were not strong enough to withstand his army, but we were strong. Was Theron now studying our weaknesses? To him, emotion means weakness. Had he sent these beings to assess our relations? The creatures today were warriors but not like the ones I had seen previously. These warriors were twice the size of any Sironian I had ever seen with very little traces of the beauty or humanity. Was he preparing for the very thing I feared the most … that William would fight?

I had known Theron would eventually send for me. There would be no way around this part of the treaty. But all fears for *my* safety were trumped by the fear I had that William would not *let* them take me. I had watched his love for me only grow stronger over the summer months. Despite all treaties, he would not stand by and allow Theron to take me away. Had Theron anticipated this and sent these strange creatures knowing William would put up a fight? I could not let him be hurt or killed defending me. I waited for William until my eyelids grew heavy. The crew often forgot that I need more sleep than the sirens, but it was rare for William to neglect my human needs. It was alarming that he had not come as he always kept his word. I began to worry.

The gentle knock on my door was barely audible over the heavy raindrops pattering along the rooftop. The sound sent my heart racing. "You're here!" I gasped. I reached for him, but he dodged the embrace. As he stepped inside, the cause instantly became evident. His thin shirt and shorts were dripping, and beads of water slid from his dark curls. "You're soaked! Let me grab a towel." I pulled down a freshly-folded towel from atop the closet and turned to find William's drenched shirt hanging on the edge of the iron bedpost. A summer together did not decrease the impact of his splendor. The view of his shirtless body took my breath away. His serious expression softened. I blushed, realizing he could read my thoughts. Oh, how I wish that he could not hear how my heart raced at the sight of him! He smiled.

"For the record, you make my heart race too," he whispered. His cool fingers slid down the length of my arm before entwining with mine. He lifted my hand to his chest where the motion of his pounding heart pulsed in the palm of my hand. "What once was broken, beats again because of you. You are my heart."

I wrapped the towel around his shoulders and brushed back a strand of dark hair from his eyes. "And you are mine," I said as he pulled me to him. "The word "love" seems too ordinary to describe how I feel about you."

"Sorry I am late. I have something special planned. This rain threatened to put a damper on my evening, but I made arrangements anyway." I giggled, as I pulled one of his white undershirts from my bottom drawer and slowly slid it onto his cool body. His eyes locked onto mine as we drew close. His chest pressed against me, sending a rush of adrenaline through my veins. He put his hand on my chest to feel the pulsating of my heart. I blushed. He started to laugh, cutting the physical tension that had begun to take over the room. "As much as I would like to stay, I don't want you to miss your surprise," I replied softly. There was nothing in the world that I wanted more than him.

"Are we walking or swimming?" I asked, barely able to speak.

"We're driving," he said as he pulled my raincoat from the closet and slipped it over my shoulders. I slipped on my shoes and began to pull my hair up in a ponytail. "You are taking too long," he laughed excitedly, as he yanked the brush from my hand and flung me on his back.

"William Avery! I take less time to get ready than any girl I know!" He laughed again and carried me to the door.

"Well, I do not know many human girls, now do I?" he said as he toted me downstairs to his new old truck. Toby had apparently replaced the other one with an even older model Ford.

"You better not know many Sironian girls either!" I teased.

"Please! Everyone knows I only date half-breeds." He winked at me as he scooped me into the passenger seat.

"Well then, you are lucky I'm one of a kind." He slid into the driver's seat.

"Two. Lucy carries the gene," he reminded me.

"True. I would hate to have to take on my five-year-old sister," I laughed.

"I don't think that would be a fair match," he teased.

"Yes, I am older … and trained by all the best Protectors you know!"

"I meant not fair for you!" he laughed. "All Lucy would have to do is summon some of her shark friends."

"A few sharks would be no match for me!" I replied, carrying on his banter. "Which reminds me … why don't we see any large sharks when we are swimming?" He started the truck and began to head away from the coast. I didn't have to ask where we were going. He was taking me to our place—to the quarry.

"They can sense us. Sharks and sirens have always shared the ocean in harmony. They have as much to fear from us as we do from them. Besides, sirens don't smell or taste very good—kind of like humans."

"I think I smell just fine actually!" I protested.

"Fine? You smell unbelievable! And taste … when your lips brush mine, it takes all of the self-control that is in me not to steal all of you. You have no idea how lucky you are to be alive." He took my hand in his, bringing the soft underside of my wrist up to his lips. I leaned in close to him, my lips pressing against his collarbone. I soaked in the heavenly smell of his neck as my lips slipped up his neck and caressed his jaw. He groaned.

"You are still very much human you know. You are tempting fate by trying to seduce a siren," William groaned.

"Luckily, my siren has tremendous self-control." I said brushing my nose and lips against his ear. He swallowed hard, a clear indication that I was pushing his boundaries.

"I am not as resilient as one might think. You better be thankful that I have super senses, or I might crash this truck right now," he said.

"Luckily, the only cars on the road at 2:00 a.m. belong to the milkman," I laughed.

"I never was very fond of milk," he teased, pulling me tighter against him.

William had taken me to the quarry many times over the summer. With the devastating effects the hurricane had on the coast, it had become our own retreat. The pathway through the woods had grown easy for me to maneuver. However, I had not attempted it at night. The dense rainfall had tapered into a light mist, and the evening rain had cooled the temperature, decreasing the stuffiness of the August humidity. The night was beautiful. "Come on! There is something I want to show you," he said practically dragging me through the dark forest. I was too excited to be afraid. Even through the darkness, the hike was relaxed with William's hand in mine. In just a short time, the trees parted and we were at the top of the quarry. I gasped at the sight. The water of the quarry was aglow, illuminating a magical blue radiance. A fine vapor mist was evaporating from the warm water reflecting the glow as it swirled up into the air.

"It's magical!" I whispered. "How is this possible?"

William smiled. "Bioluminescence. After a hard rain, these illuminating bacteria can be carried from the ocean's disphotic zone through the subterranean water tunnels of the quarry, essentially becoming trapped here. The bacteria create this magical glowing effect."

"It's unbelievable! Why haven't you shown me this before?" I scolded.

He laughed. "This only happens when the conditions are perfect—perfect like tonight."

"But why does it glow blue?"

"Blue is the only color that can penetrate to such depths. Over time these organisms have evolved to radiate this color from the small amounts of light traveling to the disphotic zone."

"Amazing!" Twinkling specks of light glistened around us. "Fireflies! I didn't see them when we were hiking," I laughed.

"They are attracted to the glow and warmth of the water. Light attracts light." He turned to me, his emerald eyes glistening against the glow of the water. I could barely breathe when he looked into my eyes. His hands cupped my face as he pulled me closer. "You are my light you know—like the fireflies. My world was dark until I found you."

"Light attracts light," I repeated softly. "Your world may have been dark, but your inner light was the beacon for *me* to find *you*," I said slipping my arms around his waist and pulling his body tightly against mine. Through the flickering glow of the quarry, I gently stroked his temple. His hand came up to meet mine, lacing my fingers into his.

"Are you ready?' he smiled.

"Ready for what?" I giggled, as he swooped me into his arms tightly and jumped off the side of the quarry into the illuminated water. I gasped as we hit the cool water.

The illumination was even more amazing from below. The tiny organisms radiated around me as William and I explored the magical water around us. For so long I was haunted by nightmares and now I lived in a dream world. I slipped away, eager to discover all that had previously been unknown to me. The reality of the world was lost as I whirled through a realm of fantasy. William found me; he grasped both of my hands and led me to the surface.

"Do you like it?" he asked. Williams hands gently brushed the beads of water from my brow.

"It's like a dream!" I gasped, casting my arms around him.

"Happy birthday," he whispered in my ear. Through the warm mist, he pulled me closer.

"It's my birthday?" I asked softly. I had never been one to fuss over my birthday. The week had been so busy that I did not realize it had arrived.

"Yes it is—it is now past midnight, making it September 2nd. I wanted this birthday to be one that you would always remember." William slipped an exceedingly large 1920s style solitaire diamond on my left ring finger. Life escaped me as I was completely drawn into a fairytale. The intricately placed tiny diamonds were woven like lace, framing the large stone in platinum filigree, before wrapping around my finger with a thin, timeless band. I was speechless as the most beautiful ring I had ever seen glistened in the moonlight. "This was my mother's ring," he whispered tenderly. "There is no creature in the world that I could present this to, other than you. I have made my intentions known, and one day I will ask you for your forever." The tears running down my face merged with the tiny beads of salty water on my face, united and forever inseparable—like William and I.

"It's exquisite!" I whispered, overcome with emotion. "Exquisite like the siren I will someday call mine forever."

"I do hope I will be that siren?" he smiled. "I am not sure that Kirby has entirely given up on swaying your affections."

"It's always been you. It will always be you." I said as my fingers gently traced the angles of his face.

"We exist in a realm not designed for us, and yet, I am alive because you seek to share this world with me. I give this to you now, as I do not know what may lie ahead. The shiva around your neck denotes my claim of you in my world, and the ring I present to you embodies our bond in yours. I can only hope that you deem me worthy of your forever," William said solemnly. I was overcome with emotion. No fairytale could be more perfect.

"I could ask for nothing more out of life than to have you," I whispered through silent tears. "You have always had my forever. William, you *will* always have my forever."

"I was too afraid to dream of you—to think that there could possibly be someone created solely for me, and yet, here you stand. The drumming of your heart is a fulfillment of an unspoken prayer—a miracle that somehow I was favored enough to win you." His words were almost a whisper. Instantly William's arms pressed my body tightly against his. His lips consumed me, as his essence joined with mine—for always.

3

———

"I can't go back to yesterday because I was a different person then," said Alice.

~Louis Carrol, Alice in Wonderland

"**Good morning, birthday girl!**" My eyelids slowly opened as William's soft lips brushed across each of them. The day marked was my eighteenth birthday. I had never liked birthdays. In particular, I had never liked celebrating *my* birthday. The concept of "growing older" was neither appealing nor repulsive. Despite this, I was aware of the implications of an eighteenth birthday. I was officially an adult. In truth, I had always felt like an adult trapped in the body of a child, but the day made it official. I rolled over and straightened the crumpled clothes I had been wearing since the evening before. "You were sleeping so hard I was afraid to awaken you." Although most Sironian slept in the afternoon and were awake through the night, James occupied most of my afternoons. I found that I could usually sleep during either parameter. However, I was always regretful when I fell asleep on the evenings William stayed.

"I'm sorry I fell asleep," I groaned. I nestled my face against his bare chest.

"Don't be sorry. You are entitled to a few hours of sleep after your siren boyfriend kept you out half the night."

"Boyfriend, huh?" I said flashing the large ring on my left hand. He smiled, but I could sense something was wrong. "What's wrong? Do you regret giving this to me?"

"Never! It is just that we have company coming today," he said.

"I know. My parents are coming. Maybe I should put it with the shiva around my neck."

"There is nothing that gives me greater pleasure than to see it on your finger, but I think it would be a good idea ... just temporarily." His eyes were leaden, and his expression twisted as if he were in pain.

"What is it that you aren't telling me, William?" He looked away. "You know something," I gasp.

"I didn't want to have to tell you this—especially on your birthday." My heart sank. William knew what I had feared. It was time.

"Theron is sending for me, isn't he?" William closed his eyes as if to block out the vision.

"I believe so. Aria entered the inlet late this afternoon to speak to Silas," he uttered.

"Aria? What did she say?" Surprise and alarm swept through me at the mention of the beauty that was once William's betrothed.

"I am not sure. After you had fallen asleep, Mace came to find me. Silas has asked to meet with us this morning. He wants the entire crew there— all but Caleb. He wanted to be sure Caleb stayed away."

"Theron's Legion will be there," I cried. "Why else would Silas keep Caleb away?"

"Silas has not divulged the details, but I can sense it. I know they are close."

"I believe I saw two of them yesterday. I was with James near the pier. They must have accompanied Aria." His concern was immediate.

"Did you recognize them?" William asked.

"No, but they appeared to be warriors of some sort. They were both pale and large, unlike the siren I have seen."

"I feared as much. Theron must have recruited some new forces—rogue Obyascon perhaps. He is correct in assuming that we will not just hand you over! If he wants a fight, then he will get ..."

"The treaty, William! I agreed to this!" I cried. William's jaw hardened. "I had to! He would have destroyed all of us."

"I will not let him take you! I cannot!"

"I will keep my word, William. Theron has promised that no harm will come to me and that I will be returned. Please, let us have no bloodshed." He swelled with emotion. I clasped his hands in mine. "William, I will come back to you, but you are going to have to let me go."

"Let us just go instead! Let's get as far away from here as possible!" he pleaded. "Theron has seen your strength and courage now. He may not destroy you, but he will stop at nothing to keep you." With urgency, he pressed his lips against my forehead. "All that I once loved was taken from me. I will not let *anyone* take that from me again." I looked up to see his perfect features twisted in pain.

"You know as well as I do that running is not an option." His eyes tightly closed as if he were trying to keep back tears.

"What am I supposed to do, watch as they take away the only thing I have left to love?"

"I will return to you … I promise," I whispered.

"You can't promise that! Despite what Theron has said …."

"Above all else, Theron values his laws. He will honor his word, but I am bound by my own vows. You know I speak truth, William."

"Are you not afraid?" he said softly.

"Yes, but I have both mentally and physically prepared myself. I am terrified for different reasons. I fear for you. My greatest fear is that I will lose you."

"He will try to brainwash you, Margo! Convince you of his laws, confuse you, and twist reality until you can no longer see the truth," William cried.

"I'm strong, William. I can do this!"

"You do not even realize what you are up against!"

"I have no choice!" I protested. "I refuse, they kill me … they kill everyone I love."

He pulled me tightly against his chest and wiped away a tear that had escaped. "There are no words to describe how I felt the night of the storm when I realized you were gone, realizing that you were sacrificing yourself and thinking I was too late to save you. The feeling was unimaginable."

"Just hold me." I cupped his face in my hands. "Hold me for now," I whispered again.

"I will never let you go," he replied. They were the words I wanted to hear … and the words I feared the most. I remained in his arms, delaying the trip we both knew I must make until footsteps neared my door.

"Come in." I said, meeting her at the door.

"Happy birthday, dear!" she smiled. "I had hoped to be the first birthday wishes of the morning, but it looks like someone beat me to it." I nervously looked behind me, but William had slipped out of sight. My grandmother motioned toward the dock. I slipped my head out to see James putting the final touches on his birthday surprise. He had spelled out "Happy Birthday, Margo!" in oyster shells along the floating dock.

"Very sweet." I replied.

"At least the boy is creative! I say he gets an "A" for effort," she teased.

"For certain," I said. I had spent the evening wrestling with how to separate James from my world. I knew of only one sure way to do it. I grimaced.

"What's wrong, dear?" My grandmother was perceptive.

"Nothing. I'm just still a little groggy." In just a short time, I would be alienating my best friend and learning my fate. Aria was waiting undoubtedly with news from Theron.

"Well, you'd better cheer up soon. Your parents will be here after lunch, and we've planned a birthday celebration for our girl!" I instantly smiled at the thought of seeing my family—especially Lucy. "I'm headed down to the market. Any birthday requests?"

"Surprise me," I said, as I closed the door behind her. I turned to see William looking out of the window.

"At least the boy is persistent," William said. I took his hand in mine.

"I need for you to do me a favor." I scowled.

"I would do anything that you asked of me," he replied. His emotions were still at an elevated state.

"After my grandmother leaves and I'm downstairs talking to James, wait for about five minutes, then take your shirt and pants off and come out of my bedroom. Then head downstairs and go into the shower." He looked dumbfounded.

"You want me to walk out of your room in boxer shorts? But that will look like …."

"I know what it will look like," I said.

"Are you sure you know what you are doing?"

"I do. I will explain later." His astonishment turned to concern. "Just trust me on this, okay."

"But Marguerite … you know what the boy's reaction will be."

"Theron is coming for me … and James is human. Hurting him is the only way I know to keep him from me. It's the only way to keep him safe." He nodded as he lifted my chin.

"Will your sacrifice never end?" he whispered. His fingers gently stroke my face.

"Not until I know for certain that all that I love are safe."

****

"Happy birthday, darlin!" James grabbed me in a giant bear hug before I reached the dock. "Eighteen. You're officially an adult!"

'So they tell me." I smiled, as I pulled away from his embrace.

"I made something for you!" He motioned towards his oyster shell birthday banner.

"Nice! That is pretty impressive!" I exclaimed.

"I wanted to be the first person to wish you a happy birthday."

"Thank you, James. I love it," I replied nervously.

32

"I made you something else." He pulled out an exquisite leather album. I flipped through the black and white photographs. There were several pages of us together as children that he had artistically edited and mounted, then some of me taken by James when he was learning photography. The pages progressed to those we had playfully shot the day we got the boat running, some of the ones I had taken of him too. Also photographs from the ill-fated prom. He had secretly snapped photos of me from across the room.

I was aware that when the gene had taken effect I had been greatly physically altered, but it was shocking to see the progression in print. In the later photos, I hardly resembled the girl I had once been. The beautiful siren in those photos had almost taken his life that night. I had lied to him. I had repeatedly put him in danger. I had not explained my transformation, and still, he loved me. I would hurt him once again. I saw what was coming like a train wreck with no way to stop it. A shirtless, half-naked William walked out of my bedroom, instantly catching James's attention from across the lawn. The siren looked every bit the part as his perfect form strode down the back steps and into the downstairs shower stall. A combination of embarrassment, mortification, and anger moved across James's face.

"I was a fool to think that I would be the first to see you on your birthday," James huffed. He began slowly then more violently kicking the oyster shells into the water. "But I guess I am just a fool, aren't I?"

"James …"

"Really, Margo! He's coming out of your bedroom … again. This time at the crack of dawn! How exactly do you plan to justify this one?" I instantly regretted the cruel plan. I fought back the mounting tears in a resolve to painfully continue with my strategy.

"I don't. I'm an adult. I don't need your permission or your blessing," I replied sternly.

"… And you don't need my friendship either!"

"James, please …"

"No, Margo! I can't do this anymore. You know my feelings for you! Honestly, I just can't pretend it is okay to watch him coming from your bedroom … friend or not! It's just too painful." He began to trudge across the lawn towards his car.

"James! Wait!" I protested.

"I'm tired of waiting, Margo! You make a fool out of me! Everything we had is falling apart, but you don't care! You are rebuilding your life … you're rebuilding it around *him*!" He looked down at the leather book in my hands. "What was the point!"

"James, please. I can't tell you what this book means to me … what *you* mean to me!" Tears flowed down my cheeks.

"But it's not enough … not for me … not anymore. Those pages represent the past. I don't even know that girl anymore!"

"You're right. I'm acting unfair towards you. I have selfishly asked too much of you!" I cried.

"… and I've never been enough for you. You aren't the same girl anymore. You've moved on. It's time that I accept the situation for what it is." His pain shot daggers through me. I slumped in defeat.

"You deserve that," I admitted through my tears.

"I do. You haven't given me any other choice," he huffed. "Goodbye, Margo." He climbed into his car and started to pull out when the engine came to a halt. He jumped out and immediately snatched me up into his arms. James looked painfully into my eyes. He held me tightly for a few seconds before he climbed back into his car and drove off.

It was done.

4

____

"The tide abides for, tarrieth for no man, stays no man, tide nor time tarrieth no man."

~ Geoffrey Chaucer

William feverishly paced the tiny bedroom. I crammed a few random items into my old book bag. It had been only a short time since Caleb had foisted the very same bag into my jeep at West Florence High School. Less than six months ago, I was just a girl—an awkward, clumsy human girl. I had known nothing of the hidden world in which I was now so tightly linked. My only glimpse of love was from storybooks. Now I stood in the very same bedroom of my childhood, the secret Sironian princess, unfathomably in love with the most desired and skilled of all the protectors.

"You're staying here! I will meet Aria alone!" he said painfully. I picked up my journal and added it to the sack.

"I won't let you do that, William!" I protested. "Aria told Silas she is here alone, to work out arrangements for my transfer, but I have seen those who travel with her. Theron is prepared if we come to fight."

"And if they have come to take you today?" William asked.

"Then I will go." I glanced down at the leather album James had given me only a short time ago. William saw the pain in my eyes—the pain I had tried to hide from him.

'I won't let them take you! I can't let that happen!" he protested. I stared into the pleading eyes of a boy who had watched as Theron had stolen everything that he had loved.

"I have a plan," I assured him. "I will agree to his conditions, gain his trust, and somehow find a way for us to be together."

"I will convince him to take me with you," William said desperately.

"He will know, William. He will realize that you are only there because of your feelings for me. You are betrothed to Aria!"

"I am betrothed to his heir—the one person in this entire world that I love."

"Theron doesn't know I am his heir. It is not safe for him to know—not yet. He will never allow us to be together, not until I can convince him that my allegiance is to his Legion. We can't risk it!"

"You are asking more of me than I can promise. Watching those monsters take you away goes against my vows as a Protector. It defies principle, duty, and above all else, it goes against my heart." I took his hand in mine. I pressed the back of William's hand against my lips.

"If I do not go, he will spare no mercy. That is a risk I am not willing to take."

****

36

I convinced William to arrive at the landing first. Given Aria's history, the less she saw of us together, the better. The crew knew to downplay any connection between us, but William's devotion remained constant. I was careful to counterbalance this by looking away when his eyes met mine. There was no need to fuel Aria's escalating animosity. Aria waited for the entire crew to assemble before she began. Kirby winked at me from across the expanse. His distraction was strangely comforting. I appreciated anything that could remotely divert my jumbled nerves. Mace and Aria glowered at each other. The summer months had not decreased his resentment of her betrayal, nor her anger over how things played out during the confrontation with Theron's Legion. I hated to see them like this. These once intimate friends had now turned into fierce adversaries. It was all my fault.

"Welcome home, Aria." Silas's greeting was formal but not cold.

"I am not sure how welcome here I am, Silas. You have assembled as if I have come to fight. I have come alone. I carry no objective other than to work out the transfer of the girl."

"Well gosh, Aria! The last time you showed up in these parts you were carrying an army," Kirby replied sarcastically.

"And a hurricane," Toby added.

"I admit my fault in the situation, but I do not take responsibility for Theron's extreme retaliation," she replied.

"We have assembled in this fashion out of caution only. We do not wish to insult you," Silas said. "However, we protect our own. You were once one of us, Aria—you still could be again." Silas's words had softened. Despite all that she had done, he still considered her one of his children. The love he felt for each of his protectors was plentiful.

Aria flashed the silver insignia on the underside of her wrist. "I am in Theron's Legion now. I am part of his council."

"You mean henchmen," Toby smirked.

"The laws you think are unjust exist for a purpose. They are to keep order both in our domain and in the human realm," Aria replied.

"They make slaves out of us all—including you, Aria!" Kirby said defensively.

"How could you do this, my sister?" Mace said. "There was no one in the world more drear to me than you. I have loved you like a sister, like a friend, and perhaps even more. The damage you caused here was more than the wreckage in our waters. You shattered the trust that we had in you. I thought the bond between us could not be untied, but you severed it with your actions and poisoned it with disloyalty." Mace turned away from her in pain.

I had to catch my breath. The hurt in his eyes was intense. My mouth fell open with the realization of the depth of Mace's feelings for Aria. He did not just love her like his sister. He had been "in love" with her. The pain in his eyes told a hidden tale. I wondered if even Mace acknowledged the depth of his feelings. Mace—the *boy* who had lost his brother had never been loved by anyone. Mace— the *teen* was used by Theron until finding acceptance and love by Silas. Mace—the *young man* had become a leader and had opened his heart to those who had become like brothers but had also opened his heart more deeply for the girl. He had fallen in love with Aria. Aria, who remained blinded by sanctioned ties and unrequited feelings for William, had missed what was so painfully obvious now. Mace had been in love with Aria all along.

William and I remained quiet. William was using all possible restraint to not rip Aria's head from her shoulders. He stood off to the side distraught and enraged. I stood in defense, trying to read the emotions of all involved—ready at a moment's notice to use any measures possible for the encounter to end peacefully. At last William spoke—his tone fused with hostility.

"You say you come alone, and yet Theron's warriors have been spotted just off the coast," William said defensively.

"I say that I come unaccompanied and still you doubt my sincerity. William, I am surprised that you would question me." Aria winced at the realization that her brothers no longer trusted her.

"What else should we expect from you, Aria?" William growled. Aria nodded in defeat.

"I suppose that is fair given recent events, but I do hope in time all will be forgiven." She looked hard at him, searching for some type of encouragement. He gave her none. Her expression hardened under the realization that once again her feelings would go unrequited. Silas sensed what was happening.

"We hold no resentment, Aria. I only hope that one day we can once again call you sister." Silas stated sincerely.

"I too wish for that, Silas. By treaty, things have been rightfully restored the way that Theron had intended." Despite his hostility, she looked possessively at William. A smug look spread across her face as she shifted her attention to me.

"Theron is waiting. Are you ready to go?" she spat. William hurdled forward as if he were about to attack.

"William, you seem to still harbor feelings for this half-breed. I must say, as your betrothed, that I am quite disappointed." He growled, crouching as if he were ready to rip her limb from limb. I spoke at last, swiftly trying to defuse the escalating circumstances.

"Aria, I will go with you as promised. I only ask that you give me until dawn to settle my affairs." She contemplated my request.

"I was prepared to leave today," she scoffed.

"Today being Marguerite's birthday, there is a celebration tonight in her honor. I think it could raise an issue with the humans if she did not attend the party," Silas said. "I will personally see to it that Marguerite departs with you at dawn."

"We are not unreasonable. Besides, I am quite tired from the journey. Your request is granted. I will meet you here tomorrow at dawn," Aria said.

"Perhaps you would like to come to the party?" Kirby added. William tensed at the proposition.

"I will have to decline. We have a long trip tomorrow. I would prefer to rest," Aria glowered at me. William was still crouched as if ready to attack. She smirked at him, and then in an instant, her beautiful form soared high into the air before slipping into the gleaming inlet water. I turned to find Mace and Toby gripping William's arms. The pain in his eyes was immense. It was painful to see him this way.

"What should we do, Silas?" Kirby asked.

"Do we just let them take Margo?" Toby added.

"No! Marguerite doesn't understand Theron's agenda," William implored.

"For now, it is the only option," Silas said gently. "I know how this pains you, William. It pains us all, but Marguerite must stand behind the treaty. He will kill her if she does not."

"Silas, you know this is some ploy!" William spat.

"Yes, there are few who know Theron as well as me. We can only pray that Marguerite's talents, wisdom, and training will be resilient enough to keep her alive."

"And that she will be able to withstand the encoding Theron will implement to coerce her into his Legion," Mace added.

"She is strong enough. I know she can do it." Toby said as he released William.

"Have a little faith, Will," Kirby smirked. "There is no way Theron could break this hardheaded female. I've been trying for many months with little results."

"But Kirby, Theron *is* the sworn ruler of the sea." Toby teased.

"Ah, he wishes he was half as suave as me!" Kirby added with a twisted grin. William tore off through the inlet waters.

"William!" I shouted after him. I was diving in when Silas stopped me.

"Give him some time, dear," Silas said tenderly.

"We have no time left, Silas!" I cried.

"Theron has promised to return you in three months' time. Above all else, he is true to his word," he replied

"You think he will try to turn me against all of you?" I asked.

"Together our small group is strong. He will do all that is in his power to dissect my family," Silas declared.

"… Because he fears us?" Toby asked.

"No. This is personal. He certainly covets all of your abilities, but ultimately, my old friend wants to hurt me. I had the one thing he always wanted," Silas said.

"What was that?" I replied, already quite sure of the answer.

"Your grandmother." Before I could respond, Toby ran up to me and flung me onto his back.

"Bet you thought we forgot!" he teased.

"Forgot what?" I asked, still concerned over William.

"Your birthday, Princess!" Kirby exclaimed as he took off after Toby who was sprinting towards the water.

"Come on, Silas! Before the hotdogs get cold!" Toby said.

"It's not even breakfast yet … and you all do not even eat hotdogs," I replied.

"I know … I have always just wanted to say that!" Toby giggled.

"You all must remember not to alert Caleb to any of this. His worrying will not bring his sister safety. It's better for him not to spend the next three months concerned over Marguerite."

"Done. We got it, Silas!" Kirby replied.

"Where are we going?" I asked.

"My house," Silas replied. "We may be siren, Marguerite, but we do know how to throw a birthday party." Silas winked as I was whisked away.

****

Silas spoke the truth. They did know how to throw a party. The crew was all there, my Knoxx Point friends, and my family. I was barely able to get a hug from Lucy before she was off with Olivia. The pair had become fast friends before my arrival. It was the first time this magical sect of siren was blended with my family. Sadie, my mother, and my grandmother swapped recipes as they filled the food tent. My father and Henry were on the porch unsuccessfully giving Toby lessons on how to blow up balloons, and Mace was kicking around a soccer ball in the yard with Kirby and Caleb. I found Silas off to the side, admiring the adjoined families.

"It has always been a dream of mine to see human and siren in harmony. In part, I get to live that dream today." He smiled at me. "You are the link between our worlds. I think the Creator has great plans for you." I had not thought about that. All my prayers recently had been for William.

"Silas, how did you know that Aria wouldn't insist on taking me today?" I said looking over the party.

"Because I wouldn't have allowed it. Today is your birthday, and you are like a daughter to me." He brushed back a strand of hair that had fallen out of my ponytail. My eyes swelled with tears as I realized that this was not just a birthday party. No one would say it, but it was also a "going away" party. I smiled as I looked over my improbable second family. Aside from James, I had never had friends before. Now, I could not imagine my life without this eccentric group of personalities. Three months away from this crew would seem like an eternity—if I was even allowed to return. William had not yet joined the party. The stress of losing me was taking a toll on him. There was constant pain in his eyes and an unrelenting sadness to his beautiful face. I had to be strong enough for the both of us. There would be time for tears when I was gone.

"This is for you, Margo," Olivia said. She and Lucy skipped up to me holding up a beautiful conch.

"It's beautiful, Olivia! One of the most beautiful I have ever seen.'"

"My dad helped me find it, and momma and I cleaned it up for you. Dad has been teaching me to swim—like a Sironian," she whispered the last part in my ear." I smiled at the dark-skinned beauty.

"Maybe we can all go swimming together," Lucy exclaimed. My breath caught deep in my throat. Henry could sense my anxiety over such a possibility.

"We will have to plan that soon, Lucy. Olivia is quite the little fish!" Henry boasted. "You will be very impressed with her, Margo!"

"I already am, Henry!" Olivia gave me a kiss on the cheek before she and Lucy ran over to join the soccer game. "Henry, as you know I am going away for a while. I wanted to tell you how grateful I am for all that you and Sadie have done for me over the past six months."

"Now we are going to have none of that talk today, missy! It is your birthday! You are part of our family and a part of our family you will stay," Henry said.

"Yes but … I am worried about William. Promise me you will look after him while I am gone. This won't be easy for him."

"Sadie and I will look out for him; you just look out for Marguerite," Henry replied. "Stay true to yourself, and remember, we all love you." I smiled faintly, once again fighting back the tears and wrapped my arms around Henry.

"Thank you," I whispered. I excused myself to go freshen up, but secretly, I was looking for William. While the others were occupied, I slipped away to the barn and quietly slid open the doors. The exquisite sailboat William had spent many years making took up almost the entirety of the barn, minus his small loft bedroom. "William?" I asked looking throughout the space. "Are you in here?" I entered the boat and climbed into the cabin. There was no sign of him, but my jaw fell open. The cabin was completely stocked with supplies, cases of dousie bows, harpoons, spears, medical supplies, and enough food rations for several months. Most of his books and clothing were aboard. Tacked to the wall just above the bed were some of the pictures we had taken together over the summer. My favorite was a strip of black and whites from the photo booth at the arcade. I tore off the bottom two and put them in my pocket. It was obvious by the massive amount of supplies and weapons that William was not just going to stand by while I was taken away. He was prepared to come for me. He was equipped for a fight. I slipped back to the party where Silas was preparing to bless the meal. We all gathered hands, and I had just closed my eyes when a wet warm hand slipped into mine.

"I am sorry I am late," William whispered in my ear. I smiled, as the familiar feeling of his skin touched mine.

"The main thing is that you're here now." I said faintly. "Are you okay?"

"I will never be at peace until we live in a world where no one or nothing will separate us."

The meal was superb, and the cake Sadie made was divine. Olivia helped me blow out the candles as the crew bantered and teased as if nothing were amiss. William and I both braved a smile. I threw in a joke here and there to make the afternoon as pleasant as possible. It was the least I could do after the time and effort my friends had invested.

Early afternoon, I asked William to bring me home to the Inlet Joy. We needed some alone time. Caleb stayed to finish his game with the crew, my mother and father stayed to help clean up, and Lucy was not ready to leave Olivia; they promised to return soon. I thanked everyone—saying surprisingly painful goodbyes to those in which I had grown to care deeply.

The afternoon sunlight danced across the churning inlet water as William maneuvered my magnificent little boat across the majestic waterway. I watched him—studying the flawless angles of his face. No amount of time away would erase my reflections as each part of his being was etched upon my soul. They could take me, but they could not separate us. He was as much a part of me as the blood running through my veins. William's sentiments mirrored my own. His pledge to me said more to me than any words ever could. A vow to William was a promise of eternity.

William anchored the boat along the floating pier and climbed into the hammock next to me. We held each other as the sun began to make its descent over the inlet. My family drove up just as the sun slipped below the horizon. Lucy darted across the lot and bounded into my arms.

"Just look at you Lucy-bug! A few more months and you will be as tall as I am!"

"No, I won't!" she giggled." I am only five, remember!"

"True. But you will be six next month, you know." Then it hit me. I would not be here to see Lucy's sixth birthday." My eyes began to swell with tears. William could read my thought and gave my hand a gentle squeeze. "Hi, William!" she continued.

"Hello, Lucy." William picked up a lock of her chestnut hair that had grown at least four inches since we had last seen her. I knew what he was thinking. The gene seemed to be accelerating in Lucy at an alarming rate.

"Have you been taking care of my friends for me?" William looked puzzled. Lucy motioned toward the inlet water that was suddenly filling with marine life. The water churned as the different species began to assemble around the dock.

William turned to me. "Wow, you weren't kidding! I have never seen anything like this! What are they coming for, Lucy?"

"Why to greet me of course, silly William." She giggled. My parents were now making their way to the dock.

"Lucy, your parents are coming. Can you tell your friends to come greet you later?" William asked.

"Sure. The others might think it's weird, huh? They aren't the same as us you know, but I don't ever say anything," she whispered before pulling out the small conch whistle William had given her. The high pitched sound was barely audible. The waters instantly calmed as the marine life submerged and dispersed.

"Wow! That is amazing! You are not weird at all, Lucy. You are very special. I just don't think you should let everyone know of your talents right now. They might not understand," I said.

She nodded. "It can just be our secret," William said.

"Ok. Just our secret," she laughed. "You know I like secrets!"

"I know you do, Lucy-bug," I said as she once again ran across the yard towards my parents. Knowing my father's ability to hear at great distances, I eyed him cautiously to see if he was listening. Caleb had joined them upon arrival. The group seemed far too immersed in the conversation for my father to be listening.

"She needs a Protector as soon as possible!" William said urgently. "I know of no one or nothing like her."

"Agreed. It is lucky that Lucy can live apart from the coast. She can still live as a human."

"Yes, but for how long? You telling me of her abilities was different from witnessing it firsthand. The gene is growing more rapidly inside of her than it did with you. With these talents, it will not remain a secret for long," William said.

"Theron cannot know of her existence, but who could we trust as her protector? Kirby?"

"Kirby is trustworthy, but he is not the strongest. There is only one other in which we could entrust her safety."

"Mace," I exclaimed. William nodded. Mace was our best option. "But would he even agree?"

"I don't know, but I will have to talk to him—tonight. Tonight is all that I have left."

William once again slipped his hand in mine as we moved across the lawn for greetings—and indefinite goodbyes.

****

The early evening was filled with family, food, and cake—lots of cake. We went to my favorite seafood restaurant before returning to the Inlet Joy for the gifts and official "blowing of the candles." Any past resentment of traditional birthday clichés vanished, as I soaked in what little family time I had left. Theron had promised to return me in three months' time but was also insisting that I eventually take my place in his Legion—*whatever the heck that may be! If I did manage to return, would I even be the same person? How would I explain my absence?* Much to my surprise, William had thought ahead on this conundrum. My family had each prepared a gift for me. Lucy made me a beautiful tan leather woven anklet. She helped me tie it into place. "Perfect! I love it, Lucy!" I made a vow to myself that I would not take it off until we were together again.

Caleb, knowing how I loved to write, found a journal with distinctive pages that would keep the ink from running when it got wet. "Thought you might want to take this to the beach sometimes," he said with a wink. His thoughtfulness was touching. The large box from my parents contained new art supplies: paints, brushes, and a large roll of canvas for stretching. It brought tears to my eyes to realize that I would not be able to take them with me. My grandmother gave me an antique, inlayed diamond band. It matched perfectly with the hidden ring around my neck that William had given me.

"It is stunning! Did grandfather give this to you?" She smiled.

"No … someone else did … a very long time ago. I thought it only right that it now be passed to you."

"It's perfect. Thank you!" I said as I slipped it on the pointer finger of my right hand. I would reserve my left hand for the day when I would wear William's ring. William, unsure of what everyone's reaction would be, had saved his birthday gift for last. The small wrapped box contained two round-trip plane tickets to Paris.

"Happy birthday, Marguerite," he said as I opened the box. "I have arranged for you to attend your senior year abroad. I know you have always wanted to go to France—what better way than to spend a year studying in Paris." Everyone was shocked. I could see the looks of protestation on the faces around me.

"But, William, where will she stay?" My mother's voice was a bit shaky.

"We will be staying with former friends of my parents. Marguerite will lodge in the home of the Bordeaux family. They live just outside of Paris, while I will be staying with another family just a few miles away. We will both attend the same private school, so I will be able to keep an eye on her." They were dumbfounded. A pin drop could be heard throughout the room.

"No one can dispute this is a superb opportunity, William. But obviously, you must understand our concerns," my father added.

"Of course, but let me assure you all that I have worked out even the smallest of details. You all must know by now how deeply I care for your daughter. I would do nothing on this earth to put her in harm's way," he said solemnly.

"We know that, William, it's just that …." A tear rolled down my grandmother's cheek. She had only had me for a short time, and I would be leaving her again. My only consolation was her rekindled relationship with Silas.

"We will miss her," uttered Lucy shyly.

"And I will miss you all greatly," I said fighting back the tears. I pulled Lucy into my arms. "But you all must admit this is an incredible opportunity. Thank you, William. When do we leave?"

"Our flight leaves first thing in the morning," he replied.

William had indeed worked out all of the details to cover my absence. I realized that when he left earlier, he was preparing for my departure. He presented my alibi so smoothly and articulately that even I began to believe the trip would take place. His enthusiasm made any reluctance from my family utterly impossible. Once all tears were shed and details picked over, excitement for me seemed felt by everyone. It would only be for eight months, I convinced them. I hoped that I would return much sooner under the premise that I missed them and wanted to return early, but William had been smart enough to create an alibi that gave me extra time.

There was one detail left to cover. Just before nightfall, William and I took Lucy on a boat ride. The sun had just begun to set when we pulled the beautiful boat William had made for me up to the landing. It was the safest place we knew to take her. Mace was waiting for us.

"I am here as you asked," he replied unable to hide the astonishment on his face at the young girl at my side.

"Mace, you met Lucy."

"Hi, Mace," replied Lucy. She jumped into the arms of the large Sironian.

"It is a pleasure to see you again, Lucy," Mace replied as he awkwardly pulled her off. She didn't notice and hurriedly skipped over the dunes and to the water's edge. He addressed William as we followed after her. "Why have you brought her here?" he asked.

"Lucy, Mace is like us. Will you show Mace your friends?" William asked.

"Are you sure he won't think I'm weird?" Lucy asked.

"Lucy, remember what I told you," I said tenderly. "No one will think you're weird. You only have to be careful of whom you show your talents." Mace's apprehension turned to curiosity.

"It's okay, Lucy. I would like very much to meet your friends." Mace's gruff voice softened to speak to the child. The introduction brought tears to my eyes. Lucy left my side and took Mace's large hand in hers. I was quite certain this was the first time he had ever held the hand of a human child. He looked like a giant next to the small girl as she led him towards the shoreline. She took out her shell and with a piercing sound, the calm waters began to stir with marine life. The display on the dock paled in comparison to what began to greet her along the smooth surf of the water's edge. Schools of large fish and sea turtles congregated seemingly unfazed by the porpoise and dolphin leaping in pleasure at her presence. Large dark billowy shadows swirled on both sides of the schools, their large fins peaking just above the rolling crest. I had never witnessed sharks of this size anywhere along the coast, and yet, they had been summoned by Lucy. The last species to arrive were the whales. Large blue whales frolicked behind the gathering as the smaller orcas pushed through the abundant water.

"Unbelievable." Mace quietly uttered as William and I both stared on in shock. Lucy began a series of high and low pitched sounds that seamlessly flowed together like a song.

"She's speaking to them?" William whispered. "Did you know she could do that?" I shook my head, too in awe to speak. We watched as she seemed to give the different species commands, the groups moving together in unison as if choreographed. We were so filled with astonishment that we did not notice the mounting species joining the gathering until the waters began to turn black as far as the eye could see from the vast amount of marine life congregating.

"You must have her stop this at once!" Mace suddenly blurted out protectively. "Such a spectacle is sure to go noticed by the forces that patrol these waters. No one must know of this! Have her disperse this display immediately!" Lucy continued her song-like utterances as if in a trance until I put my arm around her shoulder to get her attention.

"Lucy, you must ask your friends to swim back to sea," I said. "So many creatures together may draw attention from the wrong people." She contemplated this for a moment before nodding and sending out commands for the gathering to disperse. The marine life seemed to do so immediately.

"We need to get her off the beach immediately," Mace insisted. "Just in case someone out there has already been alerted of the girl." I took Lucy's hand and began to lead her back over the dunes to the landing when she stopped and turned back to the water. All animals had dispersed except for one large shadow circling just past the breakers. Its dorsal fin was higher than any I had ever seen, with the total length of the shark no less than eighteen feet.

"Wait!" Lucy exclaimed, "My friend is hurt!" She broke free of my hand and had run down to the water's edge before I could protest. She raised her left arm, and the waves ceased altogether. With her right arm, she motioned for the water to come forward and with a high pitched tone ushered the large animal towards her. We sprang in horror as she approached the shark, but she turned towards us, and with an outstretched hand we were immobile. "He will not harm me. He is only here for my help," she said softly as we remained motionless on the sand. She turned back to the animal, and as the water receded, it was quite evident that the animal was indeed in trouble. A large fishing net was wrapped around the tail and hindquarters of the shark, cutting into the dorsal fins. Lucy unwound the net from the beast as she expressed calming sounds to the creature.

"Oh no! This net has cut into you!" she exclaimed. "Here! Let me help," and with those words, the child placed her hands on the animal's wound. Before our eyes, the wound began to close and instantly heal. "All better," she whispered to the animal that we could now identify as a massive tiger shark. "My, my ... you do seem to get into some trouble, don't you!" Lucy exclaimed as she observed a long scar that stretched across the right side of the shark's body. "I will call you Scamp!" she giggled. "That name fits a rascal like you! Off you go, Scamp, but I will see you soon!" The massive shark looked at the girl once more before swimming off into the deep. She turned back towards us, and with a wave of her hand, we were mobile again.

"How did you do that?" Mace asked as he flexed movement back into his fingertips.

"Very easily," she giggled. "I can do lots of things."

"You know, Lucy, most humans are afraid of sharks," William said as we walked back over the dunes to the landing.

"Well, that's just silly," she said, "And I'm like Margo you know; I'm not like other humans," she said proudly.

"No, you're not, Lucy-bug! You are very special." I replied, trying to hide the awe I felt for what I had just witnessed.

"William, will you take Lucy back to the boat?' Mace asked. "I would like to speak to Marguerite alone." William nodded.

"It was nice to see you again, Mace," she giggled.

"It was a pleasure to see you too, Lucy. I hope to see more of your talents in the future."

"Alright. But you can't tell anyone," she whispered. "If the humans knew what I could do, they may not let me see my friends anymore."

"True. That is a very good point. You are a very smart girl. I am very happy to get to know you."

"You too, Mace! See ya!" She began to giggle as William scooped her up and flung her on his back as the pair made their way back to the boat." Mace and I stood alone.

"I know what you have come here to ask of me," Mace said.

"Yes. You are our best hope for her safety," Mace said.

"But she does not live here. How can I protect a child that lives several hours inland?" Mace asked.

"Not yet, but eventually she will be called to the ocean, just as I was called. The gene within her is very strong. Her time living solely amongst the human population is limited," I replied.

"There is no one I have ever witnessed that could command sea dwellers other than Theron. Kirby has a rare connection with marine life. He seems to understand them, but his abilities pale in comparison to this child," Mace said.

"She is Theron's granddaughter, just as I am, though her talents are quite different than mine."

"We must keep her away for as long as possible. We must keep Lucy hidden from Theron and any others who could mean her harm," Mace said. My brow furrowed.

"And if we can't keep her away …."

"I will do what I need to do," Mace replied. "I am a Protector, and she is the greatest treasure I have ever seen."

"Then I have your word that you will help to keep her safe?" I pleaded.

"More than that … you have my vow. No harm will come to the girl as long as I stand as her protector," Mace promised.

"Then I leave her in your protection tomorrow. Thank you, Mace—this promise means more to me than you will ever know."

"Marguerite, I would do anything needed to protect your sister, but I am not just doing this for her. You were willing to sacrifice your life for all of us. There are not many who would do that. I am doing this for you."

"I know … and for that, I give you my eternal gratitude," I replied.

"Just find a way to make it back to us. William is not the only one who will miss having you around," he said. I nodded.

"I will." A single tear rolled down my cheek. "I will find a way to make it back to all of you."

5

———————

"Life is a predicament which precedes death."

~Henry James

William held me as the night sky filled with stars—his body pressed so tightly against mine that I could scarcely breathe. He had left my side for only a few hours, giving me time to say my goodbyes to my family. This mythical creature had gradually become the most real thing in my life. The moonlight beamed through the picture window outlining the most perfect being I had ever known. My fingertips gently traced the creases of his hand, gradually moving over the dips between his muscular arms and working the curves of his broad shoulders. His lips parted with my touch. I gently caressed the lines of his neck before moving my fingers slowly across the edge of his jaw. I treasured every inch of him, studying each line, filing each inch of him to memory.

The scent of his skin was intoxicating. I wanted all of him—forever, and yet, I recognized the possibility that our forever may end at dawn. He knew this too as he had barely spoken all night; I could feel the urgency in his touch as if each second we shared could be our last.

"You know, there is always that chance that Theron will never let me go," I said pulling his body tightly against mine. For the first time all day, the flicker of a smile crept across his lips.

"I know what you are doing, and believe me, the thought crosses my mind about four times a hydrosecond," William whispered in my ear.

"If I recall, you are constantly insisting on me crossing off life experiences," I teased. My knees parted beneath the weight of his body. William covered his face with a pillow in frustration. I rolled over to playfully straddle him. I pulled away the pillow and moved in for a kiss. William stopped me. His expression was serious.

"I do not just want just parts of you—I want all of you. I want all of you every second of forever. I do not know if such is possible between us, but I will not risk losing you. I will not do it this way ... and not before that ring is off of your neck and permanently on your finger for the whole world to see," William said solemnly.

I sighed pressing my lips into his shoulder. "Not even for my birthday?" I smiled batting my eyes. He laughed aloud. It was good to hear him laugh.

"Not even on your birthday," he said, as he buried his face in my hair.

"Fine." I teased, "Oh and, William, ... how long is a hydrosecond?"

****

I fought until I could hold my eyes open no longer. My fear was justified; when I awoke, William was gone. *Damn this whole human sleep thing!* A note rested beside my pillow.

~ This is larger than we feared. Please stay here.
Above all, I will forever be your Protector. Forgive me.

Endlessly Yours,
William

I swiftly snatched my two backpacks, adding my journal, letters to my family, and James's album. I was even able to cram two paint brushes and few tubes of oil paint into the side pocket. The stars hung low in the sky, signifying it was still several hours before dawn. From the top of the porch, I could see my boat was gone. I would have to swim. It would be impossible to catch him, especially with my bag. I dropped the one that contained my shoes, flinging the other bag on my back. I took the stack of zip-locked letters in my hand. These "Parisian" letters were not only my alibi to be mailed weekly by Sadie, there was one in particular that I had spent the early evening wrenching over. I had decided that James deserved to know the truth. William's fears were rational, and if I did not return, James should know the true reason. It was all I had left to give him.

I was a half a second from diving off the dock when I stopped myself. William may have greater speed in the water, but I could *run* faster than any Sironian or ordinary human. I took off through the night sky, over the dunes, and onto the firm sand. My hair flamed behind me as the air streamed at my sides, my feet pounding faster and faster as I hurdled the three-mile distance to Knoxx Point. Within minutes, I was over the sea wall in front of the estate that was like a second home to me. The grounds were dark except for a dim light just off the back terrace and beaconing light from the newly-repaired crow's nest atop of the main house.

Careful not to wake Henry, Sadie, or Olivia, I positioned the large envelope containing the letters next to the back door and took off running towards the south terrace overlooking the point. I would have to plunge across the mouth of the jetties, then swim south through the dark inlet waters, before reaching the marsh trails that would take me to the landing. My heart began to race at the challenge before me, but fear would not conquer the possibility of losing William.

I slipped off my shoes and stuffed them into my only backpack. The jetties were radiant at night as the light from Knoxx Point glistened on the rocks. I once again secured the pack and was about to dive in, when a different kind of light caught my attention. Out of the corner of my eye, beyond the smooth waters of the inlet and past the oceanic breakers was the unmistakable flicker of Sironian eyes beneath the surface. What I thought was one pair multiplied into over fifty pairs of white glowing orbs.

Aria had lied. Theron had sent an army for me, an army standing by to take out the Protectors at a moment's notice. My mind raced, maybe that was Theron's plan all along, to have the Protectors in one place to attack. We had been scattered the night of the hurricane. We were outnumbered, but it would have been difficult to take us all. How easy we were making it for him this time! We would be an easy target, waiting together for a "peaceful transfer" that would never take place. I was slowly figuring out what William most likely already knew. That is why he must have left this morning, to reassemble the crew for a fight! My only consolation was that Caleb was safely asleep in his bed—or was he? My boat was missing! I assumed William had taken it to prevent me from coming to the landing. Had Caleb discovered the plans and taken it instead?

Through a beacon of light illuminating from Knoxx Point, the shapes of two sizeable figures partially lifted out of the water. I recognized them instantly as the two sirens I had previously perceived watching me. There was no beauty about them like those in Theron's Legion. Their white skin and dark eyes only confirmed the fact that Theron had sent a more powerful army this time. But the fact that they were here, still off the coast, proved that I was not too late.

I plunged across the mouth to the south side of the point. It was here that the army appeared to be slowly moving down the coastline—watching. Silas's training served me well as I rapidly climbed the rocks at the deepest part of the jetties, paying little attention to the barnacles piercing and slicing into my feet.

As I reached the highest peak, one of the siren saw me. He turned and summoned creatures about him. In numbers larger than fifty, they simultaneously eased their monstrous heads above the water's surface. My heart sank as they readied to attack.

"Are you the half-breed?" he growled.

"I am ...." My heart was pounding so swiftly that it was all that I could do to keep my voice from shaking. I would not give them the satisfaction of seeing the utter fear I felt inside. "I have seen you watching me and now you bring an army. I am here alone."

"Alone?" he seemed surprised by my words. "As tales go, your forces are great."

"As I said, I stand here alone. Have you come solely for me or are you prepared for battle?"

"We have come to collect you," the creature growled. In an instant the monster sprung from the water. As if the incredible distance between us was nothing, he effortlessly landed on the rocks just a few feet away. His pale form, though human in shape, was larger than any mortal I had ever seen. Along his back, pointed bone-like fins protruded down his spine.

"Then collect me you shall! Peacefully, if Theron's men retreat completely from the area," I boldly stated. My hands shook.

"Theron? We do not answer to Theron," the monster laughed.

I stumbled backward in shock just as the second large creature bounded from the water and landed behind me. I had been mistaken. I had foolishly thought the assembled army belonged to Theron. What stood before me was the very thing Theron accumulated forces to protect against—the Obyascon. Theron had sought to obtain my talents before the Obyascon could use me against him. William had known—he had known since the first Obyascon appeared in inlet waters months earlier that they were looking for something—someone. All of the intense training, all of the extra precautions were in part to keep me out of the hands of these evil creatures—and I was mistakenly handing myself to them.

The first creature lunged. I front flipped over him to an adjacent rock. His dagger-like claws narrowly missed me, which only seemed to anger the beast. With a growl the two hulking figures simultaneously attacked. I flipped backward again, each hand balancing on the slippery boulders. I launched each foot into the stone-like chests of the Obyascon. One creature was thrown completely off the jetties, but the other caught himself along the rocks and charged again. His long arms lashed out at me, but I leapt upward to dodge the impact. As I landed, I slipped on the wet footing allowing his daggers to slice through my jeans and into my shin. I shrieked in pain.

"We would prefer to take you alive, but if you insist on rebellion, your head will suffice," the beast huffed.

I crouched like a mountain lion preparing to attack. "My head isn't going anywhere!" I hissed. I snapped launching a swift kick to the groin. The pain knocked him backwards long enough for me to locate the other Obyascon who sprang back out of the water towards me. I met him mid-air, clawing and tearing at the beast; my strength growing with anger. I would rip him limb from limb as I had done to Maris! My feet pressed my body away from the spines of the beast. I angled my hands beneath his jaw to tear it from his shoulders, but I was not fast enough. We hit hard down on the rocks, the weight of the creature pushing a razor-sharp fin though my shoulder blade. I moaned from the impact and cried out in pain as I thrust the creature from me.

I fleetingly glanced into the waves; the army was there—waiting to attack if needed. I was not naïve; I could not fight off an entire army alone. I needed an escape! I needed to run, but I had inadvertently cut off my greatest option in choosing the jetties as my reveal. The clashing water was not an option as I would be surrounded in seconds.

The two relentless Obyascon blocked the only waterless way off of the stony peninsula. Again they attacked simultaneously but were unexpectedly blinded by the beacon from Knoxx Point as its light unexpectedly shined down upon us. The deep-sea creatures wailed as the beam hit their eyes. As they tried to refocus, an arrow shot one beast in the shoulder blade and the other clean through the side. Both were knocked to the ground. I was not alone!

"Henry!" I gasped at the sight of my dear friend as he appeared lugging a dousie bow.

"Are you alright?" he asked.

I nodded. "Sadie sent word to the crew, and they are on the way. Aria has even sent word to Theron that the Obyascon are on the attack. We just have to hold them off until they get here," Henry said. He was still breathing heavily from his efforts to get to me.

"I am so sorry," I cried. I thought they were Theron's forces coming for me. I didn't want a fight."

"Silas received word last night that the Obyascon were moving up the coast. He signaled the Protectors, assuming they would attack after the transfer. A traitor reported your existence to the Obyascon. We have to get you outta here!"

However, it was too late. Horrific pale creatures with long bone finned bodies were climbing out of the water on all three sides. All genetic parallels to the human race had been so mutated and distorted that these monsters more closely resembled disfigured dinosaurs than the humanlike siren I had known. The only escape was blocked by the two enraged creatures before us. Their eyes had changed—some type of a protective lens now covered them as they evolved for dark waters.

"They must be defeated!" I cried, charging at the beings. Henry fired the dousie bow again, this time missing them altogether. Henry was trained in medical care instead of combat and was ill-equipped for this fight. I engaged one of them while Henry defended advances from the other.

Morning hues began to creep ever so slightly along the horizon. How ironic that I had just a few moments earlier dreaded dawn, and now I prayed for it. Caleb and William would be arriving any second. Could the Protectors defeat such an army? The infantry remained on the rocks near the water's edge, leaving me to believe that like most sirens, they were unable to part from the water. But could the Protectors even get to us? Henry had managed to make it through undetected, but the forces had surrounded us now. I had to finish them off! I landed blow after blow with my only good arm, careful to avoid his razor-sharp claws. I was swift with both my arm and my feet. My dexterity, strength, balance, and speed far outmatched the beast. The Obyascon began to weaken as his energy was spent. I was about to deliver the final blow when out of the corner of my eye I saw the horrific scene. The other creature had Henry around the neck threatening to cut off his head at any moment.

"Wait! Leave him alone! You have come for me; just let him go!" I shrieked. He paused contemplating my proposal.

"And you will stop your resistance?" he mumbled in a strange archaic dialect.

"Don't, Marguerite!" Henry shouted.

"I will go with you! Just leave my friend unharmed!" I pleaded.

"We accept." He growled as one of the infantry grabbed me by the ankle and pulled me into the water where I was seized instantly. But my sacrifice was in vain.

I screamed as the Obyascon rammed his fin into Henry's chest—straight through his heart. Through my anger, I ripped myself from my captives. Blinded by the pain at the loss of my friend I wailed against my captors. More and more forces attacked me until all I could see was Henry's lifeless body slipping between the rocks and into the clashing water.

My world went dark.

6

———

"Yea, all things live forever, though at times they sleep and are forgotten."

~She, H. Rider Haggard

I blinked, trying to bring the world into focus. I could only see pain. I frantically reached for my necklace. The shiva hung safely around my neck, next to the engagement ring William had given me. I began to cry out of relief, pain, and sorrow. The hollowness filling the pit of my stomach was my only proof that I had survived. I was alive—Henry was not. I leaned over the bed to get sick. Much to my surprise, there was a long slender arm there holding out a bucket. I regurgitated a large amount of salt water before sinking back into a lumpy feather bed. I closed my blurry eyes to once again escape into the darkness. Nothing mattered. Henry was dead. Sadie no longer had a husband. Olivia would grow up without a father. It was all because of me. I wept. Someone was close by. I could hear their breathing, but I was too distraught to care—too distressed to move. I cried until I fell asleep again.

This pattern continued for the next few days. As I became more and more lucid, the vomiting was replaced by agony, and the tears exchanged with grief. The physical suffering was intense. I knew that I was severely injured, but the emotional anguish trumped any physical discomfort. My friend was gone. Through it all, soft thin fingers nursed my wounds and wiped away my tears. On the fourth day, my anguish was replaced by a longing—a longing for William's arms around me. Scar tissue had begun forming over the loss of Henry. The hole was there. It would always be there, but another concern took center stage. I could imagine how William must be suffering. I would find a way back to him.

I tried to focus, but the room was blurred. I closed my eyes, envisioning the perfect lines of William's face. I would do this for him. I opened my eyes again, this time with greater resolve. The cold, dimly lit room slowly began to take shape. The walls and ceiling were made of roughly cut dark stones. Weathered bronze sconces illuminated the windowless room. A pair hung on each side of the bed and another by the doorway. The door appeared to be centuries old as did most of the furnishings in the room. The eclectic array of contents could have been salvaged from a sunken ship. Several ancient oil paintings hung on the walls, and an old ornate mirror rested atop a battered washboard. I looked around me. The large brass feather bed was green from age and tarnish, but the pale cream linens were spotless.

In the corner sat a young teenaged female. She was sleeping. I was surprised to see one of the books from my bag lying across her chest. She was beautiful. Dark copper curls fell around her ivory pale skin, and an antique white dress hung on her extremely thin frame. A basin of blood-soaked water rested on the nightstand, a clear indication that the girl had recently been dressing my wounds. I watched her sleep for some time. She was distinctly not an

Obyascon but far too beautiful to be human. *She must be a Sironian.* I stirred to get a better look at her but instantly realized the severity of my injuries as the pain nearly took my breath away. I groaned in a failed attempt to sit up; the girl stumbled to her feet knocking my book to the ground and instantly hurried from the room, her head cast downward.

I painfully inched my way backwards until my head was resting against the headboard. For the first time, I was able to look at my wounds. I was badly bruised all over with a ghastly slice across my shin. The cut was several inches in length and was severed to the bone. Tiny neat stitches had pulled the skin back together. The worst of my injuries was to my right shoulder. The spike of the Obyascon had pierced it clear through to my back. I could barely move my arm without excruciating pain. The wound was sanitized and packed with gauze to drain. With such care, it was likely that the Obyascon wanted to keep me alive. But why had they come for me? I could guess the answer. The Obyascon were aware that Theron wanted me so they had seized me first.

"I have to find a way out of here!" I thought, losing my balance as I tried to stand. I was Sironian, and I had been here days! *"Why have these wounds not healed?"* I did not realize I had spoken aloud until I was startled with an answer. A young, handsome man stood in the doorway. I had never seen him before.

"Who are you?" I asked. He entered my room and stood at the foot of the bed.

"I would like to ask the same question of you. The Obyascon left you in these tunnels a week ago. I found you and brought you here."

"I'm Marguerite Westley."

"It is a pleasure to meet you. I am Brooks." He fumbled nervously.

"Were you both also captured by the Obyascon?" I asked. Brooks nodded.

"My sister and I have been held captive here since we were very young."

"Your sister? The one reading my book?" I glanced towards the novel now on the floor.

"Anna? She is quite excited and intrigued that you are here, but I can assure you she is not reading your book. She is blind."

"Blind? But I saw her …?"

"She loves books … the smell of them … the feel of them, but Anna has been blind since we were taken here. She was so small that we speculate that the rapid change in pressure burst the vessels in her eyes."

"Oh," I replied. "I'm sorry."

"The Obyascon do not pardon the life of many. Why do you suppose they spared your life?" Brooks asked.

"I don't know," I replied, not wanting to reveal myself to this inquisitive stranger.

"So you are from the Protector line?" he asked.

"Huh?" I was surprised that this boy knew so much about sirens.

"I made that assumption since you are a land dweller," he probed.

"Oh, yes. I am a Protector," I replied proudly.

"Of whom do you swear allegiance?" Brooks asked. My brow furrowed.

"The only allegiance I have ever sworn was to the United States of America," I replied.

"So you are sympathetic to the humans, and yet, you carry the mark of Theron?" I glance at the silvery insignia above my wrist. "I suppose that would make you quite a target indeed."

I was anxious to end this line of questioning. "Did you do this?" I pointed to the stitches on my leg?" He nodded.

"I did. When you have as much time on your hands as Anna and I, you study many things. There are medical books in the adjacent cove—a library of sorts," Brooks said.

"Thank you. I appreciate you saving my life."

"You are welcome. It is not often that we have visitors." He moved across the room and took the seat his sister had occupied earlier.

"So you are prisoners here?" I asked.

"Yes, though we do not often see our captors. Life here is all we have ever really known," he replied.

"But the Obyascon are keeping you here?"

"We are not free to leave, but in truth, even if we were granted our freedom we would have no place to go. Our parents broke Theron's one child policy when Anna was born. Theron came to take us. I was only seven at the time and Anna just an infant. Our parents escaped and put us into hiding, where we were later discovered by the Obyascon. They brought us here, and we have been trapped ever since."

"The Obyascon do not come into the caves?" I asked.

"No. They brought you to the entrance to the tunnels and left you. I found you and brought you here. Anna has no memory of them. They are water bound, except for a select few who carry a gene similar to those in the Protector line."

"Why don't you try to escape?" I protested.

"There are many miles of oxygen-filled tunnels and caverns. I continue to explore them, but the only known escape tunnel is heavily guarded. Anna could never make it out of the caves without being detected."

"You have lived here since you were a child and have not located an escape?" I sank.

"This place is a sheer labyrinth of winding passageways. Even if I did discover an unguarded escape route, Anna has never been taught to swim."

"But she is a siren? I thought all sirens could swim?" As soon as the words came out of my mouth, I knew the answer. I had once been like her. She was afraid of the water.

"She will not leave the caves. The closest she comes to water is the natural saltwater pools that form under the stalactites and rock formations," Brooks explained. I thought back on the last time I was severely injured. William had held me through the night in the saltwater pools at Knoxx Point. Each memory brought me back to him. I had to get home to him!

"Brooks, I need your help." I pleaded. "I have to find a way out of here!" I shivered.

"I don't know of a way," he said bluntly.

"Where are we? It is so cold in here!" I uttered.

"I have never actually made it all the way through the cave tunnels, but I've made it far enough to identify several deep-water fish and rare species indigenous to southeastern North America. The rock formations of these caves are not consistent with those of the northern provinces, and its mineral content suggests that we are just above the abyssopelagic zone."

"I thought the Obyascon were from the Polar Regions?" I asked.

"They are? This must be one of the southern outposts," he said.

"We have to get out of here!" I hissed as I unsuccessfully tried to pull back the ancient covers.

"You are still very ill, and I would never leave Anna behind." I shivered, both at the thought of being trapped and because the cavern chamber was freezing.

"You're shaking?" Brooks asked curiously.

"I am. It's just cold in here." I shivered again. He seemed puzzled.

"How are you cold? Maybe your injuries have caused damage to your temperature regulators?"

"I have none. I am not only Sironian; I am human as well." He stared at me in astonishment.

"Impossible! A siren cannot mate with human! They have not the self-control nor the capacity to do so!"

"And yet, I am proof of the contrary. I was born a human but also carry the genes of a siren," I replied.

"But the poison from their fins should have killed you!" Brooks exclaimed.

"True. Perhaps I carry some type of immunity."

"I have never heard of that happening before."

"And you have never heard of a half-breed either!" I replied. "I have no other explanation for being alive. I blacked out right after the attack. I remember very little before waking up here today. You say I have been here a week?"

"Tomorrow will mark the day," he said.

I ached. William would be sick with worry. *How could I have been gone a week?* I beheld my attire—a white gypsy style shirt pulled low on the shoulders for my wound and loose black palazzo pants. I blushed realizing that I would have been completely under Brooks' care this week.

"I'm dressed like a pirate," I said dryly. "You dressed me?" My eyes narrowed as I glared across the room at him.

"I can see your concern," he replied swiftly. "I could not tend to your wounds in your other clothes. Do not worry. Anna dressed you and took care of your personal needs. Though blind, she is more than capable."

"I appreciate that," I said as my expression softened.

"If what you say is true, it makes perfect sense as to why the Obyascon kept you alive. You must be of profuse value to Theron." I shivered again. "Anna!" he called out, and the girl appeared in the doorway.

"Can you warm up this room for our new friend?" Brooks asked. Anna's eyes were sealed shut, but it did not stop her. The girl appeared. Anna placed both hands on the frames of the doorway and concentrated fiercely. Heat waves formed around her slowly passing from stone to stone until the entire room radiated warmth. My mouth dropped open in amazement.

"Thank you, Anna," I replied, astonished at what the young girl had just done. She hurried back out of the room.

"Anna does not speak to anyone but me. She has always been this way. When Anna was a child, she would wake up screaming in fear of the Obyascon. I tried many things to calm her fears, but nothing calmed her fears until she learned to play the piano. She hides herself in her music."

"Music … at the bottom of the ocean?" I asked.

"Yes. We have many things here. I made friends with one of the Obyascon. Quan is exclusively a sea dweller. We met when we were boys. I was exploring the tunnels and found a portal to the ocean.

None of the Obyascon are aware of our friendship. He has been bringing us salvage off of ship wrecks ever since.

"You say there is a portal?" I asked. "Is that where you found me?"

"There is … quite a distance from here. But Quan says there are guards patrolling nearby. He brought a piano for Anna when she was five. I meet him each afternoon. He brings us food, books—all kinds of things really. The key is to allow them dry out. It helps to have a sister who can supply her own heat source."

"I imagine so," I replied. "So you read to her?"

"Every night … and she plays the piano for me."

"I use to read to my own sister," physical pain swept through me at the thought of my sweet Lucy. The innocence of this new girl reminded me of her. "Do you think Anna will play something for me?"

"Sure. Once she gets to know you. How old is your sister?" Brooks asked.

"She will turn six next month. I also have a younger brother. We are close too—like you and Anna." Reality began to set in. My family had no idea what had happened to me. If I remained trapped in this underwater prison, they might never know. The Obyascon weren't planning to use me against Theron; they were planning to hide me—at least until they had use of me. Had these two sirens been trapped down here for all of these years? I began to panic.

"I have to leave! Brooks, I have to get out of here!" I tried to stand but instantly crumpled over in pain.

"There is nowhere to go, Marguerite—especially in this condition. The main thing is that you regain your strength. Just rest and I will go get you something to eat." I closed my eyes wishing for the love I once had … and the life that had vanished.

I was not getting better. Four more days passed and I was barely able to sit up in bed. My wounds were not healing, and my vision would still go blurry from time to time. I could not understand it. As soon as I would begin to improve, another round of flulike symptoms would set in on top of the other ailments. I began to wonder if Brooks was right with the Obyascon venom being lethal to humans. Maybe I was more human than siren after all. Maybe I was dying a slow death.

Anna loomed awkwardly in the doorway for the first day, but I had slowly begun to gain her trust. She still had not spoken, but I could sense she was close. Her longing for female companionship was evident. Anna seemed to like being my caretaker. As Brooks was skilled in medical care, she left part to him, but she aided me in every other need. Anna brushed my hair several times a day and would help me with all my personal care. She would play the piano for me—filling the tunnels with intricately executed music pieces, and I would fill the afternoons by reading my favorite books to her. I would try to hide the occasional tear that would escape whenever I would get to one of Lucy's favorite parts. Despite her blindness, she would catch the tear as it reached my chin. Anna loved to hear stories about my family. I also told her all about the Crew, James— and William.

Brooks left late each afternoon to meet Quan for supplies and was absent until late evening. Anna became the most attentive during that time and rarely left my side. My wounds would not heal. The sores became inflamed, and a high fever took hold of me. I knew an infection had spread through my body. I was dying. I waited until Brooks left and devised a plan. I knew what my body needed.

"Will you help me, Anna? I need a saltwater basin. Brooks mentioned you bathe in the pools. Could you bring me to one?" She seemed skeptical at first but reluctantly helped me from the bed. It was the first time I had ventured from the room since arriving.

"I will take you there," she responded softly. It was the first time I had ever heard her speak. Anna helped me through a series of stalactite-covered mazes before leading me to a small saltwater pool. I watched as the girl swirled her hands in the water. Steam began to rise as she swirled her fingers atop the water's surface. "It's ready now," Anna said with a smile. She helped me disrobe and held my arm as I eased into the water. I sat upon a hefty rock formation and eased myself backwards so that the water covered my body from the chin down. I winced as it filled my wounds, but the pain was short-lived. My injuries were not healing. I knew of no better cure than the saltwater. I soaked in the pool for over an hour as Anna kept me company. She was beginning to open up to me. The once quiet girl began telling me about her music and her studies and in turn asked me question after question about life on land. She was immensely curious about how I was created. I told her all that I knew. She helped me to my room. I could already feel a drastic improvement as the pain faded from my wounds. The fever within me dissipated.

"I will let you get some rest." Anna said, "But it is probably best not to tell Brooks about today. He asked me to make sure you did not leave your room." Her admission was my first cause for alarm where Brooks was concerned. I would have to be more guarded, at least until I could figure out for sure if he was trustworthy.

"Well, I would not want him to be angry with you," I said. "Thank you, Anna. Will you take me again tomorrow?"

"Yes. I will wait until Brooks goes to get supplies from Quan, and I will bring you again. He meets up with him every day at the same time. Quan can't come into the caves you know. He is sea bound, but they have a special place where they can meet up without alarming the other guards. It takes him nearly an hour to make it there through the caves."

"Well, that should give us plenty of time then." When Brooks came to take a look at my wounds, I pretended to be asleep. Later when he returned, Anna hastily spoke up that she had already attended to them.

"Ok. Anna, just be sure to put this ointment on them twice a day before dressing them." He left a small brown bottle on the bedside table. I had seen ample improvement from soaking. Anna kept her promise and returned day after day to sneak me down to the pools. I replaced the strange contents of Brook's ointment with straight seawater. The wounds began to heal almost instantly. Each day I made excuses for Brooks not to redress my wounds. Much to his protestation, I convinced him Anna was fully capable. I knew that at this pace I should fully regain my strength in only a few more days. I began to wonder if Brooks was sabotaging my healing. Maybe my skepticism was unjust, but I just had a strange feeling about him. Anna and I on the other hand had become fast friends. I spent the majority of my days reading to her or telling her stories, and she spent the other half playing the piano for me. Nothing took away the constant pain I felt from being away from those that I loved, nor lessened the longing I felt for William, but Anna's presence was my one comfort.

On my twentieth day, my strength had almost entirely returned, and all physical signs of my fight with the Obyascon had vanished. Anna came charging into my room. "Ok, Brooks has left, so you can stop playing the sick patient." Anna had picked up on my scheme. "Look, I know you are completely healed, and yet, you continue to make Brooks believe you are still bedridden. I can only guess this is part of some plan."

"I mean no slight to your brother, Anna. I just know he talks with the Obyascon guards. It is best for everyone to believe I am too ill to escape—this includes your brother."

"When you leave will you take me too?" Anna whispered. My heart sank.

"Anna, I am not even sure if I can make it past the Obyascon, and even then, I have no idea where we are. We could be hundreds of miles from land. My home could be on the other side of the world."

"Is it because I am blind?"

"No, Anna." I swiftly replied. "Look, a very close friend of mine died at the hands of the Obyascon. I care about you and would never want to put you in harm's way."

"You care about me?" She welled up with emotion. "No one that I can remember has ever cared about me before … except for Brooks."

"I more than care about you, Anna; I love you like my own sister. Which is why I cannot risk any harm coming to you."

"But you would leave me here alone again," she cried.

"I could find my friends. Then we could come back for you and your brother!"

"Teach me to swim, Marguerite! Teach me as William taught you!" Tears began to flow from the girl's sealed eyelids. It was the first time I had seen her cry. I knew what she was thinking. If I could teach her to swim, then there was a possibility that I would take her with me.

"Alright," I said as I took her hand in mine. "Let's go turn you into a mermaid." She clasped her hands together and beamed with excitement.

"But, Marguerite, … everyone knows there is no such thing as mermaids."

"You know, I have heard that somewhere." I smiled as I led my siren friend towards her destiny.

7

"After all, the truth seeing is within."

~ Middlemarch, George Eliot

"**D**on't let me go underwater!" Anna said as her feet began to flutter faster and faster beneath the water.

"Let you go underwater? Anna, your feet are moving so swiftly I think you could fly away."

"So you think I am doing well?" she giggled.

"Like a fish to water." Anna smiled, meticulously executing every step that I had taught her. How could she not be an excellent student? My teacher had been the best. Every ounce of my being longed for William. The features of his face permeated my every waking thought. Every memory I had of William infiltrated the painful dreams of my restless sleep. I was sentenced to endless night—for he was my sun.

"Marguerite … Marguerite?"

"What? Oh. Keep moving. The power comes from the feet."

"You're thinking about William again."

"I am always thinking about William." Anna stopped paddling.

"Tell me about it." She leaned against the rock next to me.

"Tell you about what?"

"About love."

"Gosh, Anna. You will have a lifetime to learn about love for yourself. You can't be more than fourteen." Anna was so bashful that her eyes rarely met mine.

"I am fifteen, Marguerite, or at least I think I am fifteen. I do not know my birthday." The small stature and mild temperament of the girl had led me to believe she was much younger. "And we both know there is little chance of me ever getting out of here."

"Anna, there are all kinds of love. I am extremely close to my family. I would do anything for them. I would give my life for them. I guess that is why your parents must have run with you and your brother. They must have loved you with that insane kind of love to try to hide you from Theron." I thought of the sacrifice made by William's parents. They had loved William and Madeline with that insane love. They had died for it.

"When I was younger, I would wait day after day in anticipation that my parents would come. I would always try to imagine what they must have been like. Brooks would never tell me anything. With every question I asked about them, he would always say that he did not remember. I finally quit asking."

"The memories must be too painful." An odd expression of doubt spread across her face as she contemplated this.

"Yes … maybe," she replied sadly.

"Your brother loves you, Anna."

"Yes. I think so. I mean, he takes care of me, and he is kind to me. He is all that I have ever known, but it is different from the romantic love from the books." She shook her head as if to erase painful thoughts. "Tell me about that kind of love—like the kind you have for William."

"Well, I guess you know you love someone when you cannot imagine your life without that person. In love, all logic is preceded by an emotion so strong that senses seem to malfunction as they no longer target you, but the object of your affection." Anna's head cocked to the side in a childlike way as she tried to comprehend logic that I could barely understand myself. I smiled. "Aside from my family, I thought there was no one in the world that I could love more than my best friend James … and then I met William. I knew I loved James because I could not imagine a life without him, but as I fell in love with William, emotion became irrational."

"I am not sure that I understand," she said. I laughed.

"It's hard to describe something that you just 'feel.' Love is complicated, and yet, so simple that every part of your body understands it perfectly except for the one part of reason—your mind."

"Do you think I will fall in love someday?" she said with a faint smile.

"I do, Anna." I saw a glimmer of hope in the face of a girl who had been without hope for many years. "And I promise you that no matter what happens, I will not leave you here."

"Because you said you love me?"

"Yes," I replied solemnly.

"And when you love someone you do not want to live in a world without them … even if it is a world far away?"

"Exactly. You deserve to know that world, Anna. I will take you there."

"You promise?"

"I promise. I never break a promise."

****

Each day when Brooks would leave for supplies, Anna and I would hurry down to the pools to practice. Each day I stood in awe as she grew in confidence and ability. My affection for the girl continued to grow, but as the days passed, I became more and more skeptical of Brooks. What Anna could not see was becoming more and more evident to me; Brooks was hiding something. Despite the full return of my strength, Anna and I continued to hide my recovery from Brooks who now only joined us briefly in the morning and at night. My presence brought him a newfound sense of freedom as he no longer had to spend his days tending to Anna. He seemed quite pleased that I was there to occupy the girl, but his frustration with me began to grow. I feigned illness or tiredness each day as his questions became more and more pointed. His carefully planned façade began to slip ever so slightly as his urgency to gain information from me began to grow.

I did not trust him, but it was not until Anna mistakenly got a paper cut when I was reading to her, that I fully began to understand the depth of his alliance with the Obyascon. Anna poured a new bottle of the antiseptic Brooks had set aside for my care onto her cut, the wound suddenly swelling and throbbing in pain. I instantly speculated that the potion was not antiseptic at all but some type of derivative from the toxin exhibited by the Obyascon. The small cut rapidly became a large laceration and was only mended when I took the girl to the salt-water pools.

I watched as the girl's wound instantly healed from the water. I was flooded with memories: William bringing me to the tidal pools to heal the night of the hurricane, me nursing William's injury from the Obyascon, William caring for me after my first attack from Theron's Legion, William's arms around me in the Knoxx Point tidal pools as he saved me during the transformation. As my mind scrolled backward through memory after memory, I remembered my first encounter with William on the beach. I could still feel his hand in mine as he led me to the water to wash the sand from my eyes. How swiftly the abrasions had healed when supplied the element needed for a siren's survival.

"Anna, I need for you to trust me. I need for you to go under water and try to open your eyes." I said anxiously.

"But I am not ready yet! I have just learned to swim," she protested.

"I need for you to do this, Anna! Trust me on this!"

"I am frightened!"

"I need for you to be brave, Anna. I know you can do this. I will be right here holding your hand!"

"No. I mean. I am not physically able to open my eyes."

"What do you mean?" I was confused.

"They are sealed." It was then that my eyes zoomed in on the tiny stitches between her eyelashes. Stitches so minute that they would be impossible for a mere human eye to see.

"Oh, Anna! Who did this to you?" As the words came from my mouth, I instantly knew the answer. The remnants of matching tiny stitches had sealed the wound on my leg," I gasped.

"My eyes have always been sealed. Brooks said it was the only way to protect me. He told me that it would be too painful for light or water to enter my eyes. Brooks explained that they were sealed for my protection." I felt as if I were about to get sick.

"Anna, that potion your brother supplied for my wounds was administered to keep me ill. What if your eyes were sealed for the very same purpose?" She shook her head in disbelief; her expression twisted in denial.

"He would never do that to me! Brooks is my brother! He loves me." Anna took off running back towards our sleeping quarters.

I began to run after her when a faint flicker of light caught my attention down one of the narrowest and most treacherous tunnels. I stepped into it, unsure if it were even passable. I began to follow the dark stalactite encrusted passageway, climbing over and around formation after formation for the greater part of a mile. The light grew more vivid with each step. At last, I stepped out into the bright light half expecting it to lead to heaven itself. The passageway led to a cove. I gasped as I realized that we were not hundreds of miles beneath the surface of the water but instead hidden away just below sea level in the remote caves of an island.

I had only seconds to gaze into the beauty of the sun against the cove before movement at the water's surface caught my attention. I hid behind a stalagmite just inside the cave as a large Obyascon surfaced carrying several large bundles under his arms. I instantly thought to make a dash for it. There appeared to be no other creature or human in sight to stop me. I had been skilled enough to take on two Obyascon larger than this one. I thought the creature little match for my abilities if it were to come to a fight.

Pristine white beaches stretched for quite a distance beneath high dark rocky cliffs. Silas had taught me to climb quite well, but there would be no need for it as it was unlikely that the creature would be any match for my speed at a sprint. I made the resolve to make a run for it ... but something stopped me. I was leaving behind the girl—a girl that had known little of life and love. I had to go back for Anna. I could not leave her behind. I had promised her! I quietly followed behind the Obyascon, hiding behind stalagmites and cutouts in the cave walls to keep the Obyascon from discovering me. He trudged on oblivious that I was traveling about fifteen yards behind him. I made the quick assumption that the creature must be the creature Brooks had befriended, Quan, but as the Obyascon grew closer and closer to our quarters, I became alarmed. Brooks was nowhere in sight. Both Anna and Brooks had told me that the Obyascon did not travel into the caves. *Something must have happened to Brooks!* When the creature was approximately fifty yards from Anna's quarters, I hastily planned my attack. I could not let this creature harm my friend! I coiled to strike, but the creature stopped.

Confused, I watched as he pulled out a change of clothes from his bundles. My eyes bulged in shock and horror as I spied the creature before me shrink down and transform into the boy I had known this past month as Brooks. Brooks was not a siren after all! He was an Obyascon—some sort of shape shifter! Could Anna be an Obyascon too? My first instinct was to run, to get as far away from this prison as possible, but what if Anna were not an Obyascon. What if she were being held prisoner here just as I had been? I could not leave her behind. After my escape, they would surely fear I would return for the girl and would possibly move her to a new location where I may never be able to find her! I could not take the risk until I knew for sure.

Unaware of my presence, Brooks first headed toward the supply room, allowing a split second to dart past him into the quarters that had served as my room. I hurriedly slipped into the bed grabbing my book off the nightstand, flopped it onto my chest, and pretended to be asleep. Blood swiftly rushed through my veins, and my heart raced so wildly that I was certain when he came to check in on me that he would be able to hear it pounding. I tried with little avail to calm my pulse. As the creature neared my room, he barely held his head in the door to reassure my presence before moving to Anna's chamber to check in on her. I could hear him from down the passageway.

"Anna? Are you unwell? It is rare that I find you in bed at this hour?" Brooks asked.

"I am just a bit tired, Brooks." Her voice was a bit unsteady.

"Perhaps tending to Marguerite is wearing on you."

"No." she swiftly responded. "I do not mind at all. I like having her here. I think I just need some rest that is all. I have already tended to Marguerite's injuries for the day."

"And how is she healing?" he asked.

"Not well. I wonder if Marguerite may need a different antiseptic than the one you provided."

"No," he said hastily. "Continue to apply what I gave you. Obyascon injuries are difficult to heal. It may take many months before she is well again."

"Alright," she replied meekly. "Do you mind if I get some rest? Marguerite and I missed slumber as we lost track of time and missed it this afternoon."

"Yes. I noticed Marguerite was still asleep," he said.

"I will attend to her before nightfall," she insisted.

"Alright. Pleasant slumber, sister!" he said leaving her quarters.

I was anxious to talk to Anna but unsure of how to confront the girl. I doubted that she was an Obyascon, but if she were truly a siren, how could I possibly tell the girl that her entire life had been a lie? The shape-shifter peered into my room several times over the course of the next hour. I did not dare move as I planned my escape. At last, all shuffling subsided and the tunnels became very quiet.

"He's gone. He left about twenty minutes ago." I was startled at Anna's whisper. I turned to see the girl at the end of the bed.

"How did you do that?" I asked. "I have super hearing, and yet, I didn't know you were here at all!"

"Just a talent I guess. I have always been able to pass quietly, but my blindness caused a rare form of super sensitivity. I do not have to see things to know they are there. I can feel the heat levels of objects. It seems to allow me to move undetected, even by those with extra hearing abilities."

"You are pretty amazing! Do you know that?" Even through the darkness, I could see the smile spread across her face.

"No one has ever given me compliments before. Forgive me if I am unaccustomed to it."

"We will learn from each other." I took her hand in mine. "Anna, there is something that I need to tell you …"

"Wait, there is something I need to say first. I thought about what you said earlier, about Brooks. I cannot help but think you might be right. Marguerite, I want you to help me." The girl held out a small pair of scissors. They were similar to the ones from my grandmother's sewing basket.

"Anna, I don't know if I can do this." I looked down at the tiny scissors.

"I know you can." She insisted as she stood to light the candles around the bed. "You can do this, Marguerite!" The girl sat in front of me and leaned in close to the light. I swallowed hard casting all nerves aside as I slowly and meticulously began clipping the tiny threads. The stitches were so intricately placed that they blended with her lashes perfectly.

"When I am finished you might not have any eyelashes left!" I sighed.

"I think I would trade a bit of vanity for my eyesight any day," she said with a faint smile.

"Anna, I am sorry if I gave you false hope earlier. My theory was only speculative. I have no idea of the severity of your condition and if it was wrong of me too…"

"Just cut, Marguerite!" she insisted. I finished one eye and began the careful work on the other. I could only imagine the discomfort, but Anna did not acknowledge the pain. When the last stitch was removed, she rubbed her eyes and slowly tried to open them. After clipping several areas that were still tacked in place, the girl opened her eyes for the first time since infancy. I was startled as the iris of her eye were pale white with only the dark color of her pupil to distinguish that there was an eye there at all.

"Can you see anything?" Tears rolled from Anna's newly-opened eyes.

"Only light and shapes … I guess that I had hoped that …." I stood and began to shove what few belongings I had scattered around the room into a bag.

"Anna, we have to leave. I found a way out earlier today. We are not at the ocean depths but in a cove just off of an island. I came back for you."

"What?" she stood confused. "What about Brooks? Why did you not tell Brooks? We have to wait for him!"

"Anna, Brooks is an Obyascon." Terror and denial spread across her beautiful face.

"That's impossible!" she exclaimed.

"It's true. I saw it today with my own eyes. Before he arrived back, he shifted back to the human form you know."

"I don't believe you! My brother …."

"I do not believe he is your brother, Anna; I think he is your captor!" Tears flowed down her milky eyes. "You have to trust me." She wept openly but at last nodded. "We are leaving—tonight. Go grab anything that is important to you.

"If what you say is true, I have nothing aside from this necklace." Anna pulled from beneath her blouse a chin that now hung like a choker with a tiny shell attached. "This was the only thing that came with me into this dungeon, and this is the only thing I wish to take with me." I brushed the tear from her cheek.

"You say that, but you may appreciate a change of clothes as I am not sure how far we are from the nearest store. I hear banana leaves can be quite chafing." She smiled through her tears leaving the room and reemerging with several clothing items that I crammed into my backpack.

"Are you ready?" I said, blowing out the last candle beside the bed.

"I've been ready for this my whole life," she said as we stepped into the darkness together.

8

———·———

*"Yet there are moments when the walls of the mind grow thin;
when nothing is unabsorbed, and I could fancy that we might
blow so vast a bubble that the sun might set and rise in it and
we might take the blue of midday and the black of midnight
and be cast off and escape from here and now.*

~Virginia Woolf

The tunnels were different at night. I thought I had known darkness, but nothing like this—never anything like this. Anna, living a lifetime of darkness, moved quite gracefully through the black caverns. I stumbled my way through, often allowing her to take the lead for the first part of the journey. We were quite a distance from the sleeping quarters, and still, there was no sight of Brooks. The further we could travel unnoticed the better. My pulse quickened as a blue light glimmered up ahead.

"We have almost reached the salt pools. I can smell it in the air." Anna whispered as she took my hand and pulled me through the darkness.

"I have never been here at night. I did not realize they were luminescent," I said in a soft voice. My heart ached as I remembered the last night I spent with William at the quarry. It seemed like a lifetime ago. *Would I ever again return with the one I loved so dearly?*

"Luminescent?" Anna asked curiously, as we trudged on towards the pool. "Water can glow?"

"It's called bioluminescence." I fought back my emotions. I would have to be tough if we were to escape. "Underwater organisms that were denied light over time developed a way to make light by absorbing what small amounts of light traveled to them. Most glow blue like this one."

"I guess it's kind of like me. Even though I cannot see, I have somehow developed my own sensory devices. My body detects the surface temperature of all around me and subconsciously maps out a grid."

"That is amazing!" I said.

"It would be more amazing if I could see the illumination of the water with my own eyes."

"Anna, are you able to trust me now?" I lit a candle from my backpack and mounted it onto a nearby rock with wax drippings.

"I just fled from my brother and the only home I have ever known to go with you," she uttered.

"So you have faith in me?" I cupped my hands together and dipped them into the pool to fill them with water. "The salt may sting a little," I said as I poured the cool water into the girl's milky white eyes. She winced and closed them, but I coaxed her to open them once more as I dipped and poured again. This time she did not flinch but turned and covered her eyes with her hands.

"Something is happening …." Her voice trembled.

"Anna, are you alright?" I said, suddenly beginning to regret my persuasion.

Her hands slowly slipped from her face. I gasped as her milky white irises now radiated from deep emerald green pupils. I gasped, almost falling to my knees, not at the sudden transformation, but that I was now staring into a pair of eyes that were identical to those that I loved. Anna's eyes were William's eyes! Tears began to stream down my face. *How could I have not seen it earlier!* William was not just in her eyes, but he was also in the crook of her smile, the lines of her hands, and the angle of her chin. I was overcome with emotion. I instantly knew without a doubt that I was staring into the face of the lost Madeline Westley. William had been right all along! Not only did his sister live, but Madeline Westley was now standing in front of me!

"I can see," she gasped as she began to sob inconsolably. "Marguerite, I can see!"

"Yes. You can!" The girl turned, looking at the cavern in all directions, then she turned to me.

"Why, Marguerite! Everything is so beautiful! The water is beautiful—you are beautiful! Oh, thank you—thank you—thank you!" I giggled in delight at the girl's newfound joy. "Let's go! It will be daybreak soon, and I have a whole world to see!" She was moving in all directions at once, her emerald eyes glowing through the darkness.

"Yes, you do!" *More than you know.* "I know the way out from here. This tunnel is a bit treacherous so be sure to stay close behind me." I had no sooner stepped foot into the channel before the girl raced ahead bouncing from rock formation to formation. She skillfully maneuvered through the maze of stalagmites and stalactites, effortlessly sliding through even the tightest of passageways. I hurried behind, trying to keep up with a girl who had just been given life.

"Look, Marguerite! I think we are almost there! I can see the opening to the cove just ahead!"

"Wait! Anna! Let me go ahead to be sure all is clear!" My words were lost as the girl's jubilance outweighed all previous caution. "Anna!" I called as she ran out of the cave and into the moonlight. The splendor of the island took my breath away. The clear night sky flickered from the light of a million twinkling stars, and the moonlight shimmered as it hit the crystalline pink sands.

"Isn't it lovely, Marguerite!" Anna gasped as she danced across the sand. I eyed our escape routes. It was unlikely that someone who had just been granted her eyesight would be able to climb the dark rocky cliffs before us. The beach route seemed like the more logical choice, but there was no shelter—nowhere to hide once the Obyascon discovered our escape. I grabbed her hand as I headed towards the cliffs. We would hide in the vegetation until dawn— then I could get a better idea of our location and come up with another plan.

"Yes, but, Anna, we have to find cover before we're ...."

"It's a little too late for that," a male voice replied. Startled, we both turned to see Brooks looming above the entrance to the cavern. I crouched defensively as he leaped onto the sand before us. "I see that you grossly exaggerated your condition, dear Marguerite. I knew I should have continued to administer the serum myself."

"You mean toxin," I spat.

"We were instructed to keep you alive—just out of commission. We did not want something like this to happen." He motioned towards the distraught Anna. "What a miracle! I see sweet sister that you have recovered your vision."

"Did you do this to me?" Her voice quivered. "Brooks, did you purposely seal my eyes to keep the water from healing them?"

"It was all done for your protection, Anna," he stated flatly. "Your abilities had to be kept within."

"You have lied to me my entire life—kept me blind and made me believe we were deep beneath the sea! All the while you knew we were a short distance from the outside world!"

"I was only doing my job." He sighed, "Look, I do care for you, Anna. Whatever you think of me now remember that I have cared for you since you were found."

"Since *we* were found you mean," she spat. Her emerald eyes welled with tears.

"I am one of the only few land-dwelling Obyascon, a shape shifter genetically mutated from one of Theron's line of Protectors. I was entrusted not only as your guard but also your caretaker."

"And yet you have lied to me my entire life—calling yourself my brother!"

"It was necessary for your comfort and trust." He took a step closer to Anna. She stumbled backward in the loose sand.

"I will not be your prisoner anymore!" she cried.

"Unfortunately, you do not have that option," he replied with a roar as his lean body twisted and erupted into the form of the Obyascon. In an instant, all the beauty of the boy dissipated as he had morphed into a monster. Anna screamed and took off towards the steep cliffs. I took off after her, once again reclaiming her hand, but Brooks caught her, ripping her from my grasp. She broke free of him, spiraling into the pink sands. "I do not want to hurt you, Anna! Do not make me hurt you!" I attacked him from behind. I was pleased to know that my strength had completely returned as with one kick I sent the creature soaring into the shallows. In an instant, I was at Anna's side.

"Are you okay?" she nodded. "Let's go!" I shouted as I pulled Anna to her feet. There was no time to escape as Brooks emerged from the water with the two other Obyascon from that ill-fated night at the jetties.

"Marguerite, I believe you have met Moxley and Bratton," he said as they materialized from the sea foam.

"… and your name isn't Brooks at all is it! You are Quan!" Anna shouted suddenly putting together another piece of betrayal.

"Very astute, is she not?" he mocked. "I have taught her well!" I leaped in front of her as the creatures charged.

"Run, Anna!" I shouted, springing towards them to give her time to escape. She took off towards the cliffs scampering up the rocks in the darkness.

They simultaneously attacked. Silas's tactical training proved invaluable as I remembered to target each opponent's weaknesses separately. Moxley had been the most severely injured in the encounter at the jetties, so I embattled him first trying to concentrate on the areas in which he had previous injuries. Several swiftly targeted blows instantly knocked back his strength before he had the advantage. I remembered Bratton's girth was easy to knock off balance. Two well-placed kicks, one to the face and one to the legs, knocked the beast to the ground and another hurled Moxley back into the surf. Quan was the smallest, but his flexibility and dexterity became instantaneous as he easily dodged each strike. It was difficult to avoid the razor-like fins so prominent on the Obyascon. I knew all too well the effects of their toxin! I had to be swift! I had to be brave! I had fought for the ones that I loved before and now must do it again. I loved Anna as if she were my own sister!

"Look out!" Anna screamed from atop the cliff as Moxley rejoined the attack. She had made it to the rainforest and yet she refused to run.

"Go, Anna!" I shouted through the darkness.

"I'm not leaving without you!" She yelled back. They had me surrounded on all sides. I flipped over Quan and landed in the edge of the surf. They attacked pushing me further out to sea. Then they were everywhere—an army of Obyascon began moving in around me. Pushing off the sandy bottom, I dove above the three assailants to get back to the shoreline. Bratton caught my ankle in midair sending my body hard against the shallow water and into the sand. The impact temporarily knocked the breath out of me. His fin was coming down atop me when Quan caught his arm.

"Stop! Merissa says we must bring her alive. We have this one. Go get the girl before our queen learns of this!" A burst of light temporarily blinded me. The Obyascon hybrids were knocked into the water, and the pressing army pushed backward. I scrambled to get my footing.

"Run, Marguerite!" Anna called out. My feet hit the sand, and in an instant, I was scrambling up the cliff. My jaw dropped open as another heat surge rocketed from Anna's eyes, hurling the pursuant creatures once again back into the surf. I gasped in awe of the girl. It suddenly became clear to me why Anna's eyes had been sealed. It wasn't just to keep her blinded, it was to keep her from learning the depth of her extraordinary abilities. In all the wonders beheld since becoming a siren, I had seen nothing like the powers of this girl. Anna and I took off into the dark running through the thick tropical vegetation. We covered several miles before realizing that we were no longer being pursued.

"Do you hear that?" I whispered through the darkness. "Sounds like running water." I pulled back several large fronds to see a break in the vegetation. The night sky glistened into a small freshwater pool filled by the cascading water of a hidden waterfall.

"It is magical!" Anna exclaimed. "Like in a storybook!" It was breathtaking! My heart ached as it reminded me of William's quarry—our quarry. I closed my eyes and tried to push all thoughts of him to the back of my mind. There would be time to ache later—much later when I knew Anna was safe. I was parched and sore. My body craved the water. I climbed down to the rocks below scooping several handfuls of water and bringing them to my lips. Anna followed and did the same.

"It's cold," I said with a shiver.

"You're freezing!" Anna exclaimed as she again touched the water of the pool swirling it beneath her fingers until it was warm to the touch.

"Thank you, Anna." I said easing my sore body down into the warm water. "And thank you for saving me today."

"You are welcome," she said easing into the dark, warm water beside me.

"How did you … did you know you could do that?" Of all the Sironian I had come across, I had seen nothing to parallel her ability. No wonder Theron had come after William's family! I finally understood why his parents had tried to hide their children.

"No," she replied somberly. "I did not know, but I am pretty sure that is why I have been kept away all of these years … blinded … alone."

"I'm so sorry, Anna. I am sorry that they lied to you for all of these years. I'm sorry about what they did to you."

"Pure evil!" She buried her face in her delicate hands.

"Not everyone in the world is evil." She seemed to contemplate this before dropping her hands into mine.

"Believe it or not, I still have hope. I have hope because since I was a little girl, I would pray… I would pray that someone would come and rescue me. Then you came. I knew it was you from the first day you arrived." A tear slid from her magical emerald eyes. It was impossible to look into her eyes without seeing William. William had dreamed of finding his sister—the very same girl at my side. Emotions that I had never felt before swelled inside of me. I was so very proud to have accomplished all that my love had dreamed but stricken with worry over the complexities of her safe return. I would find a way to return his sister to him!

"I will get you out of here—off this island—to a safe place."

"I believe that … I believe in you, Marguerite." We soaked for only a short time before I once again felt revived. Oddly enough, the clear water seemed to take away my soreness, and the bruising began to diminish. Was it possible that like the salt water, fresh water now carried a similar healing property to my body? It made sense as I was after all still part human. I would have to run the theory by Silas— that is *if* I ever saw my mentor again.

We remained cautious throughout the night, but there was no sign of the Obyascon. I discovered a small cave that was whittled away beneath the waterfall that would serve as a temporary shelter. Anna collected leaves to line the floor and heated the walls as she had done in my chamber. She radiated heat—like she was the flame itself. Even the tiniest of bugs vacated the cave at her presence. I convinced the girl to take her afternoon slumber while I watched cautiously for any sign of Obyascon. I was extremely appreciative of both Anna's ability and companionship. I had not known this level of friendship since James.

I missed him. Not in the way I missed William, but in a different way—like there was a hole left in my heart. I would find myself filing away things to tell him before remembering that my dearest friend was lost to me—maybe forever. By now he would have gotten my letter. He would know the truth—if he was capable of believing in such crazy mythical creatures as the siren. Deep down I didn't actually question if he would believe. I think somehow that he already knew. He had known something was inhuman about me since my transformation. My letter would only verify what he had been trying to reconcile as impossible.

The afternoon turned into evening, and still, the girl slept. I smiled, immensely pleased the girl was getting some much-needed rest. I curled up against Anna, pulled James's album from my backpack, and lit one of the candles that I had thought to smuggle from the caverns. To say it was a bit worse for wear was an understatement as the pages had gotten wet quite a few times. The corners of the photos were worn and peeling, but the content and memories behind each photograph were there. All of the feelings were there. The girl in those pictures was me—me when I was a real girl. They were of me before fairytales flew from their pages and nightmares came to life. They were of me before I had known the sensation of being in love and the heartache of loss. The boy in those pictures was James before I had broken his heart—before lies and secrets began to separate us.

Anna's eyes slowly began to open as she propped herself up next to me. "It is already nightfall. I can't believe I slept so long."

"I am glad you did. You needed the rest," I replied tenderly.

"Yes, but you do too. You look exceptionally tired."

"I will sleep when we are safe." She leaned in closer and looked at my album.

"Who is the boy in these pictures? He is very handsome—to be human."

"Yes, he is very handsome. He is my best friend James or *was* my friend. He is the one I was telling you about."

"Oh, I remember. I remember every detail of everything you tell me. Not sure if it is a gift or just because I have little life experiences of my own to fill my head," she said.

"I once did the same with books. Now it seems that I have little time for reading, and my own adventures trump those from my novels," I replied.

"Tell me everything … from when you first began your transformation … every detail right up until where we are today."

"But I have already told you most everything about my life."

"Yes, but do it again, with more details. I want to know as much as I can about everyone—in case this plan actually works, and I get to meet them someday," she pleaded.

"Plan? But I don't have a plan yet."

"Oh, but you will. I know you will, Marguerite." The girl stretched her long limbs out next to me. Her copper hair shimmered in the light of the candle as she eagerly awaited my story. I began, but all the while, my mind was looking not towards the past, but to the future. I needed a plan. She was depending on a plan. I had none.

"Anna, I need for you to tell me everything you know about the Obyascon," I said. She sighed and her brow furrowed again.

"All I know is the history Brooks told me, so there is no way I can authenticate its truth."

"Fair enough—just explain to me all that he told you."

"Well, supposedly the Obyascon originated from the polar region, north I think, in the Artic. They were a very powerful and peaceful race of deep-water sirens that had little to no contact with humans or sirens. Legend has it that the Sironian ruler, Theron, traveled to the region to secure their loyalty, most likely in an attempt to abuse their forces, but discovered a young rebellious

Sironian from the Protector line, Bain, was being hailed as their leader. A battle ensued, and many Obyascon were killed. Theron killed the young Sironian in the name of treason and claimed his young wife Merissa for himself. Bain and Merissa had a small child—a boy. Once back with the Sironians, Merissa refused to marry Theron and fought to free herself and her son. Merissa tried to escape and was gravely injured in the resistance. Theron seized the boy from her and left her to die, but it is speculated that someone took pity on the girl and helped her escape. The Obyascon have been at odds with Theron's Legion ever since. Merissa returned and took her place as queen and sent the Obyascon around the globe looking for her stolen child. The once peaceful Obyascon turned dark with fury and learned to feed on the humans for strength."

I felt sick. How could I be the granddaughter of someone that had caused pain to so many! I had told Anna everything about myself except for my true linage. I refused to admit to my dear friend what I could scarcely admit to myself!

"It is heartbreaking to think of the lives Theron has destroyed. Why do you think the Obyascon have held you prisoner all of these years?" I asked.

"I can only speculate it was to keep my abilities out of Theron's hands."

"I tend to agree, but I can't help but wonder if there were more to it than that. Why go to all of that trouble. They could have easily killed you as an infant if it were just to keep you out of Theron's hands."

"I do not know," she said. "I do not believe anything anymore."

"We will straighten all of this out. I'll help you." She curled up next to me and closed her eyes. I wanted to tell her about William. I wanted to tell her what I knew of her real family. I did not. Until I could be assured of her linage, I would not give her false hope.

Somewhere out there was a boy that had not ever stopped looking for her. I knew he was now out there looking for me too.

The hours passed slowly. I was in and out quite a bit searching the perimeter. Despite wanting to help, Anna respected my wishes and remained safely in the cavern. "What's wrong?" she asked as I returned from my fourth run of the night.

"Everything is fine; it's just that being here reminds me of a place in which William and I use to go," I whispered.

"The quarry," she said eagerly recalling my stories from the night before.

"Yes. It reminds me of the quarry—the clearness of the water and how the ripples dance right up to the stones.

"You really love him … I can see that everything makes you think of him."

"The word love seems too ordinary to describe my feelings for him—like calling a tiger a kitten. I feel for him so fiercely that nothing common could encompass emotion this fervent." Her brow furrowed as if she were trying to uncover the answer to a math equation.

"The love between the two of you far surpasses any emotion that I have ever read. I cannot comprehend such sensation because I have nothing in which to compare. I doubt any comparison exists." I reached down and picked up a smooth shell that hung around my neck, then slipped my finger through the brilliant ring next to it. I removed my finger and held it close to my chest.

"Sometimes I try not to think about him," I confessed. "I close my eyes and just try to picture darkness … nothingness. However, he is there bringing the beauty to the dark. He is always there—even in the darkness."

"I hope that I get to meet him someday," she said taking her hand in mine. "I hope that I get to tell him all of the miraculous things you have done for me."

"I hope you get to meet him too," I replied softly. I wanted to tell her that the very person we spoke of shared her amazing green eyes … shared the bend of her smile, and shared her pureness of heart, but I did not. It would be William's place to decide if this girl were truly his sister—though I had little doubt that the beauty before me was anything other than the girl he had been seeking. I only had to find a way to get her to him. I had to find a way to return us both to him.

9

———

'Greater love has no one than this: to lay down one's life for one's friends."

~John 15:13

"**So, what is the plan?**" Anna asked as the sun began to rise. "Do you think they were out last night looking for us?"

"No, the island is small enough that I would have detected if they were searching," I replied.

"That's a relief!" Anna boasted a little too loudly for my comfort.

"The quiet jungle is unsettling," I whispered.

"How so?" she asked as she lowered her voice.

"Well, if they are not actively pursuing us, it can only mean one thing."

"What?" she asked.

"That they have the island surrounded. If their history proves correct, the Obyascon do not have the forces to cover the land. They only have a few land dwellers in their numbers, and they realize you outmatch their abilities," I replied.

"You were not doing so bad yourself!" she giggled. "I now know why Theron prizes you!" Her comment sparked another chance to tell her all that she still did not know about me. She had enough at hand about which to worry.

"Our top priority should be to find a way off of this island. The Obyascon generally sleep during the day and move at night, therefore we should do the opposite. They will still have the area surrounded, but they should have fewer numbers patrolling during this period. I will hike down to the coast to see if I can decipher a location while you see if you can round us up something to eat. I'm famished!"

"But don't you think it's best if we stick together?"

"I think there is a greater chance of scoping things out unnoticed if I travel unaccompanied. Are you afraid to stay here alone?" I asked.

"No. I am more concerned that you might need my help if you run into trouble," Anna replied.

"I will not go far. Keep an ear out, and if I am discovered by the Obyascon, I will call for you."

"Alright … what should I do if I need you?"

"You can always blast a flaming fireball into the sky or something," I replied with a smile.

"Are you teasing me?" she asked. I laughed.

"Only a little bit. You have to admit that your abilities are pretty cool."

"Alright! Fireball it is! You think I can really do that?" she asked.

"At this point, there is very little that would surprise me," I replied with a chuckle. It felt good to smile and even better to laugh. I had not laughed in so long that it felt out of place. How could I possibly smile in a world in which William and I were apart? I shoved my fists into my pockets and trudged off quietly into the rainforest. It was an easy hike to the coast. The beauty of this tropical paradise was surreal. How easy it could be to get caught up in the splendor of my surroundings! Foreign vegetation laced every inch of this wonderland. Beautifully painted creatures adorned the landscape with small tropical birds there to greet me at every turn. As the undergrowth split, I discovered the shore was separated from the rainforest by high rocky cliffs at every angle. I was surprised to see other landmasses nearby. Several mountainous islands were situated only a short distance away with even more islands along the horizon. The dark igneous rock proved that the island was volcanic.

I could have been taken to any part of the world, but highly unlikely. The crystal blue water was a red flag that the Obyascon did not primarily reside here. If the Sironian prefer the murky waters of Murrells Inlet, the Obyascon would also prefer the darker, deeper waters for cover. There was little chance they would expose their ghastly white forms if there were a risk of being discovered. I racked my brain trying to think of all of the tropical islands off of the Eastern Coast. I suddenly wished I had paid close attention in World Geography. If I had only known a year ago that I would be whisked away to an unidentifiable deserted island, then I might not have hidden my novels inside of my Geography books during class. I trekked along the perimeter of the island before returning to the waterfall. Anna was anxious to see me. She had managed to catch several small freshwater fish and had collected a few coconuts and some fruit similar to a mango. I devoured the small meal in only a few bites, which seemed to please my new friend immensely.

"What did you see?" she asked curiously, as she sipped the fresh coconut milk.

"The island is undeniably beautiful. I have never seen anything like it. However, it appears to be uninhabitable. The narrow shoreline wraps around almost the entire perimeter, but the insanely high cliffs make it unlikely that anyone occupies the island."

"What about boats? Is it possible someone could reach us by boat?"

"Thick shallow coral reefs encompass the island no less than a quarter-mile out. Only the smallest of boats could make it through the labyrinth of coral."

"And the Obyascon?"

"They would not expose themselves in the daylight, but I know they are waiting in the depths below. There is a multitude of other islands at a distance that could very well be inhabitable, but it would be impossible for us both to make it through their forces without detection."

"This island was chosen as my prison for a reason." All the hope in Anna's face seemed to vanish. "I might not be able to escape, but you can…."

"Anna, even if I could make it, I would not leave you. If I decide to go, you are coming with me," I replied.

"My body radiates heat. The Obyascon would detect me within seconds. You are our only chance."

"They would smell me as soon as I entered the water," I said.

"You said there were other close islands. If we were able to mask your scent long enough to get you past the reef, then you could make a dash for it. I could not swim fast enough but you can! You can outswim them if you could only get into open water! I know you could make it!"

"But what if I can't? I'm confident enough to fight the land dwellers, but my abilities are completely untested against the Obyascon in water. Even if I could hold them off, I would still be no match against such forces."

"You can do this! Do it for me," she cried. My head hung low as I considered the impossible task before me. The more time I had spent with the girl, the more I was convinced that Anna was indeed William's sister. She was like him in so many ways, and yet her abilities were as unique as his. Her extraordinary abilities could help us escape, but her inexperience put her at great risk. I was a Protector now. I could think of no greater responsibility than the safety of William's sister. "I know you can do this for us." Anna's soft fingers lifted my chin as her eyes met mine. "... and for William."

It was decided. I would escape at daybreak.

****

As the sun began to rise, the glowing eyes of the Obyascon began to move further out to sea. The crystal waters lacked the needed disguise promised by the ocean depths. I would plan my escape as soon as the Obyascon moved into deeper waters; with a bit of luck, I would escape to a neighboring island in hopes of finding someone who could contact William or Silas. If help were unavailable, I would secure shelter and return to retrieve Anna before sunset. At the very least, a new location would add distance, making discovery more difficult. My biggest concern was leaving Anna, but it promptly became evident that we had no other options.

The rustle of their footsteps against the tropical foliage was barely audible over the surging waterfall. I knew that they would come. Anna and I had disguised the cavern so well that it would be difficult for the Obyascon to discover us, but masking our scent posed a greater problem. We had collected as many fragrant flowers and berries as possible, but I was concerned that they would be able to track us despite our efforts. Anna bit her lip nervously and huddled closer to me beneath the foliage as the three Obyascon neared. Brooks was among the search party. I could only imagine how hard it was for Anna to see someone she once thought was her brother transformed into a monster. My eyes narrowed as I spied the two monsters responsible for Henry's death. I would one day avenge Henry, but there were more pressing matters at hand. I would bring William's sister home safely to him.

As soon as the sun made its descent, I slipped through the dense foliage to the highest point of the island. The Obyascon would least expect an escape from the high rocky cliff. I hoped their numbers would be fewer along this rocky coast. William had taught me well. Remembrances of the quarry brought both pain and accomplishment. How pleased William would be that his cliff diving lessons would prove so valuable, but here was no time to get lost in memories of the quarry as I would need every possible second to execute my plan.

I swiftly surveyed the landscape. The usually translucent water now displayed an eerie hue as it clashed against the rocks below. I easily located the deepest section and with one swift motion launched into the water below. In an instant, my eyes had adjusted to the warm foreign water. I remained perfectly still until the bubbles had cleared in an attempt to draw as little attention to myself as possible. A quick survey detected no visible presence of Obyascon. I charged through to crystal waters, realizing that I had little time before my scent was detected. I had traveled just half of the distance to the targeted island before the Obyascon descended. They attacked with none of the grace of the Sironian but with clumsy brute force.

The first small group that reached me were unskilled in the art of battle. They were quick but lacked power. With a few tough blows, I effortlessly fought off the unskilled sect. The next faction encompassed me; this group was better trained but still proved to be poorly matched against the combat training that Silas had provided. I was too quick and too resilient, easily outmaneuvering the creatures. I broke from their clutches only to find their numbers mounting. With no place to escape, I knew my only option would be to fight them all. Adrenaline raced through my veins, as the motion of the water fell into sync with my body. Body after body attacked. My fierce movements did not stop until, at last, the water was still around me. I briefly surfaced to get a look at the island before me. It was then that I saw it—a surge of heat exploded into the air from the direction of our camp. Such a display could only mean one thing—they had found Anna! I turned from the safety of the new island, barreling back toward the rocky coast—and the Obyascon.

I expected the army to attack as before, but there was no sign of my adversaries until I neared the coastline. There they awaited my return, meshed together like a wall, their bodies assembled in formation. I braced for an attack, but the creatures loomed in the shallows like gargoyles atop a cathedral. My heart sank deep within my chest. Had their plan been to separate us all along? Quan slid out of the surf and onto a large rock. I rose atop the water, still separated from the barricaded island.

"You could have made it you know … to safety … and yet, still you refuse to leave the girl," he said.

"Where is she?" I hissed, lunging toward him.

"She has been returned safely to our care, Marguerite."

"Care? You call what you did to her 'care'! You are monsters!" He laughed as he motioned toward my reflection atop the water. "We are all monsters, now, are we not?" My eyes radiated an intensity in which I had never seen. The twisted face before me was also that of a monster.

"Let her go!" I demanded.

"Your objection is noted," he replied calmly. "So, tell us how this is going to end, Marguerite. Are you going to come peacefully, or will we have to kill both you and your new friend?" On land, I would have been able to fight against the few land dwellers, but I would be no match for the assembled army that was now before me.

"You schemed this from the start, didn't you? You planned to separate us!"

"Of course," he said blankly. "You proved yourself quite an adversary on land. I thought if we could get you in water, there was a possibility to split up the two of you. Who would have thought you would make it so easy and leave the girl behind?"

"I will not leave her!" I spat.

"Then surrender, and I will take you to her." I eyed the insurmountable army that now separated me for Anna—*Madeline*. I refused to leave behind William's sister!

"You leave me no choice," I hissed. Within seconds, the line parted and I was forcefully pulled into the shallows. Moxley held me down while Bratton tied my hands behind my back. The ropes had been coated with Obyascon venom, in an attempt to keep me from breaking free. The restraints burned through my skin, and I winced in pain.

"A necessary precaution … you understand," Quan added with a smirk.

I expected a climb back to the top of the island, but a piece of clothing was draped over my head, and I was forcefully pulled behind some rocks and into a cavern. I could see nothing but could immediately feel the cool dampness of the cavern as I was carted over the rocky terrain. I stumbled through passageway after passageway as they led me blindly deeper and deeper into the island.

"You said you were taking me to Anna," I scolded.

"All in good time." Quan replied as I was blindly hauled around another turn. At last we stopped and the drape was removed. My mouth hung open in amazement at the beauty of my surroundings. Massive candles lit the entranceway to a large room. The panels of the entrance were adorned with large carved sections of mother of pearl that surrounded finely detailed mosaic walls. The mosaics consisted of heavily jeweled images of marine life, oceanic currents, and images of Sironian. Massive marble columns served as support beams throughout the great room. The floor glistened from the specks of mica and garnets that made up the polished oceanic granite floor.

"Do you like my chamber?" a woman's voice echoed from behind me. I turned to see a woman that was neither human nor Obyascon. It was immediately obvious from her inhuman beauty that she was Sironian, though her face was deeply distorted. Large sliced scars ran just below both cheek bones and another diagonally across her forehead. Long lavender hair fell well below her shoulders with the remainder of her body masked by a dark green gown, gloves, and cloak. Her green eyes pierced through the dim lights of the underground palace.

"Where is Anna?" I immediately asked.

"She is safe. The girl is no longer your concern."

"She's my friend. I would die before I left her here with you!" I hissed.

"Greater love has no one than this: to lay down one's life for one's friends, John 15:13," she recited with a smirk. "You are a fascinating creature indeed!"

"And you must be an evil sea witch," I spat.

"Evil witch is quite harsh; don't you think? My dear, we are but just getting acquainted. I am Merissa, Queen of the Obyascon and Ruler of the Northern Seas."

"I have heard of you and have been told tales of your unfortunate circumstances," I responded bravely.

"You, girl, have ignited tales of your own. I had heard rumors of a half-breed girl with unimaginable power, and here you now stand before me. Is it true that you have stood alone against Theron's forces?"

"I have," I said bravely.

"Well then, girl, you and I appear to be the only two alive who have lived to tell that tale."

"How dare you compare yourself to me! I am nothing like you!" I spat.

"So you say, girl. So you say."

"Let me and my friend go!" I hissed.

"Did it ever occur to you that both you and Anna were being held for your protection?" She raised a perfectly arched eyebrow as her mesmerizing emerald eyes met mine.

"That should mean we would be free to go at our request," I demanded with newfound courage.

"I said no such thing. I do not wish to take your life, nor can I grant your freedom," Merissa replied calmly.

"Then I am to remain a prisoner—like Anna?"

"Theron would either use the two of you for his power or ultimately he would destroy you. If Anna's abilities were ever known to Theron, she would have been exploited or killed. She has been kept here for her own safety—her eyes sealed in an effort to hide her," she explained.

"And me?"

"Rumors of your existence reached our ears. I sent scouts to confirm your existence, one of which did not return."

"I am sorry for your loss," I said blankly.

"It was then that we discovered Theron was taking you into his regime. I am sure you can understand that we could not allow such an event to take place, so we intercepted you before you were handed over to the Legion."

"But why me?" I asked.

"Theron wants nothing more than to defeat the Obyascon. You see, we refuse to answer to him. Your abilities as a half-breed are unknown. We cannot have such forces built against us."

"So essentially you are saying …."

"You will either stand with us or die. I had hoped to keep you hidden away, but you are far too resourceful for your own good. If I caged you again, I do not doubt you would escape."

"I will not be caged, nor will I stand with an army who hunts my people as an energy source," I hissed.

"Hypocritical human! You find little objection to your fields of cattle and barnyards of swine!"

"I will not align myself with monsters!" I spat.

"I am sorry to hear that. Moxley, Bratton—unfortunately our guest has chosen the option of death." Instantly, I was cast to my knees by Bratton as Moxley drew a sword to the back of my neck. I would die without William ever learning of my fate or that of his sister. I had no time for objection and no mind to scheme for my life. I closed my eyes and braced for my death. I felt the air beneath the sword as it made its descent to my neck. I inhaled expecting the worse, but the blade halted abruptly. The Queen of the Obyascon grabbed me by the hand and pulled me to my feet. I opened my eyes to find her staring at my ring—the very ring William had given me upon our secret engagement.

"Where did you get this, girl?" she demanded. I slowly opened my eyes.

"A Sironian boy by the name of William Avery," I whispered.

"William Avery, the son of Morgan and Robert Avery?" she asked.

"They are deceased, but yes, the very same," I uttered, trying to breathe.

"The boy is your betrothed?" Merissa's voice trembled as she spoke. I looked into her eyes and then closed my own. My body relaxed in defeat. William's face smothered all dread. If death were to come, it would not rob me of my final thoughts. They would not be in fear but of love. His love had given me life, and my love for him would be my last profession.

"Yes. I am betrothed to William Avery." My eyes narrowed as I stared into her face once more. "You may take this life, but you will not take his love from me. I have fought the worlds that have tried to separate us; if need be, I will fight the heavens as well," I confessed boldly. She eyed me carefully, but her expression morphed into all seasons at once. It shifted from shock to fear, then from admiration to pity. At last, she spoke.

"Quan, safely return Marguerite to the coast in which you found her!"

"But, Your Majesty, I don't understand. We cannot allow her to live! Theron will ultimately try to use her against us!"

"Return her immediately! That is an order!" I had only time to gasp before the cloak was once again upon my head, and I was rushed from the chamber.

10

———

"Sometimes even to live is an act of courage."

~Seneca

I was dragged beneath the water with my face covered and my hands tied behind my back for many miles—possibly hundreds of miles. At first, I tried to track the distance, but the change in velocity and shifting currents made it impossible. My Obyascon captors paid little attention to my need for oxygen and only surfaced when I would begin to grow limp. My throat became raw from gasping, and exhaustion set in after the first few hours. I would black out periodically, but thoughts of William kept the spark of life within me. The only thing that kept me fighting for life was the promise of love. When the struggle would become too great, I would fight through the darkness to see the light. His face was my light. I finally understood what toll the tortuous journey had taken on my body the first time. No wonder I had arrived at Anna's chamber unconscious! I was lucky to have arrived alive at all!

At last all movement came to a halt as my three captors surfaced. I came up gasping once again as it had been many miles since they had brought me to the surface for air. Though I could not see, I knew I was still in foreign waters. The viscosity and temperature of the water were all wrong to be close to the South Carolina coast.

"We've traveled far enough. Let's do it here," growled Moxley.

"The area is devoid of Obyascon. There is no one to send word back to Merissa that we have killed her," affirmed Bratton.

"I agree that it is too great a risk to leave her alive, but Merissa would have our heads for such disloyalty. I say we continue on our task and deliver her as instructed." Quan replied.

"The Queen's orders have nothing to do with this. She and I have a score to settle," Moxley grumbled. "And this time, only one of us is walking away." I did not speak. I was unsure if I even had the energy to do so. I could smell the rusty scent of my blood as it ran from my tethered hands into the water, but I had no feeling left in them. No strength to fight, no pain to remind me I was still alive.

"Do you hear that?" Quan said. "I thought I was imagining things, but I swear something has been trailing us for the last thirty miles."

"I hear nothing out of the ordinary," Bratton gurgled.

"The swooping of large fins against the current," said Quan.

"I smell it. Smells like a shark, but I turn, and nothing is there," Moxley huffed.

"Sharks fear us. They flee from us," Bratton continued.

Quan argued, "Something is out there!"

"Let's kill the girl and head back to familiar waters." Bratton uttered on his very last breath as something grabbed him from beneath the water. The Obyascon roared in pain. The sound continued underwater for a few seconds and then was no more. I could see nothing. There was a swift current below and the sound of breaking water. Quan shrieked in pain, and he released his grip on me. Mass chaos, screeching and growling ensued. I struggled to find the energy to stay afloat. My body was stricken with fear. If the remaining Obyascon did not kill me, whatever was below certainly would. But what came next was worse than the cries from my captors—silence. With my tethered hands I pulled the cloak from around my face. I immediately gasped for air, but the breath caught deep in my throat. The water around me was heavy with blood. The severed arm belonging to Quan floated atop the water nearby.

It was then that I saw it, the massive form of a shark circling below the water. Its presence was contrary to all that William had told me. *Sharks stayed clear of Sironians!* My body was so weak that I knew that if it attacked, I would be easy prey for the massive beast. It circled again from below. I braced for impact, struggling to free my hands from the ropes. But there was no impact. As the creature circled to the surface, its marred dorsal fin peaked above the surf. I was washed with relief and jubilation. I knew this creature—*no not I*, Lucy knew this creature! It was the very same shark that she called Scamp. Its fin marked it as the beast Lucy had saved in the surf. I instantly knew Lucy had sent it to find me—to save me. The tiger shark circled again taking the rope into its mouth that I had been hastily unwinding from my wrists. I was gravely injured, but I grasped the rope as tight as possible as the massive creature dove deep within the sea.

I searched the depths for some sign of home. All seemed foreign. Instinctively, the shark traveled to the surface regularly to provide me with oxygen. The beast, which many thought a mindless predator, proved not mindless at all. We traveled for the greater part of the day and into the evening. I was emotionally exhausted and physically wrought. I became nervous as the sky grew darker and darker. *There is nothing comforting about the ocean depths at night and even less comforting when attached to a massive tiger shark.* The shark shifted directions, and much to my surprise, let go of the rope and passenger in tow. A burst of adrenaline swept through me as I searched nervously for the shark. It was gone. I scrambled to the surface to find myself waist deep in water with a small island just ahead. A dim campfire flickered from the beach just ahead. *Was it possible that this beast had purposely brought me to safety?* I tried to get my footing, but my feet were numb. I toppled into the shallow surf in sheer exhaustion. I felt my body slipping beneath the waves. *God, had I narrowly escaped only to now drown from fatigue.* I cried out for help, but my lungs filled with seawater. I was no siren after all, I thought, as I began to drown. With little consciousness left, I felt my body lifted from the water. Soft lips blew air back into my lungs, and the water was compressed from my chest. Slowly the world come into focus.

As if by miracle, they were there. Kirby's flawless face came into focus first as it had been his lip against mine. He had breathed life back into me. He smiled and released a sigh of relief as I coughed the salty water from my body. I turned to see Toby's dimples and the deep-set eyes of Mace. I could read the severity of my situation in his expression.

"Hurry! Get her to camp!" he said to Kirby who promptly pulled me from the shallows. I was still coughing up water and catching my breath as Toby wrapped me into a thin cotton blanket.

"Are you alright, Margo?" Toby asked with genuine concern. "We've been in the area searching for you for weeks now. Kirby picked up on something from a shark. We thought he was crazy having us track a shark, but here you are!" I tried to respond but began coughing again.

"You look just awful, Princess!" Kirby said as he wrapped his arms around me from behind. His long fingers brushed my matted hair from my face. My eyes began to focus. I scanned the beach for William.

"Look at her wrists!" Mace exclaimed as I pulled my arms from beneath the blanket. "They have had her tied up."

"Wouldn't the water have healed that?" asked Toby.

"Not if dipped in the poison excreted from the Obyascon's fins. The poison delays the healing process," Mace responded.

I tried to speak. My throat was raw. I took a shallow breath and began again. "William? Where is William?" They looked at each other. No one responded. My heart sank in my chest. They each held the same odd expression, but no one offered up an explanation.

"I said, where is William!" I repeated. Kirby responded, his eyes shifting from mine."

"Uh, you will have to get all of the particulars from Silas, but Margo, he has been gone since just after you disappeared." I died inside.

"Gone?" Mace continued.

"Margo, your blood was all over the jetties. To be honest, we all assumed you were dead especially with Henry …."

"Yes, I know. He died trying to save me." I ached.

"William insisted you were alive despite our doubts. He was going crazy looking for you. Your scent was everywhere at first, all through the water making it impossible to track, then nowhere. It was as if you had completely disappeared." Mace paused and took a deep breath.

"You have to tell me, Mace. Where has he gone?" I pleaded.

"Margo, he felt like he had no other option," Mace replied.

"What are you saying?" I pleaded.

"He returned to Murrells Inlet when he realized he could not track you," Mace said.

"What did he do, Mace? Tell me!"

"We think he has gone to join up with Theron's Legion," Kirby responded.

"What!" I gasped.

"Margo, Theron's Legion would be his only chance against the Obyascon. He saw it as the only way to find you," Kirby said.

"I don't understand," I cried.

"The Obyascon took you before Theron could, Princess! Theron has laid claim over you." Kirby gently lifted my bloody wrist. Theron's insignia shimmered above the wounds. "The Obyascon took what belonged to him."

"Rumors are stirring that Theron's forces are preparing to move against the Obyascon," Toby continued.

"Theron's Legion is planning to fight the Obyascon over me?" I shrieked.

"The bad blood between Theron and the Obyascon has existed for centuries, but your capture has intensified the conflict," explained Mace.

"Tell me what you know!" I demanded.

"Silas can give you more particulars when we return," Toby replied.

"But William? How is he involved? Mace, you must tell me something!" I begged.

"Before he left he vowed to find you alive or to avenge your death no matter the cost," Mace continued.

"Meaning …."

"He is now tied," he replied.

"How so?" I asked.

"Like I said, you will have to get the details from Silas," Mace scowled.

"But you think he is in trouble?" I repeated.

"He is in deep, Margo." Mace sighed. "Forgive me, but you will have to talk to Silas."

"Then take me to Silas now!" I demanded.

"We are many miles from home, and you are in no condition to travel! Princess, tell us what happened to you!" Kirby said.

"Tell us where you have been!" Toby added.

"There is plenty of time for that," I replied, but images of William in harm's way transcended all other thoughts. "Where are we?" I asked.

"We are on a small island that is part of the Turks and Caicos Islands. We are around seven hundred miles off the coast of Florida."

"Such a distance! How did you know where to find me?" I asked.

"I am embarrassed to say," Mace replied.

Toby grinned.

"The shark?" He laughed.

"You're kidding, right? You tracked a shark for such a distance in the chance that it would lead you to me?" I leaned back in disbelief.

"Not just any shark. Lucy's shark. She said it would lead us to you," Mace explained.

Toby shrugged, "We had nothing else to go on."

"Lucy!" I cried. Tears began to run down my cheeks at the mention of my family. "Mace, Lucy knows of my capture?" he nodded. I felt sick at the knowledge that I had caused my little sister such worry and pain.

"She was the one who told me you were alive," Mace said.

"But how did she know?" I asked.

"I really can't believe I am saying this aloud, but she said her "friends" told her," Mace blushed a little. It was the first time I had ever seen him blush.

"Mace, please tell me she's safe—that my whole family is safe," I pleaded.

"They are," he replied. "They left the coast not long after your capture."

"And Caleb? Does he know?" I asked.

"No. Lucy thought it best not to worry him. They returned home the day after you were gone, so they're in no immediate danger."

"Even so, Lucy must be sick with worry!" I cried.

"She is a very strong little girl. She was confident that we would find you," Kirby continued.

"I need to get back to civilization, to call her and assure her I am alright." I added.

"We will make it our top priority," Kirby said tenderly. My stomach churned from worry, pain and a few gallons of seawater. I stumbled into the dunes and got sick. Kirby helped me back to camp. He eased me onto one of the logs that surrounded the fire and pulled me close. I didn't have the energy to resist, even if I had wanted to.

The night sky was clear. The blue flicker of the campfire flame reminded me of the first night I had met the Crew. We had all changed since then. I had changed the most. "Do you mind if I just close my eyes for a while? I have had very little sleep for quite some time now," I said.

"Rest," Mace replied. "But I need to clean those wounds to remove any traces of poison. We have quite a distance to travel, and you are currently in no state to do so." I closed my eyes as Mace cleaned the open wounds. He tore strips off of his black t-shirt and wrapped them securely around my wrists and forearms. I leaned back against Kirby's chest. His scent was wonderful—but all wrong. It wasn't William's. I closed my eyes. I would sleep for just an hour or two. I was finally safe, but my safety meant nothing without William. My thoughts drifted to Anna. I was breaking my promise to her. Tomorrow I would be leaving her behind. The night sky was bright, but I sensed my world growing dark.

11

"My heart has already been stolen—It is no longer available for thievery."

~Marguerite Westley

I awoke to the distinct sound of waves rolling peacefully onto the island shore. My brow furrowed as I fought to hold onto my slumber. In my dreams, William and I were at the quarry nestled beneath our tree. I curled my face into the nape of his neck as his fingers gently stroked the curves of my face. However, the sun was unrelenting as it seeped into the corners of my eyes. I nestled into the warm fantasy for one last moment of peaceful slumber.

"Good morning, Princess," Kirby whispered as he stroked the side of my cheek. I jumped backward out of his arms with such velocity that my behind hit the soft sand. "Hmm, you did not seem so quick to discount my embrace while you were sleeping," he teased.

"That's because I was dreaming of someone else," I mocked.

"And you weren't so quick to cast off my lips earlier," he grinned.

"I was unconscious," I laughed. "CPR can hardly count session."

"A guy can dream, can he not?" he shrugged. I laughed again and bent over to kiss him on the cheek.

"Thank you for saving my life, Kirby," I said.

"Not how I had imagined our first kiss, but …."

"It wasn't a kiss!" I huffed. Kirby only laughed. I scrambled to my feet and looked around for Mace and Toby. The island was much smaller in the daylight. "Where are the others?" I asked, as I brushed the sand off my behind. It was then that the full scope of my physical state hit me. Every fiber of my body ached, and I was painted from head to toe with deep purple bruising.

"Well, Mace is scoping the area to be sure there are no Obyascon tracking you, and Toby is out rounding up some breakfast," Kirby said.

"I don't know if I can eat anything," I groaned.

"Still feeling a bit rough, eh?" he asked.

"Like someone who was drug underwater for fifty miles," I replied.

"We think the distance to where they were holding you was a greater distance from here. Over the past few weeks, we have scanned about a fifty-mile radius from this base point with no sign of anything. We speculate that the Obyascon were holding you on one of the islands of the Caribbean," he said.

"That is such a distance!" I sighed, "Now, the real question is how long will it take us to get home?"

"It is a good two- to three-day trek from here if we only stop briefly to rest and recharge. I am not sure if you are well enough to make the seven-hundred-mile trip," Kirby said.

"I've been gone too long! I can make it! I want to go home!" I cried, as I hastily began to make my way to the water's edge. However, my eagerness to return to the familiar waters of Murrells Inlet was laced with guilt. I would be breaking my promise to Anna. Perhaps with my help, Silas could help locate her. "Let's go, Kirby! The others can catch up!" I had barely made it into the water when strong hands gripped my waist. I instantly tore from the grip tumbling backward onto the shoreline. I growled and readied for an attack. Laughter pierced the air. Kirby strode across the sand to my side. He motioned towards the waters with his signature smile. Mace appeared from the shallows.

"Easy there," Mace said. "I think you were about to take my head off!" he chuckled. It was always surprising to hear Mace laughing.

"That wasn't funny," I replied, still on the defense.

"It most certainly *was* funny," he said. "Or it would have been right up until the part where you tore my arms off; you are pretty strong you know," Mace said.

"I don't feel very strong," I said. "I still don't feel like myself at all." I sighed.

"You are Sironian now. You will never again feel completely human," Kirby said with a smirk.

"Gee thanks. I think I finally understand that part. That is not what I mean. My body feels so weak," I groaned.

"You may *feel* weak, but I can promise you anyone who can pry my hands off of them is pretty damn strong," Mace said.

"You have been through quite an ordeal, Princess, It's perfectly understandable that you feel unwell," Kirby said. "Look, here is Toby now!" We all looked up to see Toby carrying an entire banana-filled tree in one hand and a coconut laden palm in the other.

"I found breakfast!" he said dropping them to the ground.

"What? No fish?" I teased.

"We thought you could use some human food to get your strength up for the trip," Toby said.

"Fish is human food," I replied.

"True, but trust me," Toby said. "We have quite a long journey. You will eat more fish over the next few days than you may ever care to eat again."

"I will eat sashimi every day for the rest of my life if you will just get me home!" I promised. As I spoke the word *"home,"* the pain and guilt of leaving Anna behind washed over me once again. Would William ever forgive me if he knew that I had left behind his sister? I knew that I would never forgive myself if any harm were to come to her.

****

My Sironian friends fully intended to swim the three-day trek back to Murrells Inlet. I was determined to keep pace, but by the time we reached Key West, it was quite evident that my body lacked the strength. I would swim for several miles, and then Toby and Kirby would each take my hand to guide me until I had the energy to continue. On several occasions, Mace would swim beneath me, and I would hold tight to his shoulders as we glided through the emerald waters. I could match their stride but not their stamina. The vulnerability I felt at sea served as a reminder that I was still neither human nor Sironian. Despite my newly acquired strength and skill, I was still a stranger to so much of this underwater world.

My body, though strong and quick to learn, was no match in the water for those born into this Sironian race. I was and forever would be a half-breed. I tried to mask the angst. I tried to hide the weariness. I tried to push through the pain. My friends saw through the veil.

It was nightfall when I got a first glimpse of the mainland. As the Crew helped me to the surface, a dim glow of lights glistened in the distance. I swelled with joy over the knowledge that I would soon be on the soil of my homeland. Mace scoped out an unpopulated section of beach for landfall. My weary body had never been more ready for the swim to shore. Adrenaline rushed through my veins as I pushed through the breakers to reach the warm sand. The Crew emerged looking every bit the siren folklore. I was confident that I looked resembled death over that of a siren or human. Kirby offered to find driftwood for me to sit and rest, but I dispelled his efforts and opted instead to curl up among the sea oats along the dunes. Mace saw that I was safely situated before he returned to the water for watch duty. Kirby took off down the beach for supplies leaving Toby to stand watch over me. I fought slumber. It was humiliating that I required such attention.

"I'm alright here, Toby—rest!" I insisted, but he only smiled.

"What kind of Protector would I be if I left such a significant creature to fend for herself?" Toby responded.

"I'm hardly significant, Toby!" I said.

"You do not even realize what you are to us, do you?" he replied.

"I'm afraid I have no idea what you mean," I responded curiously.

"You represent *hope*, Marguerite—not just for the Protectors, but for all Sironian," he said. The proclamation took my breath away. His words echoed through the empty walls within me. He believed the lie that my existence had facilitated. I was just a girl, a mere girl whose only reason for living was love.

"I put you and anyone in contact with me in constant danger. I will forever have to live with the knowledge that I killed Henry," I cried.

"The Obyascon killed Henry!" Toby exclaimed. "You can't beat yourself up over that!"

"If it had not been for my poor judgment …," I whimpered.

"Life is full of regrets," he said tenderly. "Your choices did not seal Henry's fate. Henry fought because he was one of us. Any one of us would have done the same thing for you. He loved you. He lived with integrity; he died with honor. There is no greater distinction than to give your life for a grand and noble cause."

"Noble cause? And what would that be?" I asked.

"You of course." He grinned. I shook my head and leaned back against the dunes. I closed my eyes to hide the tears threatening to peek. Toby was mistaken. I had failed Henry. I had failed Anna. I had failed William. I had failed myself. My scattered thoughts blurred from exhaustion. The feel of the Floridian sand was all wrong. The smell of the peninsula, not quite right, and yet, there was a comfort to know that I was back in the states. The security was enough to succumb to my body's outcry for rejuvenation. I slept.

****

My restless slumber shifted to an abrupt reality. The loud, thunderous, unnatural rumble of an engine shocked my senses into gear. I scrambled to my feet and looked out into the water. Kirby was behind the wheel of a forty-foot cigar boat. I hurried to the water's edge to gaze at the surreal spectacle before me. He waved from the monstrosity. I covered my ears from the uncomfortable whine. Kirby cut the engine.

"Your chariot awaits, Princess!"

"What is this?" I exclaimed.

"A boat of course!" He winked at me and motioned with his lean, muscular arm to join him. I grabbed my backpack and dove through the breakers towards the boat. I took his outstretched arm as he swung me into the odd vessel. It was fitting that Kirby would choose a speedboat.

"I thought we were going to swim it?" My cheeks flushed realizing that the crew practically had to *pull* me to get me this far.

"Forgive me for saying this, but you look pretty worn out. I thought it best if you we carried you the rest of the way home," Kirby smirked.

"So you bought a boat?" I exclaimed.

"Of course! I purchased it off of a guy at the marina last night. I thought we might need a new form of transportation," he replied.

"You just bought *this* boat off of a guy?" I was confused. I looked over the sleek, shiny boat.

"Sure!" he laughed. He seemed to enjoy my amazement. These sirens always found a way to astound me.

"What, with your endless supply of gold doubloons?" I teased.

"Are you kidding? Do you know how heavy those things are?" Kirby teased. "I carry one of these!" He pulled a fancy black credit card from his pocket. "Waterproof and mobile!" Mace and Toby appeared with an armful of supplies and hurled themselves into the boat.

"You put a speed boat on a charge card?" I asked. They all chuckled. "A cigar boat? These cost as much as a house—an expensive house!" I continued. Kirby only laughed.

"I like speed … and I like nice things. Besides, I thought you were anxious to get home Princess?" he smirked.

"I am," I quickly replied. "I've just never seen one of these in person, that's all."

"Speed boats are quite common here. Lots of people are smuggling things into the country from these parts," Toby said.

"Smuggle things?" I questioned. "Like drugs?"

"Or in our case a beautiful half-breed?" Toby teased.

"Very funny!" I said. Kirby kicked the deafening engine into high gear, as the cigar boat split through the pounding waves.

I spent the better part of the morning trying to overcome the motion sickness that accompanied their reckless driving in choppy open seas. The boys were as excited behind the wheel as a group of frat boys watching a rivalry football game. Kirby and Toby took turns at the captain's wheel. The competition of who could catch the most "air" proved that I would have been much safer trying to swim back home. Only Mace noticed as I got sick over the edge of the boat.

"You are positively green." He smiled as he bounced into the seat next to me.

"I've felt better," I mumbled in a voice barely audible over the roaring engine motor. The acuteness of his specialized ears picked up the sound anyway.

"I bet. These morons forget that you are still half human."

"I'll be fine," I said as I heaved over the side again.

"There is a cabin for sleeping in the bow—not a lot of room but enough to lie down and get out of the elements. You are quite sunburned." I hadn't noticed. Sirens never burned, but though my skin seemed to defend itself from some of the sun's rays, I would still burn with extended exposure. I sighed once again realizing I would never truly fit into William's world.

"A bit of sunburn I can take. Kirby and Toby's driving, now that's a different story. Probably should keep clear of the cabin in case they flip the boat."

"Good call. Never know when we will have to swim for it!" Mace laughed with a smile so stunning that it nearly took my breath away. A notable change had happened between Mace and me during my first summer as a Sironian. All of the extreme opposition of kinship was replaced with a genuine sense of loyalty, respect, and friendship. Now on the other side, I could easily see that his hesitations were just. His concerns had indeed come to pass. My presence threatened their way of life, and yet, his heart was so pure that he had found the fortitude to love me nonetheless. I could ask for no worthier of a friend. I could enlist no greater Protector for my dear Lucy. He took off his shirt, draped it over the back of my head and tied the arms beneath my neck. "At least this will keep some of the sun off," he said just before Toby hit the top of a massive wave launching the boat high into the air. The hull smacked down hard against the clashing water.

"Will you excuse me?" Mace politely asked before smacking Toby in the back of his head. The boat jarred to an idle.

"Ouch! What was that for?"

"For being an insensitive moron!" All three turned to see my face green with motion sickness.

"I forgot you get sea sickness, Princess!" Kirby replied as I heaved over the side of the boat.

"Looks like you guys owe me a new shirt." Mace sighed over my heaving.

My system calmed a bit as Mace took the wheel. Kirby and Toby kept me company as he gingerly maneuvered the vessel through the surf. The midday sky began to deepen into dark golds and streaks of fire. The water also began to change as we headed north. I was glad to leave behind the tropical turquoise shades for the deeper gray-green hue. Darker waters symbolized that home would be soon on the horizon.

We stopped only a few times to refuel. As the sun fell beneath the clouds, Toby suggested we pull into a harbor and dock for the night. I urged our party to travel onward. The more miles behind us, the closer I would be to Inlet Joy. The crew agreed but stopped for an hour for the party to recharge; Mace and Toby dove into the deep Atlantic. Kirby started to join them but stayed behind with me. The closer we got, the more my emotions began to rise. I struggled to brush away thoughts of my family—and William. I was aware that neither would be waiting for me, but despite logic, I harbored a glimmer of hope that all whom I loved would be waiting for me. There was one, however, that I knew would not be waiting—Henry. I secretly brushed back a tear. Kirby saw me stroke it away. He draped his arm around me and pulled me close.

"You know, Princess; there would have been many fewer tears if you would have chosen me." I smiled, as I openly allowed a second tear to roll down my face.

"The heart has as much control over love as the shore does over the tide," I said as I regained a friendlier distance between us.

"The mere reason I still carry a glimmer of hope—still waiting for the tide to shift in my direction." I laughed. Kirby's majestic smile could, without a doubt, capture the heart of any girl. "My heart has already been stolen—it is no longer available for thievery." Kirby smiled.

"He loves you too, you know?" Kirby motioned towards the water where Mace and Toby were playfully wrestling. Mace tossed Toby into the air before diving down again.

"Mace? You have lost your mind!" I protested. I was taken aback by his proclamation. "He is not in love with me," I protested. "I'm pleased that he has learned to tolerate me."

"Maybe not, "in love" but he does have strong feelings for you. I have only seen him show such loyalty to Aria … and his brother." I brushed aside Kirby's theory and quickly changed the subject.

"How did he lose his brother?" I whispered, making sure that Mace was out of listening distance. Kirby leaned closer as he began the tale.

"Mace had a childhood that was very similar to ours. He was taken from his parents at a young age, just as we all were, but unlike us, he had a twin. The boys were kept together for training, but his brother's talent began to develop in extraordinary ways. Theron caught wind of his extra abilities and whisked him away to join his army."

"What was his extraordinary talent?" I asked. I was now enthralled.

"He can communicate with other sirens telepathically—a talent that only Siron possessed," Kirby said. *Similar to what Lucy can do with animals!* No wonder Mace had agreed to be Lucy's protector!

"Remarkable!" I gasped. Kirby seemed pleased to hold my attention as he continued with the story.

"When he turned fifteen, Mace left to find his brother but returned a few months later to tell us that his brother was dead," Grief swept through me at this revelation. My heart ached for Mace.

"How did he die?" I asked.

"We did not ask the particulars," Kirby continued. "Mace was so distraught that I doubt he would have shared any more information, even if we had asked. He seemed almost emotionless until you arrived."

"But he hated me!" I exclaimed.

"No," Kirby replied. "Mace saw something in you that scared him."

"What was that?" I asked.

"Purpose. You, and now your sister, brought meaning to the life that Mace had given up," he said.

"Please, tell me more!" I demanded.

"There is no more legend. It is up to you to fill the blank pages of this fairytale," Kirby said before slipping into the water to join his friends.

I closed my eyes but could not sleep. My imagination pieced in all of the blank pages of his childhood and youth. I doubted an opportunity would ever arise that would be appropriate to ask him for such personal details, and even if such an occasion should arise, I would most certainly lack the courage.

****

The morning sun broke the watery horizon. We were about a mile off of the coast when the distinct patterns of familiar landscape played out before my eyes. I rubbed my dry, tired eyes as if it were a mirage.

"Do my eyes deceive me? Tell me that what I am seeing is real!"

"Your eyes tell the truth. You are home," Mace said as he gently put his hand on my shoulder. I was on my feet as we neared the jetties. My hand clenched the side of the boat as if it were the only thing still holding me in the hull. Then I saw it—anchored in the channel near Knoxx Point was William's sailboat. My hand released.

In an instant, I was on the bow of the cigar boat. I could hear the protestations of my friends as my body soared off into the churning water. With rapid speed, my body glided through the familiar water towards the sailboat. When I reached the rear, I fluttered my feet rapidly as William had shown me to gain the vertical height needed to grasp the rear rail. I flung myself into the hull.

"William? William?" I tore through to boat searching for the prefect features of his face. His books and clothes were present and the paintings I had given him, but the boat was empty. There was no indication that he had been onboard recently. I buried my face into a nearby pillow. The familiar smell of my love filled me—making his absence all the more painful.

"Margo?" The cigar boat pulled up alongside the sterns. "I'm sorry. I should have given you notice earlier. A week after William set off to find you, Silas received word that his boat was adrift about twenty miles off the coast. He sent us to retrieve it." Mace said. He looked away as if to avoid the fear written in my eyes.

"Adrift? That doesn't sound like William," I protested, "He built this boat himself! He wouldn't just leave it!" I could barely stand.

"Silas had the same concerns," Mace admitted. "But we have had alternate confirmation of William's location."

"Mace, please tell me what you know! I feel like I'm going crazy!" I begged.

"As we told you earlier, you will have to talk to Silas," he stuttered. "The word is that he is with Theron's Legion. I really know little more than that."

"I need to find Silas!" I shouted.

"He is most likely with your grandmother," Toby grinned.

"Well, let's get going!" I said as I leapt back onto the cigar boat and forcefully took the wheel. Kirby tenderly stopped me.

"Margo, you don't need to see your family like this," he said gently.

"Like what?" I responded. But I caught my reflection in the glass panes of the boat. I barely resembled my former self. My hair was severely matted and my body badly sunburned. I had partially healed lacerations on almost every limb, and my clothes were as tattered as if I had been adrift at sea for months. "Oh," I cringed. I was embarrassed that I hadn't thought to check my appearance since my rescue. I knew where I needed to go but also how difficult it would be. My eyes shifted to Knoxx Point. William would not be there waiting for me, but Sadie and Olivia deserved to know that I was alive. I had not been there to mourn with Sadie and Olivia. I had not been there to witness their grief. I hadn't been there to confess the burden I would always carry over my role in Henry's death. Knoxx Point would be my first stop.

"Tell Silas that I will be at Knoxx Point," I said as I soared off the side of the boat and into the water. I surfaced briefly.

"You know, you don't have to keep doing that! We would have taken you to the shore." Toby joked.

"This way is faster!" I shouted back before gliding beneath the water.

12

———

"The wound is a place where the Light enters you."

~ Rumi

Sadie fell to her knees when she opened the door. She gazed at me as if she were looking upon a ghost. I collapsed into her arms, and we wept together. We wept over the loss of Henry. We wept together over my miraculous return. We wept over the absence of William. I confessed to her my guilt over Henry's death. She harbored no blame, only an acute sense of loss that no words would ever heal. I shared with her the story of my past months, careful to omit the details of Henry's death. I told her only he had died saving me. He would forever be my hero. She asked for no further specifics. It was evident that she was not ready to hear them, nor I to tell them. I wanted to see Olivia but thought it best to clean up before reuniting with the girl. Sadie confessed that Olivia had understandably taken her father's death very hard. She had not spoken a word since the news. Tears streamed down my face as the gravity of their loss was before me. She was broken. I was broken. Together we would strive to heal.

Sadie led me up to the familiar room in which I had first stayed at Knoxx Point and disappeared to run a bath. I had protested, but I knew her strong caring nature would prevail. She took from the drawer a bottle of sea salts and poured half of the bottle into the waters. She glanced over at my battered frame. Sadie smiled faintly before dumping the remainder of the bottle into the water.

"It's that bad, huh," I asked.

"If possible, you look worse than you did when I first saw you—and you were still human then," she said. I giggled. We both began to laugh … and laugh. We laughed for several minutes on that bathroom floor. The laughter did not dispel our grief but was somehow an extension of it. We laughed not to begin to heal but because sometimes there just aren't enough tears to be cried. The concentrated sea minerals once again repaired my broken skin and rejuvenated my battered body. I somehow managed to pick through the mounded mess of hair. Sadie trimmed off the tattered edges.

"You are starting to look like the girl I recognize, but you're rail thin. I am going to have to fatten you up a bit if you are to ever pass for an aspiring Parisian!" she teased.

"I do need to call my family. How will I ever explain why I haven't called them?" I grimaced.

"Long distance is expensive from Paris," she suggested.

"I'm not sure they would believe that," I shrugged.

"Well, they believed your initial story," she assured me. "There is a stack of letters for you on the bedside table."

"Letters? From my family? But how?" I asked.

"William purchased an address in France and attached it to the return labels of the letters you dropped off to send your folks. Any mail that arrived was forwarded to us here," Sadie replied.

"And the letters to them?" I asked.

"I took care of that," she said proudly. "I typed them so that they wouldn't doubt the penmanship." I was overfilled with gratitude. Her thoughtfulness brought tears to my eyes.

"How do I ever repay all that your family has done for me?" I cried.

"There is nothing to repay. We are family."

****

It had been quite a while since I had felt a real bed beneath my body. It was heavenly. I pulled the first letter from the top of the pile. It was from Lucy. My heart ached from missing her.

Margo,

I know you aren't in Paris, though Mom thinks you are. Not so sure about Dad. I don't think he thinks you are in Paris either. He doesn't say much. Caleb is worried about you too. I know you are off on some big adventure. Take me next time. I sent my friend Scamp to look after you. You know—the shark. Sharks are pretty strong. I miss you. Come home soon. Oh, bring my shark back. I Love You.

Lucy

The letter was too well written for a girl Lucy's age. The rate in which she was maturing was alarming. How long would it be before she could no longer pass for an ordinary child? I carefully folded the letter and picked out another. It was from Caleb.

Margo,

I have been pacing the floor for days. The only word I have received from you is a phony letter. What the hell? William has disappeared, and the others aren't telling me crap! I don't know if I am more pissed off at you or worried about you! Please write to me or call me and let me know you are safe.

Caleb

There were several letters from my mother, all of which were full of love, small talk, and generic motherly advice. None of her letters carried any sign of worry. My father's letters were a different story. He undoubtedly was aware that the Paris trip was a cover for something but had no clue of the gravity of my situation. I was relieved that he was spared from knowledge of all that had happened. My father had no idea about the treaty with Theron, nor did he realize that I had been discovered and taken away by the Obyascon. He was aware that being Sironian could put me in danger, but I had kept him in the dark about how that danger was continuously finding me. How long could I keep him in the dark?

As soon as I finished the letters, I would call my family. My eyes began to close. I was exhausted. I wanted to stay awake. Despite being wrought with worry over William, I was clean. I was safe for the first time in months. I fell asleep.

****

The smell of apricots and jasmine filled the room. As I opened my eyes, Olivia was curled up next to me. She instantly sat up as I began to stir. Our eyes met. We embraced.

"I am so very sorry about your father, Olivia," I whispered. A tear rolled down her cheek. "He saved my life, you know. He will forever be my hero." The girl nodded but did not speak. I wiped away her tears. She wiped away mine. Olivia picked up the palm of my hand and pressed it into the palm of hers. Waves of energy passed between us. All at once, I could hear her without her words.

"I am so glad you are here. I was scared the Obyascon had killed you too. I have missed you so much—William too! Do you know when he will come back to us?" Her gift was astonishing!

"I am so very glad to see you too, Olivia! I've missed you as well! Right now, I don't know how to bring William back to us, but I promise you I will do everything in my power to find him." She smiled faintly, but her eyes carried a world of pain. Olivia had been forced to experience the kind of pain that a child should never have to face—the same kind of pain William had known. "Olivia, how do you *do* that," I asked eyeing our jointed palms. Once again, the child did not speak to me directly but through my mind.

"I don't know. It just happened." Sadie smiled faintly as she entered the room.

"Olivia, dear, your lunch is getting cold." Her arms wrapped around me again before she hastened out of the room.

"She's remarkable! When did her ability surface?"

"A few weeks after Henry died. Olivia stopped speaking altogether. She rarely left her room. Olivia's tearstained face was buried in a pillow. I took her hand in mine to comfort her. Suddenly, I could hear her thoughts as clear as if she had said them aloud," Sadie explained.

"Amazing!" I gasped.

"Though Sironian, I had no rare gifts in my bloodline. I am unaware of any exceptional gifts in Henry's genes either, though I have long suspected he may have omitted certain things about his past." I wanted to question her further, but her mention of Henry's secrets reminded me of my own—Lucy. Both Olivia and Lucy were developing abilities at an abnormal pace for Sironian. My mind raced with questions. I would have to talk to Silas, but first, there was an important phone call that I needed to make—to my family.

"Sadie, I would like to talk with you further about Olivia, but I'm sure my family is quite concerned that I haven't called," I said.

"Yes, you certainly need to call them. The phone is waiting for you in the kitchen. Let me know if you need anything," She took my hand in hers, then pulled me into an embrace once more. "It is a miracle that you have returned," Sadie said

"I owe my life to Henry," I whispered. She closed her eyes as she took my hands to her lips. She squeezed me tightly once more before quickly leaving me. I hurried to call my family.

When Caleb heard my voice on the other end of the phone, he scolded me relentlessly. I wanted to explain my reasoning for not calling. I could not. I wasn't sure who was on the other end of the receiver. The less involvement Caleb had in any of this, the better. I assured him I would fill him in on my "trip" as soon as we were together. Lucy took the phone and began talking loudly into the receiver as if I had only been gone for days. She then whispered into the phone in a voice barely audible.

"Did my friend reach you—you know, the shark?" Lucy asked.

"He most certainly did," I responded. I wanted to tell her how her action had saved my life, but I could not. I would tell her—one day when she was older. "Thank you, Lucy. Your friend helped me get home to you. I love you so much," I said with an effort to contain my emotions.

"I love you too, Margo. When can I see you?" she said.

"Soon, Lucy, soon," I promised.

My parents were up next. I had lied so much over the past year that I was finally getting better at it. Details about my time in Paris rolled off my tongue with ease. My mother wanted to know about everything—the family, school, and culture. My father on the other end of the phone mainly listened. I was not fooling him with any of it. My mother put down the phone briefly to respond to something Lucy had asked. At last, he spoke. "Marguerite, when will you be returning?" he said flatly.

"I'm not sure, Dad. See, there is this internship that I am thinking of applying for and ..."

"Stop the lies, Margo. Just tell me that you're alright!" he scolded.

"I'm safe, Dad," I said with as steady of a voice as I could muster.

"Yes, but for how long?" he replied. "I know there is a lot that you aren't telling me. I wonder if it would be best to tell your mother the truth—about all of this." My father had no idea that I was captured and held all of this time. He had no idea of the treaty with Theron. He had no idea how many times my head had been on the chopping block.

"No, Dad!" She can't know! Not now!" I cried.

"Then tell me where you have been—the truth!" he demanded.

"I have been in a school of sorts—training as a Sironian. I have been training with Silas," I said. It wasn't a complete lie. It wasn't the truth either.

"Training for what?" he asked before my mother picked up the phone again. Then it hit me. When the Obyascon didn't return, would Merissa come looking for me? Would Theron learn I had escaped and trace me back to my family? They were all too close. I would have to distance myself from them as much as possible, at least until I could come up with something.

"Marguerite, honey, when are you coming home?" my mother asked.

"Actually, Mom, I was recently offered an internship with a publishing company here. You know how I love to write!" I responded. "I was thinking of staying for another semester."

"Oh, but, Marguerite, we miss you so much!" she cried.

"I know, Mom. I miss you guys too. I've just been thinking a lot about college. If I want to go to an Ivy League school, I'll need to beef up my applications. This internship would really help me do that," I explained.

"Ivy League? This is the first time you have mentioned going to an Ivy League school," she said. My lies were growing bigger by the minute.

"Yes, well … uh … being around the culture here has really broadened my horizons. I just want to make sure that I get the best education possible," I said stumbling over my words.

"Is William staying another semester too?" my father asked.

"He is. He has an internship at one of the hospitals here. I think he wants to go into medicine." I was completely making things up at this point.

"Sounds like he is a very smart young man," my mother said.

"He is, Momma. I love you. I better go. You know how expensive overseas calls can get," I said in a hurry. My lies were building by the minute.

"Yes, but, Marguerite, please don't wait so long before calling again. I love you," she said.

"I promise, Mom. I promise."

****

The evening sky was painted in swirling purple and grey hues. Small reflections of golden rays were barely visible along the narrow horizon. The beauty of the inlet was bittersweet without William. I sighed and closed my eyes. Just a few feet away were the dunes on which William and I first met. My life had been a whirlwind ever since—I would not take it back.

I needed to see Silas. I desired to see my grandmother. I wanted to see James. I longed to see William. My heart ached to think of Anna. I had promised not to leave her behind—a promise I was not able to keep. Now what? Silas would know what to do. He had promised in that hospital room so many moons ago that he would take care of me. I am certain at the time he never guessed how hard that challenge would be. He had chosen for me the strongest of his Protectors—the one he loved like a son. Because of me, he is now gone, and I must find him—find Anna and reunite him with his sister. Such a task seemed impossible! I had faced impossible. Backing down from "impossible" was no longer an option with my heart now displaced from my soul.

A small wooden boat appeared through the marsh reeds. The silhouette of the vessel was one I had seen many times. My insides churned. My breath stuck deep in my chest. Would I forever be watching boats and shadows—waiting for him to one day reappear? As it broke through the marsh reeds, I recognized Silas as the captain. My grandmother was in the passenger seat. She looked more beautiful than ever. Her hair had grown, now hanging well below her shoulders. Her cheeks had a glow about them that made her look ten years younger. She was stunning. A tear slipped down my cheek as she stepped out of the boat onto the sand. We embraced.

"I was afraid I would never see you again!" she said as she took my hands in hers.

"There were times that I feared that as well," I admitted honestly.

"Miraculously you have been returned to us safely!" Silas said.

"I have, but there is another who did not return with me—a girl that I believe to be William's sister."

"Could it be true?" Silas was astonished. "I feared her dead, as my contact from inside Theron's Legion has reported nothing of the girl."

"That's because Theron doesn't have her—Merissa does."

"Merissa! The Obyascon! I never dreamed that they retrieved the baby!" Silas uttered.

"And she has been hidden away in caverns ever since! They held me there too, but I escaped—with her help."

"We have much to discuss. I have news for you as well," Silas said.

"Yes. I am aware that William has joined forces with Theron."

"Unfortunately so. He thought it the only way to save you from the Obyascon—if you were even still alive."

"I am very much alive."

"Alive, yes, but Marguerite, I can physically see the toll this event has taken on you. You need to rest. You need to heal."

"I need to go find William and then get his sister back!"

"Come, my dear. There is much to discuss." Silas said as he led me back to Knoxx Point. I spent the evening telling Silas about my experience with the Obyascon. I, in turn, gleaned information concerning William's whereabouts. He had very little information. Theron had placed William as an officer in his Legion. He was heavily watched, and the Legion was planning an attack on the Obyascon. My existence had once caused Theron's Legion to destroy the coast. Now, my existence has paired the two most powerful underwater armies against each other.

And I just wanted my boy back.

13

"We travel, some of us forever, to seek other states, other lives, other souls"

~Anais Nin

I **did not return to the Inlet Joy** with my grandmother but remained at Knoxx Point. I needed to distance myself from it as much as possible. The Crew was keeping watch over the mouth of the inlet. There were no signs that we were followed by the Obyascon or the Legion, but I wasn't naïve. I was aware they could easily find me. It was decided that I would go to Theron. This time I would follow Silas's instructions. In a week's time, I would sail out to meet Silas's informant. He would take me to Theron as an ally. I would do anything possible to get to William. I would join his Legion.

Silas spent the next week preparing me physically and emotionally. When I wasn't training with the Crew, I was soaking in the tidal pools at Knoxx Point. I spent most afternoons with Sadie and Olivia. They were a part of my family now. Olivia still wouldn't speak. I also did a lot of sleeping. Gradually my strength began to return. The deep-set circles under my eyes began to diminish. The scars began to fade. I knew that I would never be the old "me" again. I didn't want to be—I was becoming a stronger version of myself.

The week passed quickly. I was nervous about the voyage ahead. There was one thing that I needed to do before leaving. I needed to talk to James. I pondered all week what I would say to him. How would he feel now that he knew that his childhood friend was Sironian?

I shivered as I slipped into the brisk inlet waters. The canal seemed particularly cool for the beginning of November. It had been almost three months since I had seen James or William. Our silly love triangle seemed like ages ago. My insecurities began to take hold of me as I streamed through the deep passages of waterway. Perhaps they had both forgotten me by now. It took only minutes before I reached James's dock. My breath caught in my throat as I spied the Inlet Joy just a few houses down. I had once been a girl playing along the water's edge. Now, I slid out of the channel like a creature from the deep.

The cool wind whipped through my tight black pants and pale grey knit. I would have to get accustomed to wearing a wetsuit. Street clothes were hardly appropriate. My body didn't regulate the cold-water temperatures like the other Sironian. It was one of my constant reminders that I would forever be a half-breed. I had only made it a few steps off the dock before I heard the back door open. I hastily hid behind a large pampas grass. Through the blades I spied my friend walking out hand in hand with a blonde—Amy. He escorted her to her car and gave her a long kiss before she drove away. Amy had finally gotten her wish. My chest felt as if someone had knocked the breath out of me. My face winced in pain. I finally knew how James felt each time he saw me with William. I had no reason to be hurt. I had no claim over James. It was wrong of me to expect him to wait for me—I loved another. But the thought of James with someone like Amy was too much to handle.

I contemplated my next move as I waited for James to go back into the house. I could knock on his door again and disrupt his life once more, or I could walk away and allow him the happiness he deserves. He looked happy. It began to rain. Cold heavy raindrops penetrated my already thin clothes. I turned towards the Inlet Joy to escape the cold rain—away from the shoreline where two silly children once played. It was time to close that door. I had left him. I had become something new. He had moved on.

I stepped into the bedroom that, for as long as I could remember, had represented home. My grandmother was not at home. She was most likely with Silas. My room was just as I had left it three months earlier. My fingers brushed over all of my favorite books, paintbrushes, and sentimental baubles that I had collected. Tomorrow I would be saying, "goodbye" to this world. I tore out the last page of Whitman's *Leaves of Grass* and grabbed a pen from my dresser. I wrote on the back.

My Family,

~Tomorrow I will be going away. Sailing into unknown challenges. Know that you are always in my heart, and that I will do my best to come back to you. I love William. I can think of no greater cause than to fight for love. If I don't return, please forgive me. Forever know that I love you too. I have to go—I hope you understand.

Margo

I slipped the page into the book and placed it on my bed. If I did not return, it would one day be found. The floor creaked. I gasped as I turned to see James standing in my doorway. The rain was beating down so hard against the porch roof that I didn't hear him come in. He was soaking wet. The last time I saw James it was raining. How fitting that we should meet again like this. He looked older—more handsome. I was stunned to see him standing there after so many months.

"You were crossing the lawn. I thought you were a mirage—or a ghost," James stuttered.

"I'm real," I replied softly. His eyes met mine, then shifted across my face, and finally to my body as he studied my features.

"Are you? You have been gone so long I can hardly believe my eyes," he uttered.

"I'm sorry I wasn't here to explain all of this to you in person— a letter is hardly fair. I just didn't know how to tell you," I pleaded.

"Tell me what? What letter?" he asked.

"You didn't receive a letter from me?" I questioned. I was pretty sure my heart had stopped altogether.

"Darlin' the last words I received from you were when I was driving away. I came back to make things right—to apologize. Your family said you had gone to Paris or something like that," he stammered.

"Something like that …," I mumbled.

"What was in your letter?" he said. A glimmer of hope flickered in his eyes.

"It doesn't matter. Looks like we have both moved on—grown up. It was bound to happen, I guess. I saw you with Amy," I said.

"Yes. I know what you are thinking, but you're wrong. Amy is nice if you give her a chance." I didn't speak. I wanted to tell him that I was happy for him. I couldn't. He would immediately see through the lie. When I didn't respond, he continued, "You see, I got sick … the flu or something. She was there. It was nice to have someone." His words seared like a hot poker. I deserved the pain.

"And your best friend just went away ... without even saying goodbye," I whispered.

"Do you even know how hard those weeks were for me?" he said. The raindrops blended with the tears swelling in his eyes. I didn't look away. I deserved to see the pain I had inflicted.

"I'm sorry. I tried to explain everything! I sent you a letter ...," I pleaded. I reached for him. He fiercely turned away. But then, as swift as he turned away, he turned back to me. James's face was different; it was no longer filled with desperation, but courage.

"I'm not here for words! I'm tired of fighting what we both know is between us!" James crossed the floor and in an instant had me in his arms. His mouth came down hard against mine. I tried to push him away, but he was stronger than I remembered—much stronger. The scent of his skin engulfed my senses. His fragrance drew me to another place. All that I had given up by becoming Sironian vividly flashed before me. James was comfort. James was laughter. James was family. James was home. I didn't want to push away those things any longer. I wanted them. I missed them. I missed him. My lips were moving against his more passionately than ever before. They stirred together slowly, then more rapidly. For the first time in many months, I allowed myself to feel. My arms wrapped around him as adrenaline filled me. I wanted to feel. Suddenly his essence began to slip between my lips and the monster inside of me began to take hold. James moaned. I fought it by pushing out my own essence into his body—trying to replace what I was stealing. *No! I would not allow this monster to take me—to take him as it had almost done once before!* I pushed James from my body so hard that he hit the wall. He fell to the floor but was conscious. He propped himself against the wall, staring at me as if I were a stranger. There was something on his face—fear? I turned and caught a glimpse of myself in the mirror. My eyes glowed a deep mystical green, and my face was snarled and twisted in a manner that was undoubtedly supernatural.

"What are you?" he uttered. His eyes danced nervously as he viewed the monster before him.

His essence still enticed my palate. I wanted more of him—all of his essence. It took every ounce of willpower I had to not take his lips to mine again—to drain him of all that my body craved. I stared at him as if he were my prey, fighting the urge to pounce. A gust of wind filled the tiny room, briefly diluting the scent. I took the opportunity to run.

Within seconds I was down the stairs and across the lawn to the dock. The rain pounded. The thunder roared. I turned back to see James staring in disbelief as the girl that he once loved dove high into the air before gliding effortlessly into the water. I was a monster. At last he knew.

****

"What does one pack when joining an underwater army?" I mumbled to myself as I rolled an assortment of items into a large backpack: casual clothes, fighting clothes, and a few of the dresses once belonging to William's mother. In the remaining space, I crammed in: a windbreaker, a sweatshirt, three pairs of shoes, my toiletries and a bottle of sunscreen. I was surprised the bag could hold it all.

It was hard saying goodbye to Sadie and Olivia. They planned an extra special meal on the evening before my departure. Silas, my grandmother, and the Crew joined us. After dinner, I escaped to the veranda to be alone with my thoughts. I had only been outside a few minutes before Kirby joined me. The evening breeze chilled as it moved atop the water. I pulled my beige cardigan tightly around my shoulders. The long-sleeved brown wrap dress did nothing to combat the rapidly cooling November temperatures. I had dressed up a bit for my last evening at Knoxx Point.

"You know, you don't have to go. We could just stay here together," Kirby said.

"Oh, could we?" I replied sarcastically.

"Sure. Theron thinks the Obyascon have you. By the time his Legion finds out you are here, you will have fallen hopelessly in love with me." By "his Legion" he meant William. I tried not to allow my blood boil over Kirby's innocent comment.

"Unfortunately, my heart is out there somewhere. I am broken until I find it again. So you see, I could never fall in love with you. I have no heart to give." Kirby sighed in defeat.

"Well then, I guess I had better go help you retrieve it." He winked at me. I kissed him on the cheek.

"Thank you," I said as I took his hand. "Thank you, my dear brother."

At daybreak, Silas and the Crew met me on William's boat. Silas informed me that the trip would consist of three days of sailing at four to five knots per hour to reach the reef. At which time I would meet his informant a mile northeast of the reef. It would then take two days of swimming at a similar pace before I reached my destination. Toby and Kirby would circle the vessel in route keeping a distance from the boat as not to attract attention. Mace would keep watch over Murrells Inlet while the others were gone. Mace was not happy with the arrangement, but Silas insisted that he remain. I found comfort in the fact that Sadie and Olivia would have Mace. It was also a relief to know that he would be there if Lucy came to the coast.

Silas gave the Crew explicit instructions that I must travel to meet his informant alone. For his safety, even the Crew must not know his identity. Both Mace and Toby agreed to abide by Silas's instructions. The informant would then report to Silas directly when we were safe. We were about to set sail when Mace growled.

"Someone is here!" he exclaimed ready to attack. "I can hear the heartbeat!" The Crew tore through the boat. Silas and I waited on deck. There was a shuffle below deck, followed by shouting. Toby and the others appeared, pulling a rattled James by the nape of his shirt collar.

"James!" I exclaimed.

"I am presuming this is a friend of yours?" Silas said.

"Let me go, dude!" James shouted as Toby tightened his grip.

"We found a stowaway. A friend of yours I presume?" They knew my relationship with James very well.

"What are you doing here?" I asked, glaring at James. James pulled out the crumpled letter I had scribbled the night before to my family. "Digging through my room apparently? How did you find that?"

"I know you well enough to know you would never leave your favorite book behind. I also know you well enough to know that if you were going to leave a secret message, it would be left in that book." James smirked. He seemed unmoved by the fact that I tried to suck the life out of him on our last encounter.

"That still doesn't explain why you are here!" I scolded.

"I had to see you! I didn't want you to leave with things like we left them the other night … you know, when you tried to eat me." The Crew simultaneously looked from James towards me with a look of humor and astonishment. I blushed.

"You shouldn't be here!" I huffed.

"Yeah, well, maybe so, but that was some kiss last night. You almost took me out with that one. I needed an explanation," he said. I was taken aback that he could make so light of the situation.

"Wait—you kissed *that* guy!" Kirby said, covering his bruised ego with humor.

"Are you kidding me?" Kirby threw his hands up in the air dramatically. James ignored him completely.

"Look, I found the letter you had written to me last night. Amy hid it before I could open it." Panic spread across my face.

"Did she read it?" I asked.

"Na. Your secret is safe. The envelope was still sealed when I found it." He held out the letter. Silas hastily retrieved the evidence.

"Well, at least now you know the truth—and why it is too dangerous for you to be around me," I cried.

"Apparently *you* know too much," Mace growled.

"Yeah, I say we take him out!" Toby glared making a slicing motion across his throat. James was alarmed.

"Wait a minute! No one is taking anyone out! James has been my best friend since childhood. He isn't going to tell anyone anything." I looked at James with pleading eyes. By telling James my secret, I had put his life in danger. "Right, James?"

"These lips are sealed," he said convincingly.

"They better be or we will seal them permanently," Toby huffed.

"Got it, scary buff dude!" James glared as he pulled away from Toby's grip.

"I still want to get back to this whole kiss thing ...," Kirby said shaking his head in disbelief. "How did you ... how did he?"

"I could have killed him—again," I said.

"Again?" James asked dumbfounded.

"The prom?" I admitted.

"Well, now things are beginning to make sense," James said. "Darlin', you deliver one hell of a kiss!" Kirby winced as he buried his hands in his face. "Do you think those kisses had anything to do with this?" James picked up a buoy from on deck and effortlessly crushed the hard foam to a powder. Our mouths dropped open in disbelief.

"Have you showed anyone else this?" The concern Silas felt filled his voice.

"No one. I just noticed I was stronger a few weeks ago—after I got the flu. But when I woke up this morning, I could tell a big difference. I gripped my toothbrush, and it practically fell apart in my hands." *How could this be? What had I done?*

"Marguerite, how many times have you kissed this boy?" Silas asked. My face flushed.

"Just twice. Once at the prom, which you all know about … and again last night." I said guiltily.

"I have questioned for some time how the boy lived after the prom incident. I can only guess that he lived by receiving some of your essence. I must admit that this crossed my mind as a possibility," Silas said.

"Is he becoming Sironian?" I asked, trying to understand the extent to which I had put James at risk.

"No. That is not possible. One must be born with the gene, but as Sironian derive strength and longevity from humans, apparently the transfer can also happen the other way. It is rare that he would survive such an encounter," Silas explained.

"Meaning you are one lucky dude," Toby added.

"More than he realizes," Kirby added sarcastically.

"Yes, he is lucky to be alive," Silas continued. "Young man, do you swim? Or have you noticed any other heightened senses"

"Nothing else seems to be different. I am just stronger," he said.

"This proves my theory. The reverse transfer would only heighten existing human muscle tissue. He should be able to run and swim faster due to increased muscle efficiency, but his genetic structure has not been altered."

"You speak as if you have encountered this before—and yet physical interaction between sirens and humans is forbidden." I then remembered how my grandmother had looked the evening before. She was altered ... younger ... stronger. Silas had given to her what I had inadvertently given to James. "My grandmother ...," I muttered.

"Yes. Your grandmother has exhibited a similar reaction through our interaction." I gasped. The full effect of this revelation came into focus. This transfer provides a certain amount of longevity and muscle strength. It also must bring about some rejuvenation as my grandmother appeared much younger. What could this mean? Healing properties? The fountain of youth? Such things would be highly coveted by humans—both for good and for evil. This Pandora's Box should never have been opened! It must stop here. Could it be undone?

"Will this fade over time?" I inquired.

"It should. Just like our bodies need replenishing. The heightened qualities in James would need this as well."

"I am understanding now why my existence has created such a stir for your people," I said. Tears began to well up in my eyes.

"Yes, you see dear, our civilization has remained hidden and separate for good reason. But you are not to blame for this. I broke our laws years ago when I fell in love with your grandmother," Silas explained.

"But I have kissed many humans ...," Kirby added.

"Not like this you haven't." Silas cut him off. "Marguerite had to willfully transfer her essence to the boy and I to her grandmother."

"I didn't mean to do this!" I gasped.

"No, you had no idea what you were doing, but your instincts knew how to save his life, even if you were not consciously doing so." Silas continued. "James, will you allow me to study you over the next few months, to determine the extent of this phenomenon?"

"Sure, anything I can do to help." He paused to look at me. "On one condition ...."

"Boy, you are in no place to negotiate," Mace growled. "I still think it would be safer to take him out!"

"That's enough, Mace!" I spat.

"Look, I am not going to say a word of this to anyone—scouts honor!" he held up a few fingers awkwardly. I was almost certain that he held up the Girl Scout sign. "All I ask is that you allow me to accompany Marguerite to the reef. I will personally bring the boat back and see that she heads off to the next leg of her trip."

"But, James, why?" I protested.

"I need to talk to you, and this may be the only chance I get," he said.

"No way!" Kirby objected.

"I have no objection to your request if Marguerite doesn't object. It appears the two of you do have a bit to discuss," Silas said.

"What will Amy think?" I asked.

"I broke up with Amy after finding out that she hid the letter you had written, and I've already told my parents that I booked a deep-sea fishing charter for the next few days. I figured it is only a partial lie ... I mean, we are on a boat ... at sea, and I'm sure there will be fish involved." I groaned.

"Alright. Fine. He can come … but only to the reef," I huffed.

"Thank you," James replied.

The Crew disembarked to begin their assigned duties. Toby and Kirby swam ahead to sweep the area. Mace reluctantly returned to his post along the jetties. I started prepping the cutter to sail. William and I had spent the better part of the summer together aboard his boat. He taught me all that I knew about sailing. I had no idea the lessons would prove so valuable. This trip was my first time taking her offshore without him. I checked the rigging to be sure the lines were in order and all cotter pins were in place. I then pulled the lines free of their wenches. James watched uncomfortably.

"I have a confession to make. Unless it has an Evinrude outboard attached, I don't have the slightest idea where to begin." I laughed. It felt good to smile.

"I had no idea how to sail either until William showed me. Here, take the outhaul at the end of the clew—near the end of the boom. Pull it, so the foot of the main is cleat."

"The whom to the what?" James said scratching his head. I laughed. It felt good to laugh. It was almost like old times.

"Here, let me show you. This small line is the outhaul; it connects the main sail to the end of the boom. See here, if we tie it like this, it will help the airflow over the mainsail." I reached over him to tie it into place. I turned to see a severe expression had spread across his face.

"Margo, why didn't you tell me all of this sooner?" His brow furrowed.

"I never knew you wanted to learn to sail." I avoided eye contact.

"I am not talking about the damn boat!" he barked.

"I'm sorry, James; I wanted to," I said. My chin dropped to my chest.

"But you didn't!" he scolded.

"I know. At first, I was sworn to secrecy and then I wanted to protect you," I mumbled.

"Come on! There have never been any secrets between us," James said. There have never been any secrets between us—until this.

"You're right, James! But how could I explain this! How do you tell someone that you are a siren!" He could see I was upset. He breathed out deeply and wiped his forehead.

"Alright well … I guess you better teach me how to secure that boom before it knocks me overboard. I am not as good of a swimmer as you … anymore." I laughed.

"If you're with me, the boom may be the least of your worries," I said with a faint smile.

"I believe that! But I'm here anyway. Let's set sail before you try to kill me again," he said.

"I promise you—you won't get that lucky," I teased.

"That's what I am afraid of," he said with a snicker. He ducked as the boom shifted overhead. I grabbed hold of the line and secured it in place. The main sail was ready. "You *are* seriously trying to kill me," he laughed.

"Gotta be quick on your feet if you are with me!" I admitted taking hold of the jib halyard. He raised the jib and began to trim the sails.

"Looks like I am doomed!" he said as I pulled anchor. The boat surged forth through the jetties into the open water.

"Doomed … from the first day you met me!" I replied.

14

———

"For a day, just for one day, talk about that which disturbs no one and brings some peace into your beautiful eyes."

~Shams-al-Din Mohammad Hafez

There was something nostalgic about having James at my side again. We could almost forget all of the changes and just be— us. Things had been simple when we were children. Nothing was simple anymore. The morning at sea proved to be quite pleasant. The robust winds calmed a bit once we were off the coast. I had taken something for motion sickness, but it helped to stay active. I passed along to James the information William had taught me about sailing. Of course, he was a pro! He promptly took over many of the duties of a deckhand. I deeply appreciated his help—and his company. The day should have been hard. James made it fun. By mid-afternoon, the surf had calmed, and we were able to relax for lunch. Sadie had packed a large basket of sandwiches and sweets for the trip. James had many questions. I tried to answer them all as honest and as best as I could.

For the first time, he learned the truth about prom night—from the kiss to the hurricane, to William's promise to protect both he and Caleb when Theron's Army was on the attack. I told him of the treaty I had made. I told him of all that has happened these past three months and of my current plans to join Theron's Legion. James became very quiet as if he were trying desperately to believe all that sounded impossible. At last, he spoke.

"You are the bravest person I have ever met," he said as the sun began to slip below the horizon. Shades of orange, pink, and purple illuminated the skyline. James took my hand in his.

"I'm not brave. I'm afraid of everything! Most of all, I'm afraid of losing all that I love—and I love you, James," I admitted. He tenderly squeezed my hand. I gently pulled it from his. He sighed. "I gave my heart to William, but that doesn't change my feelings toward you. I know it's selfish when I am in love with someone else, but I want you in my life," I confessed. He breathed deeply. His face beamed from my profession.

"I've turned my back on you twice, but I promise you that I will never do it again," James said reverently. His sunburned brow furrowed. "I didn't understand then, but I realize now," he continued. "Do I wish you had never met up with these Sironian? I do, but I also know that they've helped you through this transformation. It was going to happen. They could have turned their backs on you—they didn't. I did, and I'm sorry." He grasped both of my hands firmly.

"Me too," I whispered as he brushed a lose strand of hair from my face. "I'm sorry that I have gotten you tangled up in this," I said.

"Don't be. I'm not." He exhaled, closed his eyes and leaned his head backwards. His hand clenched slightly as he closed his eyes for a moment. I waited. It was his turn to let out his feelings. He opened his eyes and leaned into me. "I'm just disappointed that I wasn't the one for you. It's hard because I have never pictured ending up with anyone other than you," he said with tears in his eyes.

"I know," I whispered. I wanted to comfort him, but my embrace would only make things harder.

"I get it. He's your sun," he said.

"You're wrong. You are the sun. You bring warmth, laughter and joy—but he is the moon. He draws me into a world of mystery that I have never known," I replied.

"Stay with the sun," he exclaimed.

"I cannot. I look to the moon," I said as I wiped away a tear.

"I know this and still I wait for my sun," James said. He shifted his weight as he looked out over the evening tide. The large sphere seemed to glow brighter in the clear night sky.

"You will know when your moon appears," I said as I looked into the sky. "Perhaps then …."

"If he loves you the way that I think he does, then you need to find him," James said. "Just promise me you'll come back."

"I'll do my best," I promised. I was moved by his avowal. His words could not have been more perfect.

"You will have to be better than your best if this Legion is as you've described," James said. His brow furrowed with concern. He was right. Every skill that I had learned would be put to the test. Theron's Legion was unparalleled. I would have to be smart to get us out of this mess alive.

****

The moonlight glistened against the peaking crests, like diamonds dancing atop the water. I could think of nothing more beautiful than the ocean at night. Toby and Kirby were out there somewhere. They were careful not to venture too close to the vessel as to call attention but near enough to keep watch for any unwanted guests. All was quiet. We anchored for the night to keep from drifting off course. James and I had decided on three-hour shifts. I slept for the first three hours and was now taking watch while he slept. I resolved that I would not wake him to relieve me. My sleep habits were all out of whack, anyway. As Sironian slept during the day, and humans at night, my body couldn't seem to pick one course over the other. It was very frustrating. It was doubtful that I could sleep at all. I was nervous over what was ahead. Would I even get to see William or would Theron kill me on the spot? Perhaps he would no longer honor the safety he had promised from the treaty now that the Obyascon now sought me. I dangled my feet off the starboard. The spray from the water was invigorating. Perhaps I could just slip beneath the waves and be absorbed by the ocean. I was a creature of the sea after all. I slid my feet closer to the water. The current lapped against my ankles. I closed my eyes. My fingers began to loosen their grip on the rail. Perhaps I would just take a dip—just a moment beneath the waves. The sea beckoned to me, and all reality was lost—swept away in the entrancing song of the tide.

"What are you doing, darlin'?" I gasped, and the trance was broken. A sleepy-eyed James had emerged from the cabin.

"Contemplating a swim," I uttered. My grip tightened, and I pulled my legs back onboard.

"In the ocean—at night?" James asked. I had but one defense. I was drunk on moonlight and enchanted by the ocean's call.

"I *am* a sea monster you know," I teased.

"Yes, I know. I've seen that side of you—pretty scary actually. I once thought you were about to eat me," he said. We both laughed.

"Not eat you. Just suck out your essence," I replied flatly.

"Great. Oh, okay. I'm not even sure what essence is." He laughed.

"… and as I recall, you weren't complaining," I teased.

"I couldn't have complained even if I wanted to! I've read enough mythology to know men are powerless against the charms of a siren," he explained.

"Fair enough," I said in agreement.

"Your turn to get some rest," James insisted.

"I'm not sure that I can sleep. Too much going through my head," I said, but my words faded when I realized we were no longer alone.

We didn't hear it creep onto the boat, but Kirby's alert echoed in the distance. It was all the warning received. An Obyascon stood crouched on the port of the boat ready to attack. His pale white skin glistened through the darkness. The razor-sharp fins coming off his back were mangled and torn, and his body showed signs of several open, deep flesh wounds. I recognized him as one of my captors, Moxley. He was severely injured from the shark attack but still resilient enough for a fight.

"What the hell is that?" James shouted backing up toward the bow.

"An Obyascon—one of my captors. I thought it was dead," I shouted.

"You killed my brothers," it growled in broken words. "I no longer follow Merissa's orders. I here for revenge." I could barely make out the creature's words as it inched closer to us.

"Then you will die like your brothers!" I replied. The Obyascon charged without warning. I ducked as it lunged with its spiky claws, then landed a swift kick to the jaw. It hit the deck then immediately charged again. This time James was there to deliver a hard blow to its abdomen. Kirby leapt out of the water landing gracefully on the bow as Toby took the rear. Kirby slid between James and me, knocking the creature off its feet. It turned to see Toby, but before it could regain composure, Toby took hold of the monster's head and abruptly snapped it from its body. The assault was over in less than a minute. The creature was outnumbered, but we were the lucky ones. Despite our safeguards, the Obyascon was able to sneak up on us. I quickly turned to James. His sunburned face had been bleached of color.

"Are you alright?" James exclaimed.

"The question is, "Are *you* alright?" I am not sure that I have ever seen your face that pale before. You shouldn't have engaged in combat! You haven't been trained to fight the Obyascon!" I hissed.

"Any boy who has survived middle school knows how to land a punch," James replied.

I softened. No one could argue with that reasoning.

"… but still," I mumbled. It was hard seeing James up against that creature. I now realized what William must feel when he watches me fight.

"If someone would have told me a week ago that a monster like that was living in these waters, I'd have told them they were crazy. We could get rich just off its carcass!"

Toby slid the creature into the water. Its body began to fizzle and dissolve into fleshy parts as it sunk to the depths. The Obyascon were designed to break apart in the water upon death. Such a feature would prevent the discovery of the race while providing food for marine animals. It was amazing and gross.

"Guess you will no longer want to go for that evening swim," James said.

"Not a chance!" I replied.

"Dude, you just took on your first sea monster!" Toby said to James. "How does it feel?" James didn't miss a beat.

"Pretty freakin' awesome!" James said giving Toby a fist pump. "So that was one of the creatures you've been telling me about?" James asked.

"It was. The very same creature that tried to kill me a week ago," I replied.

"I think I'm still in shock. I've never dreamed something like that existed!" James was understandably still a bit rattled.

"I will walk you through it—at least as much as I know. You have been a witness to a creature not found in these parts. They primarily reside deep in the waters of the Arctic. A small army has been stationed in the tropics to guard a young Sironian girl that goes by the name Anna."

"She must be *some* girl!" Toby bellowed.

"She's remarkable!" I exclaimed. She can channel heat energy through her hands and her eyes." Their mouths fell open in disbelief.

"No joke?" James asked. "Heat energy? Like a fire starter?"

"Something like that. There are quite a few Sironian with special abilities," I said.

"But heat channeling—that would make her quite a treasure for Theron," Toby said.

"Exactly! Which is also why the Obyascon has her heavily guarded," I replied. I decided to leave out her relations to Merissa and William. The last thing I wanted to do was toss around false information if she turned out not to be William's sister.

"Do you think we should expect any more visitors, Princess?" Kirby asked.

"It would be highly doubtful," I said. "This one was not here on orders but for revenge. I killed the others—with a bit of help from a very large shark."

"Shark? You left out the shark part when you were telling me about your time with the Obyascon," James said.

"If you've heard one shark story, you have heard them all," I teased. I winked at him. Kirby didn't like it at all.

"Looks like Mace missed all of the fun after all!" Toby flexed his muscles,

"Well, we better get back out there, just in case there is more trouble on the horizon," he said.

"Thank you, guys! You were amazing!"

Kirby smiled.

"Don't mention it, doll! We are Protectors. It's what we do," Toby replied before they slipped once again into the dark water.

The remainder of the night passed without incident. The water was quiet—peaceful. Dark hues were replaced with lighter skies. Soon the sun began to peek over the horizon.

I wondered how anyone could start the day without bearing witness to the glistening rays of sunlight atop the water. To do so would rob nature of its most prized gift.

James took over the sailing duties as I went below to freshen up for the day. It was hard not to think of William when his scent permeated the cabin—his clothes, his books. Every inch of this boat was William. His slender hands had sculpted every timber. Now it was taking me to him. Had that been his plan all along? Had he returned his boat to Knoxx Point in the hopes that, if by chance I would return, I would use it to come to him?

We dipped into the Georgia coastline by late afternoon. The first leg of the trip was completed in remarkable time. James found me preparing my backpack for the next phase of my journey. "Silas's informant isn't expecting you until morning," James said. He was visibly upset.

"I know, but he could be early. I don't want him waiting for me. I will not know if he is there until I get to the reef." I rambled on nervously. "The calculations put the meeting spot just a few miles south of here. I can easily make the trip in no time."

"We're early," James said. "Don't go—not yet. Besides, if he isn't there, you'll be alone on the reef until sunrise. After last night's visitor, we both know that would be a bad idea." James was right, but his insistence aggravated me. I was a skilled Protector! I didn't need anyone telling me what to do!

"You promised you would see me to the reef. We are here," I said flatly.

"Look," he could sense my annoyance. His tone softened. "We are right here along the coast. I'm sure there is a marina just along the way. Let's dock this evening … grab a bite to eat … just relax a bit."

"James, this is something I need to do …," I pleaded.

"I know that. All I ask is one more night." He ran his fingers through his copper hair. "I don't know when I'll see you again," he begged. "You cannot promise me that I will ever see you again. One night, just give me one night." His eyes were pleading, and his hand reached out for mine.

"One night," I said taking his hand in mine.

****

As soon as the boat ventured off course, my two Sironian friends appeared onboard. They were alarmed.

"Are you trying to give us a heart attack?" Kirby said as he shook the water off his shirtless chest. His khakis hung low on his hips. Talk about heart attacks! The sight of him glistening in the afternoon sun was enough to stop any girl's heart. I looked away. It was hard to look away. I did not want to give him the satisfaction of knowing I was admiring him.

"Dude, the reef is the other direction," Toby said.

"We decided to dock and grab some dinner. The informant isn't expecting me until daybreak, so we have the evening to relax."

"Hello, civilization!" Kirby said as he stretched out onto the deck and put his feet up on the rails. "I have been craving a steak for weeks."

"Aren't you supposed to be some type of marine mammal? I thought all you guys ate was fish?" James grumbled. I could sense he was a bit aggravated that we would have company for the evening.

"And aren't you supposed to be human—as in … not be here," Kirby spurted.

"Ouch, that one would hurt, if your opinion mattered," James shot back.

"He told you!" Toby laughed. Toby liked anyone who could rattle Kirby a bit. I was impressed that James could hold his own with these guys.

"Easy! Look, let's go and have a nice meal tonight. You two better behave, or we will be eating leftover sandwiches again!"

James had brought clothes. The others had not. Kirby fit nicely into William's white button down and cargos—too nicely. I ached for William. Having Kirby parade in William's attire was torturous. Toby could not fit into any of his button downs or pants but managed to squeeze into a pair of his tan shorts and a knit pale blue

T-shirt. It clung very tightly to his excessively built frame. I slipped into one of the dresses from my backpack—a tan 1940s style fit and flare that buttoned up the front. It was one of my vintage gifts from Knoxx Point.

We turned quite a few heads as we stepped onto the dock at the marina. All eyes were on us as we made our way down the marsh walk. There was active nightlife all up and down the boardwalk with plenty of eateries right along the water. James chose a place called the Lone Dog Saloon. The server ushered us to the back of the restaurant. She only briefly took her eyes off my dinner dates to size me up. I was sure she was trying to figure out my relations with the group. The group was famished, ordering enough food for twice our number. There was a small dance floor in the center of the floor with a local band playing covers off to the side. After we had ordered, James asked me to dance. I was not in the mood for dancing but accepted his request. His arms pulled tightly around my waist, reminding me of all of our evenings together as young teenagers. Here we were again on the dance floor. I closed my eyes. The dance had changed. We had changed, but the memories brought me right back to that place—bare sandy feet, sun-blanched porch planks, and an old radio.

"I think you have monopolized this beauty long enough," Kirby said. "May I cut in?"

"Not happening," James said, twirling me effortlessly across the floor. His movements were so smooth I would have guessed him Sironian. He was no longer the boy I had remembered. Though I would forever miss the clumsy, young boy from my youth, the man before me captivated my attention. Kirby huffed back to his seat. The meal had just arrived, and the Crew began to dig in.

"The meal is here," James said.

"Just one more song." I replied momentarily taking the lead. The moment felt good. I had been torn up inside for months—I didn't want to let go of the feeling.

"You know, you could always stay." He stopped, and his eyes met mine. "I know I am not equipped to ward off sea monsters, or whatever the hell this is that you are facing, but I do know that I am not afraid to face it with you." I closed my eyes, breaking how his eyes bore into mine.

"I couldn't stay with you. My heart would always be someplace else," I whispered.

"But maybe your heart could eventually find its way back?" He swiftly replied. His eyes still carried a glimmer of hope.

"You deserve someone with a whole heart. My vessel is empty. The remnants that remain are hardly worthy of you. James, I would never deny you knowing love—whole love," I confessed. He sighed and loosened his grip from around my waist.

"You made up your mind a long time ago. I'm not stupid. I also know that once your mind is set, there is little anyone can do to change it, but I wanted you to know that you have another option," he said firmly.

"You should never be just someone's option. That is why you keep walking away. You warrant better," I replied. "You could never find contentment with parts and pieces of love. Nor could I."

"I would carry your half-emptied heart and spend my days filling it again," he whispered in defeat.

"My heart is too broken to fill," I replied. "Your efforts would be in vain. You know this. It's why you have mended the spot that I once held. You moved on with Amy. You require more than a broken soul."

"You're wrong! Your soul is not broken!" James exclaimed. "After I read your letter, I had hope ... that if I could only get you to agree to let me go with you, then maybe I could convince you not to do this crazy thing you are doing. Did you ever think that maybe love shouldn't be this hard? That maybe if the forces of nature are trying so hard to keep you apart that maybe you should listen?" He had an excellent point, but my resolve was firm. Even if he was right, I knew there was no turning back. I would be leaving soon—possibly forever. I thought James had found resolve through our last discussion, but there was more battle within him.

"I am willing to fight for this love, beyond sense, logic or reason, I know it's a love worthy of the fight," I replied.

"Pray that I will find that kind of love one day," he replied in defeat.

"I have … and I will," I whispered.

15

____

*"I did not know how to reach him, how to catch him ... The
land of tears is so mysterious."*

~ The Little Prince, Antoine de Saint-Exupery

A low fog drifted along the dusty gray morning hues. There were
neither blinding rays nor glistening waters, only a tear and a
hug. He watched me swim away. I did not look back. There were no
"goodbyes." We had said all that needed to be spoken. I pressed
forward into the unknown waters. It glided across my body more
swiftly with each stroke. With each smooth motion, I moved closer
to my destination—and with all hope, my love.

Just as promised, he was waiting for me, hovering just above the
surface. All of the nervousness I had been feeling over the past week
released in the form of a giggle. He seemed as shocked at my
reaction to him as I was. He wore a mask as if he were a sword
fighter from an old black and white movie. I knew he was a
Protector, as his skin was a golden tan, unlike the Sironian of the

deep. He was more muscular than the typical siren as well. Most sirens are long and streamlined for swimming. The informant was built similar to the Crew. His head of thick brown hair crooked to the side at my response, which only made me giggle again. *What was wrong with me? Had I completely gone mad?*

"I am assuming you are Marguerite Westley, the uh … girl, I am here to retrieve," he said.

"You would be correct," I swiftly responded. "I am assuming you are the uh … the informant that is here to whisk me away?" A crooked grin spread across his face.

"I'm a bit baffled as to why you instantly find humor in our meeting" he said. "Are you mocking me?"

"Forgive me. I do not mean to do so; I can only claim it to be a nervous energy … and the mask you are wearing. I thought 'masked men' went out of style when the color television was invented," I muttered nervously. He laughed.

"You are a very bizarre girl—even for a half-breed," the mysterious creature said.

"Is that so? Have you met many half-breeds?" I asked. "I was under the impression that I was one of a kind."

"I have met no other half-breeds, though your 'one of a kind' status probably has little to do with your genetic make-up. From the stories I have heard of you, I was expecting one with the beauty of Aphrodite and the strength of Hercules." He shrugged. "You are a girl." Little did I know that the fight would begin so soon. My tongue was equally as quick.

"Well, I was expecting some great warrior from Theron's Legion … not Zorro," I spat.

"Who says I am not a great warrior?" he asked.

"… and who says I am just a girl?" I hissed. We stared at each other. His eyes narrowed, I raised my eyebrows. He looked at me puzzlingly. He defiantly responded by raising his eyebrow, breaking the tension. We both laughed.

"I can see I am completely outmatched by your wit," he snickered.

"Well, then we better get started. How far is the swim?" I asked.

"About thirty miles from here. I will be with you for the first twenty; then you will make the last ten alone," he said.

"And why is that?" I asked.

"To prevent the risk of being discovered as an informant. According to Silas's plan, you will report to Theron alone," he replied.

"What will I do, walk up to his front door?" I asked.

"Not exactly," he said. "When on land, Theron resides on Sapalo Island. Naturally, Theron owns the land, so aside from a few natives, it is virtually uninhabited. The island is surrounded by Theron's men. You will be intercepted as you near the island. I will swim ahead, and integrate back into the patrol to prevent any overzealous siren from trying to rob you."

"Rob me? Of what?" I asked.

"Your essence of course. Your human characteristics, compounded by Sironian genes, would be a highly sought-after cocktail for my kind," he said flatly.

"I can assure you that I would not give in readily!" I boasted. "You may think I am only a girl, but I have been able to hold my own against both Sironian and Obyascon." He laughed.

"I have no doubt. If you were not a powerful force, Theron would have no use for you. But don't be foolish, a single girl, no matter what her ability, would be little match against his army," he said.

"I take it you were not present when Theron attacked my home coastline?" I huffed.

"I was not. Theron appointed me over our territory during the altercation. He was afraid to leave our region unguarded," he replied.

"Then you are unaware that I am not afraid to take on an army," I said sticking my chin confidently in the air.

"Alright! Don't get your fins ruffled, girl!" he laughed. "If I concede that you are a badass, will you please let us get out of here?"

"Fine," I said. "But answer one more thing."

"Alright," he agreed.

"Who are you that Theron would so entrust his region?" I asked.

"I am his personal Protector. I am Michael."

****

As we headed southward, it became evident as to why Theron had chosen to reside in this remote area. Small barrier islands were nestled all along the dark waters of the coast. Some islands appeared to have a few houses; most seemed virtually uninhabited. I swam the first nineteen miles without a break but began to tire midway through the last mile. Michael sensed my fatigue and suggested we stop on one of the small landmasses off of the coast.

"How are you holding up?" he asked. I brushed my wet hair back over my shoulders.

"I'm alright—nervous. I'm a bit tired … and anxious." The giggles were gone. Everything had become very real. Michael repeated his earlier instruction taking care to make sure I knew the details Silas had put into place.

"When you are ready, you will swim down the coast for about another six miles. Theron's men should pick up your scent and come to you. Tell them immediately who you are, and that you have come to see Theron. I will be nearby to take over from there," Michael instructed.

"Alright. "I said, suddenly realizing that my hands were shaking. Michael noticed, but instead of mocking me, he nodded in encouragement. With a final look of comfort, he disappeared into the surf. I was alone, and about to face one of the most difficult challenges of my life. In training, Silas had taught me to count off a mile through my strokes. I had never had to put the skill to practice. My heart raced faster and faster in my chest as I completed the fourth mile. Even as I neared the calculated area, I was unprepared for what was to come. It came without warming. It came with extreme force.

The first siren grabbed hold of my ankle, spinning me head over heels. I was face-to-face with the unmistakable face of an angel. Its porcelain face and deep blue eyes were framed by swirls of copper hair. The beauty of the creature astounded me. I started to rise to the surface so that I could tell the siren all that Michael had instructed, but it took hold of my ankle again, this time pulling me down with greater force. It let out a magical cry beneath the water. I tried to fight, but I was mesmerized. The melody captured my senses. My body drew closer to the siren, as its arms intertwined around me. I was drawn to it.

She took hold of my head tilting my face backward with her long white fingers. I was aware of what she was planning to do to me, but her melody made it impossible to resist her. I tried to think straight. I tried to think of anything other than her song—and then William's face swept through what little consciousness remained. I would not leave him looking for me forever.

I fought free from her hold, as I desperately thrashed to the surface for air. Her claws tore into my ankles as she thrust me downward again into the dark water. I was no longer face-to-face with an angel, but a demon. All beauty was transformed into a creature of nightmares. I was flooded with memories of Maris. I had defeated that monster; I would end this one as well. I growled and surged towards the beast, knocking it so hard that it was barely visible beneath the depths. All trace of humanity was transposed as I became all that I feared. My features twisted into a creature like the one before me. She shot through the surf toward me, her sweet song replaced by a piercing howl. I positioned for attack. She froze before contact. Her eyes once glowing with fury, now riddled with curiosity. We drifted towards the surface.

"What kind of creature are you?" she hissed. "Your scent is that of a human and yet my eyes do not deceive in that you are siren?"

"I am both human and siren—perhaps you have heard of me. I am Marguerite Westley, and I am here at Theron's request!" I growled.

"I have heard legends of a half-breed girl but until now doubted your existence," she spat.

"As you can see, I am very much real. Now take me to Theron!" I commanded.

"Theron's guests rarely arrive without notice or entourage," she replied as she circled me as a carnivore would its prey. "I know nothing of your visit, which means Theron knows nothing of your visit."

"He was expecting me months ago. The visit was delayed. I am here now," I replied firmly.

"So he is unaware of your arrival?" she hissed. The siren circled faster, slithering around me like a sea serpent. "I am not sure that I can pass on such an opportunity. Your essence could give me the power of the gods!" I braced for her attack.

"There is only one God, and I can assure you that your power would never come close to His!" With a deafening howl, the creature pounced, her eyes wild with malice. I struck her hard across the face. Her body hit fast into the depths. I gasped, trying to calculate her next move. She rocketed from the water; her fangs ready to sink into me. Her strength was no match for mine as I hastily took hold of her limbs. The creature within me was fiercely gauged to tear her head from body when a party of Sironian appeared above the water.

I knew the face of the party's leader well … *"Mace,"* I started to exclaim but stopped myself. The body before me, though carrying all of the characteristics of Mace, was different. His hair was longer. His eyes were slightly more deep-set. The being before me looked like my friend—but was not. I knew he had to be the brother that Mace had only briefly spoken of—the brother he implied was dead. He spoke. It was a voice I knew—Michael's voice,

"Are you aware, Morphia, that the girl who has you in her grasp is the very same girl who killed Maris?" I did not loosen my grip.

"She did not!" she gasped.

"I would suggest picking your prey more wisely," Michael said sternly.

"Marguerite Westley, will you please release her so that we may escort you to Theron. He was expecting you to report for duty months ago." I played along and released the siren. She slithered back with the others.

"How do you know this girl, Michael?" a pale albino-colored siren asked.

"The question, Luke, is why you do not know this creature. She is legendary."

16

———

"Courage is the resistance to fear, mastery of fear
~ not the absence of fear.

~Mark Twain

We arrived on Sapalo Island just before sunset. There was an immense plantation house about a hundred yards from the shoreline. I wasn't sure what to expect from the home of the most dominant underwater ruler, but this was not it. The white four-story mansion could have easily been struck from the pages of *Gone with the Wind* with its large frontal windows and endless wraparound porch. Two enormous sets of dormers garnished each side of the upper level. Michael escorted me across the plush lawn towards the estate.

"Welcome to Kingston Plantation," Michael said. "I think he was showing off a bit when he named it that a few hundred years ago."

"It's a plantation house?" I asked. The grandeur and history of such a home made it a bizarre choice for a sea ruler. Michael laughed. "Yes, one of the oldest plantations in the United States, but Theron keeps it updated with the latest amenities and styles."

"Theron? The ruler of the sea lives in a plantation house?" I said in disbelief.

"We are sirens. We reside in the ocean, silly girl. Nevertheless, Theron has many homes for entertaining land dwellers. He also prefers the sunshine during the warmer months," Michael explained.

"Is he here now?" I asked.

"There is no one on the island, except for you and I. Theron keeps a small staff of Gullah natives. They have been a part of the land here before Theron arrived."

"Do they know of the siren?"

"Yes, the Gullah-Geechee live close to nature. Those on the island accept and respect us and we them," Michael responded. The realization that we were now alone on the island prompted the question that we both knew would come.

"Michael, how could you not tell me you were the twin brother of Mace? You undoubtedly wore the mask to hide this from me on our first meeting," I scolded.

"The mask was a necessary precaution ...." I cut him off.

"Mace said you were dead," I said flatly. I instantly regretted my tone. I could see the agonizing impact of my words.

"I was not sure if the other Protectors had followed you to the reef. If I am dead to Mace, I will not contradict his proclamation by showing my face," he said. His words were emotionless, but his eyes foretold a different story.

"You would prefer to live a lie?" I pressed.

"Are we all not liars?" he responded. "You spout out judgment, and yet, your presence here is a lie in itself."

"What do you mean?" I gasped.

"You claim to be here to make good on the treaty—to train with Theron's Legion. Are you not actually here for love?" he said. Michael's eyes met mine. I was unsure what Silas had told Michael in regard to the reasoning behind my arrival.

"Silas told you …?" I asked.

"No, your eyes did. The moment you stepped foot on land your eyes immediately began searching for someone—someone not Theron. As our only recent arrival from your area is the young William Avery, I presume it is him that you seek," Michael smirked. It was the first time we had spoken of William.

"Please tell me all that you know of him!" I shamelessly pleaded.

"William arrived three months ago with news of a large rebellion growing within the Obyascon forces. He claimed the Obyascon had retrieved a powerful weapon. William revealed it to be the very same half-breed girl with which Theron had recently made a treaty. He insisted our army go after the hybrid so that her forces could not be used against us. As our sea dwellers have little expertise against the Obyascon, Theron placed William over the training of our dwellers. In addition, he has demanded William honor the treaty you set in place last spring in regards to marrying his granddaughter."

"Have William and Aria wed?" An affirmation would have made my heart stop altogether.

"They have not, though the date has been set," he said sympathetically.

"It was agreed that he did not have to wed for two years!" I cried. Michael softened.

"Apparently, that agreement has been revised as William is set to marry Aria in two months' time," he said tenderly. I was unable to speak. I was broken—again. "You have been through quite an ordeal today. Let me show you to your room." Michael placed his hand on the small of my back and guided me through a garden towards the rear of the estate. Three small guesthouses stood off to the side of a large pool. Michael led me towards the middle guesthouse.

"I'm not staying in the main house?" I mumbled, feeling almost too sick to stand.

"When on land the Protectors stay here. I assumed you would prefer this to the opulence of the plantation," Michael responded.

"I would," I agreed politely.

"Fine. I will be staying here." Michael motioned towards the furthest house. "I will notify the staff of our arrival and seek to notify Theron of your presence here. He hasn't been about the estate for the past few days, but I am assuming he is in the area."

"Do you think he will kill me?" I asked.

"Contrary to what you may believe about Theron, he abhors killing. He is not evil, misguided in his rendering of the law perhaps, but not evil. I see no reason, as of yet, in which he should take your life." He softened. "I will be back in a few hours. Dry out your clothes. Take a shower and relax if possible. I have a feeling your adventure here has only just begun." He smiled and opened the door to my suite. There were no locks. It made no sense to lock doors when Sironian hands could easily twist them apart.

The room was simple but elegantly dressed with a classic whitewashed four-poster bed, with colonial blue linens. A small white rattan nightstand and matching chair were to the side of the bed and a richly-stained vintage armoire across the room. The room was bare of pictures and accessories, except for a few books shelved beneath the nightstand. A small clean bathroom housed an old porcelain tub. A copper sink basin, fitted with current amenities, was in the corner.

I took each clothing item out of my backpack and washed it with soap. I hung the articles around the bathroom to dry. A hairdryer I pulled from the washboard helped to speed up the drying process. I concentrated on the cotton forties' style dress that I had worn the evening before. It was thin enough to dry quickly.

I pulled out a granola bar from the front pocket of my backpack and slipped in the warm tub water. The warm water was soothing to my tired muscles. After swimming such a distance, I was surprised I could stand at all. Relaxation was not an option. I was unable to think of William's reported engagement to Aria without getting sick. Was it possible that he could be on the island? I became frustrated with myself for not pressing Michael for more information. My fingers brushed along the shiva, then to the ring that hung close to my heart—William's mother's ring. *He could not marry Aria! He had already given that promise to me!*

I had no sooner slipped out of the tub and into the tan dress when there was a knock at the door. It was Michael. His presence filled the small room. Michael was every bit as handsome as Mace. He shared the same chiseled face as his brother, but Michael had a softness about him. Michael had apparently showered as well, as he had on fresh clothes, and smelled of cottonwood soap.

"Theron and his Legion returned to Sapelo an hour ago. He has requested your presence for dinner in the main house at eight o'clock," he said.

"Well … what did he say?" I asked.

"I explained to Theron that his men recovered you four miles off the island, that you had come to him, and that you were here for the duty as agreed upon by the treaty," Michael replied.

"What was his reaction?" I asked.

"He was greatly surprised by the news. He said that he had much to consider. Then he told me to ask you to dinner," he responded.

"Well, what should I do?" I asked him.

"Finish drying your hair for starters...."

"Yes of course but ...."

"You are a smart girl! You have survived an attack from Theron and escaped from the Obyascon, all on your quest of forbidden love. I think you can handle yourself for dinner," Michael smirked.

"Will you be there?" I asked him. Michael reminded me of Mace. His presence provided an odd comfort. This stranger instantly felt like a friend.

"Of course. I am a Protector, remember," Michael replied.

"That's a small relief," I said. I bit my lip anxiously. He laughed.

"I am not there to protect *you* from Theron, silly girl! I am the sworn Protector to the ruler of the sea. I am there to guard *him* against *you*."

****

Michael led me up the sweeping steps of the house to the large front door. "I will see you at dinner," he said as he turned the knob and ushered me into the drawing room. The staff hurried about, utterly indifferent to the new half-breed in their presence.

"You are leaving?" I asked, my heart pounded loudly in my chest.

"Yes, but only for a short time. I will return soon," Michael said.

The inside of the Kingston Plantation was every bit as opulent as the outside. An array of ancient carpets adorned its aged

194

hardwood floors. I stepped from the foyer to the drawing room. The walls were ornately decorated with countless gilded paintings. The private collection displayed many of the artists that I had studied in Art History class. Priceless antiques from different periods accentuated the eclectic royalty of the interior. Theron was a collector. Kingston Plantation was a secret museum, whose treasures were hidden away on this deserted island.

"What do you think of Kingston?" a voice said from behind me. I turned to see Theron standing behind me. He was tall and slender, wearing a fitted pair of khaki slacks, and a linen-button down that was open at the collar. His hair was neither blond nor brown but a rich golden tone. His high cheekbones accentuated his narrow ice-blue eyes. I had seen him only once before, during the hurricane, but never up close. He was my grandfather, and yet, he looked no older than forty.

"It's like a museum." I uttered, praying that my voice wouldn't crack.

"I am a lover of many things," he said smoothly. "At the top of these things would be art, history, and literature."

"Well then … it appears we share these interests." I said casually. *How could I be like him?* I wanted to cry. My greatest passions were passed to me by my grandfather.

"See now, we are already off to a good start," Theron said. My heart raced. I knew that his keen ears could pick it up no matter how cool my tone. "There is no need to be nervous. I only wish to get to know you better."

"I wish to know your world better," I muttered. I tried to breathe slowly in an attempt to slow my heart rate.

"Well then, would you mind accompanying me to the study?" He gently ushered me into the next room. The large room was closer to a library than a study as the mahogany shelves were filled from top to bottom with books. My mouth hung open in awe.

"Do you mind?" I asked stepping closer to the shelves.

"Not at all. It is a pleasure to meet someone who can truly appreciate my collection," he said. I picked up classic after classic, all copies I had never seen before.

"These are all first editions!" I gasped. I felt like I had stepped into a dream. "Are those Biblical scrolls?" I asked of the ancient manuscripts carefully displayed in glass enclosures. Theron smiled.

"Yes, all that you see are first editions or in some cases, original manuscripts."

"How did you collect all of these?" I gasped. He laughed.

"An endless supply of funds and plenty of time on my hands," Theron replied with a smirk. He was amused at my reaction to his library. "I travel frequently—a job requirement, I suppose you would say. It helps to know important people from around the world." His eyes narrowed, and his smile widened as he watched me.

"It's a miraculous collection. If I lived here, I doubt that I would ever leave this room," I replied as I gazed through the titles around the room.

"You are welcome. I do hope that you will spend some time here. What you see is the largest collection of its kind in the world. I am quite old, my dear. I predate the majority of volumes you see," he said. I turned to see Theron studying me carefully. My guard had slipped ever so slightly—it returned. "I assumed Silas would have schooled you a bit more about me."

"He has. You just look so young. It is easy to forget your age," I replied.

"I should say the same about you" He did not take the seat behind the desk but instead took one of the more casual reading chairs. I followed his lead and took the seat across from him. "But as they say, one should not judge a book by its cover," Theron said as he gazed upon me through crystal eyes. I refused to allow him to shake me.

"Though a bit cliché, I believe that to be extremely wise advice," I said.

"Take for instance the hybrid girl. This half-breed should not be underestimated. She appears unintimidating, yet she was able to orchestrate a quite effective plan against my Legion with only a handful of troops," he said flatly.

"Perhaps she was just lucky …," I replied nervously.

"I had almost convinced myself of that," Theron said. "However, I was quite concerned to discover that the girl was captured by the Obyascon. I, of course, instantly regretted my decision to let her live and began orchestrating a plan to retrieve her. You see, I feared that she could be used as a weapon against us. A strange fear, I know, but we do fear the unknown. Though unintimidating, the hybrid is quite a mystery." My heart began to beat faster.

"Or maybe the hybrid is very much like a siren, only a bit stronger due to the human gene," I muttered.

"Perhaps … but then she arrives on my doorstep today, without the need of an army to rescue her. Shockingly, she apparently was able to rescue herself. Should such a creature be allowed to complicate our infrastructure and potentially put the Sironian population at risk?" He broke from his hypotheticals. His crystal eyes bore into mine. "How am I doing?" He leaned in towards me. I swallowed hard. Would he kill me right here?

"You are correct. I was captured by the Obyascon, and I did manage to free myself, but I am no apparent threat to the Sironian. I am part human—yes, but I am also siren. I am here as we agreed upon to train for your Legion. All I ask is that you give me the opportunity to live. You gave your word in the treaty," I said.

"I did so, and I do not break my word once given. However, if I were to sense an inherent risk to my people, I would be obligated to disavowal," Theron replied. Our negotiation was so finely woven that it was hard to believe that we were bartering over my death. There was a ringing sound from the other room. "Ah, the dinner bell! We shall continue our conversation later. Be not alarmed, I rarely make rash decisions. As you can see, I am a collector of rare and beautiful things. How lucky for you that you are both," he said as he reached for my elbow to lead me to the door. I shuttered at his touch. Theron seemed unmoved.

The long passage leading to the banquet hall was laden with medieval tapestries; I was too anxious to notice. Classical music channeled throughout the house. We reached the double doors leading into the banquet hall. The music at the entrance hall was extremely loud. "Forgive the loud composition; I didn't want to spoil your arrival by allowing our dinner guests to hear our conversation."

"Dinner guests?" Theron swung open the double doors and there, seated around the table, was his Legion. They arose at our entrance. I saw nothing but the face I had spent every waking moment longing to see. It belonged to William. His face blanched as if he had seen a ghost. His breath quickened, and his nostrils flared. I thought for a moment he was about to leap across the table and grab me into his arms. His eyes met mine with a longing that immediately took my breath away. For that moment, the rest of the world disappeared. I wanted to shout out his name. I wanted to run to him. I wanted to cry. I wanted to take him into my arms to feel his body pressed against mine. I just stood there. I could not pull my eyes from him. Theron introduced me to his Legion one by one. I heard nothing but the sound of William's racing heart.

"... and I believe Marguerite you know Aria," Theron said. The name caught my ear, snapping me back to reality. For the first time since entering the room, I tore my eyes from William. Aria's face was as pale as mine. Her eyes bore into me as her chest heaved. She glared as if she would attack me at any moment.

"Yes," I tried to speak. I nodded, unsure if I could get the words out. "We trained together." My words were no louder than a whisper. My eyes traveled down Aria's arm. Her hand was clutching William's tightly. Pain and jealousy struck my body like a knife. I tried to breathe slowly. The monster inside of me fought to come out. I wanted to rip her from limb to limb. William opened his mouth as if he were about to speak. Aria bore her nails into the side of his hand. Of course, Theron made William's introduction last.

"And William, seeing Marguerite must be the biggest surprise for you!" Theron continued to his Legion. "As I have been explaining to young Marguerite here, William has been training our troops for a battle against the Obyascon to recover you. However, it appears our treasure has come back to us on its own," Theron smirked.

"A blessing ...," he muttered. William's teeth were clenched. His eyes didn't leave mine.

"You see, William also trained with Marguerite," Theron explained to his Legion. "He was appointed as her Protector until the Sironian gene developed and she was trained by Silas as a Protector. Is that not so, William?" Theron asked.

"Yes. I am her Protector. No time, space, or genetics will change that." William showed no fear. His words were a warning to Theron.

"Looks like she may have put you out of a job, eh, Will?" Michael said as he entered the room. William's eyes did not waver from my face. Theron took his seat. His Legion followed. Michael took the seat next to me. "The girl managed to escape on her own. Perhaps our confrontation with the Obyascon is unnecessary after all." It took all the strength I could muster to find my voice. I scarcely sounded like myself.

"Actually, I think …."

Theron interrupted, "Clearly there is much we can learn from your time with the Obyascon, but there is plenty of time for such affairs. We gather tonight for the sole purpose of celebrating. We rejoice that Marguerite has come to join us!" The staff was ushered in with the first course.

"Do you really think it wise to bring a half-breed into our midst?" Zander's words did not hide his disdain at my presence. "Does this girl's life not go against what our laws protect?"

"Come now, Zander," Theron interjected, "let us not be rude to our guest."

"The laws clearly forbid the physical interaction between siren and human. Her existence, and mixed bag of abilities, stands proof as to why these laws stand," he scoffed. William growled at Zander. Aria sat speechless. Zander continued, "Suppose the Obyascon had used the girl for breeding … to create some sort of super race. Are you ready to give up your reign to a mixed race of beings?"

"That is enough, Zander," William snarled. His jaw was clenched so tightly, I feared he would strike. Theron arose to settle the tension.

"I have not fully decided the appropriate course of action in the matter. In the meantime, young Marguerite is here as our guest and will train with us as agreed upon under the treaty," Theron replied firmly.

"You must consider how her presence will appear to our people," Zander huffed. "You set the laws, and yet, you reward the offspring of a criminal with positions in the Legion. I say we end this matter!" William hurdled from his seat and was at Zander's throat in an instant.

"It appears William still honors his vows as the girl's Protector," Theron said with an artificial smirk. There was fear behind his eyes when he bore witness to the potency of such love. "Silas was wise to choose someone so loyal. Is it loyalty that has caused such a strong reaction—or something else? Dare I say, love?" William did not respond but kept his focus on Zander, who looked as if he was prepared for the fight. "Certainly you wouldn't slight your future bride with such an admission." William snarled as he held tight to Zander's neck.

"William!" Aria exclaimed.

I was dizzy. I felt as if I may faint at any moment. I somehow found the courage to speak. "Theron, you must forgive me, but I must cut this celebration short. I am feeling unwell. I will leave you all to decide my fate in my absence," I said sarcastically. "I hope you all find your meal appetizing. Goodnight," I said swiftly. Everyone stood as I strode out of the room. I took two steps down the hall before my eyes began to well. My feet moved faster and faster, until at last, I was running. I tore into my room and flung myself onto the bed in tears. I had seen him. He was here, and yet, we were once again separated. I had moved mountains to get to him, only now to have an entire race of beings standing between us.

There was a knock on my door. Adrenaline rushed through my veins at the possibility of William walking through my door. It was Michael. My heart sank. He carried a silver tray of food. "You have been crying." His demeanor softened.

"I'm fine," I mumbled.

"Theron insisted that I bring your meal," he said.

"Laced with poison I presume," I said.

"There is only one way to find out," he said removing the lid. He playfully took a bite of each entree. He shrugged his shoulders. "Nope, no poison, I feel fine."

"I don't think I can eat anything," I whimpered.

"You swam thirty miles today—not to mention all you have experienced emotionally. Your body needs to refuel, especially if you plan to join us tomorrow," Michael said. He was right. My strength was important. I relented. The meal was delicious, a perfect blend of fish and scallops atop risotto with a tomato-based garlic sauce. The fish was a species that I had never eaten before. There was a layered caramel cake for dessert. I picked at the food for a moment. My body craved nourishment. Small nibbles became large bites, and soon I had devoured the entire tray. Michael laughed. "Atta girl!" he said removing the tray and placing it outside my doorway. "Your body thanks you!"

"My body feels like it has been run over by a truck," I uttered.

"But nothing a little rest and relaxation can't cure."

"That is a tall order at the moment. What happened after I left tonight?" I asked. Michael sighed. I could tell he was stalling, as if to try and figure out what was acceptable to tell me.

"Where do you want me to start?" he said.

"How about from the time I left."

"Well, uh … William started off after you. Then Zander made a smartass comment, so William punched him—almost took his head off! Zander, who is no match physically for William, started to invoke a lightning bolt. Theron stopped him and scolded him quite rigorously for his behavior towards you," Michael explained. My jaw dropped open.

"Yes, I remember from our last encounter that he had that ability. He tried to kill me," I uttered. "Was William alright? What happened next? Where did he go?"

"I'm not sure. William stormed off leaving Aria behind. She is staying in the main house, but he darted off so abruptly, I did not see where he went. He was pretty angry. I doubt he is staying at the plantation or anywhere close to Theron."

"Theron obviously didn't tell the others that I was coming tonight; I can only speculate that he did it to get a rise out of William," I said.

"Or to test him. No one would have anticipated such a reaction," he added.

"I need to see him! Michael, please find him for me!" I pleaded. "Can't you communicate with him telepathically or something!"

"The telepathy gift only works underwater," Michael said.

"Will you find him?" I asked.

"You know I cannot do that," he said.

"Can't or won't?" My eyes narrowed.

"Both. Look, I need you to listen to me! I know that we have only known each other for a short time, but I consider you a friend. Both you and William made it quite obvious tonight that the feelings you share run deep. You are in love with him, I get it, but Theron has chosen him for Aria."

"He doesn't love Aria!" I protested.

"Yes, he made that clear tonight also. Love is not a factor when a Sironian chooses a mate. You are walking the edge of a sword. It is not the time to make yourself disposable. Do you understand what I am saying?" I reluctantly nodded. "I will help integrate you into his Legion, but you have to work with me on this. We cannot have a continuous display of what took place tonight. Theron is threatened by both you and William. He is not a fool. He knows you both are loyal to Silas. Once he comprehends the extent as to how he can utilize you, your head will be off of the chopping block ...."

"So I am expected to stand by as my love is forced to marry someone else?" I cried.

"I do not have all of the answers, but I don't want this to end badly for you," he said. "I promised Silas I will look out for you, but Theron cannot discover that I am still linked to his Protectors. You are going to have to do this on your own. You must be smart if you expect to survive here. Stop parading your heart around for all to see!" He looked into my eyes. He saw the pain. He softened. "I am sorry if I was harsh. I am a bit out of practice in the sensitivity department."

"You're only speaking the truth," I mumbled. "There is nothing more agonizing than to have the one thing you desire ripped from you, except for the knowledge that the antidote is out of reach.'

"I do not know about that kind of love, but I do know what it is like to have someone ripped from your life." Michael became quiet. I wanted to press him further, but it was obvious that we were both emotionally spent. "I am glad that you ate something. Try to get some sleep, and I will come get you in the morning around eight." He started to leave.

"Michael … thank you … for today," I said. He smiled and gently closed my door behind him.

17

"There is nothing more agonizing than to have the one thing you desire ripped from you, except for the knowledge that the antidote is out of reach."

~Marguerite Westley

I **knew that everything Michael had said was true.** To reunite with William would place a target on both of our backs. Could I give him up to protect him? Seeing him tonight without being able to touch him was agony. I tossed and turned fighting sleep until I could take it no longer. I slipped on my flats and hurried out the door. The night sky on Sapelo was as dark as the island on which I was captive. The only lights on the island came from Kingston Plantation. I darted off down the pathway away from the main house. It curved through a grove of date palms and back toward the silver dunes. I trekked through a great stretch of thick ridges before making my way onto the beach. I removed my shoes, tossing them atop a large mound and stepped onto the beach. The night sky was filled with a multitude of gleaming stars. It was alive with the flickering of each tiny beautiful light. I smiled. The waves were breaking far out in the depths, trickling down to a gentle foaming lap by the time they reached the shore. The beauty of the ocean could almost sooth the turmoil of my heart—almost.

I looked towards the east. My heart stopped as I saw his silhouette off in the distance. I felt as if I were dreaming. I could recognize each curve and angle of his body—a scene reminiscent of the first night in which I saw him on the dock. He did not see me. I wanted to run to him, but I was frozen. I watched him from the shadows of the dunes with a longing in which I had never known.

To hold him would be heaven …
To touch him—divine,
But fate would pull him from me,
Oh, this shattered heart of mine.

Would fate ever allow us to be together? For William to publicly renounce his engagement to Aria would be suicide. Theron would never allow it. He would use any means in his power to control William. He would use my feelings for William to control me too. The circumstances seemed impossible. I contemplated the pain I had experienced these past three months. I would wish this pain on no one! Perhaps in time, he would forget me. I thought back on the look in his eyes tonight. William had learned how to love. His heart of stone had melted, but those same emotions were destroying him. We would be ripped apart again, and if the pain of losing me did not kill him, Theron would. I felt myself slowly moving away from the beach—away from the one thing I wanted most in the world. I closed my eyes and stepped away. I had slipped further into the shadows of the dark island foliage. Leaving him would be hard. I would slip away at first light.

The force that took hold of me propelled me into shock. His body pressed against me so fiercely that it sent me tumbling backward into the soft dunes. I tried to open my eyes, but the world seemed a blur. I was immediately intoxicated by his scent. The fragrance of his skin engulfed my senses leaving me completely at his mercy. This was no ordinary siren; he was my own apparition from heaven. My body responded to his touch, my arms grasping him with the same intensity. His arms moved from my shoulders to the small of my back pulling me even closer to him. I could scarcely breathe as my face pressed against the tight muscles of his neck.

"I fear this moment a dream," William mumbled. His face buried into my disheveled hair. My lips responded gliding along his firm jawline.

"This is no dream … my subconscious is incapable of such wonder," I whispered as all senses were overtaken.

"Then let us never sleep," he responded with every part of his body.

The heat from his body left me breathless. All logic was lost under his touch as his face glided towards my hairline and swept across my cheek. I shivered. Warm lips gently caressed each part of my face before softly nuzzling against my lips. I gasped at the sheer exhilaration of his touch. His hands slid into my hair pulling my face towards his with severe intensity. I was his prey with no desire to fight. I would readily welcome this death. All softness was lost as his lips surged hard against mine. My lips parted, allowing the fervent flow of my essence to be stolen. He could have all of me. Reality faded. The flickering starlight diminished. Heaven drew closer. He caught himself. His draw slipped, momentarily allowing his essence to reach my taste buds. Desire began to stir as my mouth seized to rob his essence. He was lost in the exchange as I fiercely engaged my prize. He was designed for me. There could be no substance more alluring than that which he offered. He gasped, returning the fierce flow of energy to his body. Could this be a dream? At last, I was one with William again.

Abruptly our lips parted—our bodies invigorated—our souls as one. He steadied me against his chest. His firm body lay beneath me. My face nestled beneath his chin. His hands gently stroked my hair. "Forgive me. I crave your essence like no other substance I have ever known. I wanted you so badly that I could have mistakenly killed you," William whispered.

"I would have hardly noticed if death would have arrived. Such punishment would be worth your lips. I am every bit the thief myself," I uttered. I nestled nearer to him, drunk from his presence.

"I thought it a miracle to see you tonight—a cruel miracle, designed to drive me mad with desire. I had no idea if you were even still alive. I knew the strong probability that I would never find you … and then by some wonderment … you walked through the door. I had spent every moment plotting to find you, and in the end, you came to me," William was overtaken with emotion. I bathed in his words and soaked in his kisses. If I could have extended the moment, forever would seem inadequate.

"After I escaped, Silas informed me of your plan. I knew of no other way than to come find you. I wasn't even sure that you would be here," I explained to him.

"But I was … praying for the miracle that arrived tonight. It took every ounce of my strength not to grab you—grab you and run far, far from here," William said in agony.

"Every ounce of me wanted you to," I admitted. He tensed.

"And yet, when you saw me out here tonight, you were walking away," he questioned. The moonlight accentuated the pain in his eyes.

"Not walking away from the love I feel for you, only from the agony our reuniting would cause you," I said.

"I would endure a lifetime of agony before I would allow you to leave me," William replied.

"Yes but ...."

"Do you not realize the depth of my feelings for you? If you left, I would never stop looking for you," he confessed.

"As my Protector, you are bound to say that," I mumbled. I turned my head from him to hide the tears in my eyes.

"No, I say that because we are part of each other. No amount of time, distance or forced promises can change that. It is not just my heart that I offer you but every ounce of me." He gently slid the shiva from its hiding place beneath my dress. He ran his fingers across the smooth shell. "You are mine, and I am yours," he whispered.

"The words you speak are the very words that I have been waiting so long to hear and yet it is a lie," I cried.

"My feelings for you are no lie!" he exclaimed.

"No, the lie is that we have fooled ourselves into thinking this is possible." I pressed my forehead against his. "How is it possible, William? How is a life together possible?" He clutched the back of my head.

"I will take you away from here," he said swiftly. "We will find the most remote beach in the world and ...."

"How long could we run? They would find us, just as they found your parents," I said.

"There has to be a way! We could keep moving ...." I pulled away from him.

"William, my absence would put a bounty on Lucy, Caleb ... my family."

"As long as they are far away from the coast, they should be safe," William said. He once again gently pulled my face to his.

"Lucy is changing at an alarming rate; I don't know how much longer she has until …."

"We will take her with us …."

"You're talking crazy. You are not thinking straight!" I uttered.

"And you are thinking too much," he uttered breathlessly.

"William, there is something else—or should I say 'someone' else." His jaw clenched with jealousy.

"You have fallen in love with someone else?" he asked. His eyes narrowed, and his body went rigid.

"No! Every ounce of my heart belongs to you." His body slightly relaxed as relief swept over his face. "William, I have been playing this scenario over and over in my head for months, but now that you are here, I don't know how to tell you this."

"Tell me what?" William asked. He pulled away. William looked fully look into my face.

"The Obyascon have a girl in captivity—an exceptional girl. They call her Anna, but I believe her to be your sister," I whispered. His body crumpled against me—the boy who could not cry wept without tears. "William? Did you hear me? I think that I found your sister," I said again.

"Is this possible?" he said at last. He shook his head in disbelief. "You must tell me all that you know. Start from the very beginning," he pleaded. I nodded. He leaned across from me and took my hand in his. His fingers laced with mine. I took a deep breath and started from that ill-fated night on the jetties. I spent the remainder of the night telling William of my time with the Obyascon. He listened intently to every word, often stopping me to ask detailed questions. The tension grew as I told him of our escape. He learned of my plot to get us off the island and how I had left the girl behind to find our escape. I told him of how I was surrounded by their army and how the ring he had given me had ultimately saved my life.

"I don't understand," he muttered. "You say that Merissa, Queen of the Obyascon, released you because of my mother's ring? How would she have known my mother? Neither of my parents had ever spoken of the Obyascon. I know only legends of Merissa."

"She asked who it was that had given it to me. When I spoke your name, she ordered my immediate release. She asked if you were the son of Morgan and Robert Avery. I assumed that you knew her," I said.

"I have never met Merissa, though tales of the Obyascon have haunted the dreams of the siren for centuries. I have no idea how she would even know my name. I know of no past relationship between her and my parents," he explained.

"Her knowledge of your parents only fuels my speculation that the girl is your sister—that and the fact that she looks so much like you. She has your eyes. She shares the same smile. She was the only thing that gave me comfort during those months away from you," I confessed.

"I suppose it is possible that she could have researched the girl, learned of my parents, but that would not explain why she had knowledge of the ring or why she released you," William said curiously.

"With your sister in captivity, perhaps she feared that my death would draw you to them in retaliation," I replied.

"It's possible, but something doesn't add up. With the presence of the Obyascon in Murrells Inlet and by kidnapping you, they have sparked Theron to act against them. We were coming for war," he said.

"William, we will have to convince Theron to continue with his plan to find and engage the Obyascon. It is the only way we will be able to rescue your sister," I said.

"I must agree with you. The Protectors alone are no match for an Obyascon army. Do you have any idea where she's being held?" he asked.

"I don't know. They covered my head. I was drug underwater for a full day, unsure of where I was going. I passed out several times. I almost drowned. Despite Merissa's orders, the rogues were planning to kill me."

"It is like daggers to the heart to hear all that you endured. Thank God you escaped!" he gasped.

"The prayers I rendered were answered in the form of a big shark—Lucy's shark," I continued.

"Your captors were attacked by a shark?" he asked.

"Yes. I thought it had killed both of them, but one surfaced on your boat while I was trying to make it here."

"Wait a minute—there was an Obyascon on my boat? I anchored it there as a beacon—with only a faint glimmer of hope that you would return. I never dreamed that you were headstrong enough to take it into open waters alone," William said.

"I wasn't alone. James was with me," I confessed. "He helped me fight off the creature." William scowled.

"Wait! James was with you ... on my boat ... fighting the Obyascon," he asked.

"Yes, he knows about what we are," I admitted. William's scowl only deepened.

"Even so, that would hardly give him the strength to fight an Obyascon."

"Actually, James is pretty strong now—like Superman strong," I uttered nervously.

"I'm confused," he said.

I continued with all that had happened to me, starting from the shark rescue and finishing with my arrival at Kingston Plantation. It was painfully difficult for him to hear about my life in constant danger; after all, he would forever be my Protector. It seemed even harder for him to learn about James and the kiss that ignited his new abilities. I finished the tale just as the sun broke the horizon. William was having trouble processing a night's worth of knowledge. So much had happened in three months.

"The sun is rising quickly. I have to go." I said as I brushed the sand off my dress. I stood. The morning air sent shivers across my body. It was cold without the dunes and William's body heat for warmth.

"You can't go. I have so many questions …," William pleaded. He grabbed hold of my hand and pulled me towards him in the dunes—my mind protested, my body did not.

"I will answer all of your questions, but for now all I can give you is a kiss," I teased. My lips gently stroked his lips, careful not to part William's mouth. We arose from the dunes, this time together. His fingers trailed mine until the last possible second before we separated in different directions. I had just rounded the stone pathway leading to the guesthouses when I saw Aria waiting for me.

"Do you know how much I hate you?" she growled bitterly.

"I am sorry you feel that way, Aria; I have always hoped that we could be friends," I replied.

"I came to speak with you this morning, to ask you to leave. How stupid of me to think you would be in your room," she scoffed.

"I was down on the beach," I uttered.

"I can smell him on you!" she snapped.

"I'm sorry, Aria, if my presence is once again hurtful to you," I said.

"You're sorry? You are not sorry!" she spat.

"Look Aria. I'm not sorry for my connection with William, only that you are continuously hurt by it," I replied flatly.

"I could go to Theron right now! I could tell him that the two of you were off together!" she threatened.

"But you won't. You wouldn't do anything that could hurt William ...." Aria winced at my words.

"But there is nothing stopping me from ripping you limb from limb," she hissed. I took my stance, bracing for her attack. Michael appeared from his room.

"Aria, you are not about to attack our guest, now are you?" Michael asked. She hissed at him. "That's enough!" Michael said more forcefully. "Aria, may I please have a word with you ... in private." She glared at him, then back at me before proceeding along the path. "Marguerite, I would suggest you shower and change into something more appropriate for training," Michael said as he walked off after Aria.

"Of course," I said, slipping off to my room. I had not escaped trouble long. Aria had confirmed my fears by discovering that I had been with William. I sighed. I would have to "thank" Michael for saving me from Aria's confrontation.

I turned on the faucet. Aria was correct. My scent was interchanged with William's savory fragrance. It was divine. Warding off the Obyascon had been hard, but for that moment, I found it much more difficult to pick up the soap.

18

"Being deeply loved by someone gives you strength, while loving someone deeply gives you courage."

~Lao Tzu

"**A**re you ready to go?" Michael said as he knocked on the door to my cabin. A wide grin spanned across his face. "You're wearing that?" he asked with a chuckle. I suddenly felt insecure. I had put on my black combat ensemble for training.

"What? What's wrong?" I asked nervously.

"Nothing. Nothing at all. You look pretty badass!" Michael chuckled as he pulled the door closed behind me, and we began off down the path towards the main house.

"Where is the training field?" I asked as we neared Kingston. He laughed.

"Well, at least now the outfit makes sense." He laughed. I was annoyed.

"Huh? We *are* training today, right?" I eyed his choice of clothing. He looked as if we were going to a lunch date.

"When I told you training, I had a different sort of training in mind. It is actually more of a meeting," he smirked.

"A meeting? I will go back and change." I turned back towards the guesthouse. Michael reached out for my arm, gently spinning me towards him.

"No … no. We have no time for that. You look fantastic," he smiled. Michael's smile was comforting. Perhaps it was because he was the closest thing that I had to a friend on the island. Perhaps it was because he looked so much like Mace.

Michael was right. When the dining room doors opened, the Legion was all in place, just as they had been the night before. I looked completely out of place in my combat clothes. They all wore the equivalent of resort wear—linen and button downs.

"Good morning, Marguerite. I am very glad you have chosen to join us this morning." He did not apologize for Zander's outburst; he only motioned for one of his staff to bring me a plate. Theron eyed my attire. "As you can see, we dress quite casually here." My face flushed. He turned towards one of his housekeepers. "Hilda, Miss Marguerite arrived with limited baggage. Will you see that some island attire is delivered promptly to her quarters?" The middle-aged woman looked me over, nodded, and curtly left the room.

I immediately noticed that William was absent. Aria stood off to the side awkwardly as the Legion studied large maps scattered across the table. They briefly looked up as I found my seat, several smirked at my attire, but all immediately continued talking amongst themselves. Theron had introduced me to them the evening before, but all I had seen was William's face. I was looking at most of them for the first time. Zander was seated next to a female, Mari, whose shoulder-length sleek black hair curled out on the ends. Her face was angular and her lips full. She was like a modern day superhero. At her left was a neatly dressed male that reminded me very much of Indiana Jones. He sported the rugged professor style. His face was golden tanned, and his sandy blonde hair was cut just above his ears. I didn't remember his name, but one of the others referred to him as Roi. The body language of the pair indicated that they were a couple. To Zander's right, I remembered Darion, Theron's "truth teller." His pale green eyes against his brown cropped hair and dark features were every bit the siren. His bone structure was so small and defined that he appeared feminine. There was another male who went by Barbour. He was slender with dark hair pulled back in a ponytail. His clothes were slightly more disheveled than the others. I pegged him as the surfer type of the Sironian world. He was sitting next to an exotic creature who had very dark skin and long silvery-white hair. Her name was Anastasia. To the left of the table was a hefty, muscular male with pale features named Isaac. His platinum blonde hair hung just above the nape of his immense neck. A female with strawberry blonde curls was leaning across the table. One of the Legion called her Julianna. She was the most beautiful of the siren, with flowing locks and flawless golden skin. I wondered as to why Theron had selected each of them. Without a doubt, each must possess a rare, prized talent. Theron sat at the head of the table enjoying a large spread of pastries, fruits, and yogurt.

"I hope you are hungry. My Legion has eaten already," Theron said. "We begin early here on the island."

"I will have to remember that," I said. I nervously picked at the food on my plate. Aria's eyes shot daggers in my direction.

"Aria, have you seen William this morning? It is very unlike him to be absent," he smoldered.

"I have not seen him," she said curtly.

"Very strange," said Theron. Michael swallowed the large piece of pineapple he had been eating.

"Oh, I was supposed to tell you that William would be running late this morning—something about a supply run." Theron seemed agitated with Michael.

"Well, there we have it. Let us get started without him. Shall we?" The demeanor of the group changed as they instantly gave Theron their full attention. "Let us start by revisiting the need for an attack against the Obyascon. Our primary justification was that they possessed a weapon that could be threatening to our civilization. As the half-breed is now with us, we must determine if the creatures still pose a threat." Zander was the first to speak.

"I would say, 'no.' There is no need to waste our time or resources on an inferior group when there is no present threat. Honestly, by looking at the girl, I hardly see the peril in the first place. Her only presumed threat would be by further intertwining our race with the humans by breeding. As this is punishable by death, it is only a matter of time before we will be forced to administer such punishment."

I swallowed hard and tried to be strong. Mari looked at me sympathetically. "I cannot object that you speak the law, but if she is prevented from entwining the races, in which race should she be associated?" the Legion mumbled amongst themselves.

"And which race would be forbidden?" Barbour added cautiously.

"That is a worthy question, one that we will revisit. However, the question I am currently proposing does not pertain to young Marguerite but to the Obyascon. Zander, you have made your stance on the girl, let us try to stick to the subject at hand, shall we? Do we invade the Obyascon?"

"We do. We attack immediately," a voice said from the doorway. We all turned to find William standing in the entrance. The sight of him took my breath away. He stared directly towards the others, not even looking once in my direction.

"Ah, William! I was afraid you were not going to make it today," Theron said.

"I had some things in which I needed to attend," he said coolly.

"It appears William and Zander have quite opposing views on the subject. As Zander has had the opportunity to present his case, I now offer up the same opportunity to you."

"Well, let us examine the facts. I met this morning with our northern survey scouts. First of all, the Obyascon have been leaving the Arctic region in droves. The entire population seems to be relocating south."

"Julianna, as leader of the Scouts, you have the floor to report."

"My men have detected a large amount of movement; however, I was unaware that the whole colony had relocated."

"Are you sure of this, William?" asked Theron.

"I am certain. In analyzing the rate in which the scouts reported their movement, multiplied by the sheer number of bodies leaving the Arctic, I have determined there is little chance of a colony currently residing there any longer."

"Perhaps you should leave the calculations to me," Anastasia said.

"I know the Obyascon have left the Arctic," William insisted.

"What would be your evidence? Have you scouted the entire region?" Julianna said. Julianna was selected as the leader of the scouts due to her extreme ability to see at great distances, both on land, and beneath the sea. She was able to see and process information hundreds of miles away.

"Do you doubt the authenticity of the data collected by your men?" William mocked.

"We do not, only your motivation for collecting it." Julianna's eyes shifted towards me. William's expression hardened.

"My question to you is why have you not done so already?" William spat. "Look, the Obyascon would not leave their home poorly guarded. Though primitive, they are not unwise. Logic proves the colony has relocated by the fact that there are too few remaining able bodies to protect their queen."

"Queen of the Obyascon, leave the Polar region? Hardly likely. No one has seen Merissa in thirty years!" Theron scoffed.

"William speaks the truth. I have seen her," I said.

"You have seen Merissa?" Mari asked.

"Yes. Merissa is currently residing on an island in the Caribbean," I said, trying to keep my voice steady.

"Where exactly?" asked Roi.

"Um, forgive me, but I do not know her exact location," I replied.

"Why is that?" Theron asked impatiently.

"I was unconscious upon my arrival, and blindfolded when they returned me." It sounded absurd. I winced at such an admission.

"A likely story," Zander smirked.

"Darion, does Marguerite tell the truth?" asked Theron.

"She does, Theron," Darion replied.

"Well, what do you know of Merissa?" Theron asked.

"Very little, I only saw her once, and it was very brief." I calculated my words carefully, aware that Darion could pick up on any falsehoods. "She introduced herself as *Queen of the Isles.*" Theron's jaw hardened when I spoke the word queen.

"Merissa calls herself the Queen of the Isles, eh?" he grumbled … and which isles does she presume to rule?"

"I suppose she speaks of the islands of the Caribbean." Theron looked at Darion for affirmation that I was telling the truth. He nodded.

"How do you not know the location in which you were held captive for three months?" Zander said viciously.

"What Zander is saying," Roy said, "is that numerous indicators can help pinpoint your location: color hues, vegetation, rock types, rock formations, shell coloration, sand content …." Roi added.

"I think she understands," William said firmly. He shuffled his feet anxiously.

"I am sorry, but these factors mean little to me. I have not the skill to establish my location by the small variances in the color wheel or by the shape of a fern leaf. All of this is new to me."

"Luckily we have someone equipped to do that. Marguerite, you will meet with Roi this afternoon. Perhaps with some books and visual aids, you two can supply the general location in which they were keeping you." I nodded.

"Julianna, have your scouts scan the islands between the Bahamas and the Caribbean."

"But, sire, what islands?" Julianna asked. If possible, she became more beautiful by the second.

"All of them!" he huffed.

"But is all of this necessary? We have the girl back!" Anastasia said.

"The stakes have changed and so has my motivation. Merissa and the Obyascon are laying claim to my territory!" Theron spat.

"There is quite enough unoccupied sea in the polar region for the Obyascon to reside comfortably. If she is relocating, there must be a cause," Isaac responded.

"Yes, power!" William said, trying to convince the other of a need for attack.

"There must be some other motivation as well. The Obyascon are not genetically engineered for warmer climate, so whatever has them on the move must be a threat to their existence," Roi replied.

"Alright, Roi, if not only power, what would you suggest as other motivation?" Barbour said. Both William and Theron listened silently.

"Safety. Diet. Climate Change. Uh—political motives. It could be numerous possibilities."

"Barbour, you are our weather expert! Is it possible that climate variables could play a factor in the Obyascon's movement?"

"Honestly, I'm not sure. Even subtle changes can drastically change the ecosystem. I have done nothing to alter their climate. I will research to see if recent natural disasters or ozone changes could have altered the climate enough to warrant movement."

"Alright, you have until the end of the week. Mari, as plants and vegetation are your specialties, look into the possibility of other species of land and marine life moving from the area. Have your research team draft up all of the possibilities, and we will revisit this on Friday. Roi, collect all of the data as it comes in, crossing all of those you feel are not a factor. Next, launch a team to study the most probable causes."

"Isaac, as leader of the Defenders, have you received word that any Obyascon has tried to penetrate our lines of defense?"

"Currently there has been no breach. The only excitement the Georgian defenders have experienced was the unexpected arrival of Marguerite," Isaac replied.

"Alright. This news proves that the Obyascon are not yet on our doorsteps. I expect the defenders to be ready for an attack if we receive word that they are moving up the coast."

"We will be ready," Isaac said.

"Anastasia, as you are over strategy and logistics, devise several options of attack. We want the best advantage possible, as it is uncertain the numbers of Obyascon that we will be facing." I immediately ascertained that Anastasia was brilliant. Her mind worked on a different level as she was able to recite facts and calculate numbers at a rate that was impossible for any human ... or siren.

I looked over the room. It all made sense—Roi and Mari, Anastasia and Barbour, Isaac and Julianna. I even believed Zander and Darion to be a pair. Theron, as security, kept his Legion in place by mating them among the group. No wonder he was so set on having Aria as a mate for William. If he could secure a union between them, he would secure William into his Legion for life.

****

It was hard not to stare at William. He rarely looked in my direction, which seemed to please Aria immensely. I understood the necessity of this, but that acceptance did not make the pain any less. The morning meetings dragged on relentlessly as the Legion discussed all variables associated with an attack on the Obyascon. As I had experienced the most contact with the species, each had their own questions pertaining to their assigned branch. I answered them all to the best of my abilities, still careful to leave out any details pertaining to Anna. It was best if they knew nothing of the girl. Theron would want to obtain a girl with such abilities, and if not, he would try to destroy her. I knew this fact all too well.

In the afternoon, Roi led me into the library where we combed through charts and maps in an attempt to pinpoint the location in which I had been held captive. William listened attentively from the back of the room. He rarely looked at me. If the Legion was aware of a romantic connection between us, his current demeanor would hardly support such rumors. The creature who could not tear his eyes from me yesterday, addressed me today with cool indifference. I tried to ignore his presence and focus on the task at hand. The mission was difficult as the one person I had been dreaming about for months was only a few feet away. Roi kept me focused. I was able to locate the approximate location of the island in which I had found the Crew. From there I was able to trace back the route in which we traveled home. They pressed me for information, but I was unable to outline the course back to where I was held captive. There were so many small islands on the map; it could have been any one of them! Mari showed me a vast array of plant matter, each indigenous to a specific location. None of it seemed familiar. She questioned me about my time on the island—what I saw—what I ate. I told her of the waterfall and of the fish we had caught. This detail caught her attention. She immediately began flipping through other books.

"There are hundreds of islands in the Caribbean and the Bahamas. It could take us many months to search them all," Roi responded.

"True. Can you think of anything else that could help us narrow the search?" Mari asked.

My mind raced. Anna needed me. I had promised her I would bring her home. Then it hit me like a lightning bolt! "Bioluminescence!" I shouted out.

"What?" Mari asked.

"Bioluminescence. It's when …."

"We are familiar with the concept, less so as to how it pertains to what we are looking for," Roi said.

"On the island, there were underwater caverns. The night I escaped the pools were lit by bioluminescent algae. The algae did not have a blue or green light as most bioluminescent matter, but a golden orange color." I turned to William. He smiled and nodded—urging me to continue.

"But how will that help us?" Roi replied skeptically.

"You see, when I escaped, the algae were also found in the surf surrounding the island. Within a few days, it was gone. It only appeared when the tide was exceptionally high—like with a full moon. The night I escaped it was on a full moon."

"Our next full moon is next Tuesday," Mari said.

"We should be able to locate the island, or at least narrow the location, as the algae you described is rare indeed."

"Well, then that doesn't give us much time," I said energetically.

"You've done well!" Roi said.

I turned towards William. He was already gone. I ached. I had given him the information he needed to find his sister. Would he leave without as much as a "goodbye"? I began to ache. We were separated again.

Roi and Mari departed to report their findings to Theron, leaving me alone in the library. The walls of this magical room were lined from floor to ceiling with literary works of art. A library such as this was once my heaven; now I dreamed of a creature that surpassed any hero that had ever been written.

"There you are!" Michael exclaimed as he entered the library. "Dinner will be served soon."

"I'm not very hungry. Do you think it would be heavily frowned upon if I skip?" I asked.

"It is rare that Theron has his Legion together. I think it would be best if you attend. It is harder for Zander to plot against you when you are sitting before him," Michael said. "Besides, Theron is displeased when we miss meal times during gatherings. I think it is a power trip kind of thing."

"I see," I sighed. I had little hope of William attending dinner. He was gone. I knew it, but I knew he would return to me. He would return, not as the gentle tide returns, but like an all-consuming hurricane. We were drawn together by a more powerful force of nature and yet ripped apart by that same fiery current. I knew that a supply run would not pull William from my side. Perhaps it was the one thing that he loved more than me. Maybe William had gone to find his sister. Of course he must leave me behind. Theron would never allow us both to leave. But for William to abandon me here—alone? I had proclaimed that I did not need a Protector. It was a lie. I needed him then. I need him now. I need him always. "Do I have time to freshen up?" I asked, in an attempt to soothe my heavy heart. Michael smiled.

"Not if you are going to lose those combat clothes. You look pretty "hot" for a hybrid—best-looking hybrid I have ever seen," he teased.

"I'm the only hybrid you have seen if I am not mistaken," I said. Michael laughed harder.

"You have a point there," he laughed. "Sure, go freshen up, and meet me back in the dining room as soon as you are ready."

"Thank you," I replied. I was relieved to have some time for myself. My first day with Theron's Legion was nothing like I had expected. I longed for it to be over. *I could make it through another Sironian dinner! Couldn't I?*

19

———

"There is a stubbornness about me that never can bear to be frightened at the will of others. My courage always seems to rise at every attempt to intimidate me."

~Pride and Prejudice, Jane Austen

The strong scent of roses filled my room. I assumed that Theron had them brought in from the mainland, as there were few varieties in bloom the second week in November. In Theron's world, I knew that anything was possible. There were flowers by the bed. There were flowers by the tub, and a basket of soaps, lotions and towels were placed on the nightstand. The staff had apparently been instructed to usher in a proper Kingston Plantation welcome. An enormous collection of clothes lay across the bed. I fumbled through the assortment of tropical inspired sarongs and linens. The style was all wrong. It all was too thin for the winter weather. Whereas the siren appeared unaffected by the turn of the season, I could not escape the warm blood running through my veins. I resigned myself to a fitted army green button up, a pair of tan linen pants, and the pale gray cardigan I had brought with me. I lingered, hoping that William would miraculously appear. My hopes were in vain. At last, when he did not come, I made my way to the plantation house. I was surprised to find the Legion on the lawn instead of the dining hall. An enormous table was lavishly dressed on the patio in preparation for our meal.

"Ah, Marguerite! We were waiting for you to begin the festivities!" Theron said. An immense fire pit was elegantly outfitted for grilling; a chef stood by waiting to begin the barbeque. He signaled, and one of his staff rolled out a cart filled with silver covered dishes.

"I am very sorry. I did not mean to keep you waiting," I replied nervously.

"No worries, my dear. We would not dream of starting the feast without you," he said assuredly. Theron lifted the lid off of one of the silver dishes. A large angora rabbit frantically leapt from the dish and took off running across the lawn. I was startled. Everyone laughed.

"I don't understand?" I mumbled, suddenly feeling quite ill.

"I often align mealtime with a bit of amusement," Theron said, as he lifted the lids off the other trays. Each dish carried another terrified rabbit; all of which darted off in different directions. One of the staff passed out long strips of black fabric to each of the Legion. The sick scenario began to play out before me.

"What is this?" I gasped.

"A blindfold, of course. As you know, sirens have exceptional sight—such an advantage would hardly be fair to our meal, do you not agree?" Theron answered.

"You expect us to hunt the rabbits?" I asked dumbfounded. I already knew the answer. I wanted to hurl. Theron's eyes beamed with excitement.

"But of course. Even sirens enjoy a bit of sport," he chuckled.

"I thought you primarily acquired your meals from the sea," I uttered.

"Most sirens do, but as this sect has adapted to land, we partake in some of its delicacies," Theron continued.

"Rabbit is often eaten by humans, is it not?" Zander smirked.

"I suppose but not in a situation like this," I responded curtly.

"You do not eat rabbit, Miss Westley?" Theron asked.

"I do not. Nor do I think this little game of yours is appropriate. These animals are terrified." They were amused by my objection.

"I gather from your protestation that you do not wish to partake," Zander said.

"I do not," I replied emphatically.

"Fine. We are not barbarians here. Both Mari and Roi are vegetarian, so you may remain with them for the hunt." My mind raced in all directions at once. What could I do to stop the event. I knew there was nothing I could do to stop him. Theron's entire purpose in this sick game was to rattle me. I refused to give his such pleasure. I tried to muster up as much courage as possible.

"I have another proposal," I said, struggling to steady my voice. "I do wish to participate in the hunt after all. Except, the animals that I catch will belong to me. The rabbits that I collect will be set free." Theron eyed me carefully; a broad grin stretched across his face. My proposal had only made the sport more entertaining for him.

"Do you hear this?" Zander turned towards the others. "Marguerite plans to rob us of our meal." They all laughed. I shifted nervously. Michael's eyes met mine. He looked upon me sympathetically. I could see that he wanted to shield me from this mockery, and yet, his hands were tied. Michael was Theron's Protector, not mine.

"What an interesting evening you have given me!" Theron clapped his hands together. "Marguerite seems to have feelings for these animals—very interesting. Most of the humans I have encountered hold little respect for life. They kill everything. They fight amongst themselves. They stand aside as their people die of starvation and famine," Theron said. I swallowed hard before carefully choosing my words.

"You are correct in that there is great depravity in humanity; however, there is more than an equal part of good in the world. It is the virtuous that I seek."

"Is that so …," Theron smirked amusedly, but I wasn't finished.

"I am quite surprised, however, that *your* species cannot see its corruption and callousness from within," I continued with as little emotion as possible. Theron's smile faded. He glared at me for a moment. I realized that at any second that he could strike me dead. My sharp tongue could be fatal, yet I refused to die without passion.

"I am not sure if I am vexed or amused by your criticisms, young Marguerite. No one has ever been bold enough to speak to me in such a manner. Most, I find, value their life. Do you not value yours?" Theron replied calmly. His tone did not match the fury that was building beneath his composed façade.

"I do, but I also value the lives of others, even those considered beneath me," I replied.

"Fair enough. We shall commence with our sport," Theron said hastily. I had proven that I could hold my own in his battle of words, and Theron had had enough. "You have my word that whatever you capture will have asylum here." He called to one of his men, "Philip, could you bring a large basket for Miss Westley's catch." A young servant scrambled into the house, returning with an oversized woven basket.

"Do you think that is necessary?" Zander smirked. "I think it highly unlikely that Marguerite would obtain her own meal, let alone capture ours."

"I would not rule her out so hastily," Michael said in my defense. "You have yet to see the girl in action. She just might surprise you." Theron came around and tied the blindfolds in place. Adrenaline rushed through my veins as he brushed the side of my face. Now that I was blindfolded, would he take my life? Would I be killed by my own grandfather? William was not here to protect me. Would I be strong enough to protect myself?

"Your heart thumps as loud as the hearts of those rabbits. Do you not trust me, my dear?" Theron uttered.

"I trust no one," I replied.

"Perhaps we have more in common than I originally thought," Theron smirked. "You have survived in our world for quite some time; such would be impossible without careful alliances. I would advise you to reconsider your current affiliations and commit to me." I could not see him, though the heat from his body indicated that he circled me like prey. I could see the warmth as it circled me; I was unaware that I possessed this talent and wondered if all sirens had such senses.

"Games such as this would hardly entice me to join your ranks," I said as bravely as possible. "You are well aware of the high price I place on life."

"This being the case, how strange it is that you treat your own with such reckless abandonment." I inhaled deeply, signaling in on the scent of the rabbits. I refocused my vision, tunneling it through the tiny pinholes of light breaking through the fabric of the blindfold.

"I am famished, Theron; are we going to begin the sport?" Barbour said rudely.

"We shall! Competitors, you are to remain blindfolded until your meal has been returned to its dish. Once the lid is in place, the meal is claimed. Aside from this, there are no other rules. Competitors ready? ... Begin!" I could feel the rush as each of the Legion rushed off in different directions. I did not. I remained perfectly still. My ploy had worked. My conversation with Theron was a vice to adjust my vision to the blindfold. I had used the time to allow my senses to locate the directions of the rabbits. Three had gone east and two to the northern part of the estate. The sixth had been the slowest of the bunch and had taken refuge under the gazebo on the west lawn. I dashed towards that one first. Georgianna had located that one as well; she was reaching beneath the structure as I approached. With two hands, I lifted the structure and hurled it aside. We both lunged for the rabbit, but I caught hold of its hind legs in one motion and immediately took off after the next rabbits. Two had tunneled under a hefty pile of brush on the north side. Barbour and Anastasia were plotting the best way to uncover them when I slid beneath the pile grasping both rabbits before either realized my presence. They both took off after me, but I was too swift. I slipped behind a tree as they sped past. I darted across the north lawn, sweeping the rabbits against trees and brush to mask my trail. I raced to the east, past the gardens, and into the woods. I recognized the scent before me. It was Michael. He had already trapped two.

"I am going to have to ask you to hand over your prize," I said. Michael laughed.

"It appears you already have a handful. You are going to have to share the bounty with me," he teased.

"I don't want to hurt you, Michael. It would be in your best interest to just pass over the bunnies." He laughed again.

"I am amazed at your confidence, friend. I am Theron's Protector you know. I don't usually fight girls, but I have been dying to test my skills against yours since we first met," he said anxiously.

"Well then, let's not delay the anticipation any longer," I smirked. We both hurled towards each other. He tried to sweep my legs from beneath me, but I flipped over him, landing softly to the ground. Michael, not so quick to be outdone, spiraled in the air towards me. I leaped into the air as well, our bodies meeting before falling hard to the ground. I landed on top of him, but in one swift motion, he rolled on top of me—pinning me to the ground. The way my body reacted to his took me by surprise. His sweet breath was warm against my face. My hands tingled beneath his grasp. His breath steadied as we lie there motionless. His blindfolded face drew near, and his lips gently brushed across mine. He approached again, this time with more urgency, but the loyalty of my heart took control. Despite how my body reacted to Michael, my heart belonged to another. I refocused to the task at hand and swiftly used his distraction to my advantage; I promptly tumbled him over. With my free hand, I effortlessly overpowered the wrist holding the hind legs of his rabbits, releasing them fleetingly before grasping them with my free hand.

I took off running through the woodland after the final rabbit. My heart was pounding. I had been completely taken off guard by Michael—and yet, I felt no anger towards him from his forwardness. He was not to blame; I had not realized the underlying chemistry between us. Aside from William, I had not felt such physical chemistry with anyone. The rabbits still in my clutch were alive but had gone limp from the shock of the conflict. I tracked it to a scrubby low-lying area that at one time had been marshland. There was, but one of the Legion left that I had not faced. Zander, of course, had gone after the fastest rabbit. He stood before me clutching the final animal.

"I had planned to track each of them down, and yet, it appears they have all come to me." Through the weave of the blindfold, I could see him motion toward the ground at my feet; a lightning bolt descended. I dove as far away as I could before the bolt made contact with the sandy terrain. The sand shielded me from the majority of the current, but a small bout of electricity passed through my body. I was slightly rattled from the jolt but held firm to my catch.

"How brave you are," I said sarcastically, "to use your abilities on an unarmed and blinded girl! I can only presume that you fear a fair fight."

"Hardly … you are just a human," Zander hissed. "Sure, you may boast of siren genes, but you are hardly fit to join our Legion."

"If that is the case, then why are my hands full?" I mocked, holding out my catch.

"Undoubtedly, you have superior skill on land, but you forget that the siren dominates the ocean."

"You continuously insult me, Zander, and yet your insults are unfounded. Do you plan to hand over your prize or shall I come take it from you?"

He held out the frightened rabbit. "Either way, I will win." He held out the rabbit in a manner that I could anticipate his move. He intended to snap the animal's neck. I surged towards him landing a roundhouse kick to his chest. The force sent him stumbling backward. He retaliated grabbing me by the neck from behind. The attack caused him to drop the rabbit, which took off into the scrub brush. I whipped forward, the force slinging him forward into the sandy terrain. I fled. Zander's growl pierced the cool night air. He motioned again for lightning, but I was ready this time, zipping for cover, as the bolt descended precisely where I had been standing. I darted off after the fleeing rabbit, easily catching up with the animal. As both hands were filled, I scooped it against my chest. I could sense the remainder of the Legion closing in and took towards the Plantation house by means of the coastline. Within minutes, I arrived at the steps of the massive house. Even blindfolded I effortlessly made my way through the house and onto the south lawn. The others were still looking for me as I assembled the rabbits into the large basket, and replaced the lid. Each member arrived back to the lawn empty handed.

"I am astonished!" Theron said as he removed my blindfold. "You have outsmarted and out-skilled them all!" Behind him, Roi and Mari were analyzing my every move. I now realized why the pair had not participated; it had nothing to do with vegetarianism. They had been studying me—my reactions, my movement. The challenge had been a test of some sort. My blood began to boil as I realized that I had been set up.

The others removed their blindfolds and were moving across the lawn when Theron presented another dish. "Young Marguerite has robbed you all of your meal. I am astounded!" He laughed. I had little time to recollect or celebrate as Theron moved to phase two of his sport. He removed the lid of the dish to reveal a large tray of baby loggerhead turtles. "As Marguerite has won your entrée, it is lucky that I brought dessert," he boasted. I gasped urgently.

"You wouldn't do such a thing! These turtles are endangered!" I boldly spat. "Obviously, you have learned of my fondness for these animals and are trying to manipulate me to your advantage! All of this was set up to pair my skills against your Legion!"

"If that be the case, then you only need to walk away from the sport. I have not forced you to do anything against your will. If you are correct and I am bluffing, then these creatures will be returned safely to the surf. However, if you are incorrect and I am not manipulating you, then they would serve as the replacement to the meal in which you have rightfully won." I had once rescued a baby turtle from the grasp of a seagull. Could I now rescue a clutch from the grip of a monster?

"I will do what I must," I boasted bravely.

"Bravo! What an evening this is turning out to be!" Theron applauded. "Who will challenge young Marguerite for the prize?" They all stepped forward impatient for a rematch—all except for one.

"I will not fight the girl," Michael said.

"What? She hurt your pride when she took you down earlier?" Zander mocked.

"No. I just think Marguerite has nothing left to prove, and I will not be a part of this!" Michael spat. The surprise on Theron's face was evident. Noticeably, he was not accustomed to Michael disagreeing with his authority.

"I will challenge her," Aria said flatly. Aria had not challenged me for the rabbits, but now, the vixen came for blood. Her deep green eyes flickered wildly as she took her stance. Before I had the opportunity to respond, she charged at me. I flipped backward over her, allowing time for my next move. She charged again. I caught her around the legs, hosting her high over my head, she twisted from my grasp, landing upon the lawn like a crouched tiger. She sprung, but I landed a roundhouse kick to the face. She was unaffected, attacking again, this time with greater resolve. I blocked the swift blows hurled at me before landing several of my own. She was struck backward but retaliated. This time, a swift kick to her abdomen knocked Aria onto the lawn. Sensing that I had the upper hand, Theron signaled his Legion to attack. They all came after me, except for Michael who was momentarily assessing the situation. I stood firm, skillfully blocking each of their advances, until they all surrounded me at once. Theron's plan had worked. He had milked me for information on the Obyascon, and now his Legion would take me out of the picture. I closed my eyes and prayed for a miracle. It arrived.

William appeared from the direction of the shore. He was the fastest siren ever born. In an instant, he stood between Theron's leaders and me.

"So it takes eight of you to bring down a single girl," he mocked. He looked at me, fiercely searching for the assurance that I was alright. His eyes were enveloped with worry, guilt, and pain. My Protector had abandoned me and had returned to find his love in the guillotine.

"She looks like a girl. However, her abilities affirm the stories," Anastasia said.

"This is no average girl … nor siren. She is a warrior!" Isaac added.

"She comes to you as your guest, and this is how you treat her?" William addressed Theron directly. "Under the treaty, you promised that she would not be harmed, and you let your Legion attack her! Do you not stand behind your word?" he hissed.

"As I recall, Marguerite had the option not to participate," Aria scoffed jealously.

"And by toying with her emotions, you would leave her no choice! Theron, your tactics show you have received ample information on the girl's weaknesses. She places a greater value on life than the Sironian race, but that does not mean that she is not one of us!" William glared at Aria.

"How could you dare say that the hybrid is one of us!" Zander growled.

"William, it is no mystery that you hold a fondness for the girl, but her strength is too great to be siren, and her body temperature is unadaptable. She would never be able to withstand the pressure changes and temperature changes of the ocean," Roi said.

"Also, her emotions run too high. She puts her heart before all logic—hardly one that would be useful in battle," Mari added.

"If she would sacrifice her life for a bowl of turtles, what would she be willing to sacrifice if something greater was on the line—say, love?" Georgiana added.

"I do believe she has already sacrificed for love, now hasn't she, or she would not be here," Darion said.

"I arrived here to honor the treaty I made with Theron!" I shouted.

"True. However, the object of her affection was you, was it not, William? Such an alliance would defy Theron, an offense punishable by death." Zander hissed.

"I have agreed to marry Theron's granddaughter. I hold fast to my word," William replied.

"And yet, your actions here today, proclaim otherwise," Barbour said.

"I was her Protector once. I do not relinquish the role for any treaty," William hissed defiantly.

"You received your Protectorship from Silas?" Theron asked.

"I did," William stated. "Silas would take the death of this girl extremely personal."

"Is that so?" Theron replied. "He and I were once as close as brothers," he continued.

"I am aware," William replied. "And as you well know, a Protector is appointed for life." The tension continued to mount on both sides.

"As Silas chose to defy my Legion, vanquish my protection and deny our friendship, I erase any vows in which you made under his care," Theron proclaimed.

"Forgive me, Theron, but my word will not be disavowed." William's words only further angered Theron. "As long as my heart beats, you will not silence hers."

"I see. Young William seems to be overly attached to his guardian." He eyed us together, then turned sharply to William. "Given your current obligations, perhaps it is best for all involved that young Marguerite becomes attached to another. There is but one in my Legion that has not been joined." He turned abruptly to Michael. "Michael, you seem to have a slight fondness towards the girl." Michael turned to me sympathetically.

"I do, but," Michael stepped forward.

"As you are unattached and without bride or partner, I betroth Marguerite to you. Think of her as … a gift … for your loyalty these past ten years." The Legion roared. William lunged at him. I struck William's chest with such force that he was sent flying backward to the ground. An attack from William was just the response that Theron was looking for.

"Theron! You can't just gift me," I hissed. Michael stepped in front of me protectively.

"But, Theron, she is human, and she is not interested in …." Theron raised his hand to silence the protestation. He did not look at me, nor would he listen to Michael.

"My word is final! I have had enough excitement for one evening. Michael, I shall leave the details of the engagement to you. Goodnight. We will continue with fight training at 6:00 sharp. Evidently, you all need to brush up on your skills before we pursue the Obyascon. Isaac, Julianna, and William, you have five days to get the factions prepared. Anastasia, I expect your strategy by sunrise! We will gather the remaining troops at the end of the week." Theron turned and swiftly made his exit. William remained frozen in anger. Aria approached him.

"Are you alright, William? Perhaps we could …."

"Now is not the time, Aria," he said as he stormed off towards the dark clashing waters.

"This is your fault you know!" Aria hissed at me as she went after him. She was right. By fighting against the Legion, William had shown Theron the depth of his emotions. William may agree to honor his betrothal, but Theron was aware of the truth. Like his parents, William would eventually defy all laws for love. Theron punished him because of it—punished him for loving me by giving me away to someone else.

"Let me help you back to your quarters," Michael said as he took my arm and began to lead me down the pathway to my suite. I pulled away. "Well, I will give it to you, Marguerite Westley; you certainly know how to liven up a party," he said. I didn't respond. I opened to door to my suite and shut it promptly behind me leaving Michael still standing on the doorstep.

20

———

"You have power over your mind ~ not outside events. Realize this, and you will find strength."

~Marcus Aurelius

The beautiful room was my prison. I balled up the collection of new clothes Theron had delivered and tossed them in the corner. I wanted nothing from him but my freedom! I had agreed under our treaty to be a part of his Legion; I bore his seal on my wrist! I now wanted no part of this! I finally comprehended Silas's reasons to break free from Theron's regime. I would find a way to break free! I now understood why William's parents had fled—for love. I would never allow my marriage partner dictated to me! Theron was trying to separate William and me, just as he had done with Silas and my grandmother. The alliance in which was agreed upon by William was not intended for Aria, but for me. It had taken every ounce of restraint not to reveal that I was his granddaughter and heir to the throne. There was too much at stake to risk the effects of such a bomb! I had failed Anna on the island; I would not fail her again.

Adrenaline washed through my veins at the sound of a knock at the door. I ached to see William—there was much that needed to be said. Disappointment swept over me as Michael stood before me. "I thought you might be hungry," he said holding out a familiar covered platter. I removed the lid to find the baby loggerhead turtles.

"I am not amused," I said, though I could not mask the thin smile that crept across my face. Despite my situation, I was relieved that the turtles had not become a meal in my absence.

"Let's go see these little guys home," Michael said with a faint smile. "Would you like to join me?" His smile warmed my icy veins.

"I would. Thank you," I replied. I slipped into my windbreaker and pulled the door closed behind me. I was still upset. I was in no mood for company, least of all his, but I wanted to be present for the release of the turtles. We were both silent as we stepped out onto the shore. The beach was darker than it was the night before—dark and majestic. The magic of the moonlit water never ceased to take my breath away.

"Alright, I think it is encouraged that they make it into the water on their own," Michael said. He released the babies just as we crossed over the last set of dunes. I hurried ahead, my hands smoothing a path through the cool sand. The little ones flipped their way through the shoreline, inching closer and closer towards the sea foam. For a moment, I was caught up in the sheer delight of the magic. All of the angst of the day was dispelled temporarily as the tiny creatures made their way home. As the final turtle had made its way past the seafoam, I turned to Michael. He was staring intently at me. I looked away. "Forgive me; it's rare that I've seen you smile. It is quite becoming," he said.

"Michael …"

"Look … I want you to just forget about what Theron said today," he said. My brow furrowed.

"How can I forget such a thing?" I gasped. Michael looked hurt. "Look, I'm sorry, it's not you; I just refuse to have whom I marry decided for me!"

"I know. Your stubbornness is quite appealing. But that is not the only reason you would not agree to the betrothal; you are already engaged to someone else."

"How did you know?' I mumbled curiously. Michael neared. His warm fingers brushed against the side of my neck gently pulling out the shiva and engagement ring from beneath my blouse. "You saw the necklace?" Michael said.

"Yes. I first caught sight of it when we were traveling here. After seeing you and William in the same room, it did not take a scholar to figure out you were betrothed to him."

"Please … I beg you not to tell Theron," I pleaded.

"I give you my word that I won't breathe a word to anyone. Marguerite, you have my trust. Look, I know today was awkward, but we were becoming friends. Can we just continue down that path?"

"How can I when Theron plans for us to be married?"

"I will handle the situation with Theron when the time comes. You have to trust me. Do you trust me?" I looked into his eyes. There were a million reasons not to trust Michael, but there was sincerity in his eyes.

"I do trust you," I replied. "It would be hard not to trust you. You look so very much like your brother." I trusted Mace with my life … more than my life, with Lucy's life. Michael turned away as if I had said something hurtful. He sat upon the shore, just beyond the reach of the incoming tide. I sat next to him. The moon hung high in the evening sky sending shimmers across the rippling sea. I was exhausted but had no desire to return to my quarters. At last, he broke the silence.

"So my brother claims I am dead?" I nodded hesitantly, not wishing to injure him further. "I am not surprised. I had hoped the years would have softened his hatred of me."

"I don't understand. Why would Mace imply you were dead?" I asked.

"Mace is full of pain. He blames me for a loss that no amount of time can erase." I could hear the hesitation in his voice. The history between them seemed painful for Michael as well.

"You must tell me. Please … from the beginning."

"Mace and I were as close as two brothers could be. As twins, our abilities complemented each other. He was able to move the currents; I was able to communicate telepathically. Our special gifts were what kept us both alive. You see, at birth, Sironian parents are only allowed to have one child in their care. Our mother refused to make the choice. Thus, we were both stripped from her shortly after birth. Theron sought early to harness our skills. We were sent to four different sects for training. I promptly developed the social skills to interact within the sects; Mace did not. His reserved nature came across as rude and arrogant. He was respected but made very few friends. We both effortlessly surpassed the other trainees of each sect, mastering the skills of the Warriors, Trackers, and Scholars. When it became evident that we were land shifters, we were reclassified as Protectors and reassigned to train under Silas.

"Land shifter? I have never heard your kind described in such a way."

"As you know, most sirens are unable to survive out of the water. Those born with land shifting abilities are chosen as Protectors."

"Once our training was complete, we were to be transferred to Theron's Legion. Neither Mace nor I wanted to leave the Protectors. We resisted when Theron came for us. Theron had expected this and was ready for the fight. What I did not know was that he had only planned to take me. Mace was too strong-minded to ever agree with the Legion but too powerful for Theron to leave alive. I discovered the plot to kill my brother. I hastily made a treaty of my own with Theron. I would join him, serving as his personal Protector if he would allow Mace to live. He agreed only if Mace remained with Silas. I could not tell Mace of the treaty. He was furious with me, assuming that I had traded my loyalty to Silas, and my love for him, for the power that Theron was offering. He proclaimed me dead to him. I eventually gained Theron's trust, but never did my devotion to Silas or my brother diminish. I have been an informant to Silas for the past eight years." I was overwhelmed with heartache over his story.

"I thought no one could understand true sacrifice, and yet, you do," I whispered.

"Yes, I understand you more than you know." He placed his hand on mine. This time, I did not pull it away. I wanted no connection with this beautiful creature before me, but we were connected by loss—we had both given up someone out of sacrifice, and both had traded our souls to Theron for love. I closed my eyes. "You are exhausted. Let me take you back to your room."

"I can't go back there—not yet."

"Well, how about a swim?" Michael asked.

"At this hour?"

"Of course. There is no better remedy for a weary spirit than saltwater." Michael grabbed my hand and pulled me to the water's edge. I resisted. He ignored my protestations. Michael pulled off his shirt. His perfect physique glistened in the moonlight. Michael was beautiful.

A figure stepped out from beneath the shadows of the dunes. Despite the darkness, I knew every curve of William's body. "Theron is looking for you, Michael. I think it would be best if you head back to the Kingston," William said firmly as he approached. Our history together did not subdue the butterflies stirred by his presence; it gave them life.

"I am in the midst of a lovely evening—perhaps Theron can wait." Michael shrugged.

"I don't think that would be in your best interest," William replied. Two pairs of emerald eyes glared at each other through the darkness. "I will see that Marguerite is returned safely to her quarters later." It quickly became evident that neither siren was going to back down.

"It's fine, Michael. I will see you in the morning," I uttered to break the tension.

"Alright. I will come for you just after daybreak." He glared once more at William before slipping into the darkness. William unbuttoned the top few buttons of his shirt before slipping it over his head. The shadows of his body took my breath away. It seemed impossible that I ever thought this creature human.

"What are you doing?" I asked.

"It appears you were about to take a swim. Since I chased off your fiancé, it is only fair that I take his place," William said. The hurt in his voice was unmistakable.

"The only man I have agreed to marry is standing across from me," I replied tenderly.

"If only he were a man, then perhaps …." He closed his eyes, as he took my hand and pressed it to his lips.

"Love is never easy. We will find a way," I reminded him. I erased the short distance between us pressing my cool body against his warm chest. "I thought you had gone after your sister," I said burying my face into his neck.

"I had. I was overcome with the news that Madeline was alive and took off after her before coming to my senses."

"Meaning?" I asked meekly.

"Meaning, that I suspected Theron would use my absence against you. I am very sorry that I left you to his devices," William said. "He is no fool. Theron is well aware that I am in love with you and that you are still under my protection."

"… and yet, he would dictate my betrothal to someone else," I whispered.

"He did so just to hurt me—to put me in my place. By giving you to Michael, he sought to assert his authority over me … and you," William said.

"He has no clue that I am already betrothed to you and that the union is sanctioned by his own treaty," I added.

"No, nor is it the time to play that card. To the world, I must appear bound to Aria and you to Michael, but be assured, my heart would cease to beat without you." William took my hands and led me into the cool water. If only my body could adjust as William's. I shivered. He led me safely beyond the breakers and pressed his body against mine.

"My body temperature runs warm enough for the both of us," William whispered. He wrapped his arms around the small of my waist, pulling me tighter against him. I moaned at the feel of his body. The current swirled around us, enfolding us into the churning water.

"You ought not to make sounds like that. I am trying to be a gentleman," he whispered.

"I thought we had already covered the fact that you aren't a man. You are a siren," I replied softly.

"If that be the case, then I should better be able to control the urges." He moaned as he buried his face in my hair.

"Perhaps I don't want you to," I said playfully. He smiled. His smiles were so rare that they were like unearthed treasure.

"I think you have survived enough danger for one day," he teased. His fingers traced the ridge of my spine lingering at the hollow of my back. I closed my eyes.

"And yet you continue to tempt me," I taunted.

"I am a selfish beast. The mere touch of your skin consumes me," he replied. "Logically, I should be searching for my sister right now. The possibility of finding her has been my driving force—until you appeared. There are a million reasons I should be going after her right now and only one reason I should stay."

"And which reason is that?" I teased.

"That I am fully and powerlessly in love with you," he replied longingly. I ran my fingers down his chest. My hand palmed his abdominals, teasing to dip further beneath the water.

"I can think of no greater reason except one," I said, as I continued to run my fingers over his tight muscles.

"And what is that?" he murmured. William' body responded to my touch.

"We are stronger together. We will find your sister together," I replied.

"Then you will need all of your strength to leave this place," he said. His fingers brushed against the scrapes I had received during Theron's challenge. For the first time, I became aware of what I had endured physically. I felt drained—tattered emotionally and physically.

William pulled me tighter against him. His fingers ran across the lines of my jaw, then gently to the side of my neck. My muscles tightened as he stroked my torn skin. His arm pressed firmly against the small of my back as he dipped me backward into the serene water. I closed my eyes—consumed with his touch. My body lay limp against his, as I swayed into the current. I was absorbed into the tide. My limbs were taken by the surge, shifting with its melodious rhythm. Bright emerald eyes shimmered atop the water, accenting facial features that no longer resembled that of a girl. All traces of humanity within me began to fade into desire. An unquenched hunger started to swell within me—a craving that only a siren would know. A low growl echoed deep in my throat. William became alarmed at the transformation.

"Marguerite, do you hear me? You have to take control of this!" He clutched me tighter. His words registered, but the creature within me had already taken the reins. I lunged at him, taking his mouth to mine with an uncontrollable hunger. He accepted me, but I abruptly began to overpower the exchange as I began to devour his essence. He pulled away. "Take control, Marguerite! I know you are in there." I lunged at him again, but this time he denied my lips. I shrieked, pulling away from him and tearing through the water in search of my next prey. My body tunneled through the dark water until at last, I caught the scent of a pod of dolphin. I shifted directions towards the dolphin, shredding through the current after my prey. William astoundingly found the energy to catch up with me. He thrust himself upon me, wrapping his arms tightly against my frame. I hissed as our bodies spiraled through the water. We tumbled as I fought his grasp until he ultimately pulled me onto the shore. William pinned me to the ground until humanity returned and was able to overshadow the monster inside of me. I closed my eyes and drifted. I drifted back to the first time I saw William. Our story played in my mind like a fuzzy movie reel. The images flipped faster and faster with each memory becoming more vivid. As the reel came to my abrupt reality, I was released. I became myself again.

"Oh, William! I'm … sorry!" I cried, as he gently stroked the sides of my face.

"There is no need for apologies. I blame myself. I had no idea the gene would ignite so fiercely. You are still changing."

"What is happening to me?" I whimpered.

"You are growing stronger. You were born to be a siren. The trigger seemed to be the potency of the water coupled with the intensity between us. But you must learn to control this."

"I don't know if it is possible. I don't know if I can control this," I cried.

"I know you can. We will figure this out together," he said.

"But how is that even possible?"

"You have to harness it—channel the creature for the purposes of good. Don't let the siren overtake your humanity. It is the one thing that sets you apart from us; it is the one thing that sustains your goodness." A tear slid down my cheek.

"Despite your beliefs, you hold all of the goodness that you stress I should maintain. You are good, William. Every drop of you, every ounce is of virtue."

"Then the evil around us should be afraid because together we will be a mighty pair." He gently kissed my forehead as he pulled me to his chest. I wanted to believe him. I had to believe him.

There were no other options.

21

———

"She had waited all her life for something, and it had killed her when it found her."

Zora Neale Hurston

Dusty **morning hues penetrated the thin cotton curtains** of my room. The faint sound of tiny raindrops pinged on the windowpanes. I reached for him in the cold space next to me. William had promised to stay by my side until I fell asleep. He had kept that promise, but when I awoke, he was gone. I sighed with the realization that we were once again apart. William was taking the necessary step to retrieve his sister; he was enlisting Silas and the Crew. He had contacted the Crew and asked them to meet him, telling them none of the particulars. They had all agreed. When William first explained his plan, I pleaded to go with him. He objected with good reason. William would be able to travel twice as fast without me and with a better chance of secrecy. The waters would be filled with Theron's army, especially now that he was aware that the Obyascon were on the move. My scent would be easy to pick up.

There was a faint knock at the door. The door cracked open partially revealing Michael's rain-misted face. His eyes were closed. "Margo, are you dressed?"

"I am, Michael. You may come in," I replied. He opened his eyes and crossed to the bathroom to intercept a towel. The view of this creature would have easily stopped the heart of any mortal, but my heart was constant.

"Did I wake you? It is very strange to have someone around here that sleeps at night," he said.

"It's strange to sleep at all. My body is so mixed up. I rarely have been able to sleep at night since the transformation, and yet, my body still prefers the night." He rehung the newly dampened towel and leaned casually against the doorframe.

"It is no surprise that you are confused. You have lived many years as a human. I do not doubt that in time your body will decide such details for you." Michael noticed the crumpled pillow and disturbed bed sheets. His eyes narrowed.

"I'm a restless sleeper," I said hastily.

"Marguerite, I am a siren. I can effortlessly pick up on William's scent."

"What's your point?" I asked defiantly.

"If I can pick up on it, so can the others," Michael replied sternly. I grabbed a pair of jeans and a knit shirt from my bag and pushed past him into the bathroom, firmly closing the door behind me.

"Is there another law I don't know about?" I called through the door. "Are visitors also outlawed?"

"Don't insult me." His tone was not bitter or confrontational but tender. "We are both aware of your emotional connection to William, and that indeed is a crime at this point. He is betrothed to Aria, and as of yesterday, you have been chosen for me—a quite astonishing turn of events. Six months ago Theron had planned to kill you."

"Yes, I am very fortunate to be alive," I said defensively.

"You are. I would like to keep you that way. I think you are a great asset both to the siren world and the humans." Newly dressed, I opened the bathroom door. Michael hovered in the doorway as I pulled my hair back into a ponytail.

"You seem to be the only member of the Legion that feels that way," I replied curtly.

"Marguerite, you bridge our worlds together. Not one can deny how special you are. Sure, there are those who fear this, but I think your arrival has been long awaited," Michael said.

"What do you mean by that?" I asked curiously. His brow furrowed and he looked at me in disbelief.

"You don't know, do you?" Michael shut the door to my room as we stepped out beneath the small overhang of the cabin. The misting rain had morphed into a steady downpour. I slipped on the thin rain jacket and tucked my hair into the hood.

"Are you saying that they have been expecting me?" I asked.

"There have been mythical stories of a half-breed girl prophesied for ages. A girl that would one day lead the Sironian, uniting all species and bridging the gap between the humans and the siren world." The fine hairs on my arms stood on end. I turned to face Michael. I was dumbfounded by his words.

"Prophecy? I have read the creation account of the Sironian and heard nothing of a prophecy," I admitted.

"Your friends have not told you?" he asked.

"No," I replied. My head was spinning. How could my friends keep such prophesies from me?

"… And William?" he asked.

"He has disclosed nothing of the sort," I replied blankly.

"Then let me enlighten you. The creation story is not the only record of Sironian existence. The vast ancient stones that mark the entrance to Siron's tomb are carved with history and revelation. They disclose our story from the beginning, and yet, they also foretell of a half-breed girl who will overthrow the power of the Legion and unite our world with the humans. The predictions were overlooked by most sirens—dismissed as lore by others …"

"Until I surfaced," I uttered. I was both surprised and miffed that William had chosen to keep these details from me. I was equally surprised that Silas had not divulged such information as well.

"Yes," Michael replied.

"Well, I can assure you that I have absolutely no desire to overthrow anything."

"This does not surprise me. You are born for a greater cause," he said solemnly.

"And what might that be?" I asked.

"Love," Michael replied. I was once again surprised by his words.

"Are you mocking me?" I scoffed.

"Not at all," he replied sincerely. When you are denied the opportunity to be shown love and equally so the prospect to give it, love becomes a rare and highly coveted treasure." Michael's eyes bore a sadness that I hadn't seen before. His eyes reflected the expression of a child who had been born into a race that was denied love. I could think of no greater agony than a body capable of love with no means to express it.

"I don't yet know your whole story, but I know of the hardships my siren friends have endured. No child should ever suffer the effects of a life without love," I uttered.

Michael looked upon me tenderly and was about to respond when Aria came upon us. Her long dark locks were dampened from the morning shower. Her feet were bare and her clothes drenched. Tiny beads of rain rolled down from her perfect features. I had never seen a more flawless specimen than this wild looking siren. Michael's attention immediately diverted to her. Aria looked upon me with the same familiar glare.

"Good morning, Aria," Michael said. His voice cracked a little.

"Michael, I have been looking for you. Theron is waiting."

We meandered through several trails and a sparsely planted grove before reaching a large field. The Legion was present, except for Zander. The events of the night before had evidently sparked a new rivalry between these eccentric warriors and the half-breed girl before them. They each looked upon me with a newly-sparked animosity.

"They don't seem very happy to see me," I mumbled to Michael as we approached. He didn't speak, but he took my hand in his, lacing his fingers between mine. I did not object. I needed something to solidify my place among the group. I would have to play the part of Michael's betrothed.

"Ah, I see the two of you are already getting along!" Theron said. "Splendid!" How fleetingly did Theron's friendly manners shift! I could more clearly see his motives. I did not tremble when his eyes met mine. One can only shudder in fear for so long until all trepidation is replaced by unearthly bravery. "How marvelous that we are all here for what I have planned today." He scanned the

Legion. His expression changed when he realized William was missing. "I see that my presumptions are incorrect. It appears young William has run off again. Aria, you should keep a better account of your fiancé," Theron scolded.

"I expect him here at any moment," she swiftly replied. "He was called away on business late last night." I swelled with jealousy. *How was it that Aria knew of William's business?*

"Business? It is very peculiar that he should be called away when there are preparations of attack at hand," Theron huffed.

"I am sure the business is directly related to our measures here," Aria swiftly interjected.

"Perhaps," Theron said skeptically. His eyes shifted in my direction. I feared he would question me on the subject. He did not. "Let's begin with morning reports. Roi, we will hear from you first."

"Certainly, Theron. Mari and I have received reports that an algae bloom has been detected matching the bioluminescent phytoplankton, just as Marguerite described, north of the Dominican Republic. The Caicos Islands are the closest landforms matching her vegetation and wildlife descriptions. This region would be the most probable area for the Obyascon to colonize as there are quite a number of unsettled, remote islands, lying close enough to a population source to feed," Roi explained.

"And how has this new information altered your activity, Georgianna?" Theron asked.

"We have scouts currently in route to the area," she replied. "They have reported an increase of Obyascon in that region, which supports the new information."

"How have your troops responded, Isaac?" Theron asked.

"We trained through the night. All forces have been made abreast of the current mission. My troops are primed and in position to move on command," Isaac said.

"Well done," Theron praised. "Barbour? Your update?"

"I have analyzed the pressure systems in the area. I am keeping track of several fronts moving in that direction so that Zander, Michael and I can make use of tidal and storm developments if necessary," Barbour explained. I eyed the Legion carefully as Barbour delivered his information to Theron. Their loyalty to him greatly reminded me of how the Crew admired Silas. I once again began to ache for my friends.

"Fine work, Barbour. Anastasia, we have yet to hear from you," Theron said.

"Given the locale of the Caicos islands, I have devised two attack routes. I propose a distraction coming in from the west. This would allow us disguised positioning to strike with factions moving in from the east. I will meet with the leaders of each sect to discuss logistics and strategies that will give us the greatest advantage among the Obyascon," she said. Anastasia continued to explain her strategies to Theron. I was distracted by the faint puttering of a familiar heartbeat.

"I will explore this with you further later, Anastasia. Thank you for your input." Theron looked over his Legion; his eyes stopped on me. "There is but only one who failed to report. If only our young William were here!"

"I am here, Theron," William said as he stepped out from a thick bank of vegetation. The rain had dampened his tousled hair. Tiny drops of water rolled down his perfect features. I froze at the sight of him. It took me back to another place—to the quarry, where he first professed his feeling. Our love was no serene cove, nor tranquil sanctuary—our love surged like gale winds churning the raging tide. My eyes met his, but only briefly as his stare traveled down my arm. William's jaw hardened as he spied my fingers laced into Michaels.

"Wonderful! I am very pleased you have joined us after all. It would have been a pity for you to miss out on the excitement." The smirk on Theron's face sent shivers down my spine. It was the same look displayed yesterday before revealing our intended meal.

"I hardly think this is the time for games, Theron," William snarled. "We should be preparing to move against the Obyascon." William's eyes narrowed as he surveyed the present forces. I studied him carefully. I saw what he saw; Theron's land forces had doubled in number.

"And so we shall! All in good time, William!" Theron said. "I will fill you in on the details from earlier, but there are tasks at hand that we must cover here first."

"Like what?" William growled. Fear swept through me—not so much for my own life, but for William's. Theron was planning something. Each of his Legion had come with reinforcements. I was surprised that so many sirens were capable of land dwelling.

Theron smirked. "I cannot be expected to send forth my Legion until I am assured that my players are loyal to me alone."

Theron motioned; two large sirens and Zander brought forth from the shadows my dearest friend in the world. I gasped aloud. The world stood still. My breath caught deep in my chest; I felt as if I were suffocating. James was shackled. His body was chilled from the rain, and his skin blanched from the cold. Deep circles encompassed his eyes from lack of sleep. I wanted to tear his captors from limb to limb, but I knew enough to hold my reaction. My mind rapidly dissected the situation as I began surveying how I would get him to safety. James scanned the assembly until his eyes met mine. I looked away. To acknowledge him would end his life for sure. I felt as if I were on a sick, twisted roller coaster, and the only ticket off was to relinquish my soul.

"Why would you bring a human into our midst, Theron?" I asked with a slight tremble in my voice. "Is it not your very laws that keep the sirens segregated from the humans?"

"How very insightful. You see, dear Marguerite, this is the very question I had laid out for you. This human was found patrolling the waters not long after you arrived. He was intercepted in a vessel which, I dare say, belongs to William. What are we to make of this?"

"I know nothing of this boy …," I stuttered. Theron turned to Darion.

"She lies," Darion said. "The hybrid knows the boy well."

"You did not let me finish," I protested. "I know nothing of this boy's design in coming." I fumbled through my words but tried to keep a stoic expression. Theron once again turned to Darion.

"She speaks the truth," Darion mumbled.

"So the plot thickens! I love a good mystery. We shall ask the boy." His eyes narrowed beneath his perfectly manicured brow. "What do you seek here?" James boldly puffed out his chest, though his eyes mirrored the uncertainty in my own.

"Margo is my friend. They could hardly expect me to hand her over to sea demons without sticking around to make sure she is safe." I was once again surprised at the depth of bravery harbored within him.

"You speak quite boldly for someone in your current situation!" Theron seemed amused. "Are you not afraid, boy?" The courage within my friend arose faster than a full-mooned tide.

"As your men are born of the sea and I am born of land, perhaps I should be asking you that question. Your sea demons are on human ground?" James said courageously. Theron laughed aloud.

"They are indeed. There are those of us that are equipped for short spells on land," Theron replied.

"But you are monsters just the same!" James responded quickly.

"Now now, "monster" is such a negative term. Since you seem to be casting labels, we prefer the term, "siren," Theron replied. He seemed to enjoy this banter.

"I don't very much care what you prefer!" James spat. Theron turned his attention towards me.

"Your friend here is quite entertaining." His glare shifted back to James. My friend was on trial for his life—we all knew it. "So what has Marguerite told you of our world?" To catch me in violation of his laws would cement my demise. James was too quick; he caught on to Theron's scheme.

"She did not tell me of your kind. We were friends before her transformation." James had chosen his response carefully. Theron again turned to Darion who authenticated my friend's words. Indeed, I had not initially "spoken" of the siren to him; the revelation was done in my letter.

"Marguerite has committed no crime!" William growled. "You have nothing with which to charge her!"

"That was not my intention, dear William. She is not held here against her will," Theron replied.

"Then, I now wish to leave here with my friend," I said boldly. I would leave behind William; I would sacrifice love … I would sacrifice anything if it would spare the life of James.

"Dear Marguerite, unfortunately, that is not possible," Theron said slyly. After that quite remarkable display yesterday, I can hardly allow such skill to go unchecked." He was not going to let me take James. I was a fool to think he would ever let me leave.

"I agreed under our treaty to train with your Legion. I have come for that purpose. I will also fight with your army against the

Obyascon—if it comes to that. I have kept my word. James has nothing to do with this! I beg for his release!" Theron seemed amused by my outcry of emotion. Theron stroked his chin and assertively paced before his army.

"Our mere existence has pivoted for thousands of years on the separation of the species," Zander glowered. "The human boy and this half-breed should be slain immediately!"

"Come now, Zander! There is no need for bloodshed here!" Theron's sly smile widened. Zander motioned towards my hand that was still laced into Michaels.

"Have you not reckoned the possibility that in betrothing the half-breed to Michael that the pair may indeed breed a mutant?" Both William and Michael looked as if they were ready to end Zander at any moment. William growled as he leaped towards them, his eyes flared, and he took the stance of a warrior. I followed his lead in preparation for a fight.

"Theron has no intention of such an alliance!" William growled. "He never has! He plans to do exactly what you wish Zander— he intends for this Legion to kill her. That was his intent yesterday when I was away. What Theron didn't count on was her skills—and me returning before the task was complete."

"And the betrothal?" Michael asked.

"Punishment set aside for me and ultimately another test for you," William replied. Michael released my hand. My fingers tingled as the blood flow returned from his tight grip.

"Were you once again testing me, Theron? To see if I would relinquish my loyalties to you for the possibility of love?" Michael asked. Theron did not answer but eyed William with an unparalleled vengeance. Any hope that I had of this situation ending peacefully began to vanish.

"How very cynical! I do not deny that I continue to assess the allegiance of my Legion. However, in this case, I would argue that Marguerite's hand would only be reparation for your loyalty."

"I will not be a trophy!" I growled.

"Well then, so be it," Theron said as he motioned towards his Legion. They arose atop the water, these creatures from the deep. Each was unique, beautiful and deadly. The perimeter was now guarded with sirens, no less than three deep. Their numbers were abundant, no fewer than fifty stood in allegiance. Their pale exquisite bodies hovered motionless along the clashing surf.

"As you can see, any effort of resistance would be futile," Theron said coolly.

William stepped towards Theron. He appeared to be unshaken by the mass assembly. As for me, I could think of nothing that would save my friend. I had bartered away my life once before. I bore the insignia of Theron. I had come as promised to join his Legion, but nothing would change my core. I would fight for my freedom, I would fight for my friend, and if need be, I would fight to the death for William.

William approached with caution. His emerald eyes glistened through the steady rainfall. His expression was steadfast. "Ah, but you see. I too have brought reinforcements," he said. Out from the brush appeared Silas's sect of Protectors, the most skilled sirens I had ever known, the dearest of friends. Toby and Kirby had come ready for a fight. Kirby fearlessly flashed his smile at Zander, who growled nervously at him. Toby smirked at the remainder of Theron's Legion as he popped his knuckles. Michael turned towards the assembly, his eyes immediately meeting those of Mace. I was unaware of how much time had passed since the brothers had last seen each other. All coloring seeped from Mace's face as he gazed upon Michael. Michael looked upon his twin as if he were a ghost. The tension between the pair was apparent to all.

Theron shifted nervously. "Ah, the long lost brothers are united at last!" Theron's attention focused on Mace. "Such an absence would have never taken place had you chosen to join my Legion like your brother."

"Chosen?" Mace hissed. "Whom? When have you ever given a choice?" Theron's eyes narrowed. A devious smirk settled across his lips.

"I see that Silas has not put a damper on your rebelliousness. I had hoped he would have been able to tame what the others had not." Mace growled. "What a pity that your insurrection caused you to be rejected by my other factions. I had once had great plans for you, Mace."

"I would have never answered to you, Theron!" he roared.

"Yes, well. Luckily, there were two of you. How fortunate for me—and for you, that your brother was willing to barter his allegiance in exchange for your life." Theron's revelation temporarily knocked the wind out of Mace.

"What are you saying?" Mace growled.

"Only that your rebelliousness gifted me quite the loyal subject. Your brother filled the spot intended for you. Any hesitation on his part was subsided by the fact that I let you live."

"You lie!" Mace spat. He turned and looked at Michael, who bore a look of confirmation. Michael's expression proved Theron's words to be the truth. "Michael traded his freedom for my life?"

"Michael's position in my Legion is highly coveted. It was a wise decision on his part," Theron replied.

"His allegiance to you allowed me remain with Silas?" Mace's voice was deeper as it now carried a greater pain.

"Of course. Though Silas may not support my regime, he is no threat to my power. I had hoped that he would tame you or, at the very least, keep you out of the way." Mace rose with a greater resolution.

"I stand in opposition to you now. I will not allow you to harm the boy—or Marguerite," Michael growled.

"You do realize that such would be considered an act of treason, an offense punishable by death!" Theron hissed at Michael's disobedience.

"I have looked upon the face of death before. I am not afraid to die," Michael roared.

"We stand together, Theron. Your forces outnumber us, but be advised, you will not take us down without substantial loss to your regime," William said firmly. Theron glanced at the faces of his Legion. There was abundant strength among those who bore his insignia but also a mixed hesitance that smelled very much like the scent of fear.

"Hardly a wise move with Obyascon moving into familiar waters," a familiar voice said. The gathering turned just as Silas appeared from over the dunes. "A good leader is capable of accurately weighing the opposition." Theron was astounded at the entrance of his old friend. He quickly regained his composure.

"Ah! Silas! How fortunate we are that you have joined our party!" Theron's voice was as smooth as butter, though his eyes shifted about anxiously. "One should ask how it was possible that you and your sect would so easily make it past my army."

"You forget, olé friend, that I too bear your insignia." Silas held out his brandished forearm. A frazzled young siren hurried from the water's edge. He paid no attention to the gathered party as he headed swiftly towards Theron.

"Theron, forgive the interruption, an unknown siren penetrated the perimeter a few minutes ago. As he bore your mark, my guards allowed him and his men to pass," he said. Theron grimaced as he motioned toward our gathered crew. The siren nervously shifted as he realized Silas and his Protectors were now before Theron.

"As you see, your notification comes a bit late." Theron raised his hand and motioned to Zander. In one swift command, a lightning bolt hit the siren striking him dead on the spot. I shrieked aloud as the siren fell motionless to the ground. Theron turned back to us. "I have no tolerance for poor assessments," Theron uttered without expression. William protectively stepped closer to me. At any moment, we could be torn apart forever. The reality of losing him was never more present.

"I remember a time, Theron, when you would have abhorred such a command. There was a time, my friend, when all life mattered to you," Silas spoke.

"True. I am now aware the bloodshed is often in order to keep the balance and laws set forth by my predecessors," Theron replied swiftly.

"And by balance, you mean your power," Silas said.

"Make no mistake, Silas, my actions are to sustain our kind. The humans have overtaken and overpopulated their lands. They are rapidly consuming the resources of the world. In the last two hundred years, their technology has advanced to the point where the sirens are no longer safe. How long until their greed has destroyed our oceans as well?"

"I cannot say that your concerns are without merit, but I have lived among the humans for many years now, and I can tell you, there is enormous good among their kind. To punish the boy for crimes of humanity is unjust. My sect will not allow it."

"Then you will defy me and, in doing so, the law," Theron's eyes narrowed. His Legion waited for the command to attack.

"Tell me how you wish for this to end, Theron," Silas said. "You can release the boy to us, in which case, we will take full responsibility for him, ensuring all that he has seen and heard here remains undisclosed, or we will stand and fight with Marguerite." Theron easily had us in numbers. However, with the addition of Silas and the Crew, we topped his Legion in skill. A battle against such forces would rage more bloodshed than Theron could justify. His eyes shifted among the group as he judiciously weighed his options.

"Silas, my friend, there is no further need for bloodshed today. If you take personal responsibility for the boy, then I will release him to you—under one condition," Theron said.

"And what might that condition be?" William promptly interjected.

"That you all stand with us against the Obyascon. We received word just this morning that they have moved into warmer waters. What other motivation could Merissa have in moving the colony into our territory than to challenge the Sironian for power?"

"It is strange indeed that the Obyascon should be moving into warmer waters. Until we are sure of Merissa's motivation in doing so, we will stand with you," Silas replied.

"You are aware that the Obyascon hold the humans as their primary nutrient source," Theron said.

"I am aware of the number of human lives taken by the Obyascon. I am also aware that your Legion also partakes in human essence," Silas continued.

"True, but our sources are regulated—restricted. The Obyascon feed at will. The threat they once harbored toward humans is insignificant compared to the loss of life that will certainly come from relocating to more populated regions. You cannot deny this," Theron replied.

"Like I said, we still do not know the cause. Perhaps the relocation is temporary. My Protectors will not attack without provocation. However, we will accept your offer for the boy and stand with you if a war is waged against the Sironian." Theron was not pleased but accepted the agreement.

"Isaac release the boy." James puffed out his chest, as he was unshackled and tossed to the ground. I was at his side in an instant. I took his hand and helped him up. The relief in his eyes mirrored my own. We quickly fled back to the Protectors. James looked ragged and exhausted, but he was alive. I was thankful that he had not chosen to reveal his extraordinary strength. The smart decision to keep his ability a secret had saved his life and most likely mine as well.

"Our forces move out at dawn. Silas, I expect your Protectors to be here and ready to fight." Silas nodded. Theron and his men turned to leave, and the oceanic assembly slipped beneath the water. Theron immediately turned back to our assembly. "Michael, you will be joining us." It was not a question. Michael's eyes met mine before briefly turning to Mace. Mace stared after him blankly as he followed Theron's Legion back to the plantation. When the last of his Legion disappeared, the rain swiftly dissipated. The dark skies cleared as if the weather itself were under Theron's command.

William came to me with urgency. His arms wrapped so tightly around my small frame that my bones could have turned to dust. His lips fiercely met mine, and for a moment, all else was erased from the world. The intensity of his response signified the gravity of what we had encountered. He had not expected us to live. I clung to him with every ounce of strength within me as our lips moved together. I clutched the back of his head, my fingers intertwined into his dampened hair. We had been granted one more day together, one more day of love, in a world in which tomorrow is never promised. His eyes bore into mine as his hands slid to the sides of my face. He pressed his face against my chilled lips before once again taking my mouth to his. I was lost in the essence of William Avery with no desire for rescue. We were united for several minutes without realizing those around us. They were all aware of the connection between William and me, but none had witnessed the passion. At last, James cleared his throat sending us back to our bleak reality. They looked upon us as if, at last, they knew us. James smiled, his expression one of sympathetic understanding. Aria looked upon us with a painful longing for an emotion that she had never experienced.

William stayed at my side. His arm slipped firmly around my waist. Silas diverted the scene. "I think it unwise to remain on the island until morning. I do not trust Theron. It would be better to find neutral territory for our afternoon slumber and return during the early hours of the morning."

"I know the island well. I spent several years here before joining Silas," Mace said. "There is a cove along the northern side that will provide proper shelter for Marguerite and James tonight."

"Is the area securable?" William asked.

"It is. The bends are visible from all angles, and the brush is too dense for any formidable sneak attack," Mace replied.

"Then you lead the way!" Silas said as he strode over the dunes towards the shore. We all followed, all but one. We turned realizing that Aria stood in the clearing alone. "You have a choice, Aria," Silas said.

"What choice do I have, Silas?" she spat, "I am of little use to Theron. You all must see how he shuns me, and you all despise me."

"We have loved you like a sister, Aria," Kirby said.

"And I betrayed you all."

"Yes, but Silas has taught us what Theron has not," Mace said.

"And what would that be?" she asked.

"Forgiveness," he replied.

"I am not worthy of your forgiveness." She looked at me with an expression that was almost sympathetic.

"It is given to you if you will only accept it," I said as her deep emerald eyes stared apologetically into mine.

"I have been the one who wrongs you, and yet, you offer forgiveness without an apology?" Aria asked.

"I want nothing of you, Aria, except your friendship," I said.

"With all that has passed between us, I can hardly see how that is possible," she replied.

"Come with us, Aria! Come with your family!" William said. His tender words caused a tinge of jealousy to sweep through me.

"You are not one of them, Aria; you are one of us!" Toby said. Aria scanned the faces of the Crew for resistance. She found none. Step by step she crossed the dunes and rejoined the sect.

We reached the cove by late afternoon. The area was breathtaking! The tide cut deep into the shoreline, hollowing out a secluded beach that dipped past the dunes and into the thick reeds and underbrush. The trek would have taken our siren friends only a few minutes by water, and yet, they traveled by foot for James and me. James was haggard and tired but never complained. He seemed to study my interactions with William and the Crew. He watched me as if he had never really seen me before. When I would catch his gaze upon me, he would flash a familiar smile and look away. I could only imagine how different it was to see me among the sirens. I wanted to talk to him. I wanted to know his feelings. I needed to learn of his interactions with Theron during his time held captive. There would be time to pick his brain once our group was settled.

Silas selected the spot in which to camp as William began gathering wood for a fire. Toby, Kirby, and Aria dove into the breakers to catch a meal. Mace pulled over several fallen trees and began to fashion a makeshift shelter. He easily snapped the brush into the appropriate lengths for the frame. James and I helped by gathering smaller branches and reeds for the roof. James picked up a large trunk, much larger than he should have been able to carry. I gently stopped him, all the while hoping it had escaped the notice of the group. It had. No more need to know about his heightened ability. By accidently altering his structure, I had proven the very thing that they had all feared. My birth had certified that on some level, it was possible for human and siren to procreate. What had happened with James verified that their fears about the mixing of the races were completely founded. I had unknowingly created a super human. I shivered at the complications that could arise if such became known to the humans or the Legion.

We finalized the remaining pieces of the shelter just as our meal reached the campfire flames. I was frozen to the core. William ushered me closer to the fire and wrapped his arms tightly around me. His brow furrowed. "You are going to get dehydrated. You need water," he said. Mace hurried off into the foliage. He returned with several large cacti. He pulled out a blade and trimmed off the thorny exterior before cutting off the top of each plant. He passed one to both of us.

"Fresh water … at least until I can locate another source." We both graciously accepted. The cactus water had an odd, but not unpleasant flavor.

"Another source has arrived," we heard as Michael strode into our camp. The muscles in Mace's body tightened at the arrival of his brother. William looked tense as well.

"What are you doing here?" William asked defensively. "Has Theron sent you to spy on us?"

"No. Theron does not even know I am here. I came to deliver Marguerite's personal belongings. I assumed that after today you had no intention of returning to your quarters."

"You assumed correctly," I said.

"Yes, well, I thought you might want your bag." My backpack slid off of his back and onto the ground near my feet. I was appreciative.

"Thank you, Michael."

"You are very welcome." He had other gifts as well. "I brought you some blankets and some bottled waters for you and your friend."

"That was very thoughtful," I replied. "Would you stay and eat with us?"

"I would not want to impose," Michael said.

"Actually …," Mace hissed.

"We insist that you stay and dine with us, Michael," Silas said as he shot a stern look in Mace's direction. Aria began taking the fish from the fire and passing them out among us. James took his seat at my right side, Michael at the left, as William hovered protectively from behind. My love triangle had morphed into a quadrilateral.

"Tell us, James, how did Theron's Legion capture you?" Kirby asked.

"After Marguerite left the boat, I got really worried about her," he said. "I had to see that she had arrived *somewhere* safely. I trailed behind her for a distance, eventually losing her. I checked the map of the area and made a guess as to where I thought she was headed."

"You made a very good guess," Toby replied.

"It wasn't that difficult actually. I just picked out the island that was the least inhabited with the greatest resources," James explained. "I never actually made it to the island. Theron's lackeys picked me up about three miles from shore."

"Did they hurt you?" I asked.

"No, not really. They saw to it that I was pretty damn uncomfortable and asked me a million questions about you, William, and how I got his boat."

"What did you tell them?" William asked.

"As little as possible. I told them I really didn't know much about anything. I explained that Marguerite was a friend of mine who was looking for William, so we took his boat to find him. They pressed for more information, but that is all that they got out of me."

"Was this guy one of your captors?" Mace asked, pointing to Michael.

"No. The first time I saw him was today," James responded.

"Still trying to make your brother the bad guy, eh, Mace," Michael said. "I did not even know that they had the boy. I was just as surprised as you were … and a bit confused as to why Theron kept his capture from me." The hurt in his expression was highly evident.

"Perhaps Theron's trust in you is not as absolute as you deem it to be," Aria said defiantly.

"Perhaps you are right, Aria," Michael said. "Theron has not tested my allegiance to him against my family until today. I did not question why I was left on protection detail when his forces came after you during the hurricane. I was relieved that I had been spared from the situation, and even more so, that it had ended with very little bloodshed."

"Our coast was destroyed," I gasped.

"Yes, but Theron had planned to wipe your sect from existence. As I knew none of you, only hearing second hand of the half-breed, I prayed only for my brother and that he would escape the conflict unharmed. I begged Theron to spare his life, reaffirming the agreement we had made years earlier," Michael explained.

"The first I have heard of this bargain was today. Is it true?" Mace asked. "Did you exchange your freedom for my life?"

"It is true. Theron felt that you were too rebellious to tame and too reckless to leave unattended," Michael replied.

"And so I was sent to Silas?" Mace's face was twisted in pain.

"Yes. Mace, what was told today was true. The only reason I accepted a place in Theron's Legion was to spare your life," Michael said.

"Come now, Michael. Do you actually expect me to believe that your rank has nothing to do with ambition?" Mace scoffed.

"Ambitious? Sure. But I would have traded it all to have my brother back in my life." Michael's words were so heartfelt that even Mace seemed moved. All was quiet except for the rolling waves and the crackling campfire. Mace strode off down the beach; Michael went after him. We all remained. There was much that needed to be said between the brothers. They needed time to heal.

William pulled out a couple of bottled waters and passed them to James and me. I did not realize how parched I had become. The cold night air hit as soon as the sun fell beneath the clouds. The sirens were unaffected by the temperature. William wrapped a large blanket around my shoulders and passed the spare one to James. He acted as if he did not want to accept it.

"Take it," I urged. "You will need it to get some sleep before the trip home tomorrow."

"Home?" James seemed puzzled. "If you all are fighting the Obyascon, I'm going too."

"James, that is ridiculous!" I spat! "You shouldn't even be here!" James looked hurt by my words.

"It would be unsafe for you, James," Silas said. "The Obyascon could detect that you were human from a mile away."

"You would be dinner!" Toby teased.

"The sirens will be traveling by water. What if something were to happen to Margo? What if she were to become injured or too exhausted to swim? She is still part human, you know," James said.

"I will take care of Marguerite," William replied.

"Look, I know you all are straight from a superhero comic book, but you don't know all that you are up against tomorrow. The Obyascon isn't the only evil force at work here. Theron has it out for all of you … especially Marguerite," James added.

"I'm not afraid of him," I protested!

"Let me finish, darlin'." He turned again to the others. "If the Obyascon can pick up my human scent from miles away, then they can pick up Margo's too. She will attract them before you even arrive."

"I will be fine, James!" I protested.

"His argument is justified," Silas admitted.

"What if she were to sail with me tomorrow, at least till you reach your destination. I could take William's boat and sail back at a safe distance from the Legion? That way, if Marguerite needed help or a safe way home, I could be nearby to whisk her to safety."

"No one will be whisking me anywhere!" I protested. "For the record, I'm kind of a badass! I can take care of myself!"

"Which is why you would be a greater target," William said.

"Don't tell me you are taking his side," I said turning to William.

"I'm just saying that he has a point. There should be a measure in place to get you to safety—just in case."

"But a boat? The Obyascon could rip it to shreds in a minute! Besides, the last time you were onboard you almost got yourself killed," Kirby said.

"True. This time would be different," James said.

"How so?" I asked.

"This time, I will have a whole sect of Protectors watching my back." He smiled at the group in hopes of finding some sort of kinship. "You would have my back, right?" He looked around for affirmation. There was a moment of uncomfortable silence.

"Any friend of Marguerite is a friend to us. James, this sect will protect you," Silas said.

"Cool. Thanks! So what are these Obyascon things anyway?" Silas began to tell James the history of the Obyascon. The Crew listened intently. William wrapped his arms tightly around me. Within moments, I was captivated by the scent of his skin. Silas' words faded as all I could think about was being closer to him. Surely, no siren could crave a being more than I craved William.

"Marguerite has had the greatest amount of contact with the creatures. What can you tell us?" Silas asked. All eyes were suddenly upon me as I was sucked back into reality. They all looked upon me as if they could read my thoughts. I was relieved that they could not.

"Well, the Obyascon have lost almost all traces of human form. As we consider ourselves monsters, they forever look the part. However, among their masses, there are a few shape shifters capable of looking like us, able to move on the ground like us. I was up against one of these shape shifters, though he seemed to be an exception. I think for the most part they lack higher logic, relying primarily on brute strength and numbers."

"You say you were up against one of them?" I turned to see that Mace had rejoined the group. Why was I saddened at the realization that Michael was not with him? I pushed aside the emotion.

"Yes, Mace, there were three of them. I was being held captive by one of the shapeshifters. There was another siren girl held captive there too. I believe her to be William's sister." Shock and surprise swept over our group.

"Could this be true, William?" Silas asked. "Is it possible that your sister is still alive?"

"You know that I have always felt it, Silas. I have always believed that she was out there," William replied emotionally.

"I know you have, though I thought it improbable," Silas confessed.

"However, I was mistaken on one fact. I always assumed that it was Theron's Legion that had taken my sister."

"If the Obyascon do have the girl, it would justify why we had received no reports of her. With no word after all of these years, I presumed she had been killed." Silas said.

"She is very much alive. She escaped with me but was recaptured before we could make our escape together. I promised I would return for her."

"Well, this finally makes sense," Mace said.

"What does?" Toby asked.

"Why Marguerite came to this island … why she agreed to fight with Theron against the Obyascon. She has seen the Obyascon army! She realized she needed his Legion to stand a chance against them! All of this is to keep your promise to the girl," Mace exclaimed.

"Yes. I made her a promise," I said. "But this will be no easy task."

"Why has the girl been held captive?" Toby asked

"She has great power. The Obyascon obviously wanted to keep this power out of Theron's hands," I explained.

"If he learns of the girl, she would be in further danger. Theron would want to destroy anything that could a possible threat," William said.

"Yes, we need to keep this rescue mission a secret," Silas said.

"Well then, it looks like we will be fighting the Obyascon tomorrow," Kirby said. "I stand with you, William."

"Let's go get your little sister back!" Toby cheered. However, one voice remained silent. We turned to Aria, realizing that we had entrusted her with dire information. *Was it possible to trust her again?*

"Aria, do you stand with us?" Silas asked gravely. The group turned to her. It was possible that she could run and tell Theron all that she had learned.

"I stand with you," Aria replied. "I will fight alongside my brothers." She turned towards William and me with a look of genuine remorse. Aria had been entrusted with profound knowledge. Now, she would have to prove herself trustworthy.

"Thank you," we both whispered simultaneously.

22

"We need never be ashamed of our tears"

~Charles Dickens

A dense fog blanketed the shoreline. I wiped the sleep from my eyes and reached out for William. My hand grasped through the heavy mist but found nothing. I called out to him without reply and then to James. There was no response. I shouted for my friends. All was silent except for the sound of the gentle waves rolling upon the shore. My heart raced in my chest as I battled through the white abyss towards the ocean. The billowy surf spilled over onto my feet. I looked at its greeting to find that the sea had been tainted. The once blue-green water ran deep crimson. I fell backward onto the sand, consumed with the horror that the sea was tainted by the blood of all that I loved.

"Marguerite! Wake up, love." I opened my eyes to the perfect lines of William's face. "It's alright. Everything is fine. You seem to be having a nightmare," William whispered. He was safe! I looked around to see that the others had assembled, all accounted for. They were all alive and well! I buried my face into William's chest. My friends were safe … for now. "Are you alright?" William said.

"I think so. I was having a dream, a dream in which the shore was thick with crimson water."

"It's over now," he said as he scooped me tighter into his embrace.

"But it isn't over," I cried. "The reality today could be far worse than any nightmare. We will face an army today. I cannot help but think my dream is foreshadowing the events to come."

"Before I loved you, I was sworn to protect you with my life. Now, you are my reason for life. My soul was an empty vessel until you filled it with hope and joy and love." My cheeks flushed from his profession.

"Oh, but how the sea tears at us, its undercurrent obsessed to sink the vessel," I whispered.

"I would conquer an entire ocean if to do so would secure your love," William replied. "Promise me forever!" The pleading in his eyes searched my face for reassurance. William and I had faced death, but he had never faced loosing me to someone else. Michael had awakened new insecurities.

"My heart resides with you alone; however, I cannot speak for my life. One can hardly promise something that can be ripped away at any moment," I said painfully.

"And for that reason, I will always be your Protector. For if your heart would cease to beat, mine would end as well," William said.

"I'm not as afraid of death, but I couldn't live with myself if I lost another one of you!" A tear slid down my cold cheek as Henry's death played over in my mind. "What if today goes horribly wrong? My decisions caused Henry's death, and now you are all in danger because of me. If only I had managed to get the girl safely away from the Obyascon …!"

"Stop it!" He brushed away the tear. "The Obyascon killed Henry—not you! And do you not see what you have done? You discovered my sister! There is a possibility that I will have a part of my family again! You have done that! You have given me hope!"

"What good is having hope if your heart does not beat long enough to see it fulfilled?"

"We have made it through immeasurable odds and look! We are here—together! You came into my life for a purpose. I know what that purpose is now."

"To find your sister?"

"No, to teach me to love." He drew my face to his and pressed his lips hard against mine. My body craved his essence stronger than it craved oxygen. There was no part of William that I didn't intensely desire. I pulled him tightly to me, savoring our last moments together. I was briefly carried away before Silas's voice snapped me back to reality.

"The boat has arrived," Silas said. William's glorious sailboat eased around the bend and dropped anchor just beyond the breakers. "Marguerite, James, you will have to swim out to it. The surf is too rough to bring it in any closer."

"That's not a problem," I uttered. My breath caught deep in my throat with the realization that soon, William and I were to be separated again."

"James?" Silas asked.

"I know how to swim—if that is what you are asking," he replied a bit defensively. "As long as your kind doesn't decide to eat me before I reach the boat." Silas smiled.

"I suppose you have a good point. We will venture first to ensure there are no eager sirens circling." As if on cue, the Crew dove through the surf. William took my hand in his one last time and pressed it to his lips. Our eyes met one last time before he parted and quickly disappeared below the surf. I ached for him. I could only part with him for one reason—to keep the promise that I had made to his sister. We would come for her.

I glided through the cool water and quickly ascended the ladder on the rear of the vessel. James was a good ten meters behind me fighting through the raging surf. The Crew had the task at hand as there was no sirens in his path. Just as he safely reached the ladder, the ship's captain emerged from below deck. It was Michael, carrying a large stack of towels. "You better dry off, or you will catch pneumonia," he said as he cast a towel in my direction.

"Why are you here, Michael?" I asked. "It seems strange that Theron would relinquish his own protector to transport two humans."

"You are hardly human, Marguerite. The Legion discussed the importance of keeping you out of the hands of the Obyascon. Theron personally sent me for the task. He has an entire army for his personal protection," Michael said.

"I don't need a babysitter," I scolded. "Especially one sent by Theron! He is pushing us together to secure his own agenda."

"Perhaps, but you didn't honestly think they were going to allow you to sail alone, now did you?" Michael said with a smirk.

"I'm with her!" James said as he ascended onto the deck.

"Forgive me," he said gallantly bowing to James. Michael turned back to me. "You didn't honestly think we were going to leave you in the sole care of a human, now did you?"

"I resent that," James said. "You are one of Theron's men. I can already tell that I am not going to like you." Michael smiled.

"He's feisty," Michael said. He gazed upon my sopping wet friend with a smirk. "I can already tell that I am going to like you." James glowered at Michael.

"He is different from the others," I replied. "James, just give him a chance."

James huffed and grabbed a towel, as he escaped below deck. Michael shrugged. "Well, let's get this show on the road, eh?" He turned and began to adjust the sails. Strong winds quickly moved the boat down the coastline. I stayed on deck, watching the water for any sign of William. It was a very short time before we neared the planned meeting spot. Theron's Plantation inched closer as we moved down the shoreline. The barren waters abruptly transformed into a sea of sirens as Theron's army hovered just below the surface. I quivered at the realization that William was in their midst.

Michael dropped anchor at a safe distance from the breakers. James joined us on deck as we waited for orders. Silas emerged first with the Crew behind him. I was overjoyed to see William safely among the group. Theron updated the Protectors on the current location of the Obyascon forces and the army's plan to move against them. I listened for any clues on Anna's whereabouts. "I must admit, I'm surprised by Theron's tactics," Michael whispered. "Usually he is more straightforward in his plan of attack."

"He was straightforward the night of the hurricane. His army came straight to kill us." I shivered remembering the event. That night seemed like ages ago, and yet, I recalled every vivid detail.

"You can hear them," James asked, "from this distance?"

"Yes," I replied. "The Sironian plan to head east and curve around from the north to catch the Obyascon by surprise."

"I see. And Theron is directing us to follow?" James asked. Theron was motioning to our vessel. William spied me from across the waves. My knees went weak at the sight of him prepared for battle.

"No," Michael replied. "They want us to take a more direct route. He has assigned a small division to travel with us for protection. We are to stop before we reach the tip of the Caicos Islands. A scout will travel ahead of us to ensure the area is secure. When they are in position in the north, we will move in to close off the area."

"So the Crew will travel with us?" James whispered.

"No." I replied bleakly. "He is separating us."

"Why would he do that?" James asked.

"We will ultimately be the bait, giving Theron's Legion the opportunity to attack from behind," Michael explained.

"He just said this? Theron just admitted that we were bait?" James huffed.

"No," Michael said, "He didn't have to; I already figured out his plan. I knew what he was up to when he so readily assigned me to your protection. He does not plan on us making it out of this mission alive."

"I realize why he wants us dead, but why you?" James asked.

"I defied him by siding with Silas's protectors. I believe he knows I have been an informant to them all along; Theron realizes that my allegiance is not to him."

"If we are conscious of Theron's plan, Silas and the Crew must realize this as well!" I said. My voice quivered.

"Yes. I am sure the Crew now recognize Theron's scheme," Michael said.

"Well, why are they just standing there?" James exclaimed. I motioned for him to whisper. If we could hear their conversation, they would be able to hear ours. "Why aren't they challenging him?"

"Because they are coming up with a strategy of their own," Michael replied.

"I am sure Silas is planning. He will think of something to get us out of this." But Silas only nodded at Theron's instructions. One look from William verified our speculation. William's eyes met mine one last time before he returned to the sea. Silas was skilled at covering his emotions—William was not. He looked as if he could rip Theron apart with his bare hands.

Barbour officially delivered to us Theron's instructions. He carried the same fatal look that we wore. Barbour realized, as we had, that Theron had selected his sect to be the sacrificial lambs. Barbour assembled his sect around our vessel. The beautiful creatures flowed beneath the surface like seaweed dancing in the current. The humanlike form of the siren disguised the fierce beasts preparing for battle. Aboard, we made our preparations. James adjusted the sails, Michael logged the coordinates, and we began the journey. Michael calculated that it would take us six days to reach the presumed location of the Obyascon—and hopefully, Anna. I had six days to get James out of this mess—six days to convince him to go back to his world and forget all of this. It would not be an easy task.

The sea proved to be relatively calm once we sailed from the shoreline. Michael was mostly silent as James and I rattled on with stories from the past. Several times, I caught myself smiling—even laughing. It felt wrong to laugh, wrong but wonderful. As nervous as I was to have him privy to the Sironian world, his presence brought me comfort. I could almost pretend we were on a great adventure, like the ones of the past—a past before sirens or monsters—a past before love had complicated things. However, James did not look well. He had slept only a few hours in the past week. As soon as the afternoon sky fell below the horizon, I encouraged him to sleep. He refused at first. It was evident that James did not trust Michael, but with some reassurance, he relented and slipped below deck for the night.

"You know, you really should join him," Michael said when we were alone.

"I find sleep difficult since joining the world of the Sironian," I replied.

"That's not what I meant," he snickered. I was taken aback.

"Are you implying that I should sleep with James?" I said, as my face turned fifty shades of red.

"It doesn't take superpowers to see that the human boy is wildly in love with you," Michael teased.

"And it is no mystery where my heart belongs!" I spat.

"Do you realize how much easier your life would be if you would only live as a human?" he said.

"You are kind of late to chime in on this debate. I've had this lecture from both William and James. I don't need it from you, Michael!"

"Did you ever stop to think that maybe they were right?" His smile faded as he looked tenderly in my eyes.

"Well, I'm not human anymore, so …."

"When you were talking with James tonight, talking and laughing, I saw a different side of you, one that I had never seen before. For those moments, when you were laughing, you were all human. You could be that way all of the time—you could choose to live as human," Michael said.

"But you cannot choose who you love," I replied.

"Or *what* you love, you mean," he said. Michael's words began to cause my blood to boil. William was no monster. I turned away. Michael grabbed me by the arm and swung me around to face him.

The fragrance of his skin caused my breath to quicken. He was close—too close. He could hear the racing of my heart. I pulled my arm from his firm hold. He exhaled deeply. "You are choosing wrong! Theron is never going to allow you and William to be together! Don't you see!" Michael said forcefully.

"Because we are strong together!" I boasted.

"No, you are not. Together you form a target. You are going to get each other killed, and when you are both dead, what will loving each other matter at that point! Choose to live!" he roared. "Escape now and live! I will cover for you! I will tell the Legion you are dead, and you can return to your family!"

"I can't do that. I will not abandon William. He is my family also—they all are!" I pleaded.

"You and Theron are not as different as one would think," Michael said. "You are both consumed with the power of love. This battle between you is over principle! The sheer principle of love! You represent everything Theron stands against." I could not deny the truth of Michael's words.

"His laws are ridiculous! Anyone should be able to love whom they choose!" I insisted.

"True, but you are trying to assign human emotions to a race that was intended to remain primitive!" Michael said, once again moving closer to me.

"That's bull, Michael! You have been indoctrinated into those same lies. Are you saying that you don't have feelings? That you have been so brainwashed by Theron that you have bought into this nonsense!" I responded, half in shock that I was able to piece together any sensible argument in the nearness of such a siren.

"This *nonsense* has been followed by our kind since creation!" Michael spat. I steadied myself and retaliated again.

"No, it has not! Silas left the Legion because of it! William's parents were killed because of it! You and Mace were separated because of it!" I shrieked.

"Yes! You have just proved my point!" Michael responded. "With such love, you lose sight of everything else! What is important to the race! What is best for creation!" His face flushed and his words grew in intensity. "You cannot defy everything that has been instilled in you since you were born!"

"So you live a life incapable of love! You support an existence void of emotion! You choose to shut off the natural emotions you were …." The space between us vanished as his lips were upon mine. I was so taken aback that I felt all consciousness slipping. His lips were hard at first, then soft with tenderness. My lips instinctively wanted to move with his but remained frozen. His hand slipped behind my head as he more forcefully coerced a response. My lips wanted to part, to withdraw the essence he was so eager to offer, but a vision blocked any temporary feelings of passion. The vision was of my true love. I pulled from him. I loved William. I realized at that moment that there would never be a fleeting passion nor new romance that would dispel where my heart belonged.

I stepped back. Michael's eyes were hard upon me. "Marguerite, I …."

"I think it is time for Margo to get some sleep too," James said from behind us. I turned to see James ready to attack. I hadn't even heard him come from below deck.

"Yes, I think you are right, James. Perhaps I should call it a night," I said as I swiftly moved past him into the cabin below. He shot Michael another threatening look before closing the cabin door behind us. I crawled into the small sleeping space. There were a few moments of silence as James stood there motionless.

"Do you want me to sleep on the floor?" he asked.

"James, you are not going to sleep on the floor. We've napped in hammocks together since we were eleven," I replied.

"We aren't eleven anymore," he said. He crawled up into the space next to me and closed his eyes. He was clearly very upset. Another few moments of silence passed between us before I could take it no longer.

"James, what did you see … between Michael and I?" I asked.

"Margo, I didn't have to see anything," James replied.

"What do you mean?" I questioned nervously.

"I've seen that look before," he said soberly.

"What look?" My eyes narrowed as I waited for his response.

"The look on your face. It was the same look you had right after I kissed you the first time," he said.

"Oh …." I was lost for words. He knew me too well and would quickly see through any justification. Another awkward moment of silence passed. "I guess I should have decked him," I said meekly.

"No you shouldn't have," James replied through his still clenched jaw.

"And why is that?" I asked.

"You would have broken your hand on his firmly chiseled jawline!" James took a pillow and crammed it hard over his face in a huff. "I frickin' hate sirens!" He said from beneath the pillow. I was pretty sure he was thinking another word other than *frickin'*.

There was more awkward silence. My mind was spinning, spinning so fast that all I wanted to do was close my eyes. The world began to fade away, but my thoughts softly surfaced through the darkness. "Sometimes, I still wish that …." I was barely still conscious.

"Wish what?" James asked in a whisper.

"That we were eleven." I sighed.

"I do too," he replied gently. "I do too."

23

---

*"Whatever our souls are made out of,
his and mine are the same."*

~Emily Bronte

The sun danced atop the turquoise water, casting the perfect light on Michael's chiseled face. He had been standing perfectly still on the bow for the better part of an hour, keeping watch over the morning horizon. I flipped to a new page in the sketchbook, pulled out a worn charcoal, and began sketching his likeness. With four uneventful days aboard the boat, I was relieved that William had not only stocked the vessel with books but also a basic set of art supplies—undoubtedly for me. Any relief from the tension between the other castaways and myself was appreciated. James was consistent with his dislike of Michael, who had mostly avoided me since our first night at sea.

James glanced over my shoulder as he came out to adjust the sails. Several minutes later, he approached Michael. "Why don't you take a break for a while. I'll take watch duty," he said. Michael shrugged and went below deck. I smiled as James took a similar position on the bow and struck a pose. In jest, I flipped to a new sheet and sketched James too.

"Be sure to get my good side!" James joked. I was sketching away as a great thud came from the back of the boat. The charcoal slipped onto the deck as I braced for a fight. James responded as well; his narrow frame arched for an attack. I turned to see Michael in the doorway of the cabin, also ready for combat.

"I am sorry; I should have given you warning that I was boarding," Barbour said.

"Yes, a bit of notice would have been appreciated, "Michael scoffed as he relaxed his stance.

"There was little time for that," Barbour said. "We will reach our destination in the next two days. I know the penalty for what I am about to do, but I need to warn you of Theron's plan."

"Look, siren creature! We figured this out a long time ago. Theron is using us as bait so he and the others can attack from the north," James boasted.

Barbour seemed impressed. "The human is correct, but there is more," he said.

"What have you come to say, Barbour," Michael asked impatiently.

"Theron provided stringent orders to my sect. They were to ensure that no one aboard this ship returns," Barbour said.

"He ordered your sirens to kill us?" I gasped.

"Yes, just before you reach the Obyascon," Barbour confessed.

"Of course! The Protectors would assume that the Obyascon massacred our sect. This would enrage your friends to avenge you," Michael hissed.

"And ensure their allegiance to his agenda," James said.

"These plans would wipe out the Obyascon, and get rid of us in the process!" I exclaimed.

"Why have you come to tell us this, Barbour?" Michael questioned. "You know that your disobedience will mean death."

"I have known you for many years, Michael. To take your life would be no easy feat besides I respect you. I have also seen the girl in combat. She would most likely wipe out half of my men, if not all of them. Theron underestimates her skill," Barbour replied.

"Perhaps he doesn't," Michael said. "Your men are some of the most skilled in his Legion. It is no surprise that if he devised such a plan, he would choose your sect to carry it out." Barbour nodded.

"There is a small island, just north of Inagua," Barbour said. "It is just a short distance from here. Theron kept a training camp there for his Legion about thirty years ago, but a storm surge decimated most of the accommodations. Instead of rebuilding, he just relocated the camp to his present-day location. We have often wondered why he abandoned the tropical waters of that region for the dark waters of the south."

"Does anyone still live there?" I asked. Barbour shook his head.

"The island is deserted, but you should be able to find some remaining shelter there. I will send half of my men out to scout north tomorrow at daybreak and send the other half south, Barbour said. "Before they return, I will make the boat appear as if you were attacked and killed by the Obyascon. You will have only a small window before they branch out in search of the Obyascon, but if you hurry, you should have enough time to slip to the island safety. You will all need to disappear—forever."

I began to protest. The idea of never seeing William again was outside the realm of possibilities for me. I needed him no less than I

needed a beating heart. I would get James safely out of this mess—
out of this crazy world, and find a way to let William know that I
was safe. "They will be able to smell me the moment I hit the water!
My scent will give us away!" I responded.

"It is doubtful. Any traces of humanity are covered sufficiently
by the fresh Sironian blood in your veins," Michael said. "They may
pick up on a human scent, but it is unlikely that it would be tracked
to you."

"What about James?" I asked. "How will he make it to the
island?"

"I do not know. It is best if I know as little as possible," Barbour
replied. He turned to leave.

"But, Barbour," Michael stopped him. "Why are you helping
us?" he asked.

Barbour smiled faintly, "Let's just say that the charms of the girl
have not escaped me. She may be part human, but she is a siren in
every sense of the word." My cheeks flushed. In an instant, he had
slipped beneath the water below. We were quiet for a moment as the
severity of our situation began to sink in.

"It seems as if your charms have come in handy once again,
Miss Westley," James teased.

"I wish it were that easy," Michael said as he rubbed his brow
anxiously. "We may now know the extent of Theron's plot, but it
would take a miracle to get you to the island without alerting the
sirens."

"Miracle, eh? It isn't like I can just walk on water!" James
exclaimed.

"James! That's it! You're a genius!" I said as I rushed to kiss him
on the cheek.

"Um. Thank you?" James replied puzzled, as Michael eyed me with a confused look on his face. I hurried below deck and pulled out the stowed away surfboard from below the bed.

"Very funny, I get the walking on water part now, but how am I going to surf my way to the island?" James asked.

Michael smiled as he realized my plan. "I hope your surfing skills are up to par. Marguerite and I are going to pull you," he said.

"It is the only thing I can think of that will keep your scent out of the water," I added.

"Looks like I will be walking on water after all!" James shrugged. I smiled faintly. I had gotten my wish. Perhaps I had found a way to get James to safety after all, but my survival appeared grim. I would not leave William to fight for his sister alone. I would get James to the island and then rejoin the quest for Anna.

****

As soon as the sun went down, we frantically began our preparations for departure. I ached at the thought of leaving the beautiful vessel built by my love adrift. By the time the horizon flickered its first golden hue, we were prepared to journey. Michael and I had packed our backpacks with a few provisions, a change of clothes, the dousie bow and two harpoons stowed aboard the ship. Just as promised, the sirens split forces—one group traveled north and the other south. A signal from Barbour gave the all clear. Michael and I slipped into the water as James climbed aboard the surfboard. We had attached an extra cable to the board so that we could both pull the board. We would have to make the three-mile stretch in just a few minutes if we were to make the trip without discovery. Following Michael's lead, I swam with all of my might, only occasionally looking behind me. I searched the water for any sign of sirens. There was nothing but the vast ocean. I was aware that our good fortune could turn in an instant.

I surfaced to see a small patch of land ahead of us. Barbour had been accurate in his coordinates.

"Are you alright?" James asked me. He looked helpless and pained that he was not able to help us with the swim. I winked at him for reassurance.

"What this? It's a piece of cake," I said before catching back up to Michael's robust stride. I lied. I was exhausted. The last mile was the most difficult. We both picked up the pace in fear that the sirens would soon be on our trail. Michael had been to the island but not in many years. I was impressed with his accuracy; a few hundred yards in either direction and we easily could have drifted off course.

James took the reins from us and skillfully surfed a sizeable wave to the shore. He smiled as the massive wave completed the journey. It was good to see him smile. The island was beautiful—equally as breathtaking as the southern coastline, but different. The sprawling marsh grasslands were replaced with dense tropical foliage, and instead of dark golden sand, the beaches consisted of pale pink grains of coral. James and I followed Michael through the foliage, eager to get as far as possible from the shore. It would only be a short time until our absence was known.

Just as Barbour had stated, there were remnants of a training facility hidden within the island. Situated behind a large courtyard was an elevated bungalow-style house. There were no less than twenty small round huts along the overgrown grounds, most in need of substantial repair. The area was so overrun that one could almost walk past the structures without notice of their existence. We peeked in on several of the huts before making our way to the largest bungalow. The huts were relatively bare; the less damaged ones still contained the remnants of a hammock, a washboard table with pot, and a small bathroom. However, the main house would have been opulent for island living forty years ago. Unfortunately, only a few rooms were left intact. The damage that the storm had caused was severe. Parts of the roof had been stripped away, so trees and shrubs were growing straight through the structure. Luckily, the interior living room and master bedroom were untouched by the elements—only time had deteriorated the luxury of these rooms.

"It's beautiful here! Like a forgotten time capsule!" I gasped.

"Yes, it is! I thought so the first time I came here," Michael said. "Theron sent me here about five years ago to remove any weapons that remained on the island. Its beauty captivated me."

"I wish I had my camera," said James, "This place is like a forgotten world!"

"I still don't understand why Theron would abandon this island," I said.

"Kingston Plantation was intended as his personal residence and this island for training purposes. Theron has unlimited funds. He could have certainly rebuilt after the storm, but for some reason, he chose not to," Michael said.

"It is a shame that all of this has been sitting here untouched and abandoned," I said.

"Yes, it is. I will let the two of you stay in the main house; I will take one of the huts near the courtyard. She needs someone with her, and well, I suppose you would be the better choice," Michael said.

"I suppose I would!" James replied. I rolled my eyes, realizing that even with our lives at stake, these two were not going to get along.

"I don't need anyone to babysit me! Besides, we need a watch on both sides of the grounds. I will take one of the huts on the other side of the courtyard and James can stay in the house," I said.

"That's absurd!" James shook his head. "I will take the hut, and you take the house," he insisted.

"Alright. I really don't care where I stay," I replied. It did not matter to me. I was escaping this place to search for William as soon as I could get some rest.

"You look exhausted, Marguerite," Michael said. "James and I will round up something to eat while you try to get some sleep." I reluctantly agreed. A fire was out of the question and so was forging food from the sea. We would avoid anything that would draw attention to our location. I ate a granola bar from my backpack and went to the bungalow to catch some much-needed sleep. The master bedroom contained a whitewashed four-poster bed. I removed the dusty quilt to find the under linens adequate. Thick mosquito netting had kept the bed in remarkable condition. It was a strange feeling to know that I would be sleeping in the room once belonging to Theron, my grandfather. There was a nightstand beside the table with a large candelabra, a dresser, dressing table with wash pot and a nice-sized bathroom. The water did not work, but the bungalow would provide adequate shelter for the night. I would be leaving tomorrow.

I fumbled through some of the items in the room. The dresser contained some unusual clothing items. Theron had evidentially collected these pieces from all around the world. In the top drawer under the clothes was a book, *Wuthering Heights*. The title struck me as I knew it was my grandmother's favorite book. In the front of the book was an inscription:

~ To my dearest Sara,
May my love travel with You,
As You part the seven seas.
I love you, Sara.
Aaron

I flipped through the pages, and an old photograph fell out. I knew the young woman in the picture. It was my grandmother! Beside her was a man that was not Silas, it was Theron. Unexpectedly, my grandmother's story did not add up. She had convinced me that Theron had seduced her in Silas's absence. She had implied that Theron had tricked her, taken advantage of her, and left her for dead. The woman in the photograph looked very much in love and so did the man. My grandmother had lied to me about her feelings for Theron. I clutched the book against my chest and closed my eyes. There had been far more between my grandmother and Theron than she had revealed. Theron had taken my grandmother to this island. I couldn't shake the feeling that she also could be the reason that Theron did not return.

I tried to sleep; William's face was never from my thoughts. It had been less than a week since we parted, but it felt like months since his lips were pressed against mine. We had finally been reunited, and now he would receive word that I was dead. I was awakened four hours later by a gentle knock at the door. I wiped my eyes, readjusting to my surroundings. It was Michael's voice. He slowly opened the door. Michael entered carrying a bowl of fruit: cut up papayas, coconuts, bananas, and a variety of berries. "Are you alive in there?" he asked.

"I was wondering the same thing about you," I teased. "I'm surprised that you and James have not killed each other in my absence."

"Actually, you don't see him here with me, now do you?" He smiled.

"I hope you are joking," I said as I munched on a ripe piece of papaya. Michael rolled his eyes.

"I am. James is safe and sound pulling watch duty," he teased.

"Thank you for looking out for him. He is very special to me."

"Well, you are very special to me," Michael said. His tone had shifted, and his face softened. "I wish that I could tell you that I am sorry for kissing you the other day, but I am truly not sorry. In fact, I have hardly been able to think of anything else," he said. Michael leaned in closer and tucked a strand of hair behind my ear. His hand did not stop there as it moved to my jawline. He gently cupped the side of my face and pulled it to him.

"Michael don't …." My body froze in protest, but he was determined. In an instant, his lips were against mine, this time with more urgency than before. I pulled away. "What are you doing? You know how I feel about William!"

"But you need to know how I feel. You need to know that you have options," Michael said. His lips were on mine again. I tried to protest, but he sensation was divine. I felt dizzy and started to become lost in his embrace. Through the growing physical desire, I could only see one face—Williams. I pulled from him again, scrambling back towards the headboard. He used this to his advantage as he pressed me against the bed. His hard body came down upon mine, trapping me under his perfect frame. I realized that I would have to stop this soon or I would be unable to resist him.

"Michael, I can't!" I pushed him off me with all of my might, sending him soaring across the room. He hit the wall hard and fell to the ground. I jumped up; I was surprised by my own strength. "I am sorry, Michael! I forget how strong I am," I said standing over him.

He rubbed his head. "I forget how strong you are too—strong in more ways than one. He sighed and rubbed the back of his head. "It is I who am sorry, Marguerite," he admitted.

"You can't keep doing this, Michael!"

"But don't you see! They all think we are dead or they will very soon," he said. "We could take off! I know places that no one would ever find us. We could begin a life together!" I closed my eyes, fighting away any visions of what he was proposing.

"I can't! I have already started a life with someone else. It is impossible to forget all that William and I have shared, all that we have been through together! I can't erase my love for him!"

"And I cannot erase my feeling for you," Michael said. "I tried to." His expression softened. "You would have fallen in love with me too. I believe with all of my heart that you would have … if you had only met me first. Tell me that I am wrong!" I looked into his eyes, and I knew that he was right. I would have fallen in love with Michael.

"I don't think that you are. I do believe I would have fallen in love with you. I think it would have been impossible not to fall for you, but you are trying to rewrite the past …"

"No, I am trying to start a future—a future with you! I struggled fiercely, refusing to fall in love with you, but I will not lie to myself any longer. You are my weakness in a battle I will lose," he confessed boldly. "How could I ever silence a newly beating heart?"

"You will have to if you want to be in my life! Michael, you will have to stop this if you want to be my friend," I stated.

"I don't want to be your friend! There is no shortage of males floating around you, all accepting of your friendship. Well, I am not of that kind."

"A friendship is all that I can offer you. My heart is no longer mine to give away," I scolded. Michel's brow furrowed. He eyed me through the silence. I did not waver for I had weathered the storms within my heart and bore the scars to prove it.

"I comprehend your feelings, but I will forever be hoping for the day in which you will feel the same as I." He looked hard upon at me with his sparkling green eyes. I had developed feelings for Michael, deeper feelings than I had realized, but ultimately, my heart remained steadfast. I heard footsteps running through the bungalow. James burst through the door to see me standing over

Michael. He spied the indention in the wall made by Michael's body.

"Are you alright, darlin'?" James asked. I nodded. He looked down at Michael and smirked. "Perhaps it is Michael who deserves that question."

"I am fine," he muttered. "There is nothing hurt here but my pride." He stood and brushed himself off. James smiled.

"And here I thought we didn't have anything in common," James said. Michael smiled. Perhaps a kinship was forming between them after all. James offered Michael a hand. Michael extended his arm to accept. James retracted his hand and walked out of the room.

Perhaps I was wrong after all.

24

———

"I'll break and forge the stars anew,
Shatter the heavens with a song;
Immortal in my love for you,
Because I love you, very strong."

— Rupert Brooke, The Call

The late afternoon passed uneventfully. Michael slept while James and I explored the island. I was pleased to find it well equipped. The land was abundant with food, and there were several wells with clean drinking water. There were a number of the huts still intact and perfectly acceptable for sleeping quarters. It was eerie that such beautiful grounds had been abruptly left to decay. James would be fine here.

I became anxious as the day turned to nightfall. Barbour would have told the Legion that we were attacked; the information would have been passed on by now to Theron—and William. The thought of how such news would hurt him brought tears to my eyes. James began to sense my uneasiness. I would need to leave and soon!

"I have made a sweep of the area, and I can find no trace of Sironian or Obyascon," Michael said. "I do not think we were followed. Theron's forces should reach the Obyascon tomorrow, so searching for three of the dead should be low on the priority list. I think we are safe for now."

"Thank you, Michael. It is good to know that this side of the island is secure. I would feel more comfortable if you did a sweep of the other side as well," I said as believable as possible.

"If it would make you more comfortable, sure. I will go check the north side," he replied. Michael had been kind to me, but he had not tried to renew the sentiments that I had rejected.

"Oh, but it is dark," I said. "James, would you go with him? I'll be fine here. I am about to retire to my room for the night," I rambled. I was a poor liar, but the guys were too at odds with each other to notice.

"Are you serious, Marguerite?" Michael huffed. "Since when does a siren need a human for protection?"

"Yeah, he will be fine without me," James agreed. "I will stay here with you." James picked up a bowl of fruit and sat down next to me. Michael eyed the two of us together. I decided to use this to my advantage. I brushed his hand against mine and leaned into him as I reached for the bowl. It worked. A look of jealousy swept across Michael's face.

"On second thought, it may be a good idea for you to come with me, James. I want to venture out a bit tomorrow, and it would be good for you to have a working knowledge of the whole island." James groaned but stood to join him. I watched as they headed off through the dense foliage. I hurried back to my room and grabbed my backpack. It was already packed with my belongings; I tossed my grandmother's book into the sealed bag and quickly headed out towards the southern shoreline. I was on the verge of the rising tide when I heard James's voice behind me.

"You're going to leave, aren't you?" I turned to see James walking down the beach.

"I thought you were with Michael," I said.

"I was, but I came back. I know you too well. I guessed that you were trying to get rid of me from your little stunt earlier with Michael. I knew you wouldn't stay here," he said.

I would not lie to him. "Yes, I am leaving," I replied solemnly.

"And there is nothing that I can say to stop you?" James asked.

"No. There is not."

"So running away to this island was just a way to get me out of the way?"

"No. We would have been killed out there on the water. You will be safe here," I said.

"But you won't … you are going right back out there, aren't you?" I nodded. "Did it ever cross your mind, that as you are trying to save me, I am also trying to save you?" His words struck me hard.

"I have never thought of it that way," I whispered.

"From the very beginning, I knew … I knew you were headed for trouble. I had no idea what kind of trouble William would bring into your life, but I knew you were heading straight for it. Not only did I see myself losing you, I saw you losing yourself."

"This is who I was born to be!" I pleaded.

"That's shit, Margo, and you know it! You were amazing even before you were a siren. I could see it; hell, anyone around you could see it! You love him! I get that! Everyone gets it, Margo! But for once, did you ever stop to think about the other people in your life! What about your parents, your grandmother, Caleb … and

Lucy! Did you ever stop to think about how they will all feel when these monsters kill you—and they will kill you, Margo! It may not be today or even tomorrow, but eventually, this world will take you out of it."

"James, I …."

"The world fears what it doesn't understand, and no one understands you. Hell, I don't understand you! I don't understand how you can do this to the people you love! I don't understand how you can keep doing this to me!" James was finished, both physically and emotionally. He collapsed onto the sand, burying his face in his hands. I sat next to him and put my arms around him. He looked into my eyes, searching for a reassurance that I could not offer. His face shifted towards mine as he moved in closer. I tilted my jaw and kissed his forehead.

"I'm sorry," I said as my fingers released his cropped, copper curls. I didn't look back. I dashed down the moonlit beach and dove into the sea.

****

My fear of the ocean was gone. A great respect had replaced all of my trepidation, but it was still a humbling feeling to realize I was alone in the middle of the ocean. I was cautious at first, but the water was quiet, void of both Sironian and Obyascon. After the first mile, the sea transformed from a dark abyss. As if by magic, the water began to radiate a soft amber glow—bioluminescence. The unique color of the tiny algae microbes was a clear indication that we were indeed close to the island where Anna was held captive. I kept the course. Swift strokes carried me through the tropical waters. The ocean at night was far too beautiful to ignite fear. As two miles turned into three, I began to look for William's sailboat. There was no guarantee that it would still be intact or even if it would still be in the area. All hope began to fade as I passed the previous location.

Then it appeared. It looked like a ghost ship swaying in the moonlight. The sails were torn from the mast, billowing freely in the wind. The railing was ripped from its bolts, sending it dangling from the side. The door of the captain's quarters was torn from its hinges and hardly any of the finely crafted woodwork had been spared. I climbed aboard the dark ship. Blood had been splattered along the deck, giving the impression that all those aboard had perished. Barbour had done his job masterfully. The contents of the cabin were tossed around as if displaced in a heady fight. This boat had been William's heart for so long! I ached to see it torn and battered. I had hoped the boat would carry me to Anna … and to William. I would have to come up with a new plan. I crawled into the sleeping quarters, feeling ill. My body was exhausted, and my heart heavy. I closed my eyes and spent the next several hours trying to figure out the next step. I needed sleep. At last, when I could wrestle with my thoughts no longer, sleep came.

****

My eyes sprung open as I heard the floor whine beneath its weight. Something had boarded the vessel and was walking the deck outside of the cabin. Its steps were slow and calculated as it moved aboard the boat. My heart raced within my chest. I was cornered. I quickly surveyed the cabin space, trying to form a plan. Once it entered, there would hardly be room for a fight. I would be at its mercy. I would have to fight! Any movement would alert it to my presence. I decided to hide. Perhaps if it were an Obyascon, it would not see me and leave. I knew a siren's keen hearing would be alerted by my heartbeat as soon as it reached the cabin, if not already. I quietly scooted between the mattress and the cabin wall and pulled the covers over me. I waited, ready to pounce, ready to fight for my life. The steps neared the entrance to the cabin and stopped as its shadow seemed to survey the door. From the edge of the blanket, I spied its shadow, too small to be an Obyascon, but too hunched and slow to be siren.

As it entered the cabin, I realized I was wrong. It stopped in the doorway as it heard the beating sound of my heart. I could hardly believe my eyes. Even through the darkness, I could recognize William's form. Every ounce of my body shifted from terror to unimaginable joy.

"Marguerite? Can it be true?" His slumped body straightened as he peered into the cabin. "Marguerite … I hear your heart." William's eyes scanned the darkness. "Please, God, do not allow this to be a dream. Show me that my ears do not deceive me and that her heart is still beating!" I stood in the darkness, also afraid that I was in a dream.

"I am alive, William. Tell me that it is truly you!" I said as I pulled back the covers. The look upon his face as he saw me was one in which I would never forget. All the pain in his face morphed into utter joy.

Instantly, I was in William's arms. His lips crushed into mine with such intensity that my legs were unable to support me. I crumbled into his arms. His legs gave way, and we fell to our knees holding each other. "They told me you were dead—that the Obyascon had killed you," he moaned, his lips barely parting from mine to utter the words.

"I am not dead. I have never been more alive than I am at this very moment—in your arms."

"The thought of you, lifeless, sent me into a rage. Theron ordered me to stay with the Legion, but I was beyond reason, beyond what he could control. No one could stop me from coming to find you," William cried. He wept without tears. "I prayed for the entire twelve hours that it took me to get here. My prayers have been answered; by some miracle you are alive and in my arms." His lips moved across every inch of my face, then to my ear. His fingers softly stroked my jawline. There was so much that I needed to tell him, but I did not want him to stop. I never wanted him to stop. My lips caressed his neck, first softly, then with more urgency. His breath quickened with every touch. I wanted him in ways that I had never known. My hands gripped his chest as I pulled him towards me. His hands slid behind my neck and through my hair, guiding me gently across his body. William wanted me. He clung to me as if he needed proof that I was real. My lips moved from his neck to his chest stroking each part of him. His hands moved to my waist pulling me tighter against him. I gasped as his fingers stroked the small of my back. My response only fueled his passion. "I was a fool to let them separate us," he said looking deeply into my eyes. "I will never let that happen again," he vowed as his mouth devoured my stomach. Each touch sent waves of pleasure through me. I wanted William to experience the sensation I was feeling. I matched his passion with each new touch, each new kiss, and each motion. His body readily accepted my response. I wanted nothing more than to remain in his arms forever.

But the night turned to dawn, and with the rising sun came the bitter reality before us. I pulled the covers up over us. William's eyes were closed. His head rested peacefully on my chest. It was a rare opportunity to get to watch William sleep during the night. I ran my fingers through his thick hair. He sighed, "Don't move. Let's stay here forever."

"Alright," I muttered, with the full realization that I had uttered a lie. Our friends would soon go to battle without us. We both knew what we had to do. We would not hide away while our friends stood on the battlefield. There was a young girl waiting for me. I had promised her that I would return. I would keep that promise. William wanted me to return to the island with James but also understood the danger of leaving me. We were stronger together.

"We must move soon if we are going to find the girl before the Legion attacks," William said. William knew of Theron's plan to move in at dusk. We decided to try to get in around the Obyascon and locate Anna before the Legion moved in. William and I would make as many repairs to the boat as possible and leave it until we were able to return. We had just gotten out of the bed when we heard it. Something had boarded the boat. We braced, ready to attack. I spied my backpack; the long end of the dousie bow protruded out of the top. The boards creaked as it moved closer to us just as it reached the cabin. In one swift motion, I dove towards my backpack and ripped out the bow. I tossed it to William who had it aimed at the cabin door before the intruder could enter. I tore out the harpoon and aimed it as the creature rounded the corner. I fired just as it entered. In a blur, I saw Michael dive to the side, the harpoon narrowly missing his chest. The spear plunged deep into the cabin wall.

"Easy! Wait a minute!" he protested. "It is me, Marguerite! Don't shoot!"

"Michael!" I exclaimed in relief. "What are you doing here?"

"You did not expect me to let you sneak off without coming to find you?" he boasted.

"I had hoped you would stay with James. I should have known that was too much to ask," I teased.

"James is a big boy; he will be fine there by himself," Michael grinned. "You, on the other hand, are constantly looking for trouble," Michael said. William eyed us both carefully.

"Look who's talking! You should have stayed on the island, Michael!" I said. William grew tense as he listened to our banter.

William relaxed his stance a bit but did not lower the bow. "Easy there, William. Don't you think you should put that thing away?"

"I have not decided yet," he said as his eyes narrowed.

"What is that supposed to mean?" Michael replied.

"Only that it is dangerous business making moves on my girl—especially when you are already presumed to be dead."

"William, stop teasing around!" I pleaded

"Who said that I am teasing?" William replied.

"For the record, we are still technically engaged," Michael shrugged. William raised his eyebrows and pulled back the arrow.

"She has been engaged to me for many months now, and you know it!" William hissed.

"Then why did she kiss me back?" Michael grinned.

"You kissed him!" William roared.

"No!" I huffed. "He kissed *me*! I threw him through the wall!"

"That is true and quite unnecessary," Michael teased. William growled. Michael walked out to the deck of the boat. William lowered the bow and followed.

"Leave my girl alone!" William hissed. I had never seen William this way. This jealous side of William was new and insanely hot.

"Perhaps she wanted me to kiss her?" Michael grinned. "Especially when James interrupted the first time ..."

"First time?" William did not wait for further details. He dropped the bow and landed a punch swiftly on Michael's jaw. Michael slid across the deck but was quickly on his feet and ready for the fight."

"Stop this!" I yelled, but neither guy paid me any heed. Michael took the next punch. William ducked, but he undercut, knocking William firmly in the stomach. William retaliated with an uppercut to Michael's jaw. I shrieked for them to stop. Then, something out on the water caught my eye. I shrieked for another reason. The water around our boat became saturated with blood. I peered overboard in horror as a wide current of blood was flowing in our direction. Through the scuffle, William saw my face. He dropped the skirmish and hurried to my side. Michael realized the alarm and joined us at the starboard. "Where do you think this is coming from?" I gasped.

"I am not sure," William muttered.

"A whale?" I asked.

"There is far too much blood in the water," he replied. Michael inhaled deeply. His expression darkened.

"This is Sironian blood. Something has happened," Michael responded.

"Perhaps the Legion attacked early?" I said.

"I do not think so," Michael replied solemnly. The current carried small pieces of debris. Michael picked up the bow and dipped it into the water to retrieve something in the debris. He recovered the end of a wooden spear carrying a medallion. We recognized it immediately as the one worn by Barbour.

"This belonged to Barbour. The Obyascon must have attacked his sect before the Legion was in position," Michael said.

"I fear the outcome of the encounter ended poorly for the Sironian," William said.

"This is awful!" I exclaimed. A single tear rolled down my face as I thought of Barbour's sacrifice. He had saved us. My heart swelled with guilt. Perhaps the outcome would have been different had we been there to fight. "Perhaps there are survivors?"

"It is possible," Michael said. "I will leave shortly and follow the current. The presumed location of the Obyascon was just three or four miles from here."

"I'll go with you!" I exclaimed.

"Perhaps you should let Michael and I go first to scope out the situation," William said.

"I'm going, William! End of discussion!" His jaw tightened.

"Fine. We will all go," William said as he swiftly went below deck. He reemerged with our backpacks and the few weapons in our arsenal.

"Time to head out!" said Michael as he disappeared into the bloodstained current. I winced at the thought of being submerged in the remnants of death. William saw the look on my face.

"Are you sure you are up to this?" he asked.

"Yes. I can do this, William," I replied as I repelled off the side to join Michael. William's brow furrowed. He took one last look over the horizon and then another at his boat before diving into the crimson water.

25

"Only the dead have seen the end of war."

Plato

It was all that we had feared and more. There were no survivors among Barbour's sect of warriors. The Obyascon had killed every siren. The bodies of these brave creatures were strewn on the ocean floor. Among the carnage, in almost equal number, were the remnants of many Obyascon. I felt sick. My head began to spin, and my hands began to shake, but I needed to be strong. I was a warrior on a new sort of battlefield. There was not the time for weak stomachs or childlike expectations. War was hideous, and I had just had my first real taste of the dreadful.

"Dear God! What should we do, William? Should we retrieve the bodies?" I said as unemotional as possible.

"No. We do not gather our dead. Unlike in the death of a human body, when we die our bodies sink to the ocean floor and decompose rapidly. In just a few days, this area will look just as it did before. Even our bones are created to absorb into the natural elements quickly. It is our way, how we were designed, to keep our oceans healthy, and as a way of concealment from the humans." My brow furrowed. He knew what I was thinking before I had the opportunity to say it.

"I wonder if I …."

"I pray that we will never find out," he quickly responded.

Michael swiftly scanned the area for any sign of Obyascon. The zone was entirely devoid of life. "The number of dead here only make up a small percentile of their population," Michael said.

"What does that mean?" I asked.

"What it means," replied William "is that Theron may have lessened their numbers, but things are not going according to his plan. The Obyascon are ready to fight."

"They anticipated us, attacked first, and have most likely regrouped. The Obyascon are expecting the battle that is to come," Michael explained.

"Michael, do you think you could get to the Legion to alert them of what has transpired?"

"I fear my presence would not be a welcomed one, considering that Theron ordered me dead."

"Then go to Silas. He will listen to you. You should be safe among the Protectors. Theron's forces should be assembling about five miles north of the island. If you can make it there before dusk, then perhaps we can prevent another massacre."

"I'll leave immediately," he said. Michael looked at me tenderly, one last time, before diving down into the abyss. William's jaw tightened, and he looked away.

"William, I …." I wanted to explain.

"There is nothing to say." William took my hand, and we traveled underwater another half mile through the swift current. As we surfaced, I saw a series of small islands around us.

"Do you remember where you were held captive? Perhaps my sister was returned to those caverns," William said.

"Yes," I scanned the islands and easily located it. "It's that one! There is an entrance to the caverns on the south side of the beach, but it is most likely heavily guarded. There is another entrance by sea," I said. "I think that if we can get close enough, I could locate the tunnel." We swam up closer, fully expecting the area to be swarming with Obyascon. There were none. We traveled further down the eastern side of the island, checking each rocky porthole for an entrance. Nothing led to the caverns. "Something isn't right. She must not be here. If she were, there would be more guards, more protection. There is nothing here."

"No, she's here," William said. "I don't know how to describe it, other than, I just know. It is a feeling that I have. I can sense that she is close."

"You feel her?" I asked, trying to grasp their deep connection.

"Yes. I have never experienced this before, but I know my sister is here. I can feel it! We only have to find the way inside!" We didn't have to look much further. The Obyascon guarding the porthole was an indication that we had found the way inside. He saw us about the same time that we saw him. We braced for a fight, fully expecting the Obyascon to attack. Instead, it disappeared into the porthole. We waited for a moment for the creature to return. He did not. We surfaced.

"Do you think this is a trap?" I asked.

"I don't know. It is quite strange that the creature did not attempt to fight."

"Perhaps he knew he was outnumbered and chose to run," I said.

"No. I don't think so," William said. The creature looked as if it were expecting us. He wants us to follow him. Why else would he so blatantly show us the entrance to the cavern?"

"Then we should follow him!" I exclaimed.

"I will not leave you behind, but we could be walking into a trap." William wore a heavy veil of trepidation. I tried to hide my nervousness; it was the only gift I could offer.

"Then we walk in together. I won't leave you, William," I whispered. He nodded and took my hand as we dove deep beneath the rocky surf. The tide was relentless as we reached the water's edge. The pounding of the surf against the rocky terrain made visibility nearly impossible. I began to panic as I got lost among the stones of the fortress. William found me. He guided me between the rocks and through the underwater tunnel leading to the caverns. We made our way through the labyrinth, at last reaching the caverns. As we surfaced, the Obyascon was waiting. We prepared to fight. The shape-shifter transformed before our eyes into human form. It was Brooks. I was surprised to see him alive. Scamp had not killed him after all, though she had left a large scar on his forehead and his left arm was missing.

"I'm not going to fight you or your friend, Marguerite. We both know that I would lose. Moxley and Bratton were far superior warriors and, as they never returned, I am assuming you took care of them?"

"They were going to kill me," I uttered.

"Well, it is no matter. Merissa did not like them anyway," Brooks responded flatly.

"Merissa?" William asked defensively.

"I am assuming that you are the allusive William Avery," Brooks asked.

"I am, but I have no idea who you are," William hissed.

"I am of no importance," Brooks replied, "Merissa has been waiting for you for weeks now; let us not keep her waiting any longer." We followed in silence as he led us through the dark caverns. Things grew familiar as we passed the chambers in which I had stayed. As we reached the end of the tunnel, Brooks opened a secret passage that led down a dimly lit stairwell. At the base of the stairwell was a set of large doors. Brooks knocked gently on the door.

"You may bring them in," Merissa replied in a low assertive tone. Brooks opened the doors that led to the massive chamber. Merissa was sitting on a long, dark blue velvet couch. She arose as we entered. A young girl was seated next to her. It was Anna. She was wearing an eye mask that covered both of her eyes. I was relieved that they had not resealed them. William was focused on the girl. The longing in his face brought tears to my eyes; he was seeing his sister for the first time since she was a baby. I turned to Merissa, who had a similar look on her face. She gazed upon William with the same intensity as he gazed upon his sister. I was the first to speak.

"You have been waiting on us," I uttered.

"I have indeed," Merissa said, "I am surprised that it took you so long to return."

"Your men tried to kill me," I said.

"How fortunate that they did not succeed! It appears you took care of them. Had I known their plans I would have killed them myself," Merissa smoothly replied.

"You let me go because you knew that I would return with William?" I speculated.

"I did," Merissa replied.

"Because you have my sister," William spoke for the first time.

"What?" Anna uttered. "Is this true? I have a brother?"

"Yes," Merissa said emotionless.

"Do my ears deceive me? I have a real brother! I do! I can feel him here!" Anna's words swelled with emotion.

"Yes. I have come for you," William said, taking a step towards Anna. He gently took off her mask. His hand slid from her head to her jaw as he cupped her delicate features in his hand. The girl slowly opened her eyes and stared into the matching pair that belonged to her brother. Anna could speak no further as she was overcome with emotion. Merissa took a step towards them." He growled at her and took his sister's hand in his as he led her from the couch.

"Do not assume that I am the villain," Merissa said. "I would not have called you here if I did not plan on safely delivering the girl to you."

"As I recall, you did not call us here at all. We came on our own," William hissed.

"Yes, well … I was aware that if I let Marguerite go, that you would return with her," Merissa said.

"I would like to take my sister and leave peacefully," he growled.

"Are you not at all curious as to why you are here? Why I would relocate an entire race of beings?" Merissa asked wryly. "Why would I hold a girl for her entire life, only to now turn her over to you?"

"I only want my sister," William hissed. "The rest is between you and Theron." Her face twisted at the mention of Theron.

"You say that, and yet, you joined forces with the one who killed your family? You now take orders from the one who stole your life?" Merissa jeered.

"I will never take orders from Theron! Your forces killed my friend, Henry, and stole my girl. I joined Theron as he was my only hope for retrieving her."

"It is unfortunate about your friend. The Obyascon who killed him and injured Marguerite acted on their own and against my orders. Contrary to what you may believe, they are a peaceful race who prefer the Arctic due to its solitude. My warriors are instructed only to kill as a means of defense," Merissa explained.

"They killed today! A whole sect of Sironian," I hissed.

"The sirens came to attack us—your Legion attacked first. Many lives were uselessly lost today on both sides," Merissa coolly replied.

"A whole sect of Sironian was killed," I replied.

"Yes, and now more lives will be lost due to Theron's quest for power. I am aware of the army waiting to attack but am surprised to find that you are a part of it, William."

"You know nothing of me!" he scoffed.

"I know everything about you. I have watched over you since infancy," Merissa said. "It was no coincidence that my watchmen were in the water the day your parents were killed. Madeline, whom we have called Anna, was not kidnapped; she was rescued. My watchmen would have rescued you that day also, but I had other plans for you. Have you never wondered why you were spared that day? We knew you were special—even then. My forces fought off the sirens for days until I was able to reach Silas. I knew you would be safe with him. Theron has sought you ever since. He has not taken you by force because my Obyascon would retaliate." William shook his head in disbelief.

"How can all of this be true?" he cried. "Theron feared Silas and the Crew would challenge him for power?" he protested.

"Think about it, William. Would Theron only fear Silas and a few partially skilled Protectors? Most of the creatures of the ocean bow to his command. You have been misled," Merissa said. "I am the only leader with an army large enough to challenge Theron. Though we may not be able to beat his forces, we would decimate his numbers in such a way that the other vigilante groups could step in and challenge him for power." William shook his head as he struggled to process Merissa's narrative.

"All of this time, you were watching me?" he asked.

"Yes, and the girl," Merissa responded. "When I learned of the hybrid, I knew Theron would use her, just as he had used me. We intercepted her that night at the jetties before Theron could take her. I did not know of your romantic connection to the hybrid. It was not until I spied the ring around her neck that I realized that the girl was betrothed to you."

"Of what significance was the ring?" he asked.

"It belonged to me, long before it was gifted to your mother," Merissa stated.

"All of this seems impossible," he muttered in disbelief.

"There is much that you do not know," Merissa said. "On the night that the hurricane hit your coastland, Theron's Legion was planning to kill the Protectors. He intended to obliterate you and your friends. We learned of his plan and filled your waters with our defense. Theron learned of our presence and thus chose to retreat." My mouth slipped open at the revelation.

"All under the pretense of a treaty with me?' I asked.

"Yes. Theron does not negotiate, especially with human half-breeds." She laughed at the notion. "No, he learned of our numbers and thought it wise to find another way out of the situation." I could not believe it myself, but on some level, it made perfect sense.

"I suppose I should thank you," I responded.

"You don't need to thank me. I equally fear the notion of sirens and humans intermixing. I spared you because of your connection to William."

"What I do not understand is, why—why me? Why have you watched over me, and what is my connection to you and the Obyascon?" William asked. Merissa inhaled deeply and looked downward for a moment before she spoke.

"I suppose I should start from the beginning," Merissa sighed. "Theron is responsible for destroying my life. You see, my husband, Bain, was once a member of Theron's Legion. He was unhappy with Theron's abuse of power, and so petitioned, and was granted a small sect of Protectors near the polar region. My husband, Bain, was well esteemed, and our group considered him their leader. We lived quietly and peacefully, but in truth, we had begun to question the laws enforced by Theron's regime. Bain began to permit our sect to marry for love. We began concealing the offspring of the new families to keep them from being separated. As our numbers started to grow, we understood that Theron would feel threatened. Bain knew that Theron would attack to weaken our forces, and so he gained the trust of the Obyascon. His Legion had decimated their numbers for centuries, labeling the Obyascon as mutants. Bain sought out the remaining Obyascon, merging them with our forces for defense. The Legion viewed this as an act of treason and immediately attacked. We were strong, but our numbers paled to theirs. The battle was short, but the loss was immense as almost all of our people were slaughtered. Many of the Obyascon escaped, but our sirens were not so fortunate. Only I and a handful of others eluded the bloodbath. The Legion rounded up their children, dividing them among Theron's sects. As most were unusually gifted, it is rumored that they are now the very ones holding the positions of power in his Legion," Merissa said.

"You are saying that the sirens that I met at Kingston are the very children stolen from the Protectors?" I gasped.

"I do believe so. Though these Sironian now lead other sects, they would have to have been born into the Protector line to be capable of land dwelling." It all began to make sense, and yet, there were still so many unanswered questions. Of course Theron would surround himself with sirens whose parents had once been a threat! He kept those capable of rising against him under his thumb. Theron collected them and brainwashed them under his law. Now he sought to collect William, the Crew and myself for that very reason. If we took a stand against him, he would destroy us just as he had done to Bain's Protectors. A shiver swept through my body. We would never submit. We will also perish.

"And you, Merissa? How was your life spared?" I asked, both out of curiosity and in search of any glimmer of hope.

"I was badly injured in the attack, extending all of my efforts to save the life of our young son. I watched in horror as Theron's final act was to behead my husband. I expected my life to be taken as well, but he imprisoned me, separating me from my son. I begged for death, to relieve me of the suffering of my loss, but Theron had other plans. Our sect had secured an alliance in which he now wanted. Though he had once sought to destroy the Obyascon, he now saw the advantage of such an association. As they had sworn an alliance to Bain, Theron hoped a union between us would accomplish the same task. With Bain's death, he assumed the Obyascon now regarded me as their queen. I, of course, refused to marry him, and he denied me the salt water and minerals that I needed to heal from the battle. I was on my deathbed when a young Obyascon shapeshifter came to my rescue. He was implanted into

Theron's regime as a spy. He was one of the very few known Obyascon capable of land dwelling. Theron was unaware that any Obyascon were capable of this and so Brooks was able to move among his Legion without alarm."

"Brooks was the Obyascon that rescued you?" I asked.

"He was. Brooks cared for me in secret, supplying me with the essentials needed to heal. Once I had regained my strength, we escaped in secret to search for my son. He was nowhere to be found. I knew that if I were to have any chance of locating him, I would need reinforcements. Brooks and I rejoined the Obyascon who were in hiding. Theron was correct in that they did regard me as their queen. It took many years, but I did discover my son. Theron had placed him under the care of a siren named Silas. I watched him in secret for many months. I discovered that this Silas was very much unlike Theron. Silas had become the father that was taken from my son. I realized that Silas was universally good and that he had grown to love my son very much. With a heavy heart, I chose to leave my son, Robert, under Silas's care and guidance. I knew that if I removed him, Theron would not cease until he had killed us both. Leaving him was the hardest thing I would ever do, and so, I watched him through the years from a distance. I saw him grow in strength, and in knowledge, and in love. I knew once he escaped from Theron's Legion with his bride, that Theron would seek him out and destroy his family, but I also knew that he was the son of Bain and would lead with his heart despite the outcome. When my worst fears came to pass and I could not save him or his bride, my Obyascon intercepted his infant daughter and fiercely guarded my young grandson until Silas could rescue him. Silas took the boy in and convinced Theron to allow him to raise him, just as he had done with his father," Merissa concluded. We were all emotionally drained from her story, and yet, we knew that she spoke the truth.

"But you kept my sister from me!" William cried. Tears streamed down Ann's face as she heard the emotion in William's voice.

"Yes. I had no choice, William. I kept your sister under my care with Brooks safeguarding her.

"But you kept her locked away! You had no contact with the girl!" he cried.

"I had no choice!" Merissa replied defensively. "The only one I could trust was Brooks. At any point, one of the Obyascon could be captured by Theron and her whereabouts discovered. The only way to keep him from discovering the girl was to keep her hidden away from everyone—including myself."

"But why would you deny your own granddaughter from knowing you?" I asked.

"I was always there watching over her. I have dedicated my life to safeguarding her, but she could not know me. I had hoped to one day reunite her with her brother. The hope of her living a normal life, a life free of Obyascon and Sironian, a life free of monsters and fantasy, far surpassed any selfish desire I might have had for her to know me … for her to love me," Merissa said.

"You sealed her eyes! You made her think she could not see!" William hissed.

"This is true," Merissa replied. "The child had not long been in my care before I discovered her extraordinary abilities. The only way to conceal her was to also conceal her gifts. I had planned to reveal them to her when she was ready."

"Or more so when you felt that the world was ready for her," William said.

"Yes, I am not evil. I have been forced to live at a distance from those that I love. Theron may have killed my son, but I have done everything in my power to protect his children," Merissa cried.

"You are my grandmother," William gasp in disbelief.

"Yes, you are my only grandson and my successor. You will soon be the rightful ruler of the Obyascon," Merissa said reverently.

"This is all impossible!" William buried his face in his hands.

"And yet, in your heart, you know that it is all true," Merissa said. I wanted to run to him and hold him.

"But there is one question that remains—why pull your people from the safety of the polar region to these isles?" I asked.

"For William. I relocated the colony for my grandson," she said. She addressed William again, "William, you are to be their future king. I do not wish for you to live as I have lived—cold and in solitude. I chose a tropical region that was remote and beautiful in hopes that you would take my place as ruler of the Obyascon." He looked into her eyes—eyes that were undeniably his own.

"But why now?" William uttered in disbelief. "Why have you ...."

"Because I am dying, William. I have a very short time left to live. My illness is terminal and without a cure," Merissa said. He shook his head again as if he were in pain.

"What do you want from me?" he asked.

"I want you to be the leader you were born to be. You have trained with the very best! You have been taught skill, patience, compassion, and now, you have learned to love. I waited for this time to arrive. You are ready to take my place as ruler of the Obyascon," she said.

I suddenly saw a change in William. He became what she knew he could be. A beacon of light radiated from him that shouted, "I am a warrior!"

"Had I known you would allow me to walk through these doors, had I known any of this, I would never have approached Theron!" William said. "How do we stop him? It is almost dusk! We only have a short time to stop what is about to transpire."

"You must decide," Merissa said. "Your first act as the Obyascon Prince—to save them. Save your Obyascon!" He turned and looked at Anna.

"The blindfold was only to protect her until she can harness her abilities. She is my own blood, William. I would never harm her. She will be safe here until you return," Merissa said.

"Go save them, William," the girl responded.

"Wait!" Merissa exclaimed, "You will need this." She removed a large medallion from around her neck and placed it around William's. She embraced him. William took my hand, and as we dashed up the stairs, Brooks was two steps behind us as we hurried from corridor to corridor. The labyrinth of tunnels twisted beneath the island like a maze.

"Which way to the north side?" William shouted to Brooks.

"There is a shortcut down this passage, sire," Brooks replied.

"Sire? Why do you call me that?" William asked.

"The medallion. You were just anointed as the Obyascon Prince," Brooks replied.

****

The passage led to another lengthy stairwell. The steps ascended through the interior of the island, until at last, the stairway opened out onto a high cliff. From the cliff top, we were able to see the gravity of the situation. Theron's Legion was poised for a battle. Theron stood stationed atop a large section of rocks with his most powerful Legion forces surrounding him. I was pleased to see Michael safely with Silas' sect. I filled with joy to see him next to

Mace. However, I was confused as to why Silas and the Protectors were among the numbers. Surely they were not going to fight with Theron?

As speculated, the Obyascon were prepared for the invasion. The creatures were scattered around the area as sharks surrounding a whale carcass. Theron had thought their numbers to be in the hundreds, but the creatures before us hovered beneath the water in the thousands. We realized, in horror, that we were too late. As Theron sent out the call to attack, his forces moved in without the realization that a massive number of Obyascon had been positioned to engage from behind. Theron was unaware that his entire army was surrounded. I felt my heart pounding in my chest because among those surrounded were my most beloved friends—the Crew.

"What do we do?" I shouted to William as the battle ensued. "What is Theron thinking?"

"He must not be aware of their numbers, or he would have never ignited this invasion," he replied.

"He is counting on the skill of Silas's crew, but will they fight?" I asked.

"We've got to end this before more blood is shed," William shouted.

"Dive down below the conflict. We must get to Theron to stop this!" I gasped and took one last deep breath.

William took my hand and together we dove from atop the cliff deep into the water below. The sea was becoming thick with the blood of war. I lost sight of William as an Obyascon attacked me from behind, sinking its claws deep into my leg before becoming lost in the fray. I shrieked in pain as another Obyascon caught hold of my foot, just as in my dreams. Through the turmoil, William appeared. With one swift kick, the Obyascon spun away and William pulled me through the churning battle. As we reached the rocks, Isaac spied us and moved to attack. "Isaac, I only want to speak to Theron," William said.

"You are a traitor and lover of the hybrid girl. Our orders are to kill you and the girl on sight!"

"Yes, well, that is not going to happen today," William said with a lightning fast kick to Isaac's jaw. Isaac landed hard on the rocks, nearly plunging into the blood-stained waters below. Isaac quickly gathered himself and sprang from the water's edge with a blood-curling yell. As William moved to intercept him, I felt several of my ribs splinter as Georgiana attacked me from behind. As she drove her arms into my body, my muscles screamed as if hot knives were tearing through my sides. Each blow felt as if it would knock the life from my body, but I refused to yield knowing that William stood beside me. I swung my clinched fist around through the haze of pain and anger and felt the blow sink into the center of her chest. As her sternum caved under the power of the blow, I watched her fall floundering into the rocks.

Before I could recover from Georgiana's attack, I felt Anastasia grab me from behind and hurl me through the air. Using the momentum of the throw, I skillfully twisted and landed hunched upon the rocks like a tiger ready to strike. From the corner of my eye, I spied the crew and Silas standing like rocks against a crashing tide of Obyascon. The masses of Obyascon falling upon them only to break apart under the unyielding strength of the Crew. I knew that their numbers would only increase. "Try not to kill them!" I desperately shouted to the group.

"And how are we supposed to do that?" Kirby responded.

"Do whatever you need to do, but these creatures aren't the monsters!" I replied.

"They sure look like monsters to me!" Toby said, "I think I'm having Obyascon soup tonight!" He effortlessly tossed one of the creatures from the water.

"Look! You have to trust me on this!" I shouted. "Just don't kill them, okay! It will all make sense soon!" The words had not escaped my mouth when I took a hard blow to the side; I fell to the ground in pain. I turned to see Silas upon the rocks effortlessly intercepting strikes from a large Obyascon. His arms moved in a blur redirecting the brute's powerful blows to harmlessly flail around him. I had never seen Silas in combat. I was in awe of how smoothly he executed each move like a carefully choreographed dance. His body a synchronized blend of power and grace. I frantically looked for William. Turning I could see he had taken out Theron's nearby forces and was heading for Theron himself.

As Theron attacked William, Kirby sprang to his defense.

"Oh, hell no! If you mess with our brother, you mess with us all," Kirby said.

"Their numbers are too great, Theron! They are coming in by the thousands from behind," William shouted.

"You are lying!" Theron said as he rammed the shaft of his spear toward William. William twisted his body to the side and struck out with his forearm deftly deflecting the blow.

"You killed my family but have never been able to kill me!" William hissed.

"A misfortune I shall now rectify!" Theron replied. Theron thrust his spear again towards William, this time with its razor sharp point aimed directly at his heart. William once more tried to shift and deflect the weapon, but this time he was not fast enough and the spear dug deep into William's shoulder. William took hold of the shaft and ripped the spear from Theron's grasp, grimly staring at Theron as he pulled it from his shoulder.

"I have not come to fight you. I am only trying to warn you that the bloodshed you are causing is without merit. Merissa has only come to hand over her regime, not to challenge yours!" William growled.

"To the new Prince?" Theron spat. "Are you speaking of yourself?" His eyes narrowed as he spied the medallion around William's neck.

"You have known all along! Have you not? That I am a descendant to the Obyascon throne?" William roared.

"Of course I have known! A ruler keeps close ties on their enemies," Theron huffed.

"I am not, nor have I ever been, your enemy! You have done everything in your power to separate Marguerite and me. You knew this day would come and feared our union would give greater power to the Obyascon," William hissed.

"Any hybrid form is an abomination! Such breeding could wipe out our existence!" Theron replied.

"Your only concern is your own power, which you are destroying this very second," William said. Silas joined William.

"The boy speaks the truth, Theron. If you choose not to call off this madness, you will lose," Silas said as he neared us. "We now know the true intentions of the Obyascon; My Protectors will no longer fight with your army."

There was a loud conch bellow from above, claiming the attention of everyone in the area. High above the water on the cliff top stood the once-beautiful Merissa. Combat ceased as she commanded the attention of the seas. "Enough of this, Theron!" she commanded.

"Ah, my dear, Merissa! The years have been kind to you," Theron said.

"I still wear the scars that you bestowed," Merissa hailed.

"I find you more lovely than ever," Theron valiantly proclaimed.

"Those are not the only scars I carry with me," she hissed.

"Perhaps time does not heal all wounds," he said.

"It does not." Merissa jeered. "Why have you come to attack us, Theron? I do not wish to overthrow your authority."

"No, you are too smart for that, Merissa. You have chosen your grandson for the job—the new Obyascon Prince," there were gasps from all as Theron motioned to my William.

"I have not come to challenge you, Theron; I only want peace," William replied.

"Peace? Did you not incite this war? I do believe it was you, William, who came to me demanding action for the infiltration of the Obyascon. Do you deny it?" Theron asked.

"I do not. That was before I knew the truth, Theron. I was wrong to incite war against this race. They mean no harm to siren or human. Let us have no more bloodshed today," William said. Theron looked out over the crimson waters. His numbers were still plentiful but so were the vast amount of Obyascon that stretched as far as the eye could see.

Zander emerged and shouted, "We shall have no Obyascon Prince!" Lightning emerged from his fingertips; the blow was diverted by the new amulet around William's neck, striking Merissa in the chest. Shrieks and screams erupted as the queen fell dead to the rocks below. William shouted and lunged for Zander, who had retrieved Theron's spear. In one swift motion, Zander lunged for William's neck. His body a blur as it uncoiled to land the fatal blow. Out of the chaos, Michael hurdled in front of William to take the blow. The spear pierced into Michael's skull, slicing through the socket of his right eye. I screamed and fell sobbing to my knees, as a part of my heart fell from the rocks and into the bloodstained abyss. Michael was gone.

Mace erupted into motion. His raw anger fueling his body as he grasped Zander's frame. In one swift motion, Mace slashed Zander's head from his body. Mace fell to the ground, overcome by grief and wailing at the death of his brother. Zander's lifeless body fell from his grasp. Kirby and Toby protectively stood over him, ready to defend their brother against anyone who dare rise against him. The remaining members of Theron's Legion coiled, preparing to attack the Crew.

Silas stepped between the Crew and the Legion. "Enough!" Silas shouted, halting the violence. "Are you now to fight among yourselves? Have we become no more civilized than animals? We were created by God as the Protectors of the sea, not as conquerors!" Theron seized his bloodstained staff and positioned its tip in the direction of my heart. My friends gasped; all were afraid to move with the knowledge that at any moment Theron could take my life. A single tear ran down my face. My eyes met William's. He was ready to pounce, his eyes darting from Theron and back to me. His heart pounded as he gauged the situation, anticipating his next response.

"We were created by God; this half-breed was not. Against my better judgment, I permitted the hybrid to live. I will not make this mistake again. Any Sironian who creates or harbors a hybrid shall be put to death. It is time to put an end to this!" Theron proclaimed. Theron raised his spear. His grip tightened as he aimed for my heart. I closed my eyes. I would die with Michael, but perhaps my William might live. Silas's voice broke my eulogy.

"Then I fear you should be the first to be sentenced for the crime," Silas grimly called. My eyes opened. Theron's expression changed, but he did not loosen his grip on the spear. Theron appeared stunned by the accusation.

"Are you mad, Silas? Are you aware of the punishment for such false accusations? To accuse me of such is treason! I have created no half-breed!" Theron protested.

"I have been studying the girl for quite some time now. There is only one bloodline capable of creating a half-breed, the one that is a direct descendant from the first known siren—your blood, Theron," Silas said.

"What are you saying, Silas? What are you accusing me of?" Theron protested.

"I am astonished that you would not recognize your own flesh and blood—such power—such beauty. You have assumed all of these years that the girl was my descendant," Silas replied.

"Silas, do you deny that you had a relationship with a human? I know of no other Sironian strong enough to have facilitated this bloodline! You deny that the girl is of your blood?" Theron scoffed. Silas sighed.

"There is nothing in the world that would have given me more pleasure, but she is not. Marguerite is your granddaughter, Theron," Silas said.

"Impossible!" Theron exclaimed.

"Look at her hand, Theron! The ring that she wears was once gifted to a young woman that we both loved—it was gifted to her by you." He motioned to the band that my grandmother had given to me on my birthday. I was unaware that the ring she had given me was a gift to her from Theron. It all began to make sense. She had gifted me the ring for this very purpose. She had given it to me to protect me from Theron.

"The woman in which you speak of is dead. I held her lifeless body in my arms," Theron gasped.

"But the child within her lived. Its spirit was so strong that it reignited a lifeless heart. The woman lived and gave birth to your child, Theron—a son. The gene remained dormant within the boy, allowing him to live as a human. He grew into a man but passed the Sironian gene to his daughter. The gene awakened within the girl, transforming her into the siren you see before you. Though a half-breed, she is incapable of living as a human. The siren standing before you is your granddaughter and rightful heir to the Sironian throne," Silas explained.

The spear fell to his side as he spied the small dinner ring on my hand. Theron looked at me, studied my features and saw the truth. The ruler of the ocean was without words. He turned and motioned for his Legion to depart. Theron looked hard at me one last time before diving into the deep abyss. The remaining members of his Legion followed, each taking their sect of Sironian with them. Within a few moments, all that remained was the Crew and the Obyascon. There was confusion among the race, as they tried to make sense of what had just happened.

"What do I do?" William whispered to Silas as he looked out over the creatures. The masses began to congregate around him for guidance. The remaining Obyascon bowed before their new prince.

"You are their leader now," Silas softly replied. "You know what to do. I have always known that this day would come. I have done my best to prepare you for it. It is your turn now."

"But how do you know I'm ready?" William asked. Silas smiled.

"William, you have been ready for some time now," he responded. William turned to me.

"Marguerite, will you go and retrieve my sister?" William asked gently.

"Yes," I said in almost a whisper.

"Take her to the island with James. I will join you when I can," he said. I nodded. I was unable to speak due to the lump in my throat. We would be apart again.

"Silas, will you go with her? Kirby, Toby, will you watch over my girls until I can arrive," William asked.

"Of course, Will," Kirby replied as Toby took my hand. I turned back to William who was staring at me as if his heart had been ripped apart. I ran to him, our lips joining us together as our souls became one. His fingers laced into mine as our bodies intertwined in a clinging embrace. At last, we parted.

"I will return to you … I promise," he vowed as our fingers slowly slipped apart.

26

———

"It's a thing to see when a boy comes home."

~John Steinbeck, Grapes of Wrath

"**A**re you alright, Anna?" I asked. The girl was sitting alone looking out over the water. It was rare for Anna to be alone these days. All of the Crew were quite taken with her charms—especially James. I sat on the dune next to her. Her brow furrowed as if she were deep in thought. "What's the matter?"

"Marguerite, I wish to be called by my birth name. My mother named me Madeline. I want to be called by the name that she selected for me." She fumbled with the shiva around her neck—the very same one that her parents had given to her. William had needed no confirmation that she was his sister, though he was overjoyed to see that she still wore the necklace. I smiled and put my arm around her.

"Alright, from here on, you shall forevermore be Madeline." She smiled but still seemed lost in thought.

"When do you think he will return?" she asked. I sighed. Just as William had requested, we had taken his sister to the safety of the island. There were no more blindfolds as Silas worked daily to help her harness and utilize her gifts. The Crew all thought her abilities were totally badass. I was equally impressed with her quick progression! It had been a busy two weeks. Once we retrieved William's boat and were safely on the island, we had spent the first few days recovering. Kirby was diligent in restoring the sailboat. He spent countless hours repairing and molding it to its former beauty. I filled Madeline's days with stories of her brother, and Silas familiarized her with the history of the Sironian. She knew some of it from the books in her chamber. Madeline clung to every word and asked nonstop questions about William and her family. I knew that she was almost as anxious for her brother to join us as I was. She loved the stories of her mother. I told her all about Knox Point and the endless closet of gowns that awaited her. The longing in her eyes never ceased. The thing she wanted the most was the one thing that I wanted the most—William.

We chose the name Dark Haven for our new home as it became our safe place from the darkness of the night and the darkness of our world. Each day it felt more like home. James, Toby, and I began repairing the buildings and structures. Silas was able to restore the plumbing to the main house and several of the huts. I cleared one of the extra bedrooms in the main house, and James helped me repair the roof. I wanted to be near Madeline, who was staying in the master bedroom. The boys filled our days with entertainment. Toby liked to show off a bit by pulling out the overgrown trees and shrubs by the roots. James no longer felt the need to hide his acquired strength, often engaging in contests to see who was able to pull out the largest foliage. James intrigued Silas. He frequently studied and tested James' ability, hypothesizing on the science behind his transformation.

Silas spent a great deal of time with both Madeline and James, which meant the pair spent a vast amount of time together too. I was relieved, as Madeline's presence relieved some of the tension between James and me. He was furious that I had left him on the island during the battle. I had severely injured his pride, and Madeline had been the perfect remedy. Within the first week, I began to see feelings developing between them. It was a magnificent feeling for two people that I loved dearly to begin to care for one another. They often took long walks together and afternoon swims in the cenotes on the island. Their happiness only made my longing for William greater.

Nighttime was the hardest. My mind wandered in all directions. I would be lying if I did not admit the impact of Michael's death on my heart. I had never acknowledged my feelings for him, not even to myself, but his death sparked a vast array of emotions that I was unaware existed. He had fallen in love with me and sacrificed his own life to save William. Michael did this out of love. Had there never been a William, I knew that I would have reciprocated his feelings. I would have been in love with Michael. Part of me would always question if I had loved him. Instead, there was a small hole in my heart that I refused to claim as lost love. There had been no closure, no goodbyes between us—only the empty void left by his absence. His body was swallowed up by the sea long before I could make a proper farewell.

There had been another casualty from our group. Aria had gone missing after Silas announced that I was Theron's rightful successor. It was possible that she was killed but more likely that she was running again. As Theron's heir, I had not only removed her entitlement to the throne, I had taken her claim over William. The engagement treaty with Theron had been to his heir and not specifically for Aria's hand. Both Theron and Aria would now have realized the ploy behind the covenant.

Theron had not acknowledged me as his granddaughter but did not denounce it either. He had just left. With the truth presented, he seemed unsure of his next move. I should have been afraid, but my body had grown accustomed to fear. By not cowering to fear, I had become fierce. I was a warrior over my emotions, with only one weakness—love.

****

It was the morning of our sixteenth day on the island. Our crew of castaways had made it our home. However, as each day passed, I grew more homesick for the familiar waterways of Murrells Inlet. I missed my family. I missed my mother's laughter and my father's embrace. I missed the special talks with my grandmother. I missed Caleb, my forever best friend, and my Lucy! I longed for my Lucy! Did she think that I had forgotten her? I thought of Sadie and Olivia, often wondering how they were doing now that they were on their own. They all needed me, and I needed them. It was as if I was caught in an epic fairytale and normality awaited outside of the pages. Part of me wished to stay, part of me wanted to leap from the pages and back into reality.

Each morning, and every evening, I would take a long walk along the shoreline. It gave me comfort to know that the same ocean rolled along the coast of my home. The very same sea lapped against my beloved. However, on this morning, I found no comfort. I began to run, running so hard and so fast that I found myself clear across the island. My body collapsed upon the shore. I laid upon the sand for the better part of an hour deep in thought before beginning the return. My eyes were cast upon the sand when, like a mirage, I saw the outline of a figure slowly moving towards me against the horizon. My heart began to beat faster in my chest, and, with each new step, I became more confident that William had returned. My pace quickened until I was running towards him. He saw me and began rushing towards me with the same intensity. At last, his body collided against mine, and we held each other for what seemed like an eternity. Our eternity was never long enough.

William gripped my waist as we slowly walked back towards Dark Haven. He told me of his past two weeks as the Obyascon Prince. Surprisingly, Brooks had been helpful in the transition, teaching him about the dynamics of Obyascon. Brooks organized the meetings between William and the leaders of each faction as they devised a way to discreetly relocate the bulk of the Obyascon back to the polar regions. William explained that an alternate food source would have to be located to sustain their population before permanently relocating any of the factions to the warmer climates. Brought from their region, the Obyascon were forced to hunt humans as an alternate food source because they were starving. Before her death, Merissa had assessed the problem and was seeking other food sources for them. William organized a team that would research other food sources for the race for each area and climate. He had also organized a new system of government among the Obyascon by establishing a ranking order among the groups. I proudly listened as he described the details of the new regime. Mace agreed to be his second-in-command. He would oversee the relocation of the factions and enforce the new government and ranks established among them.

I told him about our weeks here at Dark Haven. I was eager to show him the work we had done to the buildings. It was his first time on the island. He had only briefly seen Dark Haven before setting out to find me. I wanted to show him the repairs that Kirby made to his boat, but most of all I wanted for him to get to know his magical sister.

By the time we returned, our friends had prepared an excellent lunch for William.

Madeline was finally able to spend time with her brother. She was shy at first to speak but eager to embrace the man in which she had learned so much.

"You look exactly like our mother," he said with tears in his eyes.

"I wish I had gotten the chance to know them," she said. "But I have been blessed to have my brother," she cried.

"And through me, you will know them. I wish to take you to Knoxx Point as soon as possible," William said.

"Can we leave tomorrow?" she asked eagerly. William laughed.

"Yes, we can leave tomorrow. At last, I will take you home."

****

"Good morning, beautiful!" William said as he pulled back the netting from my bed. I opened my eyes and grabbed him, pulling him on top of me. He wrapped me in his arms.

"It would have been a much better night if you would have stayed." He winked at me. I buried my lips against his neck.

"Of that I am certain, but I did not want to give my sister the wrong impression." I flipped him over on the bed and straddled him.

"Sleeping in the same bed with me has never bothered you before," I said as I ran my finger down his chest, across his stomach and just below his navel. He moaned and pulled a pillow over his face. In one swift motion, he was on top of me again.

"I have never had a sister in the room next door before," he teased, as he ran his strong fingers under my shirt and up my sides. I leaned into him pulsing my lips against the hollow of his neck.

"If you would like, I can assure her of my chastity and yours," I whispered, my lips never fully parting from the folds of his skin. He groaned. At any moment he would give in to what we both wanted. My lips retreated, and my eyes narrowed as I gripped his chiseled jaw in my hand. "I am assuming I can include you in the assumption of chastity?" I teased. He laughed at my interrogation.

"There has never been, nor will there ever be anyone in my bed other than you. I am not sure that either of us would be considered chaste after the last night we spent together, but technically, I suppose we can claim the title." The recollection only fueled what William had ignited. I slipped my hands beneath his cotton t-shirt and slipped it over his head. His lips fiercely took mine. The entire world disappeared.

"We should not do this," he groaned as I ran my fingers down his back, drawing him to me. You are my universe, pulling me to you by your inner gravity." His body's reaction contradicted his words.

"You are a siren. I am fully under your spell," I whispered as my tongue ran across his chest. His breath quickened. He moaned, his body tightened both from pleasure but also from resistance.

"But unlike a siren, I will not take what doesn't belong to me." He sighed, drawing away from me.

"I belong to you. My heart has always belonged to you," I said as I clutched him tighter. William's hands moved to my face as he gently tilted my chin towards his. His eyes stared into mine as if he were looking at a lost treasure.

"If that be the case, then marry me," he said. His body braced, and his expression became serious.

"I have already agreed to marry you," I teased as I went in to kiss him. He stopped me.

"I am serious, Marguerite. I want you to marry me when we reach Knoxx Point." They were the words of my dreams, and yet, seriousness on his face sent a whole new wave of emotions through me. Thoughts of the outside world echoed logistics into our dreamland fairytale.

My head began to spin. The sincerity in his voice and the steadfastness in his expression indicated that he was waiting for affirmation. "That is unrealistic. I can't marry you now," I replied lightheartedly. He did not waver.

"There has been nothing about our courtship that has been ordinary. We live extraordinary lives; I am only asking that we live them together from this point forward," William said.

"Perhaps in a year or …."

"Are you questioning your feelings towards me?" he asked defensively.

"No, It's just …."

"Is it Michael? Do you still harbor feelings for him?" William asked. His jaw hardened. His question blindsided me. The truth was, that Michael's death had caused me far greater pain that I would ever admit. Had there never been a William, I would have fallen in love with him. I could not deny the intense chemistry that I had had with Michael, nor the constant ache his death had left behind. I had learned that love carried many different levels. He had stirred my emotion and fractured my resistance, but I carried an unbreakable love. William would forever be my only true love. I put my finger to his lips.

"William Avery! There has never been anyone to consume my heart other than you." He looked relieved. "I just thought we were going to wait for marriage." He propped his body up and eyed me seriously.

"By waiting, we only give them the opportunity to try to tear us apart again. Intentional or not, Theron's authority sanctions our union. At any moment, he may try to undo the treaty." He grasped my side and pressed me against him. He was right. Theron would seek to separate us now more than ever.

"You're right. Theron will not think favorably on the Sironian Princess marrying the Obyascon Prince …"

"Another reason not to delay." He groaned.

"Another? I would think Theron would be our primary concern," I said.

"Perhaps he is, but as for this moment, all my mind can think of is you. I want you in every sense of the word," he said as he engulfed my neck with warm, passionate kisses.

When at last I could speak, I replied, "I have always been yours. My heart has never strayed from you, but I need some time to heal."

"From Michael?" William's jaw hardened. I slowly nodded, afraid to look into his eyes. "It pains me to know that he carried any measure of you with him. I want no other man to have any part of you than me," he groaned.

"I know," I whispered. "Which is precisely why I don't want our marriage to begin like this. My heart still harbors the loss of him."

"Then I will kiss you until all of you belongs to me again," he said as his lips came down hard on the back of my neck, "I will fight forever until you agree to marry me." His lips moved across my chest. Each time he touched my skin, I slipped a little further towards our future.

"I had already agreed to marry you," I moaned, "I only ask for time."

He looked up at me. "Alright, I will give you the time you need and then I will claim your forever."

27

———

"There is a kind of magicness about going far away and then coming back again all changed."

~Kate Douglas Wiggin

I **inhaled the magical marsh air** as the small sailboat pulled into the familiar harbor of Murrells Inlet. We arrived home on Christmas Eve. William thought it best to keep our return a surprise. Sadie fell to her knees in jubilation over Madeline's return. I was overjoyed to see her and Olivia. Madeline was in awe of Knoxx Point. William immediately began combing through photographs of their parents. He began to fill her in the cracks of her heart, or perhaps, it was the girl that filled his. My soul was full of joy as I watched the pair together. At last, the tinge of sadness that was always in William's eyes disappeared.

As soon as we reached Knoxx Point, I called my family to let them know I had arrived from Paris for Christmas. They scolded me for not giving them time to meet me at the airport and anxiously jumped in the car to come. Madeline stayed with Sadie and James while William, Silas, and I went to Inlet Joy. I'm not sure if my grandmother was more excited to see Silas or me. She wanted to know all that had happened while we were away. We each told parts of the story, watering down each time our lives had been in danger. She buried her face in her hands and began to sob as Silas explained how Theron learned the truth of my existence.

"I've always known that one day that he would learn the truth. I'm not sure if I should feel relieved or frightened," she cried.

"You have nothing to fear," Silas assured her. "Whatever Theron is feeling, it is doubtful that he would harbor any anger or blame towards you," Silas said.

"I don't fear him; I only fear any repercussions towards my family," she sobbed.

"If you haven't noticed, I am utterly and completely in love with your granddaughter," William replied, "You are my family too. There is no greater privilege than to protect one's family."

My grandmother dried her tears as the rest of my family arrived for the festivities. I screamed aloud in joy as Caleb and Lucy walked through the door. Caleb looked as if he had been living at the gym since I had been gone. His muscles were well defined; he had begun to resemble a siren. Lucy had changed too. She was a head taller. Her cheeks had thinned, and she now looked more like a young girl than a child. I fought back the tears as there had been many times over the past few months that I thought I may never see them again. The look in their eyes divulged that they felt the same thing. I dished out a suitcase of faux gifts that my grandmother had bought to help perpetrate the illusion of my time abroad. The only one still under the Parisian artifice was my mother. It was best to keep her in the dark. No mother should suffer through the details of all that I had endured. I was so lost in fabricated Parisian adventure stories that I did not see William lead my father out onto the back porch.

They had never been alone before. My stomach filled with butterflies when I realized they were deep in discussion. A few minutes later, they rejoined us. I was anxious to know what William was discussing with my father. When he went downstairs to bring in the Christmas tree, I hurried after him.

"Dad, wait up!" He turned and looked at me. "I saw you talking to William. What did he say to you?" He sighed; I could see his frustration.

"Because you have been so forthright with information?" he replied sarcastically.

"I am sorry, Dad. I don't mean to lie to you all; I didn't think Mom could handle the truth."

"Perhaps not, but I deserved to know," he said. I nodded and took him down to the dock where I told him an abbreviated version of what all had transpired. He listened intently, asking only a few questions. "So Theron knows I am his son?"

"He does, but I don't know how he feels about siring a half-breed son. When the evidence was presented to Theron, he left." My father nodded but did not say anything. "And William? What did he say to you?"

"I'm not sure," he smiled, "He was very nervous and started rambling on about his feelings for you. Before he left, I think the boy was asking for my permission to marry you! Isn't that absurd! To think of marrying at your age!" I gulped, and my eyes began to tear up. I looked away to keep my father from noticing.

"Yes, I guess it would be absurd," I mumbled. "What did you tell him?"

"I told him that, in the future, if he would ever be so fortunate to gain your hand, then I would be happy for you both." I kissed him on the cheek and hurried back towards the house. He shook his head as he watched me walk away.

****

I took a long hot bath before retiring to my room for the night. I almost felt human again—almost. I fumbled through the things around my room before crawling into bed. I could still recall the unique smell of the old pages in each book. I could feel the worn paintbrushes between my fingertips. I could recall the feeling of the bed sheets on my skin, and yet it all felt as if it belonged to someone else—a person from long ago. There was a faint knock at my door before it creaked open. I expected it to be William. It was Lucy.

"Lucybug! What are you doing awake at this time of the night?" She came and crawled into bed with me.

"Can I sleep with you?" she asked softly.

"Don't you think Mom will be afraid if she wakes up and you're not there?" I asked.

"No, she never wakes up at night, and if I hear her stop snoring, I just slip back into my room."

"You don't sleep?" I asked.

"I pretend to. I usually take a nap in the afternoon, when mom thinks that I'm playing," Lucy giggled. I scooped her into my arms. She was becoming more the little siren every day. My brow furrowed with worry. Theron would know about her soon—if he did not already.

"I love you, Lucybug!" I said as I kissed her soft brow.

"I love you too, Margo," she giggled.

"Can I ask you a question?" she asked solemnly.

"Of course," I said, afraid of what she would ask.

"Can I have your room when you marry William?" I laughed, breathing a sigh of relief. "Because it is the only room that has a window to the inlet. I want to stay close to my friends," she asked. My laughter was replaced with worry again.

"Marry William? Lucy, I think you will have to wait for that one," I smiled but my brow furrowed. "Of course you may have my room, Lucy, but it is a very special room, so you must take very good care of it." I smiled at her and kissed her again.

"Margo, can I ask you another question?" she looked up at me. Her big brown eyes carried far too heavy a burden for someone so young.

"You may ask me anything, Lucybug!"

"Were you scared fighting those Obyascon?" she asked softly.

"Lucy, how do you know about the Obyascon?" I felt my breath catch deep in my chest. Would this child someday face the demons I had battled?

"I know about a lot of things; my friends tell me," she said.

"You still talk with them … the creatures of the ocean?"

"Yes, silly, they are my friends," she replied.

"Yes, but I didn't know they talked back!" I gasped. She giggled.

"Of course they do, silly! So will you tell me about it?" she asked as she curled up against my side. I brushed back a long strip of glossy chestnut curls from her face. "The real stories, not those fake ones about Paris," she whispered. I thought about it. She deserved to know about this world. As much as the thought frightened me, she would soon be a part of it."

"Alright," I said, "But the stories may get a little scary," I replied.

"That's okay. I am not afraid. I never get afraid," Lucy said.

"Everyone is afraid sometimes. Fear is the greatest gauge for the things you value the most," I said, as I pulled her tighter. Her big brown eyes stared excitedly into mine, as I began to tell her my real life fairytale.

****

My eyes slowly opened, catching the tail end of the thin white curtains whipping beneath my open window. The gentle roll of the ocean waves, combined with the soft morning cry of the gulls echoed in the distance. I smiled as I looked down to see Lucy's long chestnut curls cascading from my pillow. Her divine scent filled the room, richer than a baby scent, but still fresh, like clean laundry warmed from the sun and kissed by the ocean. Soon Lucy would awaken to a Christmas tree full of gifts. I sighed. How much longer did this beautiful child have before her innocence was taken away? How long did Lucy have until she must face the monsters from my stories? I would protect her for as long as possible. I gently pried Lucy's small fingers from my waist and eased quietly from the bed. I did not remember leaving the window open last night. As my fingers pressed down the frame, I spied the inhumanly perfect frame of William Avery waiting for me on the dock. Harboring behind him was his sailboat, now restored to its former glory. I snuggled the quilt around Lucy and hurried down to meet him.

A deep grin spread across William's face as I crossed the lawn. "I wanted to be the first to wish you a Merry Christmas," he said. William wrapped his arms around me. I snuggled tightly against him. I was underdressed for a winter morning.

"Being in your arms is the best Christmas gift ever," I uttered.

"You were wearing that white gown on our first encounter," he said as he pulled me closer.

"As I seem to recall, you were too brooding to stick around," I teased.

"Because you thought I was a monster," he laughed.

"Yes, and now that I know you are a monster, I can't seem to get enough of you," I said as I nuzzled my lips against his muscular neck. He palmed the back of my head with one hand and scooped the other around my waist.

"Perhaps you should have stuck with your first instinct," he teased.

"I was under your spell from the moment I saw you," I said. "You are my siren."

"Very true. If only I could cast a spell to convince you to marry me today," William smiled.

"Today? On Christmas Day? I can't plan a wedding for today," I laughed.

"We are finally together! That's all that matters!" he replied softly.

"Yes, but I have had many hours alone to plan out our wedding in my mind."

"You have? Tell me about what you see," he replied. I closed my eyes and drifted there in my mind.

"Well, I can't see the details, only the sensations. I feel it is in the evening, with magical scents and beautiful linens. The crisp night ocean breeze is whisking through a simple white gown, and there is candlelight. I hear lapping waves and soft music. But, the element that I feel the most is the radiation of love—love from all who came to share the union with us." William was silent as he began to share the magic that I could see in my mind.

"I am at a loss for words." A wide smile spanned across his face. "I had only envisioned the honeymoon," William teased. We laughed. William slipped a heavy, thin, sold gold chain around my neck. The round links were ancient. The gift was undeniably a priceless artifact from a shipwreck. "A Christmas gift," he said. "It's priceless, like you."

"It's beautiful," I gasped. He buried his face into my hair as I held him tightly. As laughter faded, I felt the butterflies in my stomach awaken. There was a reason William was here so early.

"Are you here to take me sailing," I asked nervously.

"If that were only the case," he whispered. My eyes shifted behind him to the magical sailboat.

"The boat looks amazing!" I said.

"The Crew did an amazing job restoring it while it was at Dark Haven. I completed the remainder of the work and restocked it last night," he uttered swiftly. I was confused.

"But why would you …." William looked out across the water. A feathery fog weaved among the marsh grass, waving goodbye as the morning sun crept from behind the skyline. I knew. William was leaving. "Please don't go," I whispered. He exhaled slowly.

"I would stay forever if it were in my power," he replied.

"I knew that you would have to return to take your place as ruler of the Obyascon, I just didn't know that it would be so soon. We only just arrived!"

"I know," he groaned. "I received word this morning that large numbers of Obyascon are missing."

"Perhaps more were lost in the battle than previously estimated."

"It is possible," William said. "But I must discover the truth for myself."

"I'm going with you!" I spat. William sighed.

"Listen to me, love. My sister deserves a bit of normalcy. She deserves a home and a family. And frankly, Marguerite, so do you." I sighed. He was right. Every ounce of my body was weary for I had slain my share of monsters. I could think of nothing more painful than to be parted from William except to look into Lucy's eyes and tell her I was leaving.

"How long will you be gone?"

"I am hoping no more than a few weeks," he said. "I need for you to care for my sister until I can return." A tear slid down my cheek. I buried my face into his chest.

"I will love her as my own sister and count the seconds until we are reunited."

28

———

*"Here you leave today and enter the world of yesterday,
tomorrow and fantasy."*

~ Walt Disney Co.

"Smile!" **I rolled my eyes** as my mother snapped the hundredth picture of the day. "Just one more picture!" she promised. I huffed. "I can't believe my baby is a high school graduate!" I wanted to say, *"You should be more amazed that your daughter is a siren, battling oceanic forces, to secure the safety of humanity,"* but I did not. I smiled and tossed the ugly cap into the air with Kirby and Toby. Lucy retrieved it, putting it atop her head and skipping around the front lawn of Socastee High School. James hurried to join us, wearing the same horrid cap and gown. He put his cap on Madeline's head before sweeping me up in a big bear hug.

"We made it, darlin'!" James said as he put me back on my feet. "There were times when I was pretty sure this day was never going to happen." I laughed.

"Ditto," I replied. "There were times when I wasn't sure we would even be alive." James put his arm around Madeline's waist as Silas came to join our fairytale family.

"You know, Princess, only you could make that cap and gown look good," Kirby teased.

"There is nothing positive about wearing this outfit," I said.

"Except for the fact that you will never have to wear it again," Toby replied. "Look! I'm bustin' out of this thing!" Toby's gown was far too small for his muscular frame. As he turned, we could see the zipper had busted. Everyone laughed.

"I am pretty sure when my time comes, I will have more of those gold cord things," Caleb said.

"You wish!" I teased. The truth was that James, the guys, and I were both lucky to have enough credits to graduate. I thought that Silas was going to have to drum up some faux class credits from my year abroad, but after reviewing my transcripts, I not only had enough classes already to graduate, I graduated with honors. James had only missed about three weeks out of his senior year and was able to make up the missed days on Saturdays. We made it!

The day would have been perfect except for one flawless face that was missing from the audience. My Obyascon Prince was absent. He had been away for many months. The death of Merissa had caused an uproar amongst the Obyascon sects. They needed to reunite. The Obyascon needed a leader. I needed my William.

I looked around for my grandmother but did not see her among the crowd.

"Where is grandmother?" I asked Caleb.

"She left after you received your diploma."

"That's strange," said Silas. "I did not even see her departure."

"Perhaps she went back to the Inlet Joy to prepare for the surprise graduation party?" I teased.

"We're not supposed to know about that!" Kirby said

"Who spoiled the surprise?" Toby pouted. Silas looked concerned.

"I am sure she is fine; she is probably prepping for the party," Madeline said. Silas appeared unconvinced.

"Marguerite, you and I will go by the Inlet Joy on the way to Knoxx Point to see if she is there," Silas said. His concern was evident. The two of them were now rarely apart.

****

Her truck was in the driveway of the Inlet Joy. As we walked up the steps to the house, we could hear a distinctly male voice talking to my grandmother. As we neared, we recognized the voice of Theron. Silas rushed through the door to see Theron sitting on the couch across from my grandmother. How strange it was to see the ruler of the sea propped uncomfortably on a faded blue loveseat. He stood as we entered. Silas immediately surveyed my grandmother's face. She had been crying.

"Ah! Silas, we meet again so soon!" Theron said gallantly. Silas growled.

"Are you alright?" he hissed, ready to pounce on Theron at any moment.

"I'm fine Silas," she said, as she wiped a tear from her face. Silas walked over to her and stood behind her defensively.

"Is there something that we can help you with, Theron?" he said.

"Actually, I was just leaving. I only came to drop off this gift for Marguerite," Theron said gallantly.

"I am not interested," I said defensively.

"Perhaps not, but you are my granddaughter, and it appears a graduation gift is in order," he replied. His smile widened, but his eyes narrowed. I did not take the bait. "I am assuming my invitation was lost in the mail?"

"It wasn't," I replied sternly.

"I see," he said, taking my grandmother's hand in his and kissing it. "Well, I see my welcome here is short lived." The mighty Theron turned to my grandmother. "Sara, it has been a pleasure to see you after all of these years. Thank you for agreeing to see me." He bowed and made his exit.

Just as my grandmother began to tell Silas and I the details of her encounter with Theron, my father walked through the door with Lucy, Caleb, and Madeline. His face was blanched, and his hands were trembling. We both were immediately on our feet. I knew his words before he spoke them. He had seen Theron.

"Was that man my father?" he asked. His eyes welled with tears as he waited for an answer.

"Yes," my grandmother replied as tears streamed down her face. Her voice trembled. "That was Theron. He is no man, but he is your biological father." His brow furrowed.

"Theron greeted me, introduced himself, and asked if this was my family," my father said. "I did not lie to him."

"So he knows about Lucy … and Caleb?" Silas asked.

"Yes," he replied, as if in a daze. "He next asked about Madeline. It wasn't until after she introduced herself as William Avery's sister, that I realized …." He buried his face in his hands. My head was spinning at the possible ramifications. "What did he say?" I said anxiously.

"Very little, but the look on his face …." My father did not have to describe Theron's reaction. I knew very well the response of my grandfather when he felt deceived or threatened.

"I thought Theron was very nice, "Lucy said. "He kissed my hand and told me he was pleased to meet me."

'I am sure he was Lucybug … I am sure he was," I said as I protectively wrapped my little sister into my arms.

"Open your gift!" Lucy exclaimed. I opened the envelope to discover Theron had brought me a legal document. Upon closer inspection, I realized it was a deed—a deed to the island Theron had once occupied. He had gifted me Dark Haven. "What does it say?" Lucy asked. I was overwhelmed by such a gift. My mind darted in all directions as I tried to process Theron's reasoning behind the extravagance. "What did Theron give you?" Lucy insisted again.

"Nothing," I replied. "Just a letter of congratulations."

"Well, that's a bummer!" she cried. "I was hoping he was going to give you something good."

****

My mother had decked out the Inlet Joy with every "Graduation Day" decoration available. She had attended to every detail. The party was perfect—almost perfect. My William was missing. But it was difficult to be melancholy with such activity and friends. The Crew seemed to overcompensate for William's absence, supplying me with ample conversation and cheer. James had become almost a permanent fixture among them. I was thrilled that the party would include him and his family. It was fitting that we would close this chapter together. I mingled among James's family and our mutual friends. How easy these sirens associated with the humans! Kirby and Toby entertained James's sisters, and I am not sure who enjoyed the attention more. I had brought two worlds together; two races that were designed to remain separate socialized seamlessly. Perhaps the prophesies were true after all. Perhaps I had been born to unite the races. I watched as the girls eyed Kirby and Toby. The pair were far more handsome than the human boys. What if more Sironian began to fall in love with humans! As the afternoon wore on, my heart grew heavy. There was one missing element that would have made my day perfect. It was not long before my feet had carried me out to the shoreline.

"Are you alright?" My grandmother found me sitting on a dune. She saw the look of longing on my face as I looked out over the ocean. He was out there—somewhere. "You are worried about William," she said.

"Yes, I'm concerned as to what has kept him away for so long. It has been over a week since William has sent word," I said.

"I'm sure that he's safe. The two of you have proven your strength time and again," she uttered.

"Yes, but this is different. It's harder to have faith when we are apart," I cried. She wrapped her arms around me.

"I know. William has quite a responsibility on his hands now. As the Obyascon Prince, it will be difficult to manage both love and duty. I am afraid you may suffer the most." She gazed out across the water.

"Is it worth it?" I whispered. My grandmother smiled faintly.

"Suffering is the byproduct of the deepest form of love. Loss, longing, suffering, death—they would have no sting, no beauty without profound love" She said tenderly.

"It is a feeling you know all too well, is it not?" I said turning to her.

"What do you mean, dear?" she asked. I reached into the small leather pouch and presented her with the book from the island. Sara

Askin's eyes began to tear as she accepted the book. As she opened the front cover, the photograph slipped from the pages."

"You have been to the island," she gasped as her mouth fell open. "I wasn't aware that the island you escaped to was our island." She brushed her finger across the details of the photograph.

"Yes, I left out those details," I replied.

"Why didn't you tell me that you had this," she asked as she looked tenderly at the photograph. I sighed.

"I am uncertain if I wished to honor your privacy or just lacked the courage to confront you," I admitted.

"You have never lacked courage, my dear. I suppose you deserve the truth." She flipped through the pages of her book, then held it tightly to her chest.

"There was something that you left out of your story, wasn't there?" I asked. "Theron didn't just seduce you. You were in love with him—and he was in love with you." She looked at the photograph and then closed her eyes, as if she were taken back in time to another place."

"You are correct. I was madly in love with him." She took a deep breath and continued, "He did not seduce me; I came to him willingly. But my earlier story was not a fabrication either. I was in love with Silas also," she said. Michael's smile flashed into my consciousness. I once thought it was impossible to be in love with two people. I now questioned that. Had I loved Michael? I mourned his death more tearfully than was appropriate. My tearstained pillow proved that my feelings for him were more profound than I realized.

"How is it possible to love someone as deeply as you loved Silas and still develop such intense feelings for someone else," I asked. I knew the answer. Though I would refuse to admit it, my heart had committed a similar transgression.

"The heart is as transparent as the depths of the ocean; One can only see until the light is gone. Silas was my light. When he was gone, my light was gone, and the world fell dark. Aaron was very attentive. Silas had been called away for so very long that I began to develop feelings for Aaron," She sighed. "It happened before I realized it. An empty heart seeks fulfillment; it longs for the joy that has seeped from it, often grasping at false hopes. Aaron was a false hope. My heart was empty, and he filled it with beautiful, magical lies. It was true that Theron deceived me, but had he not I would have fallen in love with him anyway. Silas was so steadfast and Aaron the reckless one. When I thought Silas was lost to me, I grasped for a new life with Theron. I ran away with him. That island was our special place. He purchased it for us. But I soon realized that Theron loved something greater than me—power. He began to change, or perhaps he had always been that way and I had been blinded. But when I learned that Silas was alive, I realized my true place was with him, at home in Murrells Inlet. I wanted safety for the baby I was secretly carrying. I did not tell Aaron I was with child. I tried to leave the island, but Aaron wanted to stop me. It was not an assault but a single kiss. My essence filled him to the point that he thought I was dead. Overcome with grief Aaron Theron fled the island, leaving behind on our very bed what he tough to be my lifeless body. The child inside of me kept me alive. Silas found me and filled me with his essence, igniting the spark back to my life. He brought me home and nursed me back to health. We both knew that I would have to leave the coast when the child was born. Theron could not know of his son. In the meantime, Theron went mad, undoubtedly my death fueling his cause, as he ripped all remnants of love from the siren. The laws once created to protect the Sironian were twisted and new laws enforced to secure his power. It was done largely out of grief but also to further distance the siren from humanity … and any traces of love."

"Why did you mislead me? You were in love with Theron!" I gasped.

"Yes, I was. Now many have suffered and died because of that love." For the first time, I realized the weight she had been carrying on her shoulders."

"But you came back. You moved back here once my father was older. Was it for Silas or in hopes of reuniting with Theron?" She smiled. Sara Askins knelt down and picked up a large grey rock the size of her fist. She closed her eyes and gripped the rock. Fresh powder tricked from her fingers like sand until the stone was no more. I gasped in disbelief. Silas had done for my grandmother what I had done for James. Sara Askin's smile faded, and she became solemn.

"I came back because the ocean called me—just as it called for you."

****

It was difficult to rejoin the party after such revelation. My eyes scanned the crowds. Someone was missing other than my William—Lucy! My heart beat quickly in my chest as Olivia skipped past me, toward the house. "Lucy!" I gasped as I spied her several houses down from the Inlet Joy. Lucy had taken advantage of the low tide and had climbed off of the bulkhead. There she was barefoot amongst the oyster shells, dipping her tiny toes into the water's edge. She was not alone. Mace stood off to the side watching after her. He smiled as he saw the look of panic melt from my face.

"Do you have such little faith in me?" Mace said. "I am her Protector you know. I do believe you appointed me to the position yourself," he teased. I smiled.

"Old habits die hard, I guess," I said as I continued towards the shore to meet her. "What are you doing, Lucybug?" I asked nervously. The vision of her toes in the water brought forth terror within me. Theron knew of Lucy. How long would it be before he would learn of her gifts too?

"Just talking to my friend, Scamp." My jaw dropped open as I saw the familiar fin of a tiger shark swimming back into the deeper waters of the canal. Joy spread across my face at the realization that the shark was alive.

"I thought he was killed!" I gasped.

"No. Scamp is pretty tough," Lucy said.

"Lucy, come out of those oysters or you will cut up your feet," I demanded. Lucy rolled her big brown eyes.

"The shells do not cut me," she responded. I turned to Mace with a scolding look. He shrugged.

"It's true. They do not cut her," Mace replied. It was difficult to see him smile. Mace shared that same smile with his brother. I climbed down off of the bulkhead and joined Lucy by the water's edge. She looked up at me solemnly. I was frightened that such a young girl could carry such a deep soul.

"Lucy, what's wrong," I whispered. I was afraid of her response. The creases of her brow deepened. "I need to tell you something; it's about William." Her small brow furrowed. There was a large battle at sea."

"A battle? Who was fighting, Lucy?" I gulped.

"Some of his groups were fighting each other. He tried very hard, but he just didn't make it." I couldn't breathe. The world began to darken around me.

"What are you saying, Lucy! What are you trying to tell me?" My knees began to buckle beneath me.

"Your graduation. William was trying to make your graduation ceremony, but my friends told me he wasn't going to make it back in time." She turned and saw my face. Tears of relief cleansed the darkness as rays of hope reappeared. "Don't cry, Margo! It's okay. At least he will make it for some of the party." She pointed towards the horizon.

I squinted into the setting sun until, at last, I saw it—the outline of a tiny sailboat heading in our direction. I couldn't wait for its arrival. I dove into the warm inlet water, leaving only my shoes behind. All traces of humanity dissipated, as the siren princess glided swiftly towards her true love. The Obyascon Prince spied me, breathlessly soaring off the bow. Our bodies collided in an embrace so powerful that our souls intertwined beneath the smooth surface. William's lips were still connected to mine as he led me to the surface.

"I'm sorry that I am late," he whispered.

"Late? Are you kidding me? You are here! My day is now perfect!" I cried, as I kissed every droplet of water from his face.

"Is there any way that you could ever forgive my absence?' he asked.

"William, the most important part of my day is happening this very second."

"I don't just mean missing graduation. I have not been there so many times when you have needed me over the past many months. I see how you have grown stronger, and it only makes me want you more. You are truly the bravest soul that I have ever known. I was crazy when you were taken from me and even more insane when I thought you loved another. I do not doubt that every moment with you will be an adventure, an adventure of insanity and strife, one that is full of passion and love. I have already asked you to be my wife; I ask now that you defy all reason, cast aside any objection and take my hand in yours forever."

In the history of the world, I was confident that there had never been a more sincere proposal. From the first moment that I had met William, I had been thrown into a world of fantasy. But despite the unbelievable realm that I now lived within, a realm of monsters and creatures, a world of hidden kings and mystic sects, there was one factor that remained true. William was my constant.

"Alright," I said, as I removed the diamond ring from the chain around my neck and slid it onto my finger. "I guess there is just one more thing to do," I whispered. The words barely escaped my lips before they were enveloped by William's embrace.

CRIMSON WATERS

Preface

I opened my eyes to the sound of pebbles hitting against my windowpane. It was James. I turned to find Lucy asleep in my bed. I smiled. *So … she sleeps after all!* I slipped on some clothes and hurried down to meet him.

"What are you doing here so early?" I asked.

"I wanted to take one last walk with you," he said as he laced his fingers through mine and began to lead me towards the beach. The morning could not have been more beautiful. The sun seeped just above the horizon, sending sparkling ripples atop the water. The seagulls, waiting impatiently for their morning meal, greeted us.

"One last walk? We will have plenty more walks together!"

"No. Not like this … I know what is going to happen today," James uttered.

"Well, that makes one of us," I said as we reached the shoreline.

"Knoxx Point has been a massive whirlwind. I've never seen such preparations for a homecoming celebration."

"Oh." I felt as if I could not breathe.

"It isn't a party that they are planning for, is it?" he took a deep breath before looking deep into my eyes. "It's your wedding."

"I … I have no confirmation of this, but I believe so. William expressed a desire to be married when we reached Knoxx Point; I just had no idea he intended it to be so soon," I gasp.

"And you are sure of this?" he asked as we walked along the sand. "You want to marry him … now?"

"Yes." The ocean air suddenly filled my lungs, as all hesitation disappeared. "James, I have never been more certain of anything." The words were as hard to say as they were for him to hear.

"Then he is the luckiest man alive," he said as he took my hand one last time. We walked along in silence, enjoying the morning air.

"Madeline has really taken to Knoxx Point. Her transition back home seems to have gone very smoothly," James said.

"You two have been spending quite a bit of time together lately," I said with a smirk.

"She is just wonderful, isn't she?"

"She is! I hope that the two of you find love, James."

"Love? Easy now! We are just getting to know each other. I have only ever loved one girl, but a damn siren stole her away from me," he teased.

"Gotta hate it when that happens!" I smiled at him tenderly. He smiled.

"No, on a serious note, I do have feelings for her. I just want to take things slowly. Think William will kick my ass for liking his sister?"

"I think that if William hasn't kicked your ass by now, then you're probably safe!" We both laughed. It felt good to laugh.

"I will miss this though—just the two of us." He took my hand and brought it to his lips.

"I know ... me too," I whispered. "Thank you, James. Thank you for loving me."

"Loving you was the easy part, darlin'; it was getting you to love me back that was so damn hard." I shook my head and squeezed his hand firmly.

"No, loving you was never hard ... not loving him, was the hard part."

ACKNOWLEDGEMENTS

There truly aren't words to describe my gratitude for the support and sacrifice my family has made during the years it has taken me to complete this novel. Had I known how much you would have to share me with the Sironians, I would have never put those first words to page. This book is not just my accomplishment; it is yours as well.

Scott, for your insanity to take on all that I throw at you! Your countless hours of edits and creative inputs were invaluable! This series would have never reached completion without you! Thank you for believing in me!

My magical daughters, Madeline, Merissa, Michaela, and Mia. You are my inspiration, my joy, and my life. Never lose your childhood imagination. This big girl fairytale is for you!

My editor Rea Myers for her expertise and polishing, and to Shelley Glasow for preparing this work for the world of eBooks.

My Mother for believing in me, and for being the first and biggest fan of this series. My Father for your motivation when I was discouraged and for raising a daughter who was free to follow her dreams.

This remarkable team of beta readers: Jennifer Dunnam, Linda Freeman, Mary Todd, Rebecca Roland Hyleman, Pamela Joy, Julianna Moxley Debbie whose careful eye and enthusiasm kept this work in motion.

Patricia Taylor for giving me one of her most prized possessions, her son…and for stepping up to help my girls through life's challenges.

My supporters: Carolyn McIntyre, Linda Coleman Lea Arnold, Margaret Baker, Sara Blumberg, Kevin and Anna Todd, Melanie and Rob Taylor. Your encouragement, love and willingness to tackle anything has been invaluable.

A special thanks to Kevin Todd, Jason Lee, and the Lee family, as well as the countless others who have inspired the characters of this book

And for those whom I have lost—you live on in these pages.

My students for their daily inspiration. Never grow too old to dream!

L. M. Montgomery, Jane Austen, Walt Whitman, Rupert Brooks and all of my childhood literary playmates…as well as the creative genius of the musicians serving as my inspiration during the writing process.

Jeremiah 29:11

ABOUT THE AUTHOR

Meredith's fondest childhood memories are of her summers along the South Carolina coast. Her love for story telling began at an early age, so it is no mystery that she combined her two loves when writing The Churning Waters Saga. She graduated from the College of Charleston where she studied Theatre and English.

When not writing, Meredith teaches Theatre and serves as a director and vocal coach. She currently resides in New Orleans, LA. During the summer, Meredith can still be found vacationing with her husband and four magical daughters along the waters of Murrells Inlet.

For more information about upcoming books in the series visit her website.

www.meredithttaylor.com

www.ingramcontent.com/pod-product-compliance
Lightning Source LLC
Chambersburg PA
CBHW070758120726
47910CB00001B/221